Karen's Closet
by Mario Rienzo

edited by Chris Caggiano

Wraparound Cover Painting: Leslie Lowe, 2018
Interior Illustration: "Self Portrait" by Mario Rienzo, 1993
Back Cover Photograph: "No Self Pride" by Rose Rienzo, 1995
"Wild Night" by Van Morrison © 1971 Warner Bros. Records
"Trampled Under Foot" by Led Zeppelin © 1975 Swan Song Records
"25 Or 6 To 4" by Chicago © 1970 Columbia Records
"Strange Brew" by Cream © 1967 Reaction Records
ALL RITES PERVERSE
P.O. BOX 1023
NEW YORK, NY 10009
Ordering Information:
Quantity sales. Special discounts are available on quantity purchases by corporations, associations, and others. For details, contact the publisher at the address above. Orders by U.S. trade bookstores and wholesalers.
Printed in the United States of America.
ISBN No. : 978-0-578-20295-2
10 9 8 7 6 5 4 3 2 1

This book is dedicated to all those forgotten, all those remembered, and all those yet to find their voice.

My Son, My Friend

The story you are about to read is by my son Mario, one of the most gifted people I have ever known. His use of words when he put them down on paper were so profound, that the reader could feel his emotions and become part of his world.

I knew Mario was very talented, but he had friends who reminded me of how far his talent went.

My son was an artist, a musician, a writer and a good friend to all who came to know him.

If you knew Mario the man, you were in for a treat, because he gave his all in everything he did.

If you practiced with him to learn a new song, and did not put enough effort into it after many tries, he made you know how disappointing the session was.

Mario was so into the groups he played with; he knew everyone's part to the songs.

I lost Mario at an early age of 48 years old to cancer on September 12, 2017. He had so much more to do on this earth, but was called away too soon.

I can't begin to express how very much I miss him, but Mario will always be with me, in my heart and so many beautiful memories.

Enjoy the book; I know you will.

P.S. Did I mention he could sing too! That was my son, my friend, my world.

Rose Rienzo

From the Artist

I consider myself a 'method' artist, that is, I approach a project similarly as a 'method' actor... I try to delve deep into the motivations and circumstances of the characters, in this case, Karen... of course I had to read the entire story before going to work on it... "Oh boy, this is rough... this is NOT a 'feel good' story..."

I recalled stories my grandmother told me about how it was her chore to slop the pigs when she was barely 9 years old on the farm she grew up on... she never tired of telling me the pigs were mean... in my mind's eye the farm was similar to the setting in which this story takes place... rough, hard, isolated...

Having read the entire story, I was that much more flattered that I was chosen to do the cover as I imagine Chris/Antimessiah, besides admiring my work, also felt that I had the emotional stamina to take on this project.

I have attempted to give Mario's work the dimension in the cover it deserves...

and I repeat "I will never eat pork again"

Leslie Lowe

A Promise to a Dead Friend

Mario Rienzo first entered my life as a rumor. It was June of 1977, I was playing alone with my toy dinosaurs on the school yard of PS81 on the borderline of Bushwick Brooklyn and Ridgewood Queens and, being the weird kid I was, I proved to be a magnet for the de facto leadership of the schoolyard gang. Not to say Gang with a capital "G," however there was a definite hierarchy, and they all knew about me. One time, the leader himself, impressed by the vivid fantasy worlds I was able to conjure, asked if I knew, or knew of, this other kid, slightly older than me, who would stalk around the schoolyard with head down, fists balled and brows knit, saying to himself or to everyone, over and over, "Very Mean – Very Mean."

That was Mario.

When next I almost encountered him, Mario was the drummer in Mister Miller's music class. I had taken that class ever so briefly in second grade – briefly, because I was thrown out of public school at midterm – and Mister Miller was a bit of a legend. Little did I know – or not at all – that my Idiot brother had been in home room, and the school band, with Mario Rienzo.

What's more, my Idiot Brother was determined to keep Mario a secret. He never let on to Mario that he had a brother and sister, and only invited Mario over when neither she nor I was home. And so I was saved from encountering Mario in person until a good 15 years later, when I was 22, living down in Flatbush, and seeking members for my band Iconicide – a band I continue slapping together to this day. At the time, he was putting out a zine – Clawmarks – which he later published my poetry, stories and artwork in, and filming an independent horror movie – Eyes of the Coven – which he cast me a bit role in.

But it was the demo he sent me for his own solo musical act Intelligence Is Bliss that sealed the deal and demanded I bring him into my band. Mario's lyrics railed against maliciously encroaching technology, warned against the horrors of witchcraft – though it was when he addressed the doomed breakdown of humanity itself that his words were most potent, with songs like "Lurking in the Darkness," and "No Glue."

The demo reeked of both Low Fidelity and fanatical dedication, and it is those two characteristics which permeated every cell and facet of Mario's being. There he was, low on the radar, panned over by many and appreciated by few; were one but to pause and take notice, one would see in that dedication abided an indomitable and compassionate spirit. As a bit of backstory to the work you are reading now, Mario won the Beast portion of his nickname Maj Da Beast by jumping a child one night who had sodomized a younger boy, and beating him half to death on a playground with a bike chain.

Since adolescence, Mario's dedication to a strict yet non societal moral code forged deep and lasting friendships, while it spurred others to brush him under the rug – most likely for fear that his scrutiny would fall upon them – most if not all of these revisionists were female. Heart of Gold or not, Mario was not the type one brought home to mother. He was however the individual one employed as an attack dog when one's honor had been besmirched. The first I had ever heard the term "No Filter" used to describe someone, it was yours truly talking about Mario. One always knew, in his presence, that he cast no false shadows.

Mario developed colon cancer in 2013, and the hospital's incomplete extraction of the invasive mass – another instance of being swept under the rug – ultimately led to his death in 2017, as it ravaged his liver and lungs. For years, Mario told me he had written a number of books which had never seen the light of day – all handwritten, all stashed away in his packrat's haven of an apartment. It never seemed to be the right time, and he never seemed to possess the resources, to type them up or publish them.

It was on his death bed, four days before his passing, when he expressed his satisfaction that I fully intended his writing to receive the attention and acclaim it had so deserved. I thank his mother Rose Rienzo for plumbing Mario's archives and bestowing upon me any scrap of artwork and writing of his she was able to find. One of the three things Mario was able to tell me on that day – September 8, 2017 – was that I reminded him of himself. Of who he was.

Mario was a compulsive and prolific writer, and his style was predominantly stream of consciousness. It is for this reason I found it necessary to insert myself into the narrative process, by tweaking grammar, word usage, sentence structure and any number of issues, perhaps dozens of times in a single page, easily thousands of times throughout the novel, reprising the role of sounding board which he had performed musically in Iconicide with aplomb.

I am not now nor will I ever be at the liberty of divulging to you, dear reader, the degree or extent to which this immersion exists – where his presence ends and mine begins. Some asides, additions, omissions and amendments were absolutely necessary to preserve thematic integrity, others were implemented as inside jokes between he and I, and at other times I merely stepped back and pointed fingers in jest when any machinations on my part would significantly derail the organic development of the story – a story Mario strove to tell when alive, which only now is being told after his death.

Read on, intrepid soul. This one has taken a lifetime.

Chris Caggiano

Also from All Rites Perverse

PRINT

SickWorld! 20th Anniversary Edition by Chris Caggiano

AUDIO

NHI-006 Iconicide "Jesus Corpse: D.N.R. = Live in Spanish Harlem"
NHI-008 Iconicide "Give Me Extinction Or Give Me Death!"

http://www.iconicide.com

Karen's Closet

PROLOGUE

David and Sharon weren't getting along lately, and both of them knew it. Sharon's constant dreams, horrible dreams, where she was being attacked sexually and physically abused, shoved and yelled at by angry evil minded faceless people – always faceless, no features of any human nature to focus on and soothe her thoughts – had made their sleeping together uncomfortable and *sleepless*, to say the least. Not that the two were intimate anymore; the last time they'd 'made love' – if they did do anything now besides cuddle and lightly kiss and fondle, more like 'just friends,' Sharon would just call it 'having sex' – was a week before they finally broke up. David propped himself up on his elbows and turned to her, sitting up on his left.

"What is it, Sha? More bad dreams?" He already knew the answer, but lately he wasn't sure what to say, or what *not* to say around her, and spouting clichés to reinforce his place in the universe in relation to another sentient being – cracked up in the head as she may be – was better than being quiet altogether. Besides, David's upbringing taught him that answering a question with a kind word or compliment was the way to her heart – not that he ever actually believed that shit for a minute now – was the chivalrous approach, an appropriate one for a … butch femme like Sharon Langhorn. They were lovers who'd lived together for a while, and both became loved with each other at the same time, putting their cards on the table as it were, complete with prepared speeches and a genuine air of decorum that was devoid of any hollering, hair pulling or pointing fingers.

They were people grounded to the point of obsession, trying eagerly to outdo one another in polite discourse and political and social conversation, pulling guests aside by their arms in their home, like two drooling brothers at the family Thanksgiving feast, snapping a wishbone mercilessly in half until said guest tired of being used in some pathetic home game of lovers' wits, would excuse him or herself from the party or get together entirely, sometimes never to return to another.

They had identical tastes, opinions and temperaments. In short, a relationship rocketing toward disaster from the outset. They did, to their separate credit, both decide to stay friends. It was better this way, though Sharon felt rejected the way a woman does when her relationship plans don't work out as she planned, eventually having to take into consideration the man's feelings as well. Someday, which always seemed to be considered negative – i.e., not conducive to monogamous union.

"No," Sharon answered finally, "Not yet, anyway I'd better leave." She rose and put on her jeans and light cotton sweater, giving an excuse of wanting to get up extra early for work the next morning. He didn't buy it, but held his disgust and ambivalence to himself. They exchanged a few more words, Sharon kissed his cheek and smiled, as if promising, even if only subconsciously to be heard – not to be so difficult. He did not care to ponder anything about her anymore, except for the view of her round, hippy rear end exiting his bedroom door. He made a mental note not to invite her to stay the night anymore, eventually calling his ...

He whispered to himself, hitting the pillow with vigor, looking forward to getting the only real complete night's sleep he had enjoyed since they lived together. Off he went to pleasant dreamland with a smile, annoying, troublesome thoughts of Sharon and her many peculiarities suppressed for the time being, and sooner than he would have thought, for good...

Sharon screamed when she felt the familiar sensation she'd come to dread these past few weeks. It was happening more and more.

"No, not again! Get off me! I HATE THIS!"

She jumped up and threw him off her – or at least she thought she did – one can never be too sure in these cases; her nightgown caught in one of the bedpost knobs as she flung herself off of the side of the bed and ripped at the seam, about four inches' worth. *That'll have to be mended right away.*

2

Sharon Silverina Langhorn didn't like unkempt things cluttering up her already cluttered closet. She yanked it up for now frustratedly, and slipped into the undies she'd left on the child's infant chair – Mark had given her a gag gift last year – the night before.

"I don't think I like this very much," she said, trembling, but as Sharon trembled; always painfully aware of staying in control – lest someone criticize her for being herself, and doing a bad job of it, besides – raising her head, pouting her full, nude chapped lips for effect, "I don't like this very much at all."

Sharon Langhorn was an actress in all areas. One had to be kind in their description of her, as describing a dinner date to a third party acquaintance upon returning to work Monday morning, the likes of whom you couldn't care less explaining *anything* to – much less your personal life – to *begin* with. Yes, she insisted on being described, "in a kind way, please." A person in her life wasn't so much a friend, or lover, or family member, than Someone to be Briefed. Anything, such as loyalty, love, friendship or sexual intimacy, was of little consequence alongside this – one of many – Sharon Fact. Leanna Summers could count herself as one of the privileged who went for days on end, sometimes, without so much as a teleprompter. You could say she was "trusted," but that wasn't in Sharon Langhorn's vocabulary. So just call Leanna a leaning post with ears and she'll take *that* as a sincere compliment.

Her psychologist says she's the complete antithesis of Sharon, which she doesn't buy at all, the two women had been best friends for the past ten years – Sharon thinks back their friendship between six and nine years; Leanna swears up and down it's at least a dozen years since they've "bonded." Sharon's memory shrinks or expands when it comes to Leanna, depending on where she falls at a given time in her Sharon Scale. She *will never*, curiously, admit to ten. Leanna's just nostalgic, and likes to remember things in a grand – and some may say 'disjointed' – fashion; Sharon, her Evil Twin, would just simply like to live in the here and now – and not turn the pages back incessantly, as is Leanna's pastime.

To understand this, however, one has to realize Leanna *has* a book in which she's written on the worn pages she now turns; Sharon the 'practical' one of the two young women, to be kind, has no interest in self documentation... the less the better, in fact. Not surprisingly, Sharon *isn't* the Quiet One.

"Leanna, are you there?"

The answering machine message was still playing, "Hi, this is Leanna Summers. I'm not here right now – please leave a message at the beep, cause I hate to miss your call. Tootles!" but Sharon spoke over it anyway. She paused two seconds before hanging up. *You're the type to screen your calls, Ms. Langhorn, not sweet Leanna. No, if she was home she'd've picked up. But, she wasn't. Okay, you'll have to just try and calm down until she gets home.*

KAREN'S CLOSET
by
MARIO RIENZO

Chapter One

The house was one of those "stately estates" – *isn't that a silly pairing?* – that many people viewed but all too few dared to venture. Didn't one need to be *invited* to such a palace?... Such stands on formality meant little to Mr. Rothstein, a "good Jewish boy who made good" – as was his hyphenated description whenever he would meet his Good Jewish Mother back in the Jew section of Brooklyn; or what *was* the Jew section of Brooklyn. Times change and people die, after all – some folks were unable to leave the past lay, but Leonard felt the obligation to Break the Jewish Chain, you could say. Not to turn his back on his kind or anything, but just so his coworkers in the tremendous vacuum that was the monstrous sixty story hi rise Madison/Perry/Shostrom Real Estate wouldn't feel his position there was 'mandated' by his last name. Jews owned, co owned, will own, or have owned – or sold-for-a-major-profit – everything in New York – and sooner or later the world – did they not? *Well, I certainly thought so*, and Rothstein had enough promotions... *"Beenies" are unsightly, topping off an Italian suit...*

Italians? Why must the best suits be Italian? Those ethnic half truths had haunted Larry-turned-adult-Leonard for some time – his mother stopped calling him Larry on his 13th birthday – the day he became a man in the thoughts of the family – chilling to think of it now – his own. So, rather than rally to anyone's particular ethnic cause or related emotional hand stand, preferred to just be American Leo, keep it at that – had anyone called him Leo, ever? After all, he had plenty of time to be a suffering Rothstein whenever late December rolled around. Oh yeah... guard down, sweats on, shoes off – Larry wanted to bust that old Chain to pieces.

Sharon was to visit the house the 12th of March. Ten days away. It was leap year, and the extra day bugged her to no end. *Why*, a February 29th, 1996. Who knows? Why did it bother Miss Langhorn so? Everybody knew the answer to that one. Her roommate Betty – or, if you heard Sharon describe her, Beatrice – she wasn't one for affectionate abbreviations – was thinking of having an inner circle "vodka straight" party – of which she was famous for – to commemorate the dear, soon to be departing of that strange, distant, uppity girl who helped her pay the rent every month.

Sometimes, to her credit, Sharon could cover her if she was short a bit with her half, if one of Betty's freelance projects failed to pay her 'what she was worth.' Again. Hours put in, notwithstanding, or lack of them – who wants to get up in the morning, Sharon! – which she had to admit, *was* a virtuous trait on her part, Betty had to admit. That wasn't enough to endear her to her fussier half, however. Although, she did try. Many of her friends tried to be a real confidant, but it was not in Sharon's nature to be forthcoming with too many details. It wasn't that she went out of her way to be a bitch; nothing that contrived. She just didn't trust other women. Sharon would not accept attendance to a party basically in her honor. Nice shot, she thought; getting drunk cause the Old Maid is going, going, gone. Ding Dong, the Witch is Dead. Enjoy it, Betty...

Sharon spent the night at David's house. David was an on again, off again boyfriend – heavy on the friend part – of Sharon's who tried to help her out with stuff now and again, not expecting her to get the hint, or anything. Sharon didn't commit. That was okay. He would wait. 12:05 a.m., March 3rd, and counting.

"David, why do you think Beatrice is glad I'm moving out?"

"I don't know if she – *neither* of us knows if she's really 'glad' to see you go, Sha. Why do you do this to yourself?"

"Oh, David," she said, rolling her eyes. "You're so blind sometimes. I just know she's jumping up and down doing cartwheels 'in my honor.' Instead of throwing a party and stocking up on liquor, which she'll invariably end up polishing off once the working stiffs have gone home to get up early tomorrow... I just wish Miss Freelance Artist would return some of that rent money I put out for her all these months! It's probably in the thousands by now! Geez, I could really use that towards the house right now, her and her fucking vodka that bitch!... Oh, David, I'm so sorry. I didn't mean to curse."

"Hey, the cursing I can take, but the yelling I just won't tolerate there, sister."

"Sorry, I just feel, I don't know... stressed"

"Oh, big surprise there... Do you see yourself? You're screaming in the middle of my living room – well, all purpose room, anyway."

David laughed nervously. "Sha, you've got to relax. I'm not good at giving people advice, or at least getting through to you's concerned."

"Ha! Then you'd better start pinching your pennies now, brother. You're wasting time mastering at Psychology if you can't even talk to a frustrated old maid, much less any worse."

"You might just have a point there. Did I say that, that I can't give advice?"

"Yes, you did."

"Well hey, it's only money."

"Then why don't you give *me* some of it? I've got a big old godawful house to pay for here. Jesus, what did I do? David, I bought a house! I can't even care for a *cat*, for Christ's sake!"

"Ah, yes. The Fluffy incident."

"I'm *serious*, David."

"I'm sure Fluffy was serious, too. If I wasn't fed for days, *I'd* start nailing the upholstery. Shit!"

"David, stop making jokes! I left my apartment to move into Dracula's Castle! How can I possibly *afford* this... Oh, man."

"You have to stop looking at things like everything you do is a mistake. Really. You have to learn to calm down... Whenever women come here, the only time I allow screaming is in the bedroom. Right over there, pointing upstairs, he laughs."

"I'm so sorry I raised my voice, but sometimes I think everything I do *is* a mistake... I don't know. I know you're trying to cheer me up, but it's not working."

"Well, if you're going to feel *that* way about yourself, I don't think anything I say *could* cheer you up."

"Does that mean you're going to stop trying, David?"

"Doctor Price – 'always on call for the needy.' If the Price is right."

"I guess I'm not being that good a house guest, am I?"

"Now let's not get ahead of yourself. You're only staying the night."

"Does that mean you don't want me to stay longer?"

"Sharon, Beatrice is the actress, not you. You don't do the 'soft female' routine well."

"Fuck you, David. And thank you."

"Go to sleep, Sha. Good night."

As Sharon tried to fall asleep under David's not-as-clean-as-it-could-be thick foam lined blanket – one of the bedroom set pieces she helped him to pick out when they were going to move in together – *Boy, that went well* – she couldn't help thinking she bit off a little more than her capped teeth could chew! *My mother made me get caps. She was hoping it would improve my chances at the State Fair Teenage Beauty Show! It didn't. And then she blamed me for how much they'd cost. Mother would say, "If your father was around we wouldn't need to hustle for money like this. Well, you'll have to live with them now... I hope you like them, Sharon. That's your Birthday and Christmas present, you know. How am I going to pay for this?"*

She jumped up, startled to have uttered the same words her dear mother did when Sharon was fourteen. "That doesn't necessarily mean I *am* like her, though. I'm not."

She slid underneath the thick comforter and tried to dismiss any old memories that so plagued her as a young adult. *Thirty. Not so young, huh?*

"Sometimes I wish I was more like Beatrice. She doesn't have these kinds of worries. She doesn't even have a steady income! How can she live with herself? Seems peculiar to me. Quite peculiar indeed. Well, might as well try to get some sleep and stop worrying about other people. G'night, Sharon."

Tossing and turning all night, she wished she had spent the night in her own bed, and not seemed so needy to David. In the morning, she shook him out of bed and handed him a fresh squeezed paper cup of orange juice before seeing herself out. She had called a cab, washed her face, went to the bathroom and dressed, treated herself to a pair of toasted white bread from David's cupboard.

She heard a car horn beep, and said goodbye and thank you to him under her breath. She had things to do and boxes to pack back home, and had to figure out how to tell the boss she needed some time off – two weeks at least – to get her "affairs in order," which of course meant she was having one of her nervous wreck bouts, as she dubbed them, and had to brace herself and let it pass before accepting her upcoming responsibilities.

Hadn't I always wanted my own house, as a little girl? Now I have a goddamned mansion practically, and I don't feel good about it. Not at all. "Is something wrong with me?" she said suddenly out loud.

"Excuse me, miss?" the driver said nervously. With all the hold ups and taxi driver shootings he had heard about lately, he would agree with anyone about anything, just as long as they got out of his cab eventually, and he could tell his wife about what another "boring day" he had.

"Oh, nothing. Sorry, I didn't mean to talk out loud."

"That's alright. You can say anything you want. It doesn't bother me. I hear all kinds of stuff... don't bother me a bit."

"Oh, I see." Sharon felt like he could read her thoughts, that he knew her fears and doubts and pathetic melodramatic build ups in her mind as soon as she stepped in his cab. "Can't wait til this ride is over. Think I'll have a brandy when I get home. If Beatrice's playmates didn't pilfer all my liquor. My going away party. What a joke! I treat her like a sister and the thanks I get... I'll be happy to be away from her." She caught the driver's eying her through his rear view mirror.

Something not right about this one. Not at all...

March 3rd. nine more days.

Leonard Rothstein called Sharon Langhorn 5:03 p.m. that night. Since she got home around eleven that morning, she moped around the house the past few days and halfheartedly packed a few small boxes with some small personal items – panties, bras, earrings, winter gloves, anything that would fit snugly. She would do her *real* packing tomorrow night and the next day – she still wasn't so sure about moving in, but she promised Rothstein she would return his call and give him a definite answer by the third. Here it was March third, and she had a bad feeling about the place.

"Now Sharon, don't start acting like your mother." She picked up the phone when he started to leave a message on the machine.

"Miss Langhorn, this is Leo Rothstein, I'm calling about your recently acquired property on 1922 Tug Hill Road. I'd like you to please call me at your earliest convenience –"

"Yes, Mr. Rothstein. It's Sharon. I'm here."

"Oh, Miss Langhorn. I wasn't expecting you to... Okay. This is where we stand as far as your credit rating against the bank loan is concerned..."

"Oh no, here we go, they're going to bring up the fire thing again."

"The dear old lady that owns the property," he said drily, "got wind of your recent dilemma, and..." The elderly Mrs. Shifton, a widow, did not seem the sociable – or sensible – type, and was being quite hard on Leo for a suitable new tenant. He liked Sharon, in his way; despite her own peculiar nature, he seemed to know she'd be quite suitable to take over the old mothtrap. In real estate for years, he could smell a flake miles away, and – though the 'old maid' type – seemed a good woman nevertheless. Sharon jumped in when Rothstein paused.

"Let me guess Mr. Rothstein... good news and bad news, right?" She sounded tired. He could tell.

"Right you are, Ms. Langhorn. Here it is from the horse's mouth." *Now, she's not a prize winner, y'know, but she's not as bad looking as all that,* Leo chuckled to himself on the other end. "She heard about the fire that was started at your previous apartment – "

"By my previous roommate," she quickly interjected.

"I believe you, Miss Langhorn, I deal with lots of folks who get stuff held over their heads like that, and I get many who are, like her, twice shy and never bitten." *Why did he use the words 'folks' and 'stuff' with her? She made him feel comfortable, in an unexplainable way.* "Sorry, I gave you the sad news first... Anyway, I can't say it doesn't make her leery, cause she's a leery typa gal, but, it won't matter to her, if she tells the bank yes and says no to any previous haggling bids on your part."

Sharon was steamed. It had been a long day, and was yet to be done with it. "In other words, for something my stupid ex roommate Tracy did, which had no police report filed about it, or went on record or *anything*, I have to pay a higher price for a place I couldn't afford at the price I was *hoping* to pitch, so... I guess I'm swimming in interest payments for a few years and leaving the cat to rot in her own kitty litter, huh?"

"That's the way it looks, yes. Can I help?" he said weakly, not knowing what he *could* do, or what she could possibly call in as a favor at this point. She was in over her head, but the commission from this concrete and wood fossil would put him on the map at his firm, and make his Mama crack a wee smile... maybe.

"I'm dreaming here, Rothstein. What should I do? Can't you talk to her? Let *me* talk to her. She's gotta be human."

"Well I'm not so sure about that," he chuckled again.

Sharon found his humor droll. Quaint, but droll.

"Look, it's been a long day for me, and I have to pack and whatever. Let me give you a call back tomorrow, afternoonish. We'll set up something with meeting Shifton. You, me, her, select bits of kitchen cutlery strapped delicately to my person. Ready to be released upon the magic word being uttered."

"No!" Leo shouted, going along, pretending to be the elderly woman.

"Maybe I don't want to have to use this! The magic word is 'bargain,' Madame. So I say!"

"Hmmm... you're tired. Call me here tomorrow."

"Uhhh... right. Will do. Bye."

"Bye."

Well, at least he's on my side, she thought. *Funny, I don't usually act sarcastic with business contacts...* He struck her as down to earth. Jewish – a little stiff, maybe, but that was probably put on to *impress*, not the 'real' him. *Yeah, he's okay.*

She flopped onto the futon couch with teenage abandon, flicking on the TV and changing channels rapidly just like those guys she knew in college and despised so much. *One channel at a time, dammit!* She remembered when she'd changed the channel normally B.R. – before remotes – and told herself she was old. *Why do I do this to myself? I hate to be alone. Damn hot off my latest birthday and I'm depressed.* She shut the TV, lay down on the couch and stared at the ceiling for a while.

Tracy. It had not been for quite a while that she had thought of *that* one. The *part time* stripper. Her dirty laundry hamper would suggest it was full time. *Now, it's not nice to speak ill of the brain dead, Sharon.* Yeah, Tracy. Not a bad girl – bad meaning untrustworthy or sneaky, that is – but, couldn't she think of something more original than that cigarette hole in the mattress bit?

I swear, I can't get used to anything but this damn futon ever since. She went out when the mattress did, both out with the proverbial trash, and a new apartment and Beatrice soon followed. The old bag said – *or was it Leo* – "recent dilemma." *Recent?! It was three damn years ago, bitch!* Yep, very long day. She decided to get to bed early. What was it, six? That was fine by her. Good night.

In a damp, weathered basement closet, a child sat in a filthy mix of soot, sawdust, animal droppings and shavings from a rusting tin sheet metal roof, an extension of the shed her father made, where he kept the pigs at night. The house wasn't built on livestock ground, and there was not much of a yard at all, but these facts never stopped someone like Daniel Nelson from thinking otherwise. He would tell anyone in the village down the long path of cobblestones and cracked, sand heavy concrete, that one day this ramshackle home he built would be a mansion, "fit for a king. I won't be put down and laughed at much longer. I have big plans in the works for me and my family... I'm telling you, the name Nelson will be famous in these parts." That name *would* be famous one day, but not in the way he'd have hoped...

Karen pressed her head up against the grimy wood walls of the tiny hidden room, too small for someone to suspect a child to be here. The neighbors and passersby never looked behind the shed, and it was a routine Karen had no choice but to get used to. She had heard her mother was killed, murdered by a man who came from over Archtop hills; a loner who had killed before – byproducts of his illustrious career as a thief – and particularly liked to tease pretty young women. None were ever in danger of sexual assault, however.

This, if Karen knew, would in some ironic way honor her unknown mother's manufactured memory, and set the two women apart forever. She had hoped in her innocent young mind that the real mother she had never known, knew nothing of the sadness she had endured – and would continue to endure for years to come – on the Other Side.

In church she was repeatedly told that the dead held court over the living, laughing and lamenting their mortal frailties, learning a level of pity and compassion, much greater than that they knew when Of the Flesh. Karen dearly hoped in her beating heart that the headmistress was wrong, and all her aids who smiled and pretended to really care for her while her father sat in a pew upstairs mocking God were wrong as well; for if her departed mother – more a saint to her, to be mentioned in her prayers along with the others now than anything else – knew of her suffering and loneliness she'd felt inside...

She hated the thought of it. *The dead are dead and no more! The earthly suffering in life ends swiftly in Death; if not, there is no hope for me. I will die soon at the hands of this monster, my father.*

She promised herself one day she would escape. The cool damp dirt between her fingers made a faint sound, and she looked up in a vain attempt to get some fresher air among that tinted with manure, as if some invisible wire above her head held the promise of a cleaner world just beyond some short distance, reachable by those bold enough to stand on their tippy toes and look for it. Or was it more of a smell? The toxic blend of scents in the air permeated the house outside the grim walls of the shed or Karen's closet, so that, even on his good days, or in his good moods, she had the good fortune to relive the filthy prison she had learned to get used to and shudder, knowing when the bad moods hit again, and the sickness overtook him, she would always return. Once he lived through the sickness she endured with him, which was the way she viewed it when the 'demon rum' – as the Sisters called it – took its effect, trying, ever harder to brace herself for what she knew would come – always the same every time. Sometimes she would go to the closet without being washed off first. That was the worst part. The awful, dirty, worst part.

Chapter Two

Two days passed without a word from her Jewish benefactor. 7:35 a.m., Sunday, March 6th, Mr. Factor's phone call would wake Sharon up from an unnaturally deep sleep, the type she wasn't used to having and certainly wasn't used to enjoying.

"Hello? Who is it?"

"Ms. Langhorn... this is Leo Rothstein speaking. Good morning."

"Why yes, Leo, uh, Mr. Rothstein, how can I help you?"

"You had it right the first time." His voice was cheerful, though not in a forced way, which she found unsettling at this hour of the morning. "And it is me who is helping *you*, Sharon."

Hmmm... the first time he'd used my first name. What's that all about? "Rothstein, I'm feeling a little out of it this morning. Excuse me for being blunt, but *why* are you calling me at this time of the morning?" Her voice was a bit gravelly and not at all her usual – forced – pleasant tone.

"Why, Ms. Langhorn... I just felt you might be under the impression that, for some of us, we're already up and running"

"No user serviceable parts inside. Gotcha."

"Good. I'm glad 'we understand each other.' Down to business. I know it's Sunday, and a day of rest and all that mess, but I, through the kind overtime of my gal Friday Lisa here, managed to get an exclusive with your favorite surrogate Grandma."

"Today? The old lady Shifton wants to talk now all of a sudden?"

"You got it. Sometime between 2 and 2:30 would be, her words, 'fair enough!'"

"I wonder what changed her mind?"

"Don't bother. Can you take the bus to Astor Place and I'll pick you up there? I have some errands to run before then. This came as a close shave to me, too."

"Sure. That's not a problem."

"Fine. Great. I'll be there by about one. Try to get the 12:30 incoming to make sure."

"Will do. Any clues to what this is all about?"

"Not a one. I do know though, that she's changed her mind about you considerably. What'd you do, cast a spell?"

"We'll see soon enough. See you at Astor Place. Thanks."

"See you later. Bye."

Try to get the 12:30 incoming? He sure spoke strangely sometimes. *And what should I expect from the old lady?*

Sharon tossed herself out of bed. Walking to the bathroom she peed, splashed her face with lukewarm water and rubbed her hands to get the circulation going. She didn't see the benefits of the Morning Shower hyperbole. Too early. A bite to eat, a touch of makeup, an outfit... By 11:44 she was locking her apartment door and heading for the bus stop.

What the old widow had in her mind to talk about was anybody's guess. Maybe she'd let the plumbing go all these years, and repairs were beyond Sharon's small maintenance budget? Maybe fleas in the mattress? Moths in the cupboard? New sitcoms on TV not the stuff that gets with her – ancient – moral fiber?

Secret jokes and would be dramas aside what could it be that would make the old grump suddenly okay her credit rating? Or was Leonard telling the truth, and not sugaring her up, unbraced for the greater fall – and shame – that could – quite possibly – lie ahead. What *did* she want? It was unfair, Sharon supposed, to address her as an 'old grump,' or 'old whatever.' She would get there soon enough. Pretty sure that her coworkers above *and* below her figured her for an early Old Maid pension, she could almost feel the widow Shifton's age on her own smooth face.

It had been a tumultuous past year, indeed, the last three or four had been too, in a different way. Each annual marking of the free job calendar's January pages bringing her a little less certainty of the extent of her feminine anxieties from the year before. Or the year before that. Thirty three wasn't 'old' by anyone's stretch but no one epic moment or event in her life – at least not one she would admit to registering such an impact within her that could be instantly be recalled made the two identical numbers seem to weigh heavier just the same.

3+3=6. 3 and 3 makes 6. 5+1 makes 6. 2 and 4 makes 6. She reminded herself to pay attention to the street signs outside the opaque window seat, nowhere near her synchronized destination just yet, but she knew if she didn't stop daydreaming now, she'd miss it for sure. *Dum dee dum...* different faces on the half filled bus of almost every conceivably stereotypical city dweller *...dum dum dum...* Middle aged heavy set man by himself, sweating profusely, probably some sort of glandular problem *...da da da...* Young blonde cheerleader type, boy in baseball cap holding radio *...oh, Astor Place.*

She quickly pressed the sensor next to the seat behind her, excusing herself to the sallow faced woman sitting there – a moody sort, good candidate for midwife, if such an occupation still existed. She stepped softly down the three steps to the sidewalk below, and as her bus pulled away amidst thick grey gas fumes, she saw her date for this afternoon's tea party hadn't arrived yet. She stood near an old fashioned barber shop window – some still stubbornly existed, despite the proliferating standard of unisex salons and multi faceted 'day spas.' These quaint shops usually located at the bottom of some old tenement building or small garage like spaces unto themselves made her slightly uncomfortable. *Many things did, however*, and she wondered why she thought of it.

Mr. Rothstein pulled up in his navy blue four seater about ten minutes later. She didn't know the make of the car, but for that of a bachelor, found the interior immaculate. "How are you, Mr. Rothstein," she said, putting on her seat belt instinctively.

"Oh, I'm fine, thanks. Had to wait long for the bus?"

"No, it was fine. The ride, I mean… I was just trying to guess why the widow would want to see me – sorry, Mrs. Shifton, that is."

"As you said, 'we'll find out soon enough, huh?'" he chuckled softly.

The ride to the simple grounds of the Shifton 'estate' was brief – the long suburban roads running one into another as they usually do, making one lose track of the time. No one was outside, and no other homes stood near the house, an abandoned recreational field – once a park maybe – overrun with weeds and wind strewn branches and some man made litter sandwiched and bordered the house from the other properties. Highly angular in design, the Shifton House bore more than a passing resemblance to *her* soon to be property, something Sharon viewed as a bit obsessive for some reason.

They parked the car in front of the walk and climbed four concrete steps to the front door. *Why would they own a house similar to the one they want to sell me?*

Mr. Rothstein knocked on the door first, a few chop quick wrist movements, as one might if their occupation required them to protect their hands – artists, for example. *Was Rothstein an artist? If so, what kind? Was Widow Shifton artistic?*

Sharon felt herself drifting, so she stepped in front of Leo without apologizing and knocked heavier, having no reason to favor her knuckles. Leo eyed her with that 'elegant writer gaze,' finding – as a Jew – her sudden movement rude. Sharon couldn't tell that, but couldn't care less. *Life demands action, or else they leave you, out there, to die!*

They both turned their heads toward the heavy front door when a rustling sound was heard by both, like someone dragging a heavy object on a sheet over hard tile floor. The front door clicked suddenly, and the impatience – or inability – of whomever was on the other end made Sharon feel a chill. They both craned their necks without realizing, as if some golden age reclusive movie celebrity was on the other side.

The door finally creaked open, and the squinted light blue eyes of the widow made themselves known. No Harlowe or Mansfield after all; just a frail little woman in a patternless house dress. They both approached the doorway, eager to be inside. The widow gestured a weak bony finger through the harsh afternoon sunlight which she wasn't accustomed to feeling on her fragile skin. Yes, these *were* the young people she'd be entertaining today. They had to be. No one had knocked on that door for ages.

"Come in… Mr. Roth stein is it?" Leo shook his head affirmatively. "And Miss Langhorn, I presume."

"You'd presume correctly. I am Miss Langhorn." *Why'd I say that?* She let the 'Miss' go unreprimanded, since seniors have a tendency not to appreciate post women's lib 'Mizz' title, probably having all out abhorrence of it, as well. "Though, if you don't mind, *Mrs.* Shifton, I'd prefer *Ms.* Langhorn."

"Yeeeeesss," the old woman nodded, already reading Sharon as a difficult young snit. If she took the invitation as an opportunity to haggle, or 'snow' her in any way, the widow hoped that the young man whom she spoke to on the phone, here now in her home, would politely restrain her. *Impolitely, if necessary.*

"Please sit down," the widow offered, "both of you. Anywhere is fine. As you can see, I have lots of chairs." Leo and Sharon both thanked her and sat on opposite sides of the old flower pattern couch. *So many elderly people seemed to have these kind, no matter their income,* Sharon thought. The furnishings were sufficiently cheery, and none of the articles that made up the living room – the first room of the house – seemed to have been custom made, like so many homes of the wealthy do.

Rothstein didn't seem interested at all. He just sat quietly. Surprisingly, the widow rose slowly from her tall wooden chair and shifted over to the couch, sitting daintily between Man and Woman. "I *do* have many chairs, and sometimes people sit in them, *maybe even now.*"

"Excuse me?" Sharon asked. Her last sentence was too low to hear, even at their now close proximity.

"Oh, nothing, dear. Just thinking about my chores for later on."

Leo did hear what she said, and moved to the utmost end of his side of the couch. Something about her reminded him of his own mother, and that made him uneasy. He wanted to keep this a nonsocial call. After all, he was the least of the three with anything to gain. Most other agents he knew – Jewish or otherwise not – didn't chauffeur their clients around, meeting them at the bus stop and all of this couch sitting business. Sharon and the widow Shifton were talking about something now... drapes or something else of womanly interest, keeping him mercifully out of it. He tried to clear his mind, and wished he could close his eyes for a while. *Sharon? Shifton?* Are they sisters? He chuckled to himself. The widow took notice.

"Something funny, my dear boy? Please share it with the rest of the class."

Did she really say that? Her accusatory tone filled Leo with his own brand of chills. "No, Ma'am. – I just noticed that, uh –"

The woman uttered a hearty laugh, making them both jump on either side of the sofa. Leo and Sharon were less embarrassed by that than interested in what the woman would say, after the laughter subsided.

"I'm sorry to make you young people nervous. I used to teach grade school, and say things like that to entertain myself at times," she said, looking at Leo, then Sharon, then Leo again.

"That's quite alright," stumbled Leo, "no need to explain. I'm a bit at a loss here, Mrs. Shifton, maybe the heat..." He wiped his brow with an empty right hand, "but I'm afraid I couldn't alert my client, Ms. Longhorn here, to the nature of our visit, since you weren't that clear on the phone with me to begin with." He began to perspire more than the women, a bothersome problem he's had – and his mother ridiculed him for – since childhood. *Maybe women just didn't sweat as much as men.*

"Of course! I could well see why you'd be inquisitive, but actually, it was more the *young lady* that I was in the mood to speak with, Mr. Roth stein." She broke up the syllables on purpose, not sure if there was a 'proper' way to pronounce it. The 'Stines' and 'Steens' always confused her; a trait of Jewish and German heritage she found puzzling. "Could I offer you something to drink? My manners, really. It's hot outside and you must be dying of thirst. I'm not used to having... guests."

She momentarily looked at the floor before her last word, grimacing. *This woman has something to hide*, Leo thought. Not the most forgiving 'nice' thing to think, but he had a weird feeling about her. This was *not* the same crab that barked demands and complaints over the phone, and yes, some people – even in this day and age – do hate using the phone, though the shift in personality couldn't be attributed to an old woman's concern of being polite and hospitable. He drew a previous opinion of her that this was a woman who gave a damn – or feared, for that matter – about *nothing*.

Now being in her actual home, thinking about her as before, the old Hollywood 'no autographs' recluse who took a rare afternoon out of her personal musings to field questions from a generations removed fan... *Was that what he felt like?*

"I'll have a cold glass of water, please," he said stiffly. He never used that tone with anyone before. What was it about this house that rubbed him the wrong way?

"And Miss – *Ms.* Longhorn?"

"Thank you. If you have anything besides water, I'll take it. I'm parched."

"I'm afraid that's all I have, unless you can wait for me to make you some tea."

"Cold water'll be fine," Sharon said, deflated. She couldn't stand drinking water in a glass, which she always found herself doing at strange people's houses, and friends' alike. She *was* a guest, on *business*, presumably, and the old woman probably hadn't had anyone but the mailman over in years. If she knew people, the widow would ply her with tea later on, anyway. *Water always tastes better running*. At work Sharon would get the usual droll kiddie humor about 'saving some for the fish.'

"I don't have any ice, dear. The freezer's broken."

Yeah, that fountain at work sure has tasty water. "That'll be fine, thank you." *I can't wait to get out of here.*

Leo leaned over fast, almost falling off the couch. "Now, Mrs. Shifton, about the matter of my client's mortgage payments."

The old woman read his face plainly. The social call was over. She sat slowly into her favorite rocker, having done so walking backwards, feeling the lacquered wood brush her behind the knee. Leo felt the chills rising again.

"There isn't going to be a mortgage," she deadpanned.

"Excuse me?" Leo said, now so far at the tip of the cushion he had to remind himself to brace his legs, and pulled back.

"You heard me, Mr, Roth steen," she said, settling on the easiest pronouncement she could remember. "No mortgage, no interest, no mile long paperwork. I want to get out of here, and get out fast! Suffice to say I have my reasons, and *Mz.* Shifton is as good a tenant as any."

"But she'll be *owner* of this property, including the grounds, not a *rent* paying tenant."

"Don't mince words with me, Leonard!"

He froze, suddenly stricken with paralysis, or so it felt. If she had not invoked his mother's not yet departed spirit, embodied her just then, then he could be sure of nothing. Even her face seemed to change!

"Didn't mean to startle you, young man. As the 'lady' said, she likes to entertain herself now and again." The sullen tone came as quickly as the other one had passed. "I don't care what *I* call it, or what *you* call it, but I just know I'm selling the place, and you can word it how*ever* the heck you want, short of wording me out of my money!"

Leo thought words – and their proper usage – was what being a lawyer was all about. Words were important. Words made him *sane*. "I understand. I didn't mean to nitpick. Let me start over."

"Frankly, Mr. Roth steen, there's not that much to say, so don't search for words or lawyer talk you feel I might view as 'soothing' or 'comforting.' I'm an old tired woman – and I don't view that as derogatory, just as it really is – and I like being spoken to in the direct approach. I *will* need to speak to the young Miss myself."

Young Miss? She sure likes to take digs, Sharon thought.

"And after I'm convinced she's a suitable candidate to hold the patriarchal torch to this ramshackle albatross, I'll gladly sign any papers you may be carrying in that expensive *handbag* of yours, or any the Law may feel necessary."

Sharon felt her monologue concise, but felt strangely on the outside looking in.

As Leo stated she wasn't applying for live in babysitter, she was buying the house *to keep*. Why didn't she feel the woman grasped the concept? She seemed that she didn't want to leave – understandable at her age – but, if Sharon was to get through this without feeling sorry for her, then she had to show her she was no dummy, and fast.

"Madame, I really *do* admire your attachment to this beautiful house – mansion, really – truly understandable. But I, and I feel Leo as well – Mr. Rothstein, that is," He turned to her surprised at the abbreviation of his given name, "aren't exactly sure why we've been called here, feeling, seemingly, as you did, that you don't really want to leave here."

Thank you, Sharon. I'm glad somebody said it.

"Well, I really… you inspire me, Mz. Langhorn. The truth of the matter is, my perceptive young guest, that there are other variables those who haven't lived here all these years couldn't possibly fathom. My dilemma in having to choose how much to say, hoping to… *warn* you isn't the right word… to keep you *abreast* of the caretaking and maintenance of this house and, on the other hand, having to explain *why* the house itself needs so much care, is so hard for a woman of my years to express to a couple of city types – and so young, too – as yourself. Please understand. It is the *house itself* that needs caring for!"

"I'm not sure I get you, Mrs. Shifton," Sharon said inquisitively.

"Mr. Roth steen, may I ask you to be so kind as to excuse a retired schoolteacher and her guest while they converse – a little girl talk – in my cavernous kitchen?"

Rothstein was flushed. *Now they're going to have secrets and try to shut me out*, he thought. Contemptuously, Leo sat up straight and looked directly at the widow. "Yes, of course, if you'd allow me to thumb through your library here." He pointed to the walls stuffed full with dusty hardcovers.

"Sure, look around. I won't keep her long." The widow walked ahead of Sharon with easy, deliberate steps that suggested a much younger woman than herself. Sharon hadn't expected her to be so alert, with a grasp of formidable vocabulary, stinging wit, and an ability to read someone so well as to pick and choose her words, like a spy meeting a strained ally over cocktails.

The widow put her left hand out without turning to see her, the mother cognizant of losing her little girl at the shopping mall, but with her mind on other matters as well. *She seems extremely motherly. I wonder if she has children.* The widow turned to her upon reaching the partition between – what was this, a den? – and the 'cavernous kitchen.' It was indeed quite large, and unnecessarily furnished more for show than working practicality. "Now, *Mz*. Shifton, please sit down. There's a few things you should know about this house."

I wonder if she has her meals out. It doesn't seem like anything's been used for months. Sharon seated herself on a dinette chair nearest to her and folded her hands on her lap, trying not to shiver. The widow paced for a minute or so, making sure not to say too much, not to give away all of her... experiences. To Sharon, a long, excruciatingly tedious minute or so. Finally, she spoke.

"It's not easy for me to find the proper words, Sharon. May I call you Sharon?"

"Sure," she said, her voice cracking. "Can I have some water, please?"

"Of course." The widow pulled a clear long glass from the exquisite brass dishholder. *Brass?*

She squinted her eyes, but Sharon couldn't see any stains or rust associated with such an ill chosen alloy for the job. This was more a room in a dollhouse – all the rooms were – than a place where a breathing human being existed, ate and slept. It was tap water, probably luke warm, in a glass, but she would drink it. "Here you are, dear."

Sharon took the glass carefully. She was sure right now if she failed to hold it with both hands she would drop it. She shivered under her sweater, and drank half the glass of luke warm water. The widow stood at the sink, her arms propped up on the edge of it as if waiting to pounce. *A woman of her age? Please, Sharon, don't be silly.*

"How is the water?"

"Oh, fine. Do you have any problem with the pipes? Rust, I mean."

"No, no. we've been quite lucky as far as that goes. Sometimes the rain, you know, the rain gets into the outside pipes out back and – I don't know what causes it. Seems to be the water gets a little bit cloudy when the rain comes, but it's never that awful reddish color, no."

The widow gave a slight shudder at the thought of it that surprised Sharon and made *her* jump too, as if *she* felt the same about rusty water, embarrassed that she'd notice and think she was mocking her.

"Never knew much about plumbing," the widow continued, not noticing Sharon's nervous movement. "That was something my husband liked to tinker with, but it was more than that... Women them days weren't allowed to do 'Men's Work' and were talked about around town if they did. Now you've got this 'Women's Lib' and everything's different. Kinda scary if you ask me... Women marrying other women, and all that. Lez Bee Ins, is that what they call 'em?" she asked, enunciating the word with clear disdain.

"Yes, that's the word for it, alright."

"Are *you* one o'them lesbeeans? Cause if you are it don't make no difference to me. Money is money after all, and everybody needs a chance to better themselves, no matter what." Sharon stifled an urge to snort, the old woman's naïveté clashing hard with her own hard line feminist views. *Was it naïveté, or just male servitude? Why doesn't she know any better? Because, that's how she was brought up, and she doesn't know any better.*

The widow was left waiting for an answer. She hadn't noticed Sharon's twitching, or shaking, or nervous jumps, but she did – the Teacher – recognize that faraway look when she saw it. Sharon widened her eyes and recognized her thought. *That's a nice way to think. It's... good to be aware of things that have happened in the past couple of decades. Don't laugh. Please, don't laugh!*

"No, I'm *not* a lesbian, but like you I don't see them any differently."

"Right, well, that's good anyway. Do you have a husband, or someone steady in mind, or will you be staying in this big old house by yourself, like me?"

Sharon didn't want any comparisons between herself and this Old Bag, but she was moving in alone, and the thought of becoming this person before her was hideous. *What answer should I give? Be polite? Brazen? Open for suggestions?* "I'll be moving in alone, yes. I can make the payments, if you're worried about that."

"No, not at all. I'm sure your Mr. Rothstein would alert me to any problems way before they happen. His people are really good that way. They take pride in their business, which my Van used to admire about them. The Jews."

Van, like in van Morrison? Wild night is calling... Don't laugh! "That's nice, Mrs. Shifton."

"Call me Dorothy, please."

"Okay, Dorothy. So," she put her empty glass down so she wouldn't fidget with it. "What was it you wanted to talk to me about?"

The woman's blank gaze told Sharon it was too late for questions, the mention of her dead husband jogging her lonely memory. "Yeeeessssss..." she said clearly, in her own head now. "My Van was a great man, as great as they come. He made me feel so safe and cared for." Still dazed, she took another glass from the brass sculpture that held them and ran the tap. Her pale blue eyes went a disturbing off grey. "...I miss those days."

She took a few lukewarm sips and suddenly bolted upright, feeling a surge of recognition that again surprised Sharon. *This woman makes me terribly nervous. I hope not too many of these 'Sunday Visits' are in order to seal the deal. My nerves can't take it.*

"Sharon, there's something you have to promise me." She sounded terribly stoic. Unlike the woman Sharon had been speaking to moments ago.

She has many facets to her, this Old Bitch, Sharon thought loudly. "And what is that, Mrs. Shifton? Are you sick? Is there something you need?" *Damned politeness to hell in a handcart. Anything to speed this trip to Grandma's House.*

Unfazed, or maybe just not caring to comment, she answered with the clear tones of a woman many years her junior. The effortless way the woman moved around her vocal cords for dramatic effect was impressive. *Old teachers never die, I suppose?*

"*No*, dear, I am *not* sick. And *I*, at my age, need nothing. The truth is, this *house* is sick, and she needs many things, not the least of all being a mistress who understands her needs. You will find that, although she requires much attention and consoling," she broke off to sip her water carefully and train her gaze on the unflinching stare of her guest. *She thinks I'm mad. That's all well and good. I'm going to retire with my nerves intact. As much as it'd like to, this old barn isn't going to kill me yet. Try your hand at it!* "This house will give you enjoyment and companionship, once you begin to *understand* each other."

She finished eying Sharon over the glass. It hadn't occurred to her to put it down yet. Sharon stayed politely still, hands in her lap, listening to this nonsense. She saw a comical scene in her mind just then; Leo, rushing through the swinging kitchen door, carrying a red hot poker in one hand, a clenched fist in the other. *Stop it! Stop it! Please get to the point, Thee of Many Wrinkles, or I shalt sticketh thee with thine porker. Yay. Verily. Forsooth! Don't laugh!*

Coolly, she said, "Really, Mrs. Shifton, I don't know *what* you're talking about, or where you're going with this."

"I'm talking about ghosts, you little fool!" the widow said, slamming the glass backwards into the lower sink cupboards, shattering the thick clear cylinder into a surprisingly intricate array of hazardously tiny crystal clear meteorites, just inches short of the part of her body where her hips might have been, long ago. Sharon fixed on the splintered shards hitting the floor, thinking, *in a parallel universe, this all made sense somehow.*

Leo slammed down the copy of *Tom Sawyer* he was skimming and found the old woman weeping. He saw the blood on her right hand and looked at Sharon with a hang dog expression she had not seen on his face – Leo, Leonard, Leonard Rothstein, Roth steen, before. "What the hell happened here?" he barked, out of character, his dark eyes now on the blood falling to the tile from the widow's wrist. *At her age, that could be serious*, he thought guiltily.

Sharon answered him, smirking, clearly overtired and not caring anymore. "Why, Leonard, dear boy. As you can see, everything's just fine."

"There's gauze in the bathroom cabinet," said the widow sharply. "I'll be fine. You two, I'm not so sure." She said it sighing heavily. *Drily?*

When they said their polite goodbyes – papers signed – the date was March 8th, the time was 3:35 p.m., and the house was now, for all visible purposes or any bit of passing small talk, Sharon's. Leo dropped her off at her building, patting her hand before opening the door for her on the passenger side. He might have done this just out of politeness, or male conditioning, or even as a passive flirt – how many movies had she seen where a case got sticky due to the attorney falling for his client, or vice versa – which she dismissed.

More than likely, he had read the shaky, sweaty palms going over and over her pleated skirt, making the blood flow warmly through her firm thighs underneath; or just the plain desperation in the eyes of a woman who was just realizing that maybe it *wasn't* so bad to live with a roommate who didn't much respect her, and who most likely respected herself – from all the amoebas with penises that sashayed their testosterone from one room to another, gone the next morning from Bea's room – less... She digressed. Bea? Sharon realized she was the only one who didn't call Beatrice Bea, or Betty – she was suddenly trying her luck with name abbreviations – Leo, for instance – and wrote her a, in her estimation, downright affectionate memo before brushing her tired teeth and going to bed.

The anxiety Sharon felt had hung off her shoulders on the Leonard Rothstein steen, she remembered, the old woman trying in vain to find the right pronunciation when so many names were infinitely harder to pronounce – chauffeured ride home, and the meeting with her widow friend was as stressed as the fragile Ms. Langhorn had reluctantly expected.

Beatrice –

I was at the house and me and the woman worked out a deal. I'll be staying there alone for the next three days. Will be back sometime in the afternoon of the 12th, maybe night. Enjoy the bottle of Sherry I left for you. Thanks for the party – no hard feelings? See you later –

Sharon

Perfect grammar or wording notes to roommates makes for a thin turnout at your funeral, she thought, not knowing why, and tried to avoid either. She set the alarm for 6:30, figuring on leaving the apartment at 8 or so, the widow was not specific about when to arrive, just 'sometime in the morning,' would do. Leonard was kind enough to, as he said, 'cell phone a pal of mine in the car game,' and had *him* cell phone an employee's beeper to have a car ready to rent, delivered to Sharon's building in the morning.

'He'll wait for you,' Leo said, like he knew the guy, and Sharon marveled – as she often did on her coffee breaks or subway rides when she forgot to bring a book to read – at how Mankind, in the latter part of the twentieth century – or was it really the 21st working an early shift? – could get so much done without the primitive notion of physical contact to complete a task, as long as your colleagues and mercenary types they dealt with were similarly 'plugged in.'

She got under the covers and closed her eyes, thinking of, among other things, what she was supposed to do in that big house all by herself for four days. Then again, for that matter, what would she do in this house alone for years to come? *Was I crazy? What do I need a crazy old mansion for, to die there? An expensive tomb maybe?*

She folded her arms over her bosom and willed herself to at least close her eyes, if sleep was to be out of the question tonight. *Just try to take it easy. It'll be alright.*

March 9th, 12:35 a.m.

Chapter Three

The barn doors flapped open with the breeze heavily, signaling the start of the storm that was soon to come. Karen was in the kitchen lighting the cast iron stove, coals splintered in the candlelight with sparkling fingers reaching out to get her, failing to get her, within the Iron Maiden bodice type shape of the burner her father had built with a man named Clifford – last or first name she could not be sure, her father called everyone he knew by one name only; it was his way... who was a blacksmith by trade, or that's what she thought by overhearing the two men talk of labor, which was often. It was a man's sense of pride to garner himself honest, steady work to 'provide for his family' – a saying she couldn't quite comprehend since she was 'provided' with so little, in comparison to the other children she'd spoken to at school now and again.

Karen Nelson, due to her father's constant yelling and strapping her to make her see His Way, didn't bother talking to those her own age as Daniel Nelson would tell her in between belt lashes that would turn her soft freckled fair skin the deepest shade of red she could imagine. When the areas she had been struck had taken time to settle and raise, the deep red would pass into a purplish blue, and she'd sit on the floor of the house, or when she got the sickness, sitting in the filth of the tin roofed shed and stare at the wounds intently and dream they were something else, as if she were changing into some mythic forest gnome or faerie creature she had read in the books she'd sneak away to look at in the small room at the bottom of the school.

Basement. Base ment. Can you use the word basement in a sentence Karen? 'I am kept a prisoner in the basement of a monster. A monster that treats his farm animals better than I, and as far as I'm allowed to know, does not subject them so to such hideous, wretched games as I must accept as a common occurrence.' No, I dare not answer my teacher with such strong, true words as this; Miss McConnell was uninterested, and reacted quite heated at times in fact, when any of her class children spoke out of turn.

'Out of turn' for an adult of course, being only sort of happening not placing them in the middle of an ever spinning universe of which their importance rivaled, if not exceeded, that of her precious Sun itself. The stars, and what she had heard of Astronomy – what some of the mothers of the children construed as Witchery – amused her. In her bleak predicament of Life with Father, few things often did.

In fact, if she could be considered dead on the spot, as she sat in her very classroom chair before her also, inked pen in hand, then she certainly *would* accept as so. Hers was the soul of a child imprisoned in an adult whore's form. The shutters were making an awful sound, rickety rak, rickety rak, that made Karen look over her shoulder intently, somehow imagining that someone – a man, a dirty man that frequented the Inns and bars, past the hills where Father went to business – might be peering in looking at her tending the fire. What he did was still completely unclear to her; all she knew was that he hadn't been home when he usually was tonight, and poking the sparkling embers within the Iron Maiden with the long branch she'd found outside on her way back from school today was a good way for her to get the nervousness off her mind.

When he came home late, that usually meant one of two things… One, that he'd had an argument with someone at Gray's Tavern, and not getting the respect he deserved, would come storming in through the storm pitted ill shaped wooden door.

It often stuck on its hinges when opening or closing, not having been properly screwed and measured when Daniel Nelson and a coworker built the doorway and nailed the boards together – boards that now looked back at her ominously, more unsettling than any old hardcover she'd read about possessions, or ghost stories, or work of demons, books Miss McConnell always found time in her teaching schedule to condemn utterly.

The Bible was the only book that was above critiques; why this was so eluded her. She knew her teacher went to church on Sunday morning. She had to; she also doubled as Christian Instructor in the dark, incensed and torch lit room below the main room with the stained glass and the Saint statuettes, where the adults congregated and said their prayers. Children had little right to live – was that too harsh an opinion? – and nowhere was that glowing observation clearer than when, not scant seconds with which to admire the beautiful colors inside the church, the pews, all in tow like women soldiers awaiting the signal of their commander; the Altar pearly white through the thick smoke of incense, which seemed to grow from the steeply raised floor of the Church.

She or the other children never stayed long enough to see where the white clouds with the thick acrid scent that tickled her nose emanated from, and – she'd be too embarrassed to ask this, but – Karen didn't think any of the other children knew either. The children were separated from their parents by a tall, slim, white robed priest who always held a staff of iron, that frightened some of the children, in his right hand and ushered past a secret passage which opened somewhere behind the priests' quarters – it was dark and Karen could never be sure of the exact place where the real wall was and the false wall began – and were left in the care of Miss McConnell for the next two to three hours.

There was a tall, beautifully engraved wall clock leaned against the ragged stone wall, as close as it could be before it would wobble on its mortar base, crashing and causing the priests to frown and wander the caverns and halls, mourning their ticking friend, who ticked no longer.

Karen's mind would wander quite a bit during these Instructions, and indeed it was her lively imagination that kept her from sinking into deep depression. *If she only knew.* Standing so straight with her pretty hemmed skirts and buttoned petticoat she bought from the Pennsylvania tailor who knew her father, if she only knew what a bleak, sad, pathetic life her pupil Karen Nelson led outside of her classroom. Although this room – if one could call it that – was scary and filled with the ghosts of the tortured and the condemned, souls who had denied Christ, the Lord and his father, the Creator, and had paid the long slow agonizing price the Church handed down for accepting to be saved without question – the tall iron staff carrying priest seemed to revel in the stories of the Hunts, when all in the streets were wicked with the thoughts of Satan's children, and the Pope had decreed those to either be saved or tortured til death – or both.

She'd gladly stay here forever, without the torches to light the shimmering stone wall, a coppery red and orange hue, if it meant she'd be away from that man, the one who terrified her so. Yes, darkness could be endured as well as other things. Why not? The darkness of the shed was the deepest blackness there was in this life, or had to be. If the sins of the father, as she'd read in the Old Testament, were as harshly abominated by God as she was told, then black, the color black, seemed to get a deeper black, til it felt like she was falling into a deep, unholy well somewhere inside herself.

All of this imagining played hell on a young girl's concentration, and, to her credit, Miss McConnell was decidedly more patient with her flock here than in the intellectually haunted walls of the local school building, a building often charged with being of little use to the town of Old Forge overall, the needs of children again meaning little in the adult world's scheme of things she could not, willed not to, understand fully. She would miss 8th grade, and any grade thereafter, due to the ultimate decision to close the school forever – their precious Miss McConnell fading into marital oblivion.

As of now the school would open its doors on schedule, a haven for the children of the lost souls from Old Forge, New York. Yes, 8th grade would pass her by like many other things but she'd prepared for this possibility – prepared for the possibility of Death itself – even – however much a fourteen year old could prepare for Death – and stabbed at the dancing coals indifferently, waiting.

Sharon arrived at the widow's estate around 9:00 a.m. The man who drove her to her destination, Sam Cornell, had been a perfect gentleman, even by Sharon's scrutinizingly peculiar standards. *You can never be too careful about men*, her mother would say. *They'll stab you in the back with a dull blade if they have to, and if they don't have that, then a couple of your broken ribs'll do just fine. They're always trying to compensate for that rib they gave to make Eve. Just jealous, I say... The only really good deed any of them could ever take credit for.* She was appreciative of Rothstein for talking the guy into renting her a car for her three day stay.

More than 'appreciative,' she was fast considering him a friend, and when all this hokey nonsense of house sitting her soon to be property – a 'courtesy arrangement', so dubbed by the Old Bag herself, to convince Sharon there definitely *was* some sort of spiritual entity or whatever; *poltergeists even*, like a certain famous feline cartoon character might say – was mercifully over with, she'd have to remind herself to ask the ol' boy in sometime. Not that she had changed her idea of Men that much. They were still Troglodytes, these rare specimens Rothstein and Cornell notwithstanding.

"You sure you're gonna be alright here?" Cornell asked, turning to look at her next to him, his eyes meeting hers. He wasn't a bad looking man – bulky around the shoulders and arms, a 'powerlifter' type, though he didn't seem like a gym junkie; longish slicked back hair that flapped quietly from the breeze coming through his open driver's side window; nice features; smiled a lot but seemed to mean it; black tight shirt, white khaki type pants – Beatrice would like him. Not the bookish type like Rothstein at all.

From talking to him on the ride over, she sensed he'd read a few novels she might have enjoyed herself, if she had the time or patience to *read* a book all the way through. Why do you meet all the nice guys and the hunks – like this one – when you're never prepared for it? She really cared little for that sort of Cracker Jack box cliché 'Sensitive Male' question, but answered him brusquely and without a speech anyway.

"I'll be fine, thanks, Mr. Cornell. Thanks so much for driving me here. It wasn't necessary."

"*Sam*," he said aggressively, startling her for a second, "and it's on me. No trouble... I told Leo not to worry about the rental... we'll square away the damage when you come back from your little vacation here." He pointed at the large estate outside.

"It's hardly a vacation, Mr. Cor – Sam." *Remember – try to be warmer with people. Who knows? It might help.* "But it *is* an unusual arrangement. Lucky I'm on self imposed sabbatical, indefinitely. Nice time to be playing hooky from work, right? Now that I have to pay off this fossil in back of me." She felt a sudden urge to throw her head into his blond chest and whine like a spoiled little rich girl in all those feminists' nightmare 50s B High School flicks, but didn't. She had never been this moody and out of control of her emotions – the only thing she felt she ever *could* control – since planning this *purchase magnifico* with Rothstein, off and on, two months back. She was late this month, and figured that was the reason, nothing more.

"Well look, Sharon – if it's okay I call you Sharon."

"Well, I really don't – "

"Let me leave you my business number," he said, not really interested in her answer. "If you have any trouble with the car, not that I think you *will*, since like you said, you'll only be taking her out for groceries and short runs up and down the road here."

He pointed instinctively to nothing in particular, just fanning the windshield of the Subaru Pioneer with his left index finger, a motion that reminded Sharon of a gunslinger. *Yeah... come from out west, by way of Brooklyn?* She felt the giggle coming through her shoulder blades before she could stifle it.

"Did I say something funny?"

"No," Sharon said, her eyes wide, "I just got a sudden case of the giggles. They come on every so often," she lied.

"Are you sure? I think it's these hands of mine. I'm always making gestures, sometimes goofy looking ones. I bet I gotcha with that pistol whip number, didn't I?" Maybe it was the early morning hour, lack of sleep, stress, nerves or whatever, but no sooner had he said the word 'pistol,' Sharon let out the loudest heartfelt laugh like she hadn't remembered doing in years. *Oh, that felt good...*

"I'm sorry but you hit the nail on the head with that one. I didn't mean to make fun –"

"What are you afraid of?" he butted in, much softer this time. "If something's funny, it's funny. C'mon, I'll help you bring your bags in, no charge." He came around to her door and opened it, pulling her two small suitcases, a large handbag, and a few plastic shopping bags of canned goods from the trunk. It was a power opener job, and Sharon thought the little Japanese car suited her fine. His right hand man Jake something followed behind the whole way. Sam of course needed a way to get back home. Was this his not so subtle way to meet women while his silent partner in tow chauffeured him home? *Beatrice would eat him up.*

After the Lincoln Town Car kicked up dust on its way back to the City, Sharon took out the single key from her purse the widow had given her the previous day and placed it in the lock, making the sign of the cross – something she never remembered doing before – before she turned the key. The heavy brass trimmed wooden door opened easily, quietly; no eerie creaking noises she half expected to hear. *Expected?* No, more like *willed* herself to hear.

I won't be bullied by this old doddering woman with her perverse psychology about wanting to move out in the worst way and yet making me agree to this stupid three day weekend mess. 'Not a good candidate for caretaker' if I can't last seventy two hours and a morning. Indeed! Thank you, Mrs. Shifton... you old bat!

That fourth morning, the 12th of March, was to be the day she took up permanent residence, at least on paper, anyway. The old woman called it 'premature' on her part to tell Ms. Langhorn she could *move* in on the 12th. Being here before or after suited her fine, she could even have a swinging singles party Friday the 13th into Saturday morning the 14th, just don't move in *on* the 12th is all.

She doubted March 12th christened a birthday, or anniversary, or any such thing associated with the widow. If it did, why the blank expression and roadkill eyes about it? Something 'special' happened on March 12th every year in this house. And, coming from a woman who didn't have a friend or living relative – in the world, God only knows what that date must have signified. *Was it really the 13th this Friday? I'm getting too old for this.*

The late morning and early evening of March 9th was no big spook out, in fact, she wished there *was* something to take her mind off the boredom and creaking walls of this old double decker – maybe that, or those, was/were the ghost/ghosts? Hey, if babysitting a couple of spirits – besides the alcohol kind – is all she had to do to close this deal, it would be fine with her. Goes over Leo's head in a way, in which way she could not exactly be sure, but in some strange way she thought he should be here as well, too. *Well, let Leo get his beauty rest – he'd done enough for me above and beyond the call*, she thought.

Sharon spent the day thumbing through a few Harper's Bazaar mags she had accumulated without looking at; she wasn't interested in catching up on her mail the way she used to, so why not get a little bloodshot eye mania on the old lady's dime?

41

At about 4:30 – she could not bother squinting around her to the next room, where the wall clock was – she dropped a few letters she had yet to open in her lap and put her head back, trying to catch a little shut eye before having to go to bed.

She laughed out loud thinking that, a little dry cough laugh that sent a cold tingle through her spine down to her fingers. There was a fireplace – the clichéd of all in the annals of ghost story history time – and she'd lighted it hours before to get used to it, since more than likely she would not knock out any walls or make any other big architectural changes, since she despised that duration from clean to clutter to clean again, even though she had not actually been through that, just breathless slob fests now and again, and decided that, really, being here seeing it now, that this house and its cozy, old fashioned style suited her fine. Anyway, the widow had requested that she not change anything including the furniture, otherwise incurring the wrath of the mysterious tenants she'd hinted so strongly about.

After daydreaming for a few hours and no television to help her get to sleep – the widow saw no good in it – at about 10:40 Sharon changed into her nightgown and slept in what she supposed was one of the guest rooms. All the rooms were peculiarly narrow and practically identical; the original builder must have had a purpose in mind, but what it could be must have died with him, if he *was* dead. She looked up at the ceiling and went quickly to sleep. Her bad dreams, however, did not go so quickly.

Still in her soft white cotton nightshirt, Sharon felt transported into another time, another version of what she was *sure* had to be the same spot – or at least close by – that she was laying in moments ago. Moments? How much time had gone by? She could see herself in the empty room, looking around, as if suddenly being placed there by the gods, without explanation, but somehow feeling she should be here. It was dark, pitch black, and the Dream Sharon could feel things brush against her feet.

Actually the hem of her *nightshirt* was brushing something, and her feet were squishing inside something cool and, as she took more steps, never ending. She put her hand before her face and saw it for a second, but then realized she *wanted* to see it. Trying to focus – *could her eyes focus in pitch blackness?* – she chanced taking broader steps, her oversized man's shirt – that Dave had given the *real* Sharon – swept back and forth with a dull *whoosh*, definitely hitting something on the sides of her, but what? A far off sound her feminine intuition – the Dream Sharon – cautioned her was the crying of a child – *a young girl?* – alarmed her, and she stood straight, hoping to be able to hear better and guide herself to the sound. The company of a sad little boy or girl, a stranger, wasn't a very cheerful thought and to witness such things made the Dream Sharon sad just thinking about it.

The Real Sharon could see herself thinking turned on her side in the guest's bedroom, too involved to simply wake herself up now. Her other self bent at the knees – there was definitely something brushing both sides of her nightshirt now – something *large* or *some*one – and, feeling bolder, reached out slowly with her right hand broadly, as a blind man might as to avoid striking their head on a foreign object, and felt skin – no, not skin. Flesh, yes, but not human. There was a thin coat of short hairs ticking her palm, and she smiled, unafraid. A guttural sound came from someplace just ahead, a sound every child learns to identify early on, an *oink*, or the sound of a pig. She was brushing a sleeping sow's bristly fur in the opposite direction of growth, dull quills that seemed to inspect her fingertips, and she obviously had awaken the animal from its own piggy dreams, but it did not stir or get to its feet as she might have expected.

The first few loud grunts were followed by softer ones, and both the Real and Dream Sharons couldn't recall hearing the sounds of a pig in mid sleep. Karen the Second kept her hand on the soft, warm belly, feeling a serene rush of – *compassion?* – of some *goodness*, as if emanating from the animal itself.

She brought her palm down in reverse and felt her hand ride over the soft hill that was its hind legs, and playfully felt for its hooves, feeling the leg thinning out suddenly – horribly she thought, the warm thick flesh replaced by a bony spare rib against her skin. She never remembered her fingertips feeling so *sensitive*, as if the sow's primal essence could be picked up by them, and through her own solidly real but dreamed form.

Finding one of the rear hooves, she tugged it slightly, grasping the point at which the bone had split off as Mother Nature had designed it. This was not met with the indifference the sow had shown before, and it suddenly tried to right itself, falling off to its side, grunting loudly once more, and regained its footing, but stayed still before her. At least she could feel it standing before her, its head in front of her midsection somewhere, its thick breath blowing little air bullet holes into her loosely hanging nightshirt. *Man's t shirt, really,* the Real Sharon said to herself, working through a separate part of brain, still very much the Observer.

Sharon II cold still hear the weeping, louder now. Yes, definitely a girl. Teenager, possibly. She turned to her left where she'd heard the sound, and realized her chubby friend was making too much noise for just one piglet, or full grown sow for that matter. There was more rustling against her nightshirt, and she was immediately aware of many *more* pigs suddenly, deftly, for what she guessed was their rather large size – pigs bred and overstuffed for slaughter – rising one at a time, awakened by the alarm clock that was swill now, her lone Pig Friend.

The freshly awoken – now – grunts reverberated in this room, bouncing off the walls, wherever they were in this cruel darkness, making her hold her ears, the scattered stover effect, as if coming from one monstrous sized pig, which, if she hadn't felt the series of overfed bodies shifting restlessly against her thighs, hooves half sleepily scratching her bare ankles, causing her to lift either leg in reflexive defense – she might think just might be true. They rustled loudly, jostling each other and almost knocking her over at least twice, her bare heels digging into the moistness beneath her she now figured must be slop, or earth, or both.

44

The gross picture this called up into her mind had not long to stay there, her immediate concern being just to grasp onto any belly or head or snout she could grab so as not to fall over. She would hate to fall into this mess below her, crashing into a filthy stew of old soggy cabbage, table scraps, dirt and pig shit face forward, ending her brief dream life painfully as the heavy sharp hooves of her new pals played a perfectly fine game of break-the-bitch's-bones, their weight on her bringing those sweet strains of Gabriel's Horn.

Their restless square dance subsided as quickly as it started, and Sharon II being in no danger of being – as she recalled the title of a late 70s Led Zeppelin tune – Trampled Under Foot – she trained her dream ears on that constant sobbing, now clearly audible beyond the stirring noises and grunts and yawns and farts – these Sharon mercifully was unable to *smell* where she was, just *feel* it – of her temporary roomies. She walked past the herd, still to her sharp left, getting closer and closer now to the origin of the crying. It was more of a *wail* now. What could this poor child be suffering through, to cry so violently? She now stumbled through the … trail, her dormant maternal instincts now to the forefront and in full bloom.

Her left foot, in mid sprint, struck another fleshy substance, and as if from all around her, the faraway sobbing abruptly stopped and a terrible screeching filled – no, *assaulted* her ear drums, the blood curdling tones of an animal being expelled from heaven, swirling round and round her head. Dizzily, more on the verge of falling now than ever – if not flat out fainting – this also subsided and was replaced by that heartbreaking young girl's weeping. Now, however, the far off fuzzy AM Radio was gone, and Sharon II was ashamed to find the sound coming from directly in front of her.

She accidentally struck the girl in the thigh as she ran to her, the girl – still invisible to her in the darkness – sitting at her feet, possibly propped up against one of the terribly acoustic walls of this black Hell. She felt a soft, clammy hand grasp hers, as if the strange night vision worked just a little, thank you, and gripped her palm firmly.

If she were trying to rise, odds were in Sharon II's cloudy state that they'd both be sprawling in the invisible moistness in a split second, this wasn't the case though, as if the grasp were more a sign of blind recognition. Another human – another *woman* – to accompany her and soothe her young troubled mind in this maze of pigs, mud, darkness and nothing else.

If there were walls, Sharon II's mind flashed in front of her, *then there had to be a door.* She found this life outside herself – as the Real Sharon watched intently outside *her*self – unendurable for much longer, and, an uncharacteristic move for the real Sharon, this alternate universe Sharon pulled the unseen girl by the forearm bending at the knees for leverage, as she did when she stroked the first pigs' fur, but the girl didn't want to leave, it seemed. She stood firm, like stone, as Sharon II froze for a moment in distinct desperation.

A blaze of light appeared as if sent by God, and the girl was clearly visible now, although the brightness forced Sharon II to cover her eyes, the lustrous light, burning on her flesh like an unendurable summer heat, the humidity turned to maximum. She forced herself to look down again, just to know the face of this poor soul crouched below her, not being able to see her through the painfully bright light. This movement was in vain, as the Hell lights beamed into a dazzling strobe now, and this space, until now only occupied by herself and her young 'guest,' as far as she'd known, was now filled with back to back bodies of future pork rinds, bacon, and ham strips – all the pigs she'd been among before seemed to catch up to her. *I didn't hear anything! They've been transported somehow.*

As she looked around in a confused panic, sow's flesh so close they seemed to support her, like an overcrowded rush hour NY subway, almost lifting her off the ground, the little girl – she saw snippets of her shape – long brown hair, straight to the shoulders, print dress or some sort of school uniform, she couldn't be sure; sweet, youthful features, big sad eyes above a sensual, pouty mouth – was now laughing hysterically, maniacally, and in the warp speed strobe she was trapped in the middle of – the awful inescapable middle – her companion's eyes reflected this devilish cackling.

The girl cringed from her, and Sharon II thought she'd noticed her among the pig army before her for the first time and, disoriented, pulled away, not comprehending.

But it was this Other World Sharon who wasn't comprehending all this, not in the least, and as her mind drifted briefly, the teenager lunged for her from her seated position, dirty fingers bent into claws, mouth opened ready to... Sharon II screamed, and just then the dream broke, and the Real Sharon was alone, and shaken awake in a cold sweat that moistened the pillow beneath her. She opened her eyes wide, and wiped away what she realized were tears; not the moistness that films over eyes. Like tears during sleep, not tears. She bolted from the bed and went down the hall to the guest bathroom, and fainted.

Daniel Nelson came home to the slight strains of a fourteen year old girl humming to herself, his distant rage upon arrival temporarily out of mind. She turned with a jolt hearing the door slam shut, not realizing he was home. The sun had come up and she'd been waiting, without sleep, for hours.

"Karen," he bellowed, "what are you doing there? Why don't you make my supper?"

"Well, I though–" Hesitating, Karen's larynx froze, the shock of him in front of her with that look. Trembling, she took a short breath and started again. "I... I thought you'd be home earlier." *About seven hours earlier.* "But if you want, I'll fix you breakfast. I had to throw out your dinner. It was burnt. So, don't worry, I'll – "

"You threw out my dinner? Bitch, what did you do *that* for? Can't you do anything without making me fucking angry? Now make me something to eat you cunt, and maybe I'll leave you alone and sleep it off." He spied the poker in her hand and, even though she'd never have the good sense to try anything like she was thinking, wrenched it from her hand roughly in his paranoia just the same. "Give me that!"

"Ow! I'm not doing anything with it."

"I'll say you're not." He pushed her, knocking her against the stove, sending a fast hot pain through her shoulder. She reached out, slumping to the floor. He was smirking the way he always did to make her feel inferior. Worse, unloved and unappreciated. Karen, despite everything, still loved her father. He pulled her up by the back of her tattered housedress and slid his left hand through the open front over her right breast. He turned her around, hiking up her skirt, stroking her young thighs slowly, lustfully.

Karen's eyes were wide. Still disjointed from lack of sleep, she expected this when he came home in a rage, no doubt angry and revved up from a deadly combination of arguing, fist fighting, disrespect, and habitual lying. She really thought, waiting up for him all night, that *this* time he would act like a father; hold her in his arms, stroke her hair, poking the embers as she did before. *Things will be alright, sweetheart, things... will be different now... So different.*

His hands paused on her small curved hips for a moment, savoring the sensation of his erection growing to maximum effect through his dungarees. Pulling his penis out of his fly with his right hand, he bent her at the waist hard. Karen thought she heard something crack. Her body had stiffened into a mock rigor mortis – part of her muscles' defenses for enduring the Act. He guided his hard penis against her, and thrusted hard at once, making Karen gasp with pain and fear. Once in, he had intercourse with her savagely, both still standing, him still holding onto her waist for leverage.

"No, please, stop... Daddy, stop, please..." Karen whispered, almost to herself. *Only to herself.*

"Quit mumbling, whore. I'm in the mood for some tight pussy, and you *know* you got the one I like. Ooh! You feel good bitch. I wanna fuck you good. Get on the floor." Bending forward, she fell to her stomach on command, petrified. He was horny, and speaking like a father did not talk to his daughter. "I'm gonna give it to you in the ass, cunt. I'm gonna fuck you in your ass til you scream, and beg me to take it out. Take it out of your young smooth tight sweet ass! Do you want it in the ass, bitch?"

48

She didn't answer. Or scream. Or beg. She grit her teeth until it felt as if they would break off at the gums, while he penetrated her anally as far up into her as he could. Drops of blood formed against his erection. And he held a muscled forearm around her neck as he climaxed within her.

Having finished, he rose, draping her dress over her behind, and slumped, giggling stupidly to himself – in the corner, quickly falling asleep. A deep sleep he'd be in the middle of until morning. *Okay, it's over. At least I didn't get sent to the shed this time.*

She tip toed out to the pump, where she cupped the rusted water in her hands and bent over, legs open, to wash herself. Afterward, she went over to the pig pen and peered in. A rush of recognition gripped her, and she fled through the field crying. Karen awoke later that afternoon from a deep sleep, looked up to the sky, and dreamed impossible dreams.

Chapter Four

Sharon called her psychiatrist from the widow's estate. Phone calls were allowed, "within reason of time and place," the widow stated, and she took the opportunity to call Doctor Haskel and let him know how she'd been doing. She needed to talk to someone. It was March 10th, roughly 3:30 in the afternoon – she couldn't see the big clock too well, the only one in the house – from where she was, a little cove below the main stairs where the Master Phone was. *The only one of those, too. I'll need to put in a couple more extensions when I move in*, Sharon thought, as she dialed the number on the quaint Princess rotary phone. If the widow let her.

No doubt she would, as all the furnishings were included in this dirt cheap deal. She heard her mother's clipped tones in her head. *Sharon, don't look a gift horse in the mouth. After all, it's not every day you get a 'mansion' for the price of a New York condominium. I'm your mother. I won't steer you wrong.*

Ring, Ring... a strainingly pleasant young girl's voice, maybe eighteen or nineteen, was heard on the other side, three-hundred-something miles away.

"Hello? This is Doctor Haskel's office."

"Yes, hello... Trisha?" Sharon grabbed the name through a fog.

"It's Doctor Haskel's office. Yes, I'm Trisha." Trisha sounded like she had a toothache. Sharon guessed that she was alone, and she was munching on some potato chips. *Wise. Unsalted. Yep, got to watch the old tum tum, Mz. Langhorn.*

"This is Ms. Langhorn. *Sharon* Langhorn."

"Oh, yes! Ms. Langhorn!" Sharon heard a rustle near the phone. A hastily crumpled junk food bag, no doubt. When Trisha spoke again, her tone returned to Concerned Secretary Mode. "How are you? You haven't been to the office in quite a while."

"Only three weeks," Sharon answered. She considered the comment intrusive, but dismissed it. "I'd like to talk to the Doctor, if he's there, please, Trisha."

"Where are you calling from?"

Why do you care, you little airhead? "I'm out in Old Forge. Calling from a ghost town."

"*Where* are you, Ms. Langhorn?"

Sharon's stomach started to softly flutter, her left temple pulsing slightly to the beat. "Old Forge! Old Forge, New York. It's upstate!"

"Okay. Up state. Will you be coming for a visit soon?"

"Well, let me talk to Robert and I'll *find out*," Sharon said, tersely. *Why he hired her I'll never know.*

"Ro – uh – Doctor Haskel isn't in right now, Ms. L. I'll give him the message –"

"Wait, don't hang up. I can't use this phone too many times. Listen. Write down this number I give you." The widow's phone number was inscribed into the small niche above the Princess Rotary. Slowly she spelled the numbers while Trisha said them back to her.

"Got it," Trisha said.

"Now Trisha. Let the Doctor know where I am and to *please call me* up here when he gets in, or when he voicemails you, or whatever. I have something to tell him about." The last sentence dragged off her tongue deathly slowly.

"Sure. I'll let him know you need to speak to him urgently. I'm sure he'll try to reach you right away. Oferge, right? O-F-E-R-G-E?"

Sharon's head had reached that fog bank again. Like when she tried to remember the secretary's name, and wanted to hang up. "Yes, that's it, that's… fine, Trisha. I'll see you."

"Have a nice day, Ms. L. Good day to you."

"Oh, and Trisha," Sharon whispered, as if telling a secret.

"What is it, Ms. L?"

"Don't call me *Ms. L!*" With that, she slammed the receiver down, and dragged her feet through the foyer. She felt suddenly wiped out, and she plopped herself onto the only couch, and went to sleep.

March 11th, 1896. It was Karen's birthday today, and she waited for the gift she would get later that night. She *hoped* she would get one anyway, since she always got something when her mother was alive. Only weeks before Karen's fourteenth birthday, her beautiful young mother's untimely death spelled a pretty bleak celebration that year. 1895 would be a terrible, unspeakable year for the adolescent – teen Karen. One – the year and the funeral – which she rarely let herself think of, let alone talk about. Her stunted emotional development – due to an overprotective mother and tyrannical, paranoia prone, story teller, hustling father – had continued to go underdeveloped once her physical being – including her fragile developing emotional, personal and *sexual* awareness she was denied from – as were all girls she knew – speaking about – was left in the not-so-tender care of Mr. Daniel Nelson. No middle name.

Many would say the same of his ambition. *Most* probably thought so, as well as *knew* a few things about the Lone Wolf widower who inhabited the godawful shack-cum-mansion he – in his mind only, it seemed – was always promising to build. The wolf *had* a cub, though, and the women in a few neighboring villages passed the time more than a few hours a week taking pretend bets on when that Little Red Riding Hood would get eaten up alive by her over hungry, awaiting, overly hairy Grandma. He hadn't eaten her all up yet, *not just yet*; that much they knew.

They saw the girl go off to school, and many of the wives had daughters in her crowded classroom. Daughters who held their mothers' rapt attention when telling of that particular wide eyed stare. A stare that intently observed and studied nothing in particular. Her motions and her bolted in neat desk could be nerves, nothing short of alarming. Sharon Langhorn's proto feminist liberated liberal Republicrat friends at the office – after a century's worth of shaping, reshaping and shaping again the ever changing, ever empowering face of the American woman – may have described Karen's body language as erratic, or possibly slightly neurotic – a buzz phrase in the century the youngest surviving Nelson would never see, or even believe could exist.

Sadly, Karen's ills were not as easily categorized into another manic depressive or clinically depressed psycho personality disorder. Karen's sexual abuse by her father, starting only days after her mother's body was relegated forever to Holy Ground, went deeper than the modern day tabloid and talk show watered-down-for-the-media versions of incest spoken about freely – if often inaccurately – in the dead end of the 20th Century.

No, Daniel meant for the physically blooming Miss Nelson, Miss Karen Daniella Nelson, to take the place of his long ill and now deceased wife, and to a man of his low caliber and misogynistic views of everything a man could possibly think of; that a man's penis could kill all manner of distress and ill will, as long as said man could take a woman's private, intimate moments, thoughts and feelings, and destroy them utterly in a savage display of sexual and biological superiority. Was his daughter any different, then?

Her firm, budding breasts, steadily forming lusciously since she was eleven or so, now full and protruding as her mother's ample bosom had been when they'd taken his attention away from the scam he'd been trying to perpetrate on some dim neighbor boy ... bring him to ask her to accompany him to a Fair Dance, which had been the first either had attended... despite the Fair having occurred every year in their small, very spacious, very boring town. Karen's mother had never felt comfortable in the presence of those her own age, especially the young men who, like Daniel, were quick to notice her outward charms and wished so much to 'spoil her' for her wedding night, unafraid of reprisal, as her father was away most of the year on some manner of business few people knew much about.

'Boys being boys,' the culprit who would deflower the pretty shy brunette could leave the village for a while if the coward dared question townsfolk of whom this person may have been. As it happened eventually, to both the 'coward' – though her father worked steadily and was a good man by all accounts – he was doomed a coward ignorantly by younger townsmen when he time and again avoided instigated and physical – and therefore violent – confrontation – and Mr. Nelson, one of her many suitors, and not the best of the lot at that, the pretty brunette could have proven both of them, if not the whole town and nearby provinces, to be very cold, uncaring, miserable men, when it came to the women in their lives, and ultimately, to themselves? But these were things that happened in another world; that Karen would never know. And that was just as well. Today was Karen's birthday. Karen's... birthday.

Sharon was finally able to reach Doctor Haskel early the next morning, and none too soon; her frayed nerves were starting to give way, the vein on her right temple that throbbed during her frequent migraines, she was sure, had burst at least three times during the night. At least. Blood was everywhere. How does one get blood out of a pillowcase? I'll have to consult Mother on that one. Yep! The voice on the other line was the even, distant tone of one who emoted little in his life, and when he did it couldn't be, by anyone's far reaching opinion, a sign of growing concern. Even if you looked and listened hard. A con man with a lab coat. The voice of a doctor.

Doctor Haskel was brief, and a bit annoyed. "Sharon, I don't know why you've put Trisha in such a state. She nearly tripped over herself trying to give me a fistful of messages this morning, like a regular late shift waitress on uppers, attacking the cook with a barrage of starved requests."

Sharon stood silent, but didn't appreciate his tone. She didn't leave all those messages to hear him act self important. What she wanted was to get his attention. "Well, Doctor," she started, focusing fast on what she'd rehearsed in her head a thousand times by now. "I'm sorry poor little Trisha couldn't make the track team, but you *are my* doctor, and if I can pull you away from your busy schedule for just a small moment, there is something I've had on my mind recently that could do with some explaining."

The doctor let out a slow, heavy sigh. Sharon was one of his steadiest customers, and he hated to see – or hear – an unhappy patient. "How can I help you, Sharon? Go ahead. I'm listening."

Satisfied that he was, she started telling him the dreams, the nightmares, the in betweens, the no sleep – or, too little sleep – and, God be praised, the fact that it was her last full day – and, dreadfully, night – in this terribly sad, sullen house. As she told him the loose theories she had fabricated at this tail end of her visit, to what very well might be her own house in a matter of hours, she could hardly imagine how it ever *could* be *her* house. Or the old woman's. Or anybody's.

The widow Shifton, as peculiar a character as she may have *been*, was one hundred per cent right in her peculiar statement about the *house itself* needing care. And how she had painstakingly, after her husband's death, put all the furnishings and little bits in place, by trial and probably mostly error, to the point that whatever this house was, or more accurately, what must have come to inhabit it in some remarkable way, in some way that, until now, Sharon would have had until now no reason to entertain, was at peace, or peace enough to leave an old woman to grieve for her dying husband in peace. Peace for both of them.

Sharon did not feel it however – whatever it was – at peace any longer with her there. What is it about my presence that could be disturbing this thing, this ghost so much? Sharon had asked the good doctor. His stock, offhanded answer – all his answers seemed to be off handed – was that there *weren't* any ghosts, and that she should leave that house as soon as possible as it was causing her great delusional distress. Also while she was at it she should seriously reconsider buying the place.

"But Bob, the old lady has the keys. That was the thing, the stipulation. She talked about me leaving for a short walk, or groceries, but she really didn't intend that at all. There's more than enough here to eat for months. Much less for just three days and a morning. What does she care if I don't get my morning jog in, as long as she has *her* fun?"

The doctor's voice became grim and forceful on the other end. Was he showing real compassion for another person, or still acting? "Sharon. Please, you've got to get out of there, for your own sake. Try to leave somehow. Out a window. Anything. Just try something. I wouldn't say something like that if I didn't think it were doing you more harm than good being there. Something is obviously bothering you, or triggering some dark, buried memory of yours you've suppressed, possibly when you were really young. You'll do no good for yourself to be by yourself, having delusions, and not be monitored or be given any medication. The *Clozapine* helped you once, didn't it?"

"Look Bob, I'm really not a big fan of all this 'suppressed memory' stuff. If you want to know what I really think, I think it's a lot of garbage. That causes more harm than good, and all your damn medication, that you doctors prescribe at a moment's notice, like the Great Cure All. A lot of hype and ... damn words, but more like a lot of crap, clear out, to me."

"Okay, Sharon. I *know* you're a little shaken up. Maybe a lot. Shaken up by whatever's going on with you. I –"

"That's just it. I don't *know* what's going on with me. That's the problem. I keep seeing this little girl. She's in an awful state; disheveled, dirty, always in this dark, filthy room inhabited by a bunch of pigs, of all things."

"Pigs?"

"Yes, pigs. And she cries incessantly. My heart goes out to her. But I don't know who she is. She doesn't really exist of course, but I think she *did* exist, once, and that maybe, and I don't want to take out on you, Doc; I may be neurotic and a social zero and full fledged bookworm, sure, but I feel strongly – and I'm not a big fan of the occult, or the supernatural, or anything... hell, I don't even have a Bible at home... but, I really do feel like – how do I say this? That there is a – God! This is such a cliché, but it's time – that there's such a *strong* presence here..." Her voice became progressively smaller, less forceful, less passionate about her new found cause leaving the doctor an 'in' to state the obvious. *Was it though? Obvious?*

"Sharon, this is highly irregular nowadays, but I think I should come out to see you. I'm afraid these delusions might get worse if you're not back on your Clozapine again soon. You know what, Sharon? You've been a patient of mine for a while now, and I'd hate to see you in a distressed state of mind. Give me the address to the house. I'll take a ride out to see how you're doing as soon as I see the rest of my patients this afternoon. I have a pen and paper. Just tell me where you are."

Sharon's chest began to heave in and out wildly, and beads of sweat formed on her forehead that weren't there a moment ago. After a long pause that the doctor waited out patiently, Sharon let her feelings be known. "You know what, Bob? Doctor Haskel?"

"Yes, Sharon? I'm still here."

"I, uh... I don't think I want you to come by here, and I'm not sure when I'll be coming to see you again after this is all over." *If it'll ever be over.*

"Sharon? Do you think that's wise?"

She answered back in a wicked, dead on parody of his emotionless voice. "No, I don't think that's wise, Doctor Potato Head, since, as I said, if you, I, or anyone comes in or out of here and the old witch finds out, the deal's off and I can forget ever having my own place. And at this price! I'd play poker with the Devil with loaded chips before I fucked – sorry – passed this up."

"But Sharon. Please hear me out. I don't think you're well. I'll come over on *my own time.* It's okay, really. I'm concerned about your mental health."

"Oh, *are* you now?" Sharon snapped, pissed now. "I think you're full of shit. Sorry to bother you, *Bob*, really. Goodbye!"

Slamming the receiver down onto the cradle, Sharon felt a part of her whisked away – harshly forced out of her body as soon as the connection was terminated. Suddenly it was painfully clear this was a new Sharon Langhorn who had emerged, formed quite shakily and hastily over the past odd two and three quarters days. Painfully clear. Now that she was a changed woman, and before she had to do what we all must, attending to the details of life after some great religious insight or some such miracle, she had a new friend with things to discuss. A friend who might be her in another life. *A past life maybe?* These were things she never paid much attention to or particularly believed in, but she knew one thing: it did exist, and it needed her help.

The doctor buzzed Trisha in the next room. "Trisha?"

"Yes, Doctor Haskel. I'm here," she replied. He could hear the faint sound of a potato chip bag rustling. She always kept a bag between her legs. At least it seemed like always. Constantly chewing. Munching on her chips. Between her legs. Like he didn't know.

"Trisha, please come in here. And throw out that damned junk food! It sounds like rats in the wires on my end!"

"Yes, sir!" she said, genuinely surprised to have been found out, and did as he said.

"Trisha?"

"Yes, Doctor Haskel?"

"I'm concerned with our mutual friend, Miss – *Mz*. Langhorn."

Trisha put her head down. At this point, she wished Sharon would just disappear. "Was that who you were talking to just now?"

"You know it was, Trisha." He raised his voice, annoyed. "You put in the call to me! ...I'm sorry to yell, but –"

"You're not yelling," she stated, cutting him off.

"Look, if I'm sorry about something, I'm sorry, alright?"

"Yes, Sir!" Private Trisha saluted him – a move she might have thought was appropriate but that he found ludicrous, just upsetting him more.

"Do we have the number to that Rothstein friend of hers? The lawyer... *Leonard*, I think was his first name."

She stared back at him, not speaking.

"Well, *do* we?"

"I think so. I'll check her file. She gave it to me once as an emergency number, but I'll have to see."

"Why don't you go do that, Trish." He nodded toward the door, and she showed herself out, wiggling her shapely behind the way she purposely did – a way to get boys to notice her in grammar school, that she continued to do without realizing it still now. The doctor did however recognize it. Hot girl, he thought. Nice body. Too bad she's such a ditz.

He remembered the Mister Potato Head crack, and a few other choice words Sharon had for him. He didn't suffer being put in his place over the phone easily – two ex wives with a penchant for the sport put him off to it indefinitely.

To hell with it. She didn't merit a visit. All the way up there to Old Forge. Three hundred miles, at least. Probably a lot more. What was he thinking that made him propose he'd come up and see her sometime? This wasn't the Doctor Kildaire Show, and he wasn't Cary Grant. Trisha waved the file with Rothstein's number in it like a racing flag. The doctor could see her through the open door, and raised a weak hand from his armchair to acknowledge her excitement.

"I got it! I got it!"

Robert Haskel called Leonard Rothstein's office at Madison Perry Shostrom Real Estate. Leo was Mr. Perry's Vice President of Building Claim Inspections; a fancy way to say that Rothstein was the House Dick. He'd always fancied himself the Sherlock Holmes type, and he got to do his walk-up-ring-the-bell-flash-the-badge act with aplomb. Not a cop. An average cop wouldn't do it for his mom. No sir. A *real estate* cop. Now that was an unusual venture, and quite hard to explain. Little consequence then, that there were no other Building Claim Inspectors that he was Vice President *of*. Even in a sixty storey monster high rise like this, the kind that, like the irritable unemployed folk who were the ants he spied down at from his wide bay window might say were a staple of the commercial machine, and which were one eyesore example of the leftover excess of the Baby Boomer plus (de)generation.

He was too young to be involved in that he said/she said/they want blood sport, and all he expected from himself – Vice Prez Fake Title or not – was to do his chosen job as best he could. He'd been going over one of the firm's new landlord neglect cases, one that had to do with a welfare hotel mogul who was putting his government checks in his pocket rather than do major repairs that were desperately needed. This kind of brazen neglect, and Giving the Law the Bird, wasn't new to him of course, but these low class characters still sent a stiff pain through his neck when he read the office tear sheets.

Raymond, an intern a couple of doors down from him, took the call.

"Okay, Ray, I've got it. Hello?"

"Hello, is this Mr. Leonard Rothstein?"

"Yes, it is. Is this a personal or business matter, Mister –"

"*Doc*tor. Doctor Robert Haskel. I'm Sharon Langhorn's psychiatrist."

"Oh."

"I had your office number in Sharon's file. *Is* she your client, Mr. Rothstein?"

"Yes, she is. Might I ask whet this is about, doctor?"

"Certainly. Before I begin though, is this a bad time?"

Leo paused for a moment. He'd been surprised to hear that Sharon put him down as a reference for an *emergency* contact, as that seemed to make little sense – and for the first few seconds thought the worst. Thinking that a doctor – analyst or otherwise – wouldn't start off terrible news with, 'Is this a bad time?' he figured it was nothing serious, smiling to the receiver at his Jewish Nature, as his mom called it. "No, not at all. Go right ahead."

"I'm not so sure about that. You took an awfully long time to answer. I can try you again later."

"No, please stay on the line, Doctor Haskel. My blood pressure's going sky high on account of all the new cases that have piled up since last week."

"Oh. Sorry to hear it."

"Don't be."

Hearing that, Doctor Haskel felt he could be frank with this man.

"It's just part of the job for a Vice P."

"Vice President! How nice for you."

Geez, Leo thought. *This guy must be a head shrinker to the bone.* "Save it. We have more titles around here than at the DMV. Doesn't mean much. I'm just a regular working guy with a generous salary for my efforts."

"I see."

Leonard started to think he was getting the run around. *He's Sharon's therapist, not mine. He called me, so I wish he'd just get on with it.* "Excuse me for being a little antsy, doctor, but I *am* still on the job. Is there something going on with Sharon that I should know about?"

"That's why I wanted to talk to you. I really don't know how to answer your question. She called me from the Shifton Estate in a wild state, left many messages, and when I finally got a hold of her she didn't sound like herself. Not the tone of voice or words – I'm used to people going a bit bonkers and taking it out on me, it's my job after all."

"Yes," Leo strained. He remembered the episode of *the Flintstones* he'd enjoyed as a kid. The one where Fred was to inherit his late uncle's creepy mansion and fortune if he, Wilma and the Rubbles spent one night. It turned out to be just Fred and Barney, running for their lives from three wacky cutlery wielding servants, who stood to share the pot in case Fred had an accident. *Then* he thought of Sharon in that house, alone, and guessed she'd gone half out of her mind with boredom – if not something more serious – and must have rung the Doc to *bust balls.* As long as they weren't his.

"Mr. Rothstein, are you still there?"

Leo realized he'd gone adrift twice in the last few minutes. Not a good sign. Maybe he'd be paying the Good Doctor's couch a visit soon after all.

"Yeah Doc, I'm here. Can you please get to the point? I can't tie up this line too long." *A good enough excuse*, he thought. *A kook. A real kook!*

"Yes, of course. It's my professional opinion that Mz. Langhorn has become delusional while staying the weekend at that big house in Old Forge."

"Hm. Hm. The Widow Shifton's place. She told the both of us her wishes while we were at her home, expecting to sign the papers over straight away, when she popped out with this little tidbit. I would have taken the time off to stay with her, but the stipulation was that she be there by herself. Besides Langhorn's not the type to ask a guy for a hand, if I read her right, I mean."

"That's exactly what most concerned me after our phone conversation. She didn't sound like the same woman. She is indeed, as you pointed out, quite an 'independent' young lady. I can't explain it. I'm extremely sorry to waste your time and take you away from your work, but I think being there is giving her a relapse."

"Relapse? How so? Are you saying Sharon has some kind of 'history'? *Problems*, I mean?"

"It wouldn't be right to breach the trust of a long time patient, but suffice to say Sharon hasn't had the happiest of childhoods."

"Haven't we all," deadpanned Leo.

"Yessss, well I'm sorry to have wasted your time, Mr. Rothstein, on a hunch."

"That's quite alright. If there's something that merits my attention, please call me at this number again. No problem."

"I'm surprised to find you at work on a Sunday to begin with."

"Real estate work is a never ending story, Sir."

"I'm sure it is. Well, I'll be in touch if she calls again."

"That'll be fine. I'm going up to bring her home tomorrow morning anyway."

"That sounds like good news. Have her call me when she gets home, and keep an eye on her, please."

"Will do."

"Okay. Thanks again."

"You got it."

"Good day."

"Bye now –"

Hm. Maybe I'll check on her a little earlier than planned, Leo said to himself. *Just to make sure.* He told his personal assistant Cheryl to postpone his other appointments for the day, grabbed his coat from the back of his chair and slipped into it while simultaneously going past the glass and metal customized cubicle front that connected Cheryl's space with his medium sized office. *The firm will understand,* he almost said to Cheryl, while barely noticing the look on her face. *I guess she just saw Superman*, he said to himself, as the elevator came down, and smiled.

Sharon sat in the voluminous living room, at the head of the longest table she had ever seen, other than in cheapo flicks about strange goings on at creepy old mansions on the Late Movie. She wasn't into the Trivia aspect of it, like the *real* fans of horror movies were, stuff like, 'Who starred in what, who was the makeup artist for this guy, who was the stunt man for that guy', and on and on.

She'd had a puppy love crush on this boy Mario, who she thought was the cutest, sweetest boy on the block – if not the neighborhood – a pre teen thinks their neighborhood is the whole *world* after all! – he was the first boy she'd kissed on the lips, and who had the choice pleasure of touching her legs and belly while she was in her tiny bathing suit, breasts still forthcoming to fill out the top of it by another two years. *Gosh how I was embarrassed and exhilarated to have a boy touch my naked body!* But he got on her nerves at times with all that movie Trivia stuff.

She did admit – at least to herself – to enjoying those old scary movies, and even some of the gorier ones that got cut to ribbons when they showed on network TV, for their entertainment value, and the better ones' attention to detail. Like those dark sullen mansions with the white screaming sheet floating down the tremendous staircase, scaring anybody at the foot of it – and were there always the *entire* house's occupants at the base of the banister when ghoulish things always happened? Wasn't there? – who would dare look up in the terrible misshapen nose putty 'n' grease painted face of the one … in question. *Yeah, those pictures were good for a laugh,* she thought, but I never thought the day would come when I would be *living* in one.

In front of her were a couple of cans of tuna fish she had found in the cupboard. She mixed in a healthy amount of mayonnaise like she did at home. It just sat there next to the napkins, knife, fork and spoon like the night before, and the night before, a long glass of rum 'n' coke that she'd mixed in a great thick metal malt shaker just like they used to have at the sweet shop in the East Side Kids movies. "Gee, that shaker's a great one. Gee, ain't this the most exciting mixed-fucking-drink on the face of the freakin earth, huh? Oh, yeah. I'm having the time of my fucking life here. OF MY FUCKIN LIFE! Tuna fish, Tuna Fish, TUNA FISH! My Kingdom for rye bread! A lousy fucking loaf of white fucking bread, okay? OKAY?!"

Sharon was speaking – actually, screaming – out loud to herself to balance the dead silence that filled every square inch of the old house. Not even the usual settling noises or drumming of boiler pipes and various plumbing could be heard.

The house was truly quiet. For a dyed-in-the-wool city girl like Sharon it seemed to go on forever. She had an unnerving suspicion that the silence was a *false* silence, possibly cancelling out those other noises in favor of something else. *Something else.* As if something might be just around the corner, waiting, lurking someplace beyond the smoking, quietly crackling embers of the fireplace. That sound, she thanked God, *could* be heard. But even that seemed be getting quieter, and Sharon was beginning to believe, if she wasn't totally sure already, that this little Weekend at the Creepers might have been the best thing for her, in a way.

Sure, the place was spookier than hell – wasn't that fabulous? – it was the fact that this was the place that she was meant to call home by morning, her new home, *a house all to herself!* Wasn't that what all little bratty, snooty girls who grew up to join the Liberation Brigade Work Force dreamed of? To own property, and without the help of a *man?* Oh, perish the thought!

This could be the defiant pinnacle of one woman's brave success, a thumb in the eye to everyone at work and at the apartment – Beatrice, really... and her wanna be stuck up model pals. 'Oh, Sharon, I couldn't *possibly* have any of your home made rice crispy – whadda you call them – *cakes?* – they're murder on the hips you know, darling. Murder!'

She abhorred – and was also technically removed from – even though she'd heard her mouth say, 'I'm leaving, I'll give you notice, I paid these bills,' blah, blah, and more blah. Had anyone been listening? Anyone at all? The tall glass of rum 'n' coke was transforming slowly into the straight stuff, as she added more rum little by little until the only coke that was left had already been swimming around in her not-so-firm-anymore – alright, *paunchy* – stomach waiting to be digested. She didn't think she'd ever felt so bad. As if it wasn't *her* feeling that way, but that Sharon was sort of 'tuning into a frequency' somehow. Could that be? There obviously wasn't anyone else in the house. *Then why do I feel so bad?*

Sharon heard the question ringing in her head but had no answer for it. None at all. High fives all around from the ... bunch or not, she had to realize by now that this place wasn't *haunted*, was it? That seemed too farfetched, even among this deadly silence she'd had to endure since the night before, when this melancholy replaced her usual bitchy confidence everybody loved so much, that this definitely wasn't the home she'd envisioned for herself, even though admitting that she would possibly be joining the ranks of New York's homeless – with little doubt – scared the damn *shit* out of her, she was sure the old woman would open those great old Pearly Gates to be met with a resounding 'No!' from her, and the Bat would just have to be content with moving back in, vacation over. *This is your type of place, bitch, not mine! I ain't dead yet,* to paraphrase the Vaudeville set. *Your type of place. Not mine.* Leo would drive her home, and she and her mom would brainstorm what to do next.

Sharon brought the now empty dish she had placed in front of her into the kitchen. About an hour earlier, it had been piled high with three cans of generic tuna fish – a brand she didn't recall hearing of before – with heaping spoonsful of *Hellmann's* mayonnaise she had found in the refrigerator – the large jar one buys when one suspects to be stuck indoors for a while. The fishy smell wasn't too *bad*, and she was glad it was the white kind of tuna with the mild taste, instead of the darker meat that was sharply tart and salty, which was the kind she did not like at all. She washed the used dinnerware – all of one dish and glass – and rinsed out the utensils she had set out but left unused, for good measure. The running water from the faucet seemed to make a humming noise, which she thought might only be the old pipes making themselves known. Soon she realized, however, that it wasn't the pipes.

Daniel Nelson went to see an acquaintance he had met at the Inn a week before; something about a bet that the man had owed him, but the deal went sour. Nelson meant to hurt him, and the news spread, until the small, nondescript man was nowhere to be found. The innkeeper had not seen him since he'd heard that Daniel had a mind to thrash him.

The dream house he meant to build still hadn't been realized. There were no supplies ordered or in storage in preparation for the momentous event anywhere to be seen in the barn, or anywhere, for that matter.

He made it a personal obsession to find this man with his money. Money he had neither seen, nor felt, nor possessed. Instead of dropping the subject altogether and dismissing the wager – whatever it was he was unable to even recall – he meant to teach this stranger the moral about Another Man's Wages, which his father had taught to him as a boy.

The elder Mr. Nelson, a man of few words – but heavy hands – imparted only a few handfuls of wisdom young David might have taken with him into adulthood, contributing some moral character or ethic to a life that was – through many headstrong mistakes – otherwise bereft of any. To the old man's credit however, the gospels he *did* share with the many blood relatives who occupied the same simple Kentucky shack, were repeated *ad infinitum*, over and over. Daniel would listen to this jabbering, loud, overweight man – at one time before his teen years he could swear remembering his father at over four hundred pounds – spew clichés that were of little practical use and far from original, even common among neighbors.

His favorite was, 'Another Man's Wages.' "They say that a man who looks after his family and provides for 'em, locks horns with another man about his property and what he has – including his women – and that other guy got less than him, then the Good Man have every right to take what he can from *that* one, bein as how he was aimin to get the first feller's goods in question first. Do a decent day's work and you'll be looked after, like it says in the Holy Bible. The Bible says all sinners will be cast out who cast the first stone... A man's wages is his own concern, less he aims to take 'em for 'is own. And without case, he gets what's comin to 'im, the poor Devil."

Daniel liked this composite tale of faceless enemies just fine. It could not truthfully be said that he had *understood* the underlining meaning however, that greed in any form, for any reason, was a sin. He just liked the part about the man who had been disrespected and challenged exacting his revenge on the wicked minded poor Devil. A 'poor Devil,' in his father's eyes, was a man who could hear the footsteps of another man behind him who was not even there yet. Who might *never* be there, but the man's deep rooted guilt would construct the predator just the same, and the most terrible looking sharp fanged, razor clawed, hulking, gigantic, beady eyed monster at that.

"And this was the way they would describe folks," as his Daddy used to say, "who'd gone a-runnin." The only reason for a man to leave his family was if he had something to hide; a man who had enough sense amidst his particular crisis to leave his family well *out* of it, or else give them the same perspired wide eyed look he suffered from – the curse of debt, some called it. That was all well and good and passé, but now *he* was the one who had the power to put the Curse to another man's mind, and it was a surge of good feeling he would not soon let go of.

Karen knew something was going on that she should not know about, seeing as how he was so deep in thought those weeks before he disappeared. Even his drinking had tapered off considerably, at least compared to the mood swings she had witnessed before, which Karen attributed to his beloved Whiskey. Out of blind concern and some sense of loyalty to this man who neglected and violated her, keeping her a slave there on the farm – and away from school more days than not that when she *did* appear for lessons, a scolding in front of the whole class and backed up school work to be made up and completed were always expected and *hated*, as she would attend every day if her father's constant cycle of helplessness-cum-abuse were not the norm – she would at times hide the bottles and canteens of drink, little tin vials also, rusty, with dirty caked fingerprints, in hopes that he would find them missing and therefore forget his dependency on them, which in turn would change his demeanor, forcing him to treat her as a father should, instead of as he had been.

All this would ever get her was a spanking over his knee, bare bottom red and bruised by the end of it, or something worse. What could it be that occupied his mind to such distraction, she thought to herself at night as she served him dinner that he would finish half or less of, when only a month before he had eaten all of the portion she had prepared for him, often scolding Karen that the meal was not enough, and that he had expected there to be more. She could only cook what he gave her, as she was not allowed to go anywhere except church and school, but such outbursts were just another way he had of putting her in her place, which he certainly must have seen as quite low and inconsequential. These nights he barely finished the dishes she placed sheepishly in front of him, and she started to take the leftover food to the pigs out back, seeing anything he had put to his mouth as tainted. Hungry as she often was for the simple meals he allowed her, she would rather scrape the remaining dinner into the pigs' trough, than to eat from the same plate as her father.

As she saw them stir from their sleep, fighting for the nourishing feast Karen dropped into their pen, so much tastier than their usual rotten vegetables and watered down stew shavings, she felt a peculiar chill creep up her back from someplace way down, almost outside her person, the feeling that this man, who was more husband than father to her, more Master than Provider, was thinking of a way – maybe several ways – to leave her. To leave her here with nothing, to pursue some new dream or fancy of his she dared not inquire about. So much was his state altered, that her bruises had all healed when she went to inspect them – as she did some mornings, having to prove to herself this sullen life she lived was indeed her own – and he had not taken her womanly favors from her during day or night for at least two weeks, or more.

Karen suspected this was as amiable as she would ever see him, and the *attention* she *had* grown to expect from him at a great reduction as it recently was, did her nerves good and helped her to achieve peace of mind as much as she could, with such a man in close proximity day in and day out.

She took to smiling more as he sat in his corner of the large sparely furnished room – what future generations might now consider a 'studio' – leaving her to her own devices; accepting his meals as before, but without insult or praise, neither raising his hands nor her dress.

She smiled not because he expected it, as a rich man might from his servant, but out of honest-to-god relief. Her schoolwork improved as her mind was clearer to do her studies, as well as her attendance since he no longer questioned her goings on. Soon, he even trusted her to run errands only *he* saw to previously, and in Karen's young mind this was a close to a 'family' she and her father – her keeper – would be. She had an idea that the worst was yet to come.

Daniel Nelson put a crude thin wood beam across the top of the doorway, made out of spare branches he had found scattered around the base of one of the elder trees. He connected the end to the opposite wall, attached on each side – and to each other – by curly end screws. He had cut off the pointy extremities before nailing them together, roughly measuring the distance with outstretched hands, as Karen curiously watched. *What was he up to*, his daughter was thinking, this man whom she hardly recognized these days.

There was a rolled up carpet her father had placed in the corner who-knows-how-long ago. It had sat on its end for months and months collecting dust. He walked over to it the morning after putting up this strange lumpy eyesore overhead, and Karen had a good idea what he had meant to use it for. He was probably going to make a partition out of it, to alieve himself from his daughter's gaze, thereby being more able to concentrate on whatever had taken hold of his senses thus far. Sure enough, he took it out to the front steps to be batted on the clothesline. Karen was surprised he had not shoved the thick wool brush in her hand to do it herself. *Must be important to him, alright.*

After a few minutes of hearing the dull sound of the back of the brush hitting the foreign dirty material, she saw him drag the carpet into the house again and drape it rather comically – due to the weight of the thing – over the crude beam. This thing that he made so impressed him that he stood back from it, hands on his hips, admiring his handiwork.

Karen had not seen her father in this position before – in an almost womanly pose – and it made her smile. She let out a tiny giggle when she saw a certain picture in her mind, but quickly dismissed it when she realized he would be furious at her for laughing at him. She shook almost immediately, crouched on the floor where she was, not moving, his eyes catching her in their deep blue glare, through the silhouette of the hard daylight. Instead of being angry, or cursing her for laughing, *or* a beating, he just tilted his head slightly, not taking his eyes off her. Expressionless. She was not completely sure this did not terrify her even more.

He seemed to enjoy her looking so terrified, as if thinking back to his days with Karen before Another Man's Wages – the great work of his otherwise useless father – and she was reminded of thinking back to when the air in the cabin was so much thicker with dread than it was now. He parted the drapery – as if it had been there all along for *years* – with a finesse she had not thought he was capable of, like the fine Englishmen with their dainty dos and don'ts she had read about in a book last year. That work – she failed to remember the title or author – made her laugh when she had read it; the 'gay' manner of its characters, quite foreign and frivolous to her, one with so little. So loose with their spending money, which seemed to be stuffed in their pockets to infinity, buying the very best; the very best of everything.

Many things that day made her giggle sadly, and for quite some time afterward they requested to be custom made she had never heard of. Did she know someone who had...? She giggled now while thinking of it, and before she knew it the curtain flapped open, announcing he was there, in front of her. On her side. She shut her lips tightly over her teeth until they hurt, reprimanding herself for being so careless. Again he showed no sign of anger, and lowered himself in a squat to address her quietly.

"Karen," he stated, holding one of her wrists gently in an uncommon gesture of – what she guessed was – affection. "I have to go out for a while. I'll be back soon. There's a matter I have to take care of with another gentleman; that is *highly* important. There's nothing to worry about. I put up this partition so you can have some privacy. You're a big girl now, Karen... I trust you can look after things, while I'm gone?"

Karen was in shock. Whomever this stranger was in front of her, who had somehow managed to take her father's form, he was not too welcomed here. When Karen Nelson saw this Impostor standing in front of her – *kneeling* in front of her then... Oh yes, he would set it all right.

"Karen? Karen, are you listening to your father?"

No, I'm listening to a crazy man who thinks he's my father, she thought of exclaiming, but dared not. Looking the stranger in the eye, with as cool an expression on her face as she could muster, the said, softly, above a whisper, "Yes, I'm listening... Daddy. Poppa, yes, I understand."

"Very well then!" the New Daniel said. "I've left plenty of food for the horses, oats and hay, not just roughage. They should eat well. We only have two, you know! And I've also left a week's worth of ripe fruits and vegetables in the garden, in the two big wicker baskets, daughter. That should be enough for you and your pudgy snout nosed friends outside. Just give them the shavings. I wouldn't want to waste good food on pigs. Just give them the usual cabbage and scrap meat. We still have the cake of stew meat here someplace, don't we?"

As if in a trance, listening to this man-who-claimed-to-be-her father's mouth speaking in such even respectable tones, unlike the growling and shouting before, her father's aggression (!) that she had grown so accustomed to so early on, she almost missed the question. It was like a *dance* of sorts, the lilting tones of his voice; up and down, so evenly released from his ragged, stubbled throat – the Adam's apple bobbing up and down like a conductor's button tip.

"*Excuse* me, Poppa, I didn't hear you correctly. Please repeat it again. I'm sorry, Poppa."

He looked at her with that same cool, tilted head expression as before, even trying to smile, that only succeeded to muster a sinister looking smirk, despite his best efforts. "Now Karen... this is very important, and I want you to stop daydreaming and listen to my provisions I've made for you. There is no need to be afraid. I am your father, and I've done much thinking over the course of this last month or so. There were... some... *liberties* I took with you in the past which were... in – uh – *inexcusable* on my part. I was a different man then, and I'm eager to apologize for any mistreatment you may have suffered my readiness to raise my hands – at any cost – to you. I have acted wickedly towards you, as a father shouldn't, for any reason, towards a daughter or son, of which I have none, so I cannot speak on that matter. Depriving myself of drink these last few weeks had shown me the error of my ways. I've been wicked, wicked towards you, and much of the state of my affairs, as well as but not limited to... this run down estate of mine – of ours. I... I've so much more to say."

He stopped then, lowering his head and... as if on the verge of tears. *Tears? Could it be*, she thought. *My father? This cannot be happening. If this be a dream, then oh mother of merciful God, let me not wake.*

On the verge of tears herself from such an emotional and heartfelt confession from this person, her father – not quite a confession, being that all details were cautiously left out, maybe only for the sake of respectability – when did Daniel Nelson – scourge of his village and laughing stock of fathers who did the proper man's work, school mates and mothers all – who did not laugh so loudly, having more than a clue of what he was up to in that cabin with a motherless shapely beautiful... daughter – ever care of decorum, propriety, or – gads! – respectability?

This 'confession,' as she called it – and believed it to be for the rest of her days to come – was far from what she saw in her dreams when a broken, doomed, waste of a man knelt before the Kreator to be told of his many sins from a great parchment unraveled in his great hands, knowing his plight and grasping at his Master's overflowing robe with grubby dirty hands, more like paws, begging the Lord's forgiveness, crying like a common beggar for a chance to redeem himself his sins, but getting no satisfaction from the Lord, who then whisks him to his just reward in the Kingdom of Hell, in the Devil's miserable company for all eternity.

Yes, that was what Karen saw in her many dreams, the only outlet a young girl could hope to have against so many injustices, perpetrated by her own father – or so she was forced to believe – unquestioned; though in her heart she wished this were untrue – no less. No, it was not the confession at the feet of God she had pretended to hear, over and over, during slumber, after going to bed hungry and soiled or nursing bruises for reasons unknown to her. It was, however – *please know this, girl!* – a voice seemed to at once boom at her, more than she ever hoped to hear. *So be satisfied with that, at least.*

This was all too true; how quickly she had forgotten his vile treatment of her when suddenly there was none, save maybe outright avoidance, a disrespect she would – and did – accept like a mother's breast milk to a baby... Yes, she was *not* God, and expecting her father's judgment to be sent down *only* by him and surely no other lest his wrath be unbound as sure as she knew... in these salty tears welling in her soft pink eyelids, sweating and more confused than ever. No, she was not God, and this was as humble a vision of her father as she was likely to see, and for that, she should be grateful.

"Please, father," she burst out, his question asked, it seemed, a hundred years before, "there is no need to say such things." The word 'apologize' seemed too risky to say to a man, much less *him*, and to say 'such things' would have to suffice as a substitute.

She reasoned, "I know very well where everything is, as, you must remember, it was I who attended to these things so long ago, before this change that came over you... Oh! Pardon me, sir, for saying so, but it is indeed a change that has taken place, for the better, if I may speak out of turn a moment."

She bit her lip, not knowing what to expect next, and shut her eyes in fear, when the gasp of air from his dirty lips released as she was about to speak again, such was her state during this tense discourse.

"It is," he said finally. "It is indeed, a change, I mean, and an all too welcome one at that. I am *sorry*, Karen, so sorry for abusing a girl's love for her father, so that nothing in the world can make up for it. When I return from this bit of nasty business I must attend to – like I said, for the good of both of us – as what I am affects you and the other way 'round, things will be changed alright. And for the better, as you so righteously said." He tapped her on the knee for closing effect, and they sat later, at the table together, eating dinner without another word from either of them, as if the sins of the past weighed heavily – like a terrible, damaging secret – on them both.

It was a weight she wanted to be lifted from her more than anything, and she would endure a lifetime's worth of silence with peace of mind, than talk and constant fear, any day, and be glad for it – *blessed*, even – most important it felt like the worst was indeed over, and as she ate this meal with her father Daniel Nelson, Karen Daniella Nelson cherished the feeling of warm protectedness she thought she felt, as if it were summer all over again instead of the – often cruel – autumn it was. She made sure that she looked at every part of this man, every part she cared to look at anyway, and blessed the saints that watched over her, in this time of contentment for *not* having to witness parts of his manhood she should never have had to see nor feel, nor be hurt by...

God, the pain when he penetrated me that first day he took me, she remembered, shuddering as from a draft. How her feelings afterward towards this man when he began taking what should only be taken from a wife or mistress, as she had heard from some of the girls at school during mischievous, private discussions behind the church walls – near the gate where the younger children ran giddily and played without care – but not – mother of God no! – from one's own daughter...

She was willing to put all this behind her now, yes even *that*, to instead focus on every feature she could manage to glimpse without staring... this sucking up and committing to memory, every line of his nose, his eyebrows, his sandy hair that was always unkempt and dirty, the shape of his fingers, calloused and worn from labor – and many brawls at the Inn – the figure he cut in his tattered shirt and patched over pants, down to his dirt caked work boots and awful smelling dry misshapen feet with their curled, thickly nailed filthy toes underneath. *Yes, commit everything about this individual to memory, Karen,* she said to herself most seriously, *for the jury in your head feels that this guilty man has made his peace with you, girl, for a reason. A terrible reason, best not discussed at this time.*

Daniel did not suspect her of eying him this way, as a girl has a way – even at fifteen – to watch a man without actually *watching* him, and quite to her surprise, finished his bowl of stew and bread she had fanned out for him – *everything* – even giving the dish a few swirls with his index finger and popping it in his mouth not once, but twice. He had not finished a dish she had put before him for the longest time, as she reminded herself – every night he did the same, but now he was obviously full, and pleased with the meal, though he did not bang the table and bark at her for another helping as he did before. There was at least another portion for him in the pot, maybe one and a half if she took no more... which she usually did not, seeing as how her options were substantially upgraded with his improved demeanor to begin with, but to add to the list of surprises and unexpected turns of event, she already had more than her share of this even though he asked for no more.

He rose, dabbing at the corners of his mouth like the Englishman in that book she had read – she could not remember the name of – and that was all she could remember after that. He left soon after, hat in hand, and that was the last she saw of him ever. The worst was yet to come.

Chapter Five

Karen nibbled at the crumbs on her dish, absentmindedly staring into space, not knowing what to expect. Only knowing that she would have to expect anything now. The air was clear on this Monday morning, and Karen brought the wooden trough with the chopped up bits of cabbage out to the pig pen. One of the good things about living alone like this was that she could wake up much later than when Daniel rattled the skillet with a spoon – which was his version of an alarm clock – right next to her ear each morning, scaring her dead awake. She was so used to the crude wakeup call anyway – having a permanent hum in her right ear to show for it – that she found herself waking at 6:00 in the morning anyway; sufficiently rested.

This was fine with her, since her father would rattle his spoon at 5:30 – precisely – according to the roosters, and neither owned a watch left her another half hour of sleep, and the pigs looked forward to their breakfast, as she well knew. This was to be the last day they got fresh vegetables however, since she knew she would have to start buckling down, and begin rationing the crops between herself and the animals. Who knew when her father would return, or what he was up to, for that matter. It had been a week since he left – hat in hand – and she did her usual chores, like looking after the pigs and the two horses, nowhere near Champions, the both of them.

She loved Thomas and Lucette dearly nonetheless, always stroking their silky manes of silver and dark brown – Lucette's and Thomas', respectively – while they chewed their oats. Sometimes in a feed bag, but mostly loose in a separate trough her father had built away from the one reserved for drinking – that one Daniel had bought at auction for two silver dollars he had obtained from one of his many gambling pigeons. Instead of squandering his winnings – money from the sky, as he put it – drink or the occasional whore like he usually did, he bought this fine piece of oak carpentry, more a table that some aristocrat might have commissioned that went wrong somewhere along the line rather than a 'real' trough, and brought it home over his head with a grin on his face from a purchase well spent.

Lucette seemed to take a special liking to the mahogany stained hollowed out tree trunk, as she would trot around it for good measure – even when she was not thirsty – in the way a burlesque dancer might prance among the downstage lights, which greeted her with their artificial warmth and security. Thomas just drank from it, with little notice of its design, as any other mare or stud would; Karen could swear she saw in his great wide brown eyes that nothing caught his interest. In fact, this of course could not be proven, but young ladies have a way of bonding with certain animals that defied the understanding of family or friend alike, and if Karen loved the two big beautiful horses she went to feed and clean up after several times a day, then surely they loved her just as much back, if not more.

The dependence on Karen by these creatures – not to mention the chickens, rabbits and assorted farm critters that were known to steal a leaf of cabbage... or scrap of stew meat from the can as the mood would strike them was all too known to her, and she attended to their needs, or, just passing by, brushed them affectionately with a warm loving palm as she would if she had a little brother or sister to look after. This most likely would never be, and upon reflection of this thought she was unsure she wanted any, seeing as how, up until recently, she had been treated at the hands of her hardworking father.

His whereabouts and who knew what kinds of adventures he was up to did of course fill her with much curiosity and nervous suspense. Karen would be lying to herself if she tried to pretend that she were not worried if not for her father's safety then surely of her own, but those thoughts – at least for the time being, were greatly alleviated and kept at bay by the needs of the farm animals – a mother to them she was – and the dear blue sky with the faint breeze that enveloped her face and ran through her hair like a mother's touch. She went inside and sat as still as she could, her eyes shut tight, trying to remember her deceased mother's face.

Daniel had left the cabin on February 16, 1896. The future would be forever changed for a scared little farm girl come the 12th of March, when her suffering would finally come to an end, and an unknown soulmate in another, far complicated world would soon come to know, in her *own* time, how much suffering this child Karen Nelson *had* endured. The air became a full on breeze, as Karen locked the stables for the night.

"I never heard back from Leanna," Sharon said out loud to no one. She was doing a lot of that lately, talking to herself. Leanna's message machine fading on the other line, her voice filled with the excited effervescence of a twenty something after a bad relationship demise with better job prospects on the horizon...

"Hi, this is Leanna Summers. I'm not here right now, but please leave a message because I'd hate to miss your call. Tootles!"

I wonder what happened to Lea. God! Everything's swimming around in my mind... hard to concentrate... Never thought I'd feel like this... What? Inside Sharon's mind or from someplace even deeper – she had no way to be sure – she saw a huge burly man, about thirty five maybe, dark hair and eyes, heavily tanned skin, muscular but mainly just the arms and shoulders – she was unable to see his back – not the body builder type of muscles, but well placed on his broad frame. A working man, as they looked years ago, *long* ago, 19th Century maybe. And those Colonial clothes? Not Colonial. Late 1800s settler type clothing. Like the men wore on *Little House on the Prairie*.

81

He was coming towards her, hands outstretched, arms heavy and glistening with sweat. Deeply tanned, almost cinnamon. A laborer's tan most likely, from working out in the sun for long periods. Skin light pink on his upper arms, showing beneath his rolled up sleeves. His face was distorted – but not grotesque – the ugliness no doubt borne of great anger and disgust, not due to a deformity – though, in the dark light that seemed to shine on this creature, obscuring his right side, like an exposed photonegative toned down – one couldn't be sure.

He meant to grab her, possibly choke her... No, definitely choke her! Sharon froze in her place, her heels digging into the ground of this nowhere place she now found herself in. *Did I 'channel' this person?* Sharon asked herself, and of course could find no answer. She was opaque, noticing her palms sweaty and exuding a faint sulfurous smell – as could he; she could see both of them, he and herself from somewhere over the back of her head, as if riding alongside a Steadicam.

She could hear a song she hated, 'Strange Brew,' by Cream. Hated in part because David played it, and the record it originated from – the original *vinyl* record, passed down from his brother's collection. The two men shared a mutual pet peeve – hating CDs – that went beyond their blood relation – incessantly, whenever she came over to visit, she would hear it, as she was hearing it now – crystal clear and now that she thought about it, disturbingly loud. *Strange Brew... Kill what's inside of you...*

This stranger was on top of her now, a low hum coming from his lips like a leopard studying his prey, about to strike. She might have just heard the growling in her head, due to fright. But *wasn't* it her head this was happening in? *Wasn't it?* His thick fingers went to wrap around her throat, or so it seemed. She tried to keep her eyes open when in this dream state, vision, or whatever it was, thinking quickly that she might be able to find out something if she just stuck it out a bit more.

He *passed right through her* as effortless and simple as crossing the street, both their bodies bathed in some cruel black light – that was the only way she could later think to describe it – his face softening almost to a smile. *No, that was definitely not a smile!* A smirk, then – a horribly *twisted* smirk, the expression of a hell bent killer or mental patient run amok, free once more from his confines to attack and threaten harm once again...

Her mind was swimming with all these images, thoughts, and more. She turned around catching a glimpse of another man, thinner, lankier built than the first – long face, short cropped hair – only this one was not grimacing, smiling or smacking his chops. No, this one was obviously scared and under the attack of the first. From the determined look on *his* face, this second man must have done the other some great injustice, the revenge of which he meant to collect right now, with Sharon between them both. She heard a scream, and she knew it was Man #2, though by the time she turned back once more to the one coming towards him and then through her, since she could not stand the sight of the pitiful look on his face – the horribly sad look of a man most likely about to die.

Sharon felt the scream get louder – not hearing it exactly, but *feeling* it – and in an instant both figures and the murder obviously soon to be committed were gone. She turned around, and did so again, repeated it, then turned once more on her heels, the way she did when she was a little girl spinning around to get a head rush at her grandmother's. The scenery that enveloped her in this 'vision' – great tall strong trees, slowly dying in a dark lonely forest filled with godawful noises of night creatures and assorted natural wonders she, the City Girl, would sooner not know about.

This chilly outdoor scene slowly regressed back into the widow's parlor, off to the side of the living room that fed right into this room she stood in now, which was unseparated by any door or partition, just open space. Not unlike the open space she had just felt herself in, the whole play taking what she thought must be a good half an hour, which most likely, in the Real World, was more like a few drawn out seconds.

The forest background gave way to the rich tapestries and detailed furnishings by way of fine sparkling mist, which enveloped Sharon and her unexpected guests until they ceased to exist entirely in her mind – or anyplace else.

That funny sort of lightheadedness she felt when these *dreams* would grip her during the day or night had let up again, and she just slinked over to the living room table, collecting herself as she took careful steps to remind herself that whatever was going on here would be coming to an abrupt and welcomed end come morning. Leo would be there to pick her up, and she just might confide some of the goings on she had experienced here to him, at least to the point of seeing his Jewish eyes sufficiently glazed over.

What manner of house is this? she thought. *Why do I have to be the one to experience these things – did they really happen? Will they happen in the future, like Christopher Walken in the Dead Zone? I'm so confused! It's beyond me how all of this can be true... Then the old gal will be here too, and I'll tell her in the most tactful and respectable manner, to take this old spook house and lump it! I mean it... I can't stay here another day, much less my entire life. No, that'll never do. Guess I'll just have to try and get along with Beatrice and her bullshit,* Sharon lamented. *Yeah. I guess I'll have to... Jesus, if she'll have me! What did I do? My life is going to Hell! What was I thinking? I can't afford this place – I can't afford shit! What am I, sick or something? Who the hell was I with my delusions of grandeur to think I could own my own damn house! Yeah, that'll happen, right? I'll just tell the old woman thanks, but no thanks...*

It's just the same old Sharon Silverina, Mz. Langhorn, the bitch, the Queen Bitch, fucking up things... and her life... as per usuale.

She slumped into the chair at the head of the table, the one she had been sitting at most lately, the only chair at the dining table she sat in – out of all fourteen of them – and slumped her head onto her crossed over forearms, feeling the psychedelic effects of another headache coming on. *Jesus, God... this really sucks.*

Daniel Nelson killed that man the day Sharon saw into, a man he hardly knew for a reason even the victim of his rage, more than not, probably was not even aware of for sure himself. A man of principles – if not an unusual, twisted version of a principled man he was – he usually set out to finish what he started most of the time. He left a dead man lying in a forgotten wilderness in an uninhabited part of the Midwest – which at that time would have described an awfully large piece of land – on one side of the state, and a scared, confused and quickly maturing teenage girl with exhausted provisions and little hope for her future of seeing her father again – on the other. Not the family type in his own eyes, this was just as well.

One day in the not so distant future, after guilt over leaving his only daughter to die of starvation among the filth of them prize winning animals he'd accumulated as payment for various gambling debts owed him, and a pathetically overgrown and failed stab at farming, in a dirt shack he had the mistaken idea of which he could build himself, not to mention the murder of this man for reasons unknown – who, in truth, it was found out, had many friends with *his own* blood on their minds – he would be found not unlike this poor wretch Sharon would feel behind her in the vision begging for mercy, sweating, shaking, face a twisted form of fear, shock and some other terrible emotion she couldn't quite place, even if she had the capacity to do so, which she didn't. The man of principles tarnished, ending as he began, a lonely sad hulk neither loved, nor with the capacity of love to give. Maybe it all would have been different if Karen were alive to hear the news of his death. The torment of her soul in that other world might never be.

Somewhere, in a sooty, foul smelling makeshift storage area, 'Karen's Closet,' as her father's drunken alter ego would call it... *Get back in your cage, you bitch. I'll come get you when I need you gain, and not before... My, what a sweet piece of ass you are. Come a little closer and show your daddy a little lovin' baby... Damn, you're tight... I'm gonna come right in your little ass, you dirty whore!*

"Nooooo!!" Sharon screamed, bolting from the bed as if pulled by some unseen force, two large calloused hands gripping her shoulder blades, pulling them from the back. Yet again, from all sides. A man's face, soon his whole figure, rose into view. His features were a wretched twisting of pain and sick satisfaction. She could see his right hand, then his left, reaching for her, touching her, first her calves, then her thighs, where they lingered for a moment. She should have felt his weight on her, but did not.

Sharon wondered how this could be, since the man was clearly at least fifty pounds heavier than she was, remembering the last time she weighed herself she was an even 136 pounds – at 5'8" she intended to adopt a diet plan but never got around to it. Then bits of the vision she had maybe only an hour before – maybe more maybe less, she could not be sure – at sometime between 'seeing' the awful murder of that pathetic, thin sad man by the other larger crazed one in the dark shadow of moonlight, and now – she had apparently gone back to her room to try and manage sleep, to *really* sleep, soundly and peacefully, as she had done all her life – at the very least half the time anyway... *We all have our little demons, after all*, Sharon heard a voice say in her head, her vision clouding until this would be rapist, half a dream and definitely a little more than a half real was a blurred hulking form, a mass hunched over, frozen – the leopard biding his time, ever ready to pounce once the rabbit made the smallest mistake – faded from view slowly, until his thick fingers could no longer be seen making slight imprints on the surface of her thighs and was gone.

I seen it! I saw his hands on me, coming closer... his breath heavy, thick, reeking of cheap liquor... did I dream it? Sharon put her head back on the pillow hard, a dull thump in stereo on either side. She cared not how she looked, nor did she bother to brush her hair out as she did every night at home at the apartment.

Home... what a peculiar thought that is, she reflected, eyes on the ancient carved plaster – *was it plaster?* – ceiling. White turned a drab gray-white from time. She considered she had not a clue to what ceilings were made from in *any* building – and an owner, of gray durable pride in aesthetic appearances when Rockefellers and Vanderbilts duked it out for top honors among the Ball going set, debutantes all in a row, that kind of excess was not at all a part of Sharon's character, though she could not help but admire the workmanship and the work involved even if the intentions of the contractors' benefactor were less than artistic. *What is artistic, after all?* Her mind grazed through the films and biography programs she occasionally caught in TV about such people, people if they *were* indeed at all like her, or someone she ever knew in life. To hear the serious hushed tones of the narrator of these descriptive 'fall of the empire' shows, ratings catchers sure to grab the attention of the wanna be Lotto winning Welfare Nation – 'We are Legion for we are many,' came to mind, from *The Exorcist III* with George C. Scott., commander in chief American Actor doing the soul saving this time and – they seemed hardly human in manner or ritual, rituals peculiarly their own.

She saw in the Manhattan streets where she was daily a well paid secretary to the 'I gots mine and I'll gets yours soon enough!' set. Ambition, if well intended and appropriately set forth, was and should be admired, the individual respected for their force of will and determination to prove something, whatever it may be, especially when against the odds – and secretly, against the individual's private better judgment – but these people, this loosely built 'clan,' for that was what they were, cut from the same cloth as any outsider to their world-within-the-world could see – though God help you if they heard you say this – you would get a passionate speech on just *how* differently treated, dyed and stitched that cloth really was, and where they were on it, in reference to family names, status, or whatever was/is important to them, if they understood the word 'important' in the deeply felt real sense of the word at all.

These glass-and-chrome cave dwellers, she concluded long ago – watching their dismayed, frowning faces when a cab ceased to stop at their Royal feet, arms outstretched, one at a time – or even both, God help us – in a Nazi-ish pose of self important grandeur. Really quite funny once you thought about it. 'Hang Hitler!' you cry, as Curly salutes the Moe-Führer infiltrating the Nazi headquarters as Larry, the most paranoid of the Stooges, peeks out the door scared to the tips of his perm fried long hair of being found out by Adolf's henchmen. You laugh as you think the same movie goers who cheered the American propaganda antics of the Stooges, Marx Brothers, Bob and Bing – or any team stuck in making throwaway fluff, painting the would be U.S. Invaders as bumbling ignorant foreigners with funny hats and mustaches – were the same who revered these rich kids, second generational snot noses who expected the riches of their relatives as their birthright, and you feel like hanging your head in shame at how easily the weak can be amused.

Injustice very much fueled Sharon's ambitions, mostly unrealized at this point, but all in her head nonetheless, the purchase of this estate – never ending continuous payments of which notwithstanding – a major step forward as part of the plan. But plans were meant to be changed, as were the rules of any game, and this beaten, melancholy disheveled Sharon – so far removed from the fresh-as-a-daisy young City Bitch, as Dave used to fondly call her, who arrived on these doorsteps not yet three days ago – was not exactly in the winner's circle of this little 'catch as catch can' game she was playing with the Merry Widow. What could that old bag be up to, anyway? And where was she?

"Didn't she know this place was haunted?" Sharon said aloud, the last word falling out of her mouth without a trace of either disdain, sarcasm or disbelief, and it was because she *said* it, and *meant* it, that she knew all help for her while she remained in this terrible old house with its horrible secrets and nightmares and screaming and pain – pain practically pouring from the walls themselves, such a claustrophobic despair having never been felt by her before... and with good reason.

Nothing had ever happened to her like this, and Sharon's nerves seemed to be saying to her, 'If it's all the same to you, honey, I can't wait till the old rag gets her wrinkled ass over here and turns the skeleton key to freedom, because as far as we're concerned, we can't wait to get the fuck out of this mess you put us in.'

Sharon had to admit to her nerves that they had a good point. *Oh, yeah...*

Chapter Six

The widow Shifton paced the floor of her friend Libby's living room, the false tile linoleum giving way in spots where the floor boards were becoming warped with age. The two women had grown up together as neighborhood children; both went to elementary, junior high and high school together; both had married young, and to similarly even tempered men, the sort not afraid of a hard day's work, nor late with a compliment to a deserving woman. As young Libby and she would play some innocent girl's game like patty cake or old maid – a card game that always made her chuckle, the 'old maid'... it struck her, while grasping her hot china cup tightly the way she did when she... hysterical to one still so full of life as young Miss Davis – later Mrs. Shifton – was, now fell into one of these spells, which was often these days, that those days were certainly it didn't seem so funny when she realized – reminded by infrequent visits to the full length hall mirror, batting her eyes as if not to see it and girls, like so many other things, this of course wasn't a passing thought, but some dragging her feet to escape its pull.

Look! Look! Look at what you've become, old thing that nagged at her like Don Quixote's donkey in the fable. Nagged and pulled and *woman... scarcely better than the spinster card, you dried up old prune!* poked at her brain.

Her Lost Youth. She supposed Libby had similar thoughts as she did on the subject, but Libby's genial manner, still the same – God bless her – as it always was, made her doubt it, at least Libby must not have obsessed on it as she did, or should she say *it* obsessed on *her*, the mirror seemed to say as she passed it, looking straight ahead most of the time, avoiding her reflection, frightened that the mirror-voice might be proven right, that the firm breasts and supple skin of the young – and she'd often been told her charms were excess of most, her hand always held out to join a handsome male suitor at a dance or chance sharing of a horse drawn cab – had been lost to the vicious past forever.

She continued pacing, mulling over different thoughts that now randomly entered her head, catapulted by the grim moments of her past and that awful truth telling mirror in the foyer. Libby had two such pieces, the one in the foyer and another in her bedroom – which Dorothy managed to escape by keeping the lights off – even her nightlight – before quickly jumping into bed as quick – relatively – as a woman in her 80s *could*, of course – fading into a troublesome sleep she was well used to by now.

After all these years alone, her distorted, confusing thoughts one part a sign of old age senility and three parts guilt and good old fashioned regret – had become a sort of macabre comfort to her, as might the black winged hellspawn perched atop a sick man's doorway in Poe's *The Raven*, had been perversely comforting during the last few moments of life for *him*. Still holding the flower printed china cup Libby had given her more than an hour ago so tightly that she almost dropped it from the strain on her arthritic hands.

"Curly top, are you alright in there?" a syrupy thick voice echoed from the kitchen, straining to be heard over the haphazard orchestration of pots, dishes, saucers and hot running water. Libby had liked soaking her hands in hot water as long as the widow could remember, and she guessed any amount of money the feeling still sent a peculiar sweet sensation down her elderly but robust spine.

There were other matters on her mind now however; matters grimmer in nature than that of dishpan hands and giddy pretty schoolgirls lost. Matters she at once had no control over, as well as being their Master.

"I'm fine, Libby, thanks. Just admiring the view of the coast from here. Quite an eyeful."

"That it is," Libby returned, warm water still tap dancing over dirty dishware full blast, "that it is indeed. When my Frank was still alive, he'd look out that big bay window for hours on end, smoking his pipe, having God knows what kind of thoughts in his head... he'd never tell me." She shut the water now, and let the remaining pieces soak, drying her hands while turning the bend that met the living room to meet her houseguest. "...he wasn't that kind of man, I suppose, to share what he was feeling or thinking with his wife, I mean. Never bothered me like it does these young brides you see on television nowadays. Always a bee in their bonnet about some silly goose nonsense, going on about how their husband isn't good enough at this, or doesn't bring home enough of that, not at all realizing how great and easy they have it compared to when we were coming up... Ah guess a wife *can* gather all she wants to know about a man – and a few choice bits she'd most likely not know about – if she had the power to go and get it back... if she lives with him long enough, for enough years. Whether he's a chatterbox or not I ain't think's got so much to do with it."

The widow liked this sudden surge in Libby's character, so much in fact, and it was enough to get her to sit down and loosen her death grip on Libby's china, the dark coffee poured into it upon her arrival long gone. Always admiring her friend's good nature, the hopeful side of the coin to her hopeless. She thought of this fact, and it made her lower her head, taking a moment for herself before answering Libby to address the little girl in her mind now, telling her to fold her little hands and kindly keep her pouted youthful lips, by any other human being, not for many, many years since her Charlie's death, closed and locked, the key in her schoolbag for safe keeping.

Libby had been standing up perfectly still in front of her, directly opposite, occasionally turning to squint her eyes into the kitchen for lack of a better way to seem unconcerned about her guest for a good twenty seconds, maybe thirty she thought, at least. Finally, Little Girl ticking her lock, knees together under her desk in her imagined classroom – why she placed the child there was even stranger to her than witnessing herself as an adolescent to begin with.

Mrs. Shifton raised her head to acknowledge her hostess. "Uh, yes Libby, I agree. I feel the same way as you on the subject." She managed a little smile to seal the deal. But Libby wasn't buying.

"You agree to *what* exactly, friend?" Libby asked in an accusatory tone that was most rare for her. "And you feel the same as I do about *what*, exactly?" Libby sat down and squinted her light green eyes, which were as clear as they were in grammar school. Mrs. Shifton didn't answer. Wouldn't answer. "What's the matter, what's got your tongue now, missy? What is it this time?" The widow had never seen her so riled up, and over what she perceived as a silly pretense of manners, at that.

"Now, Libby, there's no reason to get so nasty, not just because I didn't feel like answering you right away. What was there to answer, anyway? You made a statement and I heard you very well. If you were waiting for an acknowledgment to see if these old ears heard you, then rest assured they did, Libby. Case closed."

"Oh! *Now* you talk, is it?" Libby got up from the table and studied her guest, squinting again as she'd always done when she thought the whole story wasn't being told. "And the *case*, Mrs. Shifton, the case is *not* closed." She caught herself wringing both hands again and again with her moist dishcloth. Noticing the widow following the movement with her eyes, she abruptly threw it on the table, not wanting anything to break what she felt was the mounting tension between them.

"Really Lib, you're acting like a child. And calling me 'Missy,' of all things? Look at my face! Do you see the wrinkles?" She put her hand to her face and lightly pressed the creased skin to emphasize her point. "And God, Libby... When's the last time you think I qualified as a 'miss' to anyone? Not for a while, I'm sure!"

"Never mind that," Libby said, guessing she'd best be getting past these frivolities and get to the underlying problem. Soon enough. A woman proud of her composure at times when all around her were always losing theirs, Libby settled herself, lowering her tone as the widow knew her friend would. "Okay. As you know, curly – Beth Ann

(?)

– I'm not in the habit of raising my tone – or my ire – 'less I think there'd be a good reason to. In this case," she said, almost in a whisper, meeting the widow's gaze with her own, "I think, in my humble opinion, that it's justified."

Doctor Haskel was, as his colleagues on the private rag tag research team he more or less headed on these three days he took off from his private practice, a sort of a throwback. The common man's idea of a 'real' doctor others in that profession for decades now had considered folly, he had one major flaw that separated him, like a leper away from the healthy, from his coworkers – to Haskel, doctors – any specialty or general practice would do – which was his humanity. He cared for his patients, genuinely, and they responded to his thoughtfulness – all of them, and it was a great source of pride and inspiration when talking to them about this, were – in kind, with whatever they could let go of within themselves, not to seem either self serving or meekly servitudinal.

He did not much tolerate the smugness his fellow psychiatrists seemed to be drunk on, no doubt cultivated somewhere between their junior year of med school and their first childish spin on the standard issue thick cushioned swivel chair in each of their private offices, all pretty much the same character.

Drab, neatly painted or plastered sheetrock walls, a painting or two or three of little mind bending artistic merit, thereby avoiding the risk of controversial individual thoughts and opinions from a patient – and with the meter running at these prices, we can't have that, now, can we? – the unsettling notion of addressing him or her as an equal, when a pleasant looking but clichéd depicted scene, meant to subdue such discourse, not invite it.

So many other things he'd heard people say about his profession, so many as to fill a three subject notebook on both sides of the page, moderate sized letters besides, not the kind detention overtimers used in their 'I'll never do this again' essays, printing only four of five words on a line, finishing a four page paper – meant, in truth, more to degrade than to punish – which surely was a thing of the past in the liberated, gun toting school system that is such a part of our culture, and has been for a number of years now. Yeah, Doc Haskell, the Good Doctor was well aware of the shrink jokes, new ones coming out every minute, faster than bunnies have babies, the way his daughter Kathy, only weeks away from her fourth birthday, went around the house saying lately.

Kids, he thought, momentarily removed from his present train of thought, are always up to something. They come up with the silliest, most endearing sayings, their innocence – at least that of his own blood blinding to him, a father not even four years now. The time went perversely – *perversely?* Yes, that was the only word he could conjure to describe the intangibility of time – fast, as he'd been warned by many his senior all his life. There it was then, fatherhood for a onetime devout bachelor, espousing the greatness of Being Alone, until he met Katherine, Sr.; and that all changed. A *gradual* change, was the proud coda he put on such thoughts, for he felt in no sense of the word *whipped* at all the picture that harsh phrase conjured in his mind – in *any* man's mind – did honestly not pertain to him.

95

He could say that without pretense; it was something, his individuality, his pride in being a man who made a point of giving considerable thought to the act before presenting Kathy the First with her engagement ring five years ago, the better part of his schooling over, diving head first into his internship rounds thinking of her, bringing her with him to every hospital ward, every ghetto, with a soon to be demolished building used as a shelter, often with no electricity or plumbing bills paid, and the inevitable loss of these necessities. All of the times he shook someone's hand, introducing himself as the therapist his mother Julie so wanted him to be, her own plans for that occupation forever cursed due to her maternal instincts taking precedent over her career ideals.

She never regretted shucking her schooling to be Robert's mother – at least he never heard her exclaim so – even though *her* parents, his dear Grandpa Bill and Grandma Julia, had the financial means to send her if she wished. They were progressive in their own way, Robert had long ago decided of them, not pressuring a daughter in the throes of the post war Big Band 'What, Me Worry?' era to marry, something his Mom's girlfriends would be ever envious of, their own parents a sign of the times, trying to get their daughters married, respectable and out of the house – by twenty five, if any of them could help it – as the great social edicts of the day proclaimed.

Those tear jerker movies about the man always being right, and don't disobey your man – more dogs than wives, they were – and always be behind your mate, right or wrong, no matter what, a woman's place is in the home, and yatta-yatta-yatta-that's all folks really planted such a seed of distrust in his mother during her teen years – before the Cold War, Korea, and the Japs' economic uprising was even a sick joke among the Lit set – of this Man's World she lived in, to such an extent that in the thick of hippiedom circa 1967 – around, before and after the mystical Summer of Love – this woman – fast approaching the venomous, much maligned thirty year mark, though not nearly as 'out of it' as these sex hungry drug induced teens might have thought – was *also* out there, flowers in hand, funky grease painted counter culture designs smeared carefully on her face – with not a small amount of artistic precision – as the rest of them.

She watched the healthy full breasted displays of girls some ten years her junior with a disassociated ease, already in the midst of something she all but never would have believed could be possible when she was their age if she wasn't then seeking it herself. "My, how they carried on," she'd tell Robert, beaming, pointing out parts of retro shows on TV and re runs where she felt she had a good grasp of, even if it was as trivial a tale as, 'I had a friend, Jeanie, who had the same exact pants as that Marcia Brady girl, as Lord knows, looked just as good in 'em from the back as she did! I, on the other Robbie, did not,' at which time she would burst into laughter. She was – is *still* – a great jokester and a master of making fun of herself which Robert, now the heralded Doctor Haskel, hoped had rubbed off on *him*, too.

A great woman, his mother was. He'd always be indebted to the woman for putting him through school in the beginning, how she scraped and saved for his first semesters at the First Community Medical School was anybody's guess. All he could think of was she must have just put it into her head to do it, and nothing he could say as a smug know it all teenager – which he unabashedly was – would change her mind. *He* would do what just wasn't in the cards for *her*, even if there *weren't* more than a few opportunities for her to buy a new deck, so to speak. Once his mother made up her mind about something, even if it was to her later detriment, then the lid was shut on the matter for good. Was this also a trait he inherited from his dear Mommy, he pondered? Most likely! 'Definitely yes,' Katherine would – *did* – say. Well, there were worse things to be than stubborn.

"Trisha," the doctor croaked into the intercom, realizing his throat was dry from being lost in thought, "will you please come in here for a minute?" He cleared his throat. *Too little too late*, he thought. *I'm sure Trisha got a nice giggle from that one. Doctor Froggy Throat.* He spun in his standard issue leather chair – a resolved give in – thinking, *Why tamper with head shrinker success?* – chuckling to himself.

Trisha, who had been looking through her purse for a certain shade of red lipstick she was almost sure *wasn't* in the bag – but looked anyway – got up and habitually straightened out her polyester/cotton blend skirt – on sale at Macy's – a real bargain buy just a week ago – and walked over to the doctor's office door, about ten paces from her desk – sometimes, she heard the juicy dirt – not private session or group though – through the wood, or she'd press her ear to the intercom turned low. *Wicked girl*, she said softly to herself. She knocked on the door, and he instructed her to come in.

She sat on the patients' chair, the only one in the room besides his – and the proverbial Shrink's Couch, of course. The doctor sat still for a moment, unsure of what to say or why he called her into his office. It was some time after ten in the morning – he liked to be in early to collect his thoughts, even though his caseload didn't begin until noon. He didn't mind paying Trisha for the extra two hours, either. There wasn't much for her to do during this time, since she mostly had to deal with patient details like taking their medical histories, medications they were on or had been taking and which doctors had prescribed them, methods of payment, what coverage or plans they used – Medicaid, Medicare, SSI, SSD – and other related inquiries.

And answering the phone. The extra twenty two dollars he had to pay to have her here earlier was well worth it to him, though. She, being young, could use the extra money, as all young people could, and she had no dependents or family business to attend to that would prevent her from coming in at 10:00 a.m. – and he liked her company.

That really was the main reason – he used Trisha as a buffer to help brace him for the coming throngs with their myriad of problems – some imagined, some real, some imagined to be real – which, he had to admit, still gave him the willies as it had when he had first started practicing.

For this, he was grateful to have her here for the first two hours of his 10-to-4 shift, even if the thought of needing some reassurance from a third party about his patients – as if he really bought into that media hype about the mentally ill or emotionally distraught being a danger to the world; a ticking time bomb that would without warning or provocation lurch over and dig their claws into the nearest available sane person at any given moment – brought him not a little feeling of embarrassment, and even anger at himself. He still wasn't the man he envisioned himself to be – the Great Healer – that he'd been so Hell bent on proving while still in school, his face beaming when his mother heard from his professors how well he was doing, knowing her money she had sweat and eaten shit for doing any odd job or temp work she could find was being well spent.

How I let my mother down, Sweet Julie; Single Mom Incorporated. He thought of this and more until he realized he wasn't alone in the room, and straightened up in the plush chair to gather what small dignity he felt he had – *if any*, he heard echo in his skull – a voice as his mother's was, exactly hers in fact. *But not hers*, his guilt reminded him.

"Trisha," he said finally, "it's good to have you here." He stumbled over the words, as someone suddenly stirred from sleep, to answer an important question better left for when he was fully awake. He felt foolish for saying something so asinine, having just greeted her for the day maybe only twenty minutes before. She looked at him curiously, tilting her head slightly. He realized he was fumbling around, hands all over the armrests, on his face, through his hair, outlining his lips – for now moistened with nervousness – and he caught a smirk trying to fight its way onto Trisha's supple pale skin, she trying desperately to curtail it.

Another day he might have been a little sore at this, but now he mentally wished her to let go of her forced composure – doubtless out of respect for him, which he appreciated – and smirk, smile, yelp, laugh or whatever. He leaned over his desk towards her, thinking this might do the trick, feeling guilty for doing so, as she might believe her behavior unforgiveable – or at least inappropriate.

Trisha suddenly burst forth with a loud gasp, a peculiar noise uttered though her teeth which he found amusing himself, and totally reasonable, given his retarded machinations this Monday morning, the 12th of March. "I'm sorry, Doctor Haskel. I don't know what came over me."

"I do," he said. "I've been acting like a horse's ass ever since I came in this morning."

Trisha's face reddened as he spoke.

"And you have every right to laugh or make whatever you call that strange noise you made, at my expense; I allow you, whole hearted."

Before he could finish the sentence, somewhere around *I allow you*, she burst into a guffaw of laughter, as when having heard a great joke from a professional comic. His intuition made him smile, feeling the morning's jitters pass through him and away as he heard her voice, hysterical as anything, and reminding himself how nice it was to have someone nineteen years his junior to remind him, from time to time, that there really was life on this planet after all.

"I'm sorry," she kept saying, over and over, still laughing whenever she looked at his face – the pathetic face, he guessed, of the Man who Didn't Get the Joke.

But he did.

"Oh," Trisha muttered, mad at herself for losing her composure this way, "you must think I'm terrible for coming into your office and laughing like this, doctor." She put her head down, expecting a rage to spill forth from him.

He took his time to study her a moment, possibly to savor the feeling of power, however small, this scene implied. *Another failed attempt at being better than the masses, my son?* Angry at himself once more, he made sure not to show it and scare Trisha.

He composed himself quickly, though he was sure he saw terror in her eyes for just a second or two, possibly having seen the transition on his face, from her actions to the voice to her again. "Now now, don't get excited Trisha. If you want to laugh, laugh. By God, I think we've had *enough* dreariness in this office lately, don't you?

She looked startled, then relieved. The giggles out of her system now, and feeling she wasn't going to be reprimanded – or fired – she confidently sat up in her chair and smiled sweetly, the way she did when greeting incoming patients. "Ye – yes. I guess we have, Doctor Haskel... I. Guess. We. Have."

The words stumbled out so slowly as to be comical unto themselves, but the doctor didn't laugh this time, as she thought he might. "Yeah, I really think it's good that you want to loosen up a bit, if that's what you're getting at, Doctor." She continued, "I – I just went into a fit, I guess, because you looked so fidgety, and that's usually not like you, you know?"

"Yes, I know perfectly what you mean, Trisha. Or should I say, what you're guessing I mean, or maybe am implying."

"Yes. Um, I think."

This made Doctor Haskel chuckle, after which Trisha, thoroughly sure her job was still secure, did so herself. "I don't know what this is all about, Doctor, but I'm glad to see you loosening up a bit!... Of course you *know* I didn't mean to laugh *at* you, but..."

"Say no more, dear girl," he said, cutting her off, the endearment coming from someplace foreign, though somehow fitting for this conversation. "It's okay, really. You're my employee, not my captive." He paused for effect. "You're perfectly within your rights as a human being, and a healthy young woman," – he wanted to add and beautiful besides, but decided it wasn't appropriate – "to laugh, giggle, *guffaw* or whatever, as the mood hits you. Not to the point of distraction, of course," – as he added this, she put her head down shamefully once again – "but within reason, by all means."

"Thank you."

"Never mind. I know I came to work this morning," – he looked at his wrist, realizing he hadn't worn his watch and, trying to pass it off as having an itch, scratched it with his free hand – "looking like a lost puppy in the woods – I'm only forty years old; God knows I'm not *dead yet*, or so jaded that I can't admit to an off day once in a while – I know. I also know I can't shake this feeling that – now bear with me because you know how I feel about Psychic Phenomena – that Sharon, that is, Ms. Langhorn, is having some sort of problem up there in that house. Do you think that sounds – I don't know – dumb?"

"No, not at all… in fact," Trisha replied, leaning forward on her folded hands, her breasts brushing against her forearms, "I had a really funny dream last night, and among other weird shi – sorry, I was about to say –"

"That's alright. Please continue." Doctor Haskel was curious as to what she had to share with him; he himself kept awake the night before with strange dreams about animals, a young girl he never met before, and Sharon Langhorn.

"Okay, like I said, I had a strange dream that involved Ms. Langhorn, but the specifics were pretty fuzzy."

"How do you mean?"

"Well." She searched her vocabulary to find the right words, "Kinda fuzzy, like I said, like a TV picture tube – squared off like a movie…"

"Go on."

"Only, I *don't know!*" Her voice showed distress, as if she sensed how interested the doctor was, like he had something to do with it all. Did he? No, it was her dream, that couldn't be possible.

"Try your best," he said, trying to sound comforting, edging close to the end of his seat.

"Well… Okay, I'll try."

"That's all you *can* do, Trisha, is try. Now go slowly."

"Am I going to be charged for this 'session'?" she joked, trying to alleviate the building tension in the air.

This amused her boss too much. "No! Hah! No… you won't be charged. Not *full price*, anyway."

"How about twenty bucks, my morning pay until twelve?" she chided him, sensing his good mood.

"I think that'll be fair, if you work through all your coffee breaks all this week."

"Deal. Okay." Trisha breathed hard, her hands pressing the skirt creases over her thighs. "It was all just so vague. I saw a little girl –"

"A girl?" he said, trying not to show alarm. *Surely this couldn't be the same girl I dreamt of.* "Go on, please," he said, taking the notebook from his top desk drawer to document her story.

"Well, I don't want to make a big deal out of this, Doc – Doctor Haskel. Really, it's not that important."

"Are you sure?"

"Yes, sir."

"Quite sure?" He looked at her balefully; he really wanted to hear what she had to say.

"Yes, I'm sure. Quite sure."

Oddly enough – or not so odd, in the long and short of things – he felt a little let down about their little chit chat coming to an end. Still, he had to respect her privacy. "Okay, Trisha. We'll talk about this some more a little later?" He paused, sliding back into his seat, tipping it back, their eyes locked in sober understanding.

She had worked for him a long time – eight months – a lifetime for a twenty one year old female – make that *beautiful* female – and she trusted him not to push after a few tender prods. A good man like her father.

"Is that okay with you, later?"

"Later'll be fine, Doctor Haskel, thanks. Is that all for now?"

"Yes, that'll be all for now. Just let me know if our Ms. Langhorn makes her presence known, yah?"

"Yah, mon capitan," she spoke in a half assed Swiss accent, "we vill keep an eye out for zee girl."

"Was that supposed to be German?

"Yah, shoor," she intoned, back to the bad Swiss again.

"That was awful!" he shouted, slapping one of the armchairs, enjoying this exchange.

"Glad you like it," Trisha said, as Trisha. She exited the office to go back to her desk.

Doctor Haskel got a feeling, a sense outside himself, something that seemed to come from outside the nearby bay windows, among the sunlight spilling in. A whisper seemed to be among the breeze, reminding him of a poem, a deeply romantic poem he had read in college. *A whisper on the wind...*

He didn't have time for this, to be listening for secret messages on the breeze, or stop to smell the roses. "I'd just better stop this daydreaming and get ready to see my clients," he said aloud to himself, hoping to snap out of this trance – or whatever it was – that had overtaken him since waking up this morning. He had never doubted his sanity; that should be obvious for the line of work he was in. Before he forgot about his morning musings and studied his patient chart for the day, one thing kept coming up that he was trying to put out of his memory. Something he didn't want to admit to.

That voice, spoken plainly, in a woman's tone, not unlike his mother's, though that wouldn't be possible… in his thoughts he wouldn't – *ha*. He could feel the irony in his next idea like a fire burning – hear voices. But it was as plain as day, just the same. *She'll be calling. Karen will be calling.*

Chapter Seven

Leonard's private line wasn't exactly ringing off the hook. The other agents at the office were off on their rounds, cut throat as ever, and Leo was staying at home base, holding down the fort. It was not too busy here this Monday morning, but the real estate game was not what it had been a year ago; anyway, Leonard had been at this job for six years, interning for two more before that, and was starting to think of checking into a different line of work. Leo might have been Jewish, but he certainly wasn't money hungry. Never the sensitive type, he thought ethnic jokes were damned funny if they made any sense, and people like those liberal 'PC' assholes who wanted to take everyone's rights away, just to protect a precious few whom they would lie through their teeth *professing* these queens to be the majority, could suck his balls as far as he was concerned, off the record, that is. He wasn't about to air his strong opinions in this highly conservative environment.

The firm he worked for was part of a larger conglomerate – *Whoever heard of a real estate conglomerate*, he said to himself, when he had first gotten the call to interview for the intern position. *How little I knew about landowner politics back then,* he reminisced – whose ultimate goal, once a pipedream of the major shareholder – Sheraton somebody; nobody saw him – who worked here and not even the Board saw him that often, as he did most of his dealings and transactions by fax – was to own all the property in the Adirondack tourist strip – seemed to be becoming a reality.

This was a dirty business real estate, and Leonard Rothstein knew he didn't have the killer instinct necessary to get the commissions and high visibility deals to make him a major player and add him to the office tale legends, thank God.

I may not be Catholic, but thank God, he sighed to himself, taking a shallow breath, blinking the lack of sleep from his eyes – last week was frantically high volume. *A lot of overtime was had by all* – as he thought about his coworkers. Those poor bastards. *What do they get out of this job*, he wondered. He found himself wondering this, pondering its deeper meanings – finding none of course – day after day, coming to no definite conclusions. How could you? In an environment like this, snakes in the snakepit, snipping at each other's tails, stealing half digested rats from each other's stomachs.

The whole mess – despite the pleasing dressing gown pulled over the buildings' outer self for tax time excess, nicey nicey designs cut into the walls and beams, care of the absolute best carpenters' services other people's money could buy – struck him as grotesque: a horrible display of corporate excess – he had no more than a minimal attachment to. *Purely a job*, he reminded himself. *This isn't me. I dress up in suits they make me buy, slick back my hair and play snake oil salesman. Or do I play the snake? It's hard to remember sometimes.* His only memorable client after all this time was his newest, Sharon Langhorn. She was a mystery to him, to be sure. Not independent enough to be considered militant, not androgynous enough to be a butch, mot manly enough to be a bull dyke – or even just a regular dyke, whatever that was anymore – Ms. Langhorn was a cliché laced enigma, and he looked forward to finding out more about her. He was dying to hear from her. It was 10:33 in the morning.

Already here for over two hours, he was bored out of his mind. According to the widow's stipulation – the whole setup was bullshit in his opinion, but Sharon had agreed to it, against his advice to the contrary – he couldn't go near the house, or contact her, or anything until at least two o'clock. They were all supposed to meet – the widow, Sharon and himself – around four.

There was no law against her calling *him* however, even though the widow would rather she didn't. The idea of her in total isolation caged up in the house she supposedly was so in love with that she was dying to move in and buy even when her credit said *no fucking way*. *Sharon* knew her savings were for shit, and *Leo* knew her savings were for shit, hell, even Shifton knew the little lady's bankroll was a joke. A joke to want to finance a place like that, at least.

Everything's relative after all, his mother would say. *One man's garbage is another man's toil. What's junk today is a modern masterpiece tomorrow, provided there's enough elbow grease in the underdog's vision,* which didn't seem likely in Langhorn's case. Add to that her money situation – Leo himself no stranger to making a good buck, would be highly hesitant to enter into such a long term payment agreement with the old woman – and he had to admire the woman for her big balls to tackle such a project. Odds were, at the current dying age being about eighty seven, it would be highly unlikely that the old woman would even see half the payments.

Wasn't that something in her favor? – he thought. She had no one else, the old woman, and more than likely she wouldn't see more than half of Sharon's money before she croaked. *Oh, was that too nasty? Too heavy handed? Too much like the truth? Well, too bad. I'm not in the habit of extending too many compliments these days.* Leo decided he'd leave early for the day this afternoon, and leave the snakes to fight over the choicest part of the tank, so to speak. It was when he got up to get his coat from the hanger, and walked over to the time clock to punch out for a quarter-to, that his phone rang. He picked it up after three rings.

"Madison Remy and Shostrom real estate. Leonard Rothstein speaking. How may I help you?"

There was a pause on the other end and for a moment Leo thought maybe the line had gone dead. "Hello? Is anyone there?"

"Yes, uh, Mister Rothstein? This is Doctor Haskel, Sharon Langhorn's psychiatrist."

The name didn't ring a bell.

(?)

Sharon might have mentioned him once or twice, but he couldn't recall right now, his mind still on the injustices of his chosen occupation.

"Mister Rothstein? Are you still there?" the husky voiced stranger on the phone inquired.

(?)

Might as well stay a little longer and figure out what he wants, Leo reasoned. "Yes, I'm still here. Doctor Haskel, is it?"

(?)

"Yes."

"What can I do for you, Doctor? I was just about to leave for the day."

"So early? It's not even eleven yet," the doctor said, smelling a brushoff. He quickly decided to give Leo the benefit of the doubt before he could be sure Rothstein wanted to get rid of him. "Surely you can't be leaving for the day so soon?"

What was this guy after, Leo wondered. Or for that *matter, was there something wrong with Sharon that he should know about?*

(?)

Was she sick? Did she have an accident at the house, or worse? He and Sharon were starting to become friends, weren't they, and he had so few of those, he couldn't care less about his responsibilities to her as an agent, although of course this *was* his responsibility and he'd better not make the mistake of forgetting it. *So let's hear the good doctor out, shall we?*

"Surely I can be, Doctor. With all due respect, I'm not feeling my best today and the grind is getting to me. I'm sure you can understand that."

"Yes, of course," Doctor Haskel responded, saying no more. He didn't really know why he called Leonard

(?)

just that he had, and would do well just to stay coherent and make something up as he went along.

"May I ask what your call is in reference to?" Leo asked in clipped tones, still in Real Estate Agent Mode.

"Why of course," the doctor said, more awake than he was a moment before. He couldn't help thinking about that voice he thought he had heard. *She'll be calling... Karen will be calling.* Who was this woman or whomever, named Karen, indeed. He'd accept the fact that he *did* actually hear the voice, inflected just as his mother's was – which he wasn't ready to do – yet.

"Why of course I understand," he intoned again, for effect. "I used to work for a living too, at one time."

This made Leo want to laugh, but he thought it was better not to. Self deprecating humor was one thing. Most doctors, whatever their specialty, weren't confident enough – or mature enough emotionally – to handle someone *comprehending* a self deprecating joke at their own expense. "Oh, did you now? That's good to know," he answered, thinking coyness was the lesser evil to a good natured ribbing. "That's all I do over here y'know, is work."

"That's good... it's the American Way, you know."

Leo started to get annoyed at this fellow on the other line – what if he wasn't Sharon's doctor after all

(?)

but some goon who was after her for something that saw her in his company? He felt it best to find out before he left for the day. "I'm sorry but you still haven't answered my question regarding my client."

Doctor Haskel knew his mind was somewhere else and he felt the fool for it. How this man must be thinking of him, he wondered; almost out the door, all of a sudden getting a call out of the blue

(?)

from his client's psychiatrist, not even telling me his manner of business. *What a fool I'm being this morning*, he added, cursing himself.

"I'm sorry, Mr. Rothstein. It's uh… a busy day here today –"

"I'm sure it is, Doctor. Don't psychiatrists start taking patients later in the day, Doctor?"

"Yes. Yes they do. But…" The doctor searched quickly for a sufficient lie to tell Leo

(?)

"…the fish are biting quickly today, is all. A lot of people with problems today. Here to start the week off sharp, y'know. Pack the register with names, or someone else might take 'em." Not being able to muster a lie, Doctor Haskel tried his best at levity. On such short notice, his delivery was pitiful.

Leonard grew tired of all this stupidity and raised his voice the next time he spoke, raising a few eyebrows at the office as well in the process. "Now look here Haskel – if you *are* Sharon's doctor, that is–"

(?)

"– I want you to tell me what you want and I want you to tell me now."

Haskel stayed silent on the other end, mad at himself for raising this poor man's suspicions. *Couldn't I just crawl back into bed,* he imagined to himself. What a morning I'm having... "Is a client agent privilege I take quite seriously and would appreciate it if you would just call Ms. Langhorn when she returns from her extended weekend."

"Yes, at the mansion," the doctor countered, regaining his composure again.

"How did you kn...

(?)

Well I guess she would've told you," Leo said, deciding this probably *was* her psychiatrist – though he couldn't recall Sharon mentioning his name before –

(?)

"since you are her doctor."

"I'll get right to the point, Mr. Rothstein," the doctor said in the best authoritative voice he could muster, "I'm having a lousy morning so far, and I deeply apologize for talking nonsense and wasting your time."

"Forget it," Leo said, waving his hand in a dismissive gesture to no one in particular. "You just caught me at a bad time. I'm not having the best day today either, although at –" he checked his watch for the precise time "–10:49, I can't believe how tired and disgusted I feel, as if the whole day's already rolled by, plus overtime. Hence, why I was on my way out, losing money in the process."

"I feel the same way – the fatigue, I mean – and I've only been here inside the hour. It feels like a thousand years have flown by since I said good morning to my secretary," he said, making Leo nod in acknowledgement on his end.

"I shouldn't be telling you, I suppose, wasting your time this way, if you'd really like to be on your way home and all."

"It's okay," Leo replied, picking up the change in the doctor's voice, and quipped, "I won't charge you for my time if you don't charge me for yours."

The doctor laughed out loud at what he had said, which made Leo jump, surprised by the new sound coming from the receiver. "That's great," Doctor Haskel said, in between chuckles, "just great." He took a deep breath, collecting himself to finally finish his thought. "Rothstein, I know I can't prove this, but..."

"What is it? I'm listening."

"I – I feel that there's something wrong with Sharon."

"How do you mean... wrong?"

"Well, I won't get into a lot of rhetoric about doctor patient confidentiality, just to say that I don't renounce them in Ms. Langhorn's case and I can't go into details without her permis–"

"Doctor *please*, what's on your mind?" Leonard demanded, banging his hand with his right palm as he did so. He was leaning against his desk, overcoat still slung over his left shoulder.

Doctor Haskel maintained a respectful silence, as before, waiting for Leo to continue.

"I'm waiting, Doctor."

"Mr. Rothstein, obviously I've put ahead the wrong impression to you, and for this you have my sincere apologies." He paused before continuing, bracing himself for further outbursts. *My friends at school were right about me not knowing how to keep things brief. Sometimes I wish I could just get to the damn point, already.* "Mr. Rothstein, let me get to the point."

"That would be nice, Haskel. I'm not as young as I was when I first picked up the phone."

"I deserve that, I suppose," said the doctor, huffing. "I think there's something the matter with Sharon – at the *house*, that is."

"Really?"

"Yes."

"Do you mean," Leo tried to find the proper words but could only come up with the most banal, "something mental?"

Doctor Haskel took this as somewhat intrusive, as well as crude, but decided that, now on the topic, it might be best to stay there. "Mental? Well, that's a relative term, of course..."

He heard Leo let out a weary sigh.

"Sorry. Straight to the point. Alright. Here it is. I feel that even though I perfectly understand the owner has made these provisions with my patient – peculiar as they may be in my profess – in my *opinion*, I think being there all alone will make her... relapse."

"What do you mean by 'relapse'?" Leo queried, finding the seat of his chair behind him with his hand, seating himself. If there was something the matter with his client that might affect the firm – and Sharon herself, certainly – then he owed it to himself to hear the doctor out, long winded or not.

Doctor Haskel cleared his throat before continuing. "It's taken me a long time – Sharon is one of my oldest patients – to get Sharon to this point, through therapy..."

"Go on," Leo coaxed sternly.

"... and I'd just hate for her to recall certain things, after it took so long to draw her –" He tried to find the right words, but like Leo, wasn't feeling too poetic this morning. "– out of her... shell."

Recall certain things? Leo repeated this several times in his head. That didn't sound too promising. Obviously there were things troubling Sharon he knew nothing about. His mind started to wander, to the many possibilities a disturbed person could find themselves in when alone. Especially in such a large house. *All alone. So many echoes. Strange noises. Oh, God – how could I have bene so stupid to agree she stay there by herself?* He checked his watch. It was three minutes to eleven.

"Mr. Rothstein, are you still on the line?"

"Yes yes, I'm still here," Leo hissed, a throbbing behind his eyes having just appeared, moments before, the same pain he got whenever he found out he had overtime without notice. It looked like he'd be getting his full hour's pay from ten to eleven, after all.

The doctor sensed that maybe he had said too much. "Mr. Rothstein, I –"

"Please call me Leonard. Hearing my last name over and over makes me cringe."

"Very well then, Leonard. There are many things you don't know about Ms. Langhorn. I feel she may be in danger in that house, alone." Leo could hear controlled urgency in the doctor's voice. "I think we should meet somewhere to discuss this further."

"Is it that urgent? I'm supposed to meet her there at four. That's when this morbid 'stipulation' is supposed to end, and the widow signs the papers over to Sharon."

"Tell me, Mr. Rothstein." The doctor's voice was suddenly grim. "Do you have feelings for Ms. Langhorn that go *beyond* client agent status?"

"Now," Leo started, putting his legs up crossover on his desk, "how do you mean that exactly?"

"What I mean by that, exactly –" he started, thought the better of it, then stopped, not wanting to offend. "Oh, it's not important... She mentioned you in a way more befitting a friend, or – dare I say it, knowing Sharon the way I do, as a romantic interest, possibly."

Leo was speechless on the other end. He put his legs down and leaned over his chair, as if whispering into the ear of child playing on the floor. "Do you really think so, that she feels that way about me?" He was so stunned that was all he could manage to say.

"I can't be sure, but she does care for you, Leonard, that much I'm certain of. She called me yesterday. Sometimes I have Sunday patients, so she probably took a chance. She had a few words with my secretary, Trisha. She's usually quite cordial to people even if... even if she doesn't that much care for a person; prides herself on it, in fact."

"That's all fine. She strikes me as a strong willed type, like she fought a lot of adversity to get where she is, but on the other side, Doctor Haskel... I don't know what this has to do with me, barring my position as go between for this transaction."

The doctor, waiting a moment before speaking again, checked on Trisha through the glass partition between his office and her desk, a wall length one way mirror.

(?)

She was busy filing her nails, biding her time until twelve, when her shift *really* began.

"So," he said, returning to the conversation, "you *also* have feelings of affection towards Ms. Langhorn?"

"Why, I like her well enough," Leo answered, not caring for the doctor's accusatory tone. "You could say she's my type."

"That's good to know. So you're leaving for the day, huh?"

"Yes, sort of... I still have to pick up Sharon at the estate. That's business, so I guess I just felt like getting my head together til then."

"You're also concerned about her too, how she's doing after three days alone, correct?"

"Sure. After all you told me now –"

"But I haven't told you much of anything."

"Even so, it was important enough to call me here, so yeah, I'm curious to see how she made out out there by herself, especially after you mentioning to me there might be cause for concern." He looked at his watch again. Eleven o three. Time to punch out. "Look, this has been a nice chat, but I really have to be going now."

"Very well, I won't argue the point. Just let her know I've been asking about her, and for her to call me when she gets back home." His voice had a trace of annoyance. *A quick study, this Rothstein*, he thought.

"I'll be sure and do that now, doctor. Don't worry – whatever you have going on between the both of you, it's none of my business," Leo said, trying to send him off the scent, "whatever she's up to, I'll have her home safe, dad."

"That's not the reason I said –"

"See ya, Doc," Leo said, putting the receiver down. On the other end of the phone, Doctor Haskel was still holding the receiver, dissatisfied with the abrupt dismissal.

"What was that, Leo?" a coworker inquired.

"Oh nobody, Frank. My client's shrink was asking around for her. Think they're an item," Leo kidded. *Hm. Wouldn't be the first time I heard that, but why'd he call here?*

(?)

117

"Whadda you got to do with it?" Frank asked.

"Beats me. You know how psychiatrists are – they're all neurotic."

"Yeah, neurotic." Frank laughed at the picture this cast in his head. "One more nuttier than the next."

"That's for sure," Leo replied, looking down at the phone, wondering. "Tell Mister Shostrom I'll be back later, will ya? I'm gonna take a long lunch before I pick up the doc's daughter," he told Frank with a wink.

"Long lunch, pick up girl, got it," Frank shot back, making the O.K. sign with his thumb and index finger. He returned to his desk as Leo punched out for the day at 11:06, catching the next elevator down to the lobby.

The doctor sat in his chair alone with his thoughts. The talk with Leo – or was it the strange happenings thus far that stirred him? – had rejuvenated him. He buzzed Trisha and asked her to step inside a moment.

"Yes, doctor," she said, her eyes wide.

"Trisha, cancel my appointments for this afternoon, and take the rest of the day off for yourself."

"Cancel? Take the day off? What's gotten into you this morning doctor, if I may ask?"

"Nothing, Trisha, and *everything*," was his reply, his heart beating rapidly as he spoke. "I'm going up to see our Ms. Langhorn. Hold my calls," he said half jokingly.

"Are you sure about this, Doctor Haskel?" wondering herself. "It's not like you to go off during the day like that."

"Well I'm going. Stay if you want, but I won't be coming in again until tomorrow morning."

"Doctor," she pleaded, eyes even wider, "be careful."

"I will," he said, and then he was gone, down the stairs to the street below.

"I'd better call the police," Trisha said aloud, "there's something going on." And dialed.

In the kitchen of the estate, Sharon stood by the sink, gripping the porcelain edge. Like many of the fixtures, the kitchen set was the original; maybe going back sixty, seventy years. The house itself was probably much older – maybe a hundred, hundred and twenty or so. It was hard to tell; Sharon wasn't much on architectural trivia, and the house was refinished, remodeled, added onto and wings subtracted so many times, that she was sure even an expert couldn't tell. It was a nice enough place, she thought, her mind racing to all sorts of imaginable and unimaginable things while in the house alone, things both seen and unseen. It was the unseen part that wasn't sitting too well with her, forcing her to vomit from the overwhelming sights and sounds around her – her body's only way to combat so many things she really didn't *believe* in, was to heave. And heave. And heave some more. She'd been vomiting off and on most of Sunday night, continuing into the next morning.

Later this afternoon, she would be free of this place for good. If Leo and his paperwork didn't like it, well, she didn't care. Whatever was going on in this house was outside both her understanding and her beliefs. She wasn't a devout Jew like Leo – although neither was he, in the strictest sense – or a shameless Catholic like Beatrice or Maureen. *So what am I?* she asked herself. *What do I believe?* Sharon couldn't give herself an honest answer, but she did know she wouldn't find out staying around here much longer. It was as if she could *feel* the *old* in this house. *Feel the old?* This made her chuckle at her own nonsensical choice of words. But hey, nothing was normal around here, so why not talk abnormal, too? It wasn't as if someone were actually watching, or was worried about her being here all alone.

Puking her guts out for hours and hours now, she was beginning to doubt that anyone – Leo, or otherwise – was going to come knocking on the door and bringing her home at all. *Locked up here* all alone. "Entombed."

The word rolled off her tongue making her giggle again, which was enough to make her dry heave, expecting something more substantial. Where was she getting all of this waste, anyway? She hadn't exactly binged while she was at the estate, hardly tasting the canned stuff in the pantry. She mainly kept herself afloat with the bottled water she had brought herself, and the widow's concentrated orange juice – a good blend – she had to get that brand when she got back home.

There were, of course, the visions; the little girl in the hallway, behind the pantry, behind the swinging kitchen doors – she shot a glance over to one corner of the kitchen where she had seen her before to see if she would be there right now – in back of the staircase landing to the attic... everywhere. Who was this person, this scared, crying young woman who appeared to her regularly, so sad and melancholy as to break her own heart just watching her... a phantom girl who so reminded her of herself – 'in another life?'

Oh, those days alone with him, she remembered. Horrible days alone when her mother would go to work – hours upon hours she would think, alone in her mother's clothes closet, hoping he wouldn't see her, knowing if she told mom how her stepfather – her mother's husband, Oh Jesus – looked at her, touched her, embraced her... then that one day, when he went farther than he had before. Even when he had put his finger in her vagina, a thick, calloused finger barely fitting in past her hymen, Sharon petrified with fright, knowing this must be wrong, that men don't pull down little girls' panties... not their stepdaughters... they shouldn't do that, touching them that way.

The way they use their innocence against them, shouting hollow threats that at the time sounded like they might have been uttered by Satan himself... who knew about these things? She never told Sharon what men wanted, she never believed her, she knew it. So she let him do what he wanted. *What he wanted.*

Sharon could feel the bile rising up in her gut once again, and heaved, gripping the edge of the porcelain for all she was worth. What he wanted... *God, how could I let him do that to me?* What he wanted. *Oh God, please go away. My mother will be home soon. Leave me alone!*

As she felt the waste rising up through her, her ribcage pounded against her muscles – a sickening, scary-as-all-hell feeling – alerting her – though she could never know it then – to the presence making itself known to her insides. Her eyes were dilated and moist with mucous, but she still focused well enough to see the little girl with the torn clothes and the sad expression reaching out to her, with small, bloodied, dirt caked hands...

As Doctor Haskel walked down the small outside ramp that ran from the outer emergency doors of the commercial building he shared with other medical oriented businesses, he wondered if what he was doing was a good idea. *Sure it is*, he heard a voice say in his head, reassuring and feminine. Was it Sharon's voice? *Funny, a psychiatrist who hears voices!... if that gets out, it's just what those therapy naysayers'll need to pickle us all.* He got his car keys out of his jacket breast pocket and opened the driver's side door, and started up the car with the deft quickness of someone who had done so many times before. *Not like that would be such a bad thing,* the voice finished. He looked out the rear view mirror. So many wrinkles; grey hairs tufting out the sides of his temples which he hadn't noticed before. No, not a bad idea, he thought, at all.

Libby removed the cups from the dinette table, dragging her feet on the Indian rug – laid out on the floor parallel to the table and chairs next to the only window in the room – as she always did since the hip operation. The widow Shifton called to her from the living room, where she was halfheartedly thumbing through the *Readers Digest*s and *Ladies Home Journal*s on the coffee table.

"Libby? Libby, dear, can you hear me?" The widow turned in her seat to try and get a look at her. She sat in a plush vinyl chair the likes of which she herself considered lowbrow and tacky. *Then again*, she ruminated, *Libby lives alone and is free to buy what she likes. I am used to extravagant things because I've been married to a man of extravagant means, and I shouldn't put my tastes onto a friend.* Satisfied with her own private observation, she managed a smile and sat back a little more into the chair she disliked so much.

When Libby, having ignored her calls, finally came into the room again, she found her asleep, and shook her tenderly awake with a moist hand, a wet dishrag in her other, moister palm. "Curly wake up, hon, you fell asleep."

"Ah!" the widow cried out, startling Libby, who threw the wet dish towel up in the air. The widow grasped Libby's wrist and looked up at her with the innocent frightened look Libby remembered her wearing as a child. Moments later, she cursed herself for being so dramatic.

"Dorothy, what is it, girl? Are you alright?" The widow bent over to try getting some air into her lungs, and Libby tried to help by patting her back – the way mothers do to burp their babies – though she really didn't know what good this could do.

"Libby!"

"Yes, Dorothy, I'm right here, honey." She took a deep breath before she continued.

"What is it?"

"It's Karen. I *have* to go to her."

"Who's Karen?"

The widow looked at Libby as if she'd never seen her before.

"Who is this Karen, Dorothy?" Libby asked more sternly, worried that her friend might be having a stroke.

"Dorothy," the widow said, finally, "I'm not Dorothy, I'm Curly Top."

"Oh dear," Libby sighed. *Something's happened*, she thought. *Something in her mind.* "Dorothy, I *call* you Curly Top," she started, her voice measured and soft, "but we only called you that when you were a little girl."

The widow leaned over to her right closer to Libby, taking Libby's hands in her own. "But Libby dear, my angel," she said, her voice light and affectionate, mimicking Libby's tone of some seventy plus years ago, "you call me Curly Top still, don't you?" In her mind, she had gone back to another time, when the two of them would play together at school. "Don't you, Libby? Don't you still call me Curly Top?"

"Well... yes, Curly – Dorothy... I mean," Libby stammered, wanting to get to the phone and call someone, but not wanting to leave the widow alone in this state even for a moment. She had read about how stroke victims can lose their sense of who they are, or regress, as seemed to be the case here. She would just have to wait for the right moment.

The widow ran her fingers through her white hair, a look of shocked surprise registering on her face. "Libby! Someone's cut my *hair!* Oh my *goodness*, who could have *done* this? Did *you* cut my hair, Lib? *Did* you?" She grabbed Libby's wrist and gave her that look again, the look of wide innocence only a pre pubescent girl can muster seriously. Libby put her own hands down and tried pulling away from the woman/child gently, but decided to use more force to do so. Mrs. Shifton recoiled, as though Libby had not firmly pulled her hand away from her own, but had slapped it.

"Libby," she whispered. "Why must you be so *rough* with me? Am I not your *friend?*" Her voice had grown louder, but was now decidedly apologetic. "Why did you slap my *hand* down like that? I'm not one of your *rag* dolls, you know." Her tone became accusatory. "I *think* you should give *someone* an apology," she continued, "especially since you cut all my *hair* off to *start* with."

"I didn't cut your hair off, Dorothy!" Libby shouted, more out of fear for her friend's state of mind than out of genuine exasperation. She immediately lowered her voice, knowing it was not the widow speaking right now, but some twisted memory of herself as a girl, or *something*. She could not be sure, but in any case she reasoned it might be best to call a professional before she hurt herself.

The widow slumped back into the chair again and closed her eyes. *Good*, Libby thought. *Maybe she'll go back to sleep and forget this nonsense. Or maybe she'll go back to sleep and never wake up!* The thought of her dearest, oldest friend dying in her plush vinyl chair horrified her and she briskly rubbed Libby's arms and shoulders, deciding this time she was definitely on the way out of this world.

"Karen!" the woman/child screamed again, clutching at Libby's left wrist with one hand and gripping at the air with the other. "Karen! She's in danger! I have to help her!"

Libby pulled away from her firm grip and shuffled to the other big chair in the room – this one quilted, not vinyl – as quickly as she could without falling down, to get a blanket for her friend.

"Karen! Karen! No, don't go in there!"

"Dorothy dear," Libby exclaimed, "why are you so upset? And who is this Karen? Eh? Who is it, please tell me!"

Mrs. Shifton did not answer, nor did she give Libby any reason to believe she had even heard her. Libby tried to push the widow back into her chair and tuck the blanket in around her, but wherever in her mind she was right now, Libby reasoned, she had gone there to stay.

Doctor Robert Haskel was driving down the pock marked road, en route to the estate. He was unsure of the address; was pretty sure Sharon had not mentioned the house number to him at all. He began to think this trek had been a bad idea and a waste of time; not like him at all.

But here he was anyway on this godawful road he had only driven over once before – to meet a patient who would not go quietly to the sanitarium he had recommended, unless he would hold her hand on the minivan ride there – and he remembered the ride in this very car, in fact – terribly uncomfortable and bumpy. Same as it was now.

Two things came to mind as he rolled precariously over this awful mass of stones, dirt, buried trash and ground in bottle caps – one, that patient he saw off to the loony bin – doctors were allowed to use mentally ill slang, just as the rest of the world were not – more than two years ago was definitely out to lunch, and two, that he was due for a new car.

Libby shook the widow as she simultaneously tried to put the jacket around her. Even though they were the same age, she felt peculiarly like she were the widow's granddaughter, doting after the senile family member. Mrs. Shifton, who was somewhere between herself and the woman/child at this moment, had suddenly stopped her aggressive agitations, and just fell limp at once. *Maybe this is it. Maybe she's dead.*

Libby walked around the living room, intently searching for that wet dishrag the woman/child had made her throw up in the air before. She turned over the couch cushions with fervor; she bent over, searching underneath the furniture with a flashlight she kept on top of the television, as she was constantly worried about burned out fuses; she even shone the light onto the *walls*, reasoning that, possibly, the rag had stuck itself to one of the papered over wood panels, as if, since the widow's sudden sickness, water now contained the identical qualities of glue.

Anything, she said to herself, *please, I don't want to deal with this right now. God, she's the only friend I have... Don't take her yet, please.* Libby clicked off the flashlight, admitting to herself her behavior was stupid. She looked over at her guest, who was slumped over in her old vinyl chair, cut up and...

Libby looked down at her dead friend's corpse, trying to disbelieve what she saw. The reality of it was, of course, that there was no chance left to do so, as there was *no time*. No time at all. She was dead. Dorothy, her beloved childhood friend, Curly Top... never to be a child again. *Maybe in another life*, she thought. Maybe in another godawful, tragic, dismal, beautiful life, Libby's friend was dead.

Doctor Haskel, meanwhile, was beside himself with guilt. *How could I have hit her*, he asked himself.

(?)

How could she have run in front of me so fast? She was so old. He reached no answer that satisfied his highly learned, structured-to-a-fault mind. This whole day was turning out badly for him so far, and there was *still* that nasty business of the rest of the day – *most* of it, he shuddered dismally – having yet to run its foreboding course.

He looked over at Libby, a stockish woman in her seventies, *maybe* early eighties, yet she had that unmistakable presence – even in what to her must have been a truly sickening experience to endure – of a woman from her time, someone who took care of her charge, whether blood or marriage related or not. No doubt he wouldn't be turned away from a fresh cooked meal or a warm hug – pressing himself against her full, reassuring bosom, having those cuddly mother type thick arms wrapped around him for comfort – by such a woman, an obviously working class jewel of a woman the likes of whom – thanks to the dragon headed reading of feminism and its assorted splinter sub projects – like the great speckled Dodo bird – will never be seen nor heard from again.

And I killed her friend,

(?)

126

he reminded himself, as if he actually needed the smallest reminder of this tragic occurrence. As he gave his part of the equation to the deputy who had made the drive down to the only two houses in this immediate area – the two homes themselves, each of them built by Libby and Dorothy's deceased husbands respectively – he couldn't help repeating this to himself, obsessively – *the obsessive psychiatrist*, another voice of his somewhere in his muddled thought processes seemed to be telling him: *what a sick, perfectly appropriate term for you!*

The distressed middle aged doctor politely excused himself from the deputy's moronic usual questions someone like himself – in his profession – so far removed from the big city crime he undoubtedly would like to stay *away* from, or at least he looked the type – a sallow faced fellow with rubber features like the extraordinarily multi jointed 'skinnies' he'd seen in a sideshow – back when they still *had* such things – freak fest. The typical atonal vocal delivery, a drone that just screamed *incest survivor*, stupid little hick who he – probably – was.

Now Doc ol' boy, don't put people down just because they're not some cock hungry fag college grad like your damn self. Ooh! Hit a nerve, did we? Well fuck you! You deserve it! You just killed that old bag lying on the ground over there! And look at her pathetic friend, the horrible voice in his head continued, *just awful! Look! She has a dishrag in her hand! The distress! And look again, old man! She's even drying her eyes with it! Youch! The horror,* it mocked, and just as the sheriff's helper – who never in his life would want to work on the real police force back in the city – was leaving, having closed the flap on his notebook and put it back into the left breast pocket of his grey polyester uniform shirt, Doctor Haskel blurted out, quite hysterically, "Would you shut the fuck up you moron, I just *killed* somebody!"

The 'uh-oh' expression on the rookie deputy's face was obvious to even the most casual observer. There were plenty of those around later too – one would be surprised how a heavily *un*populated area gets heavily *populated* when the smell of blood – crazy *old* blood no less – is in the air.

Many women, children and men – most on disability or retired or largely both – came out from their shacks, from their respective towns – the nearest five miles away, the farthest twenty – to see the widow Shifton dead, the oldest member of the Province known collectively as Tug Hill Acres among the born-theres – which, as the quasi nickname implied, was exactly what it was – cheaply purchased dry soil acreage with hills as old as God surrounding them – was dead, more importantly for various morbid reasons, she was *murdered* and, accidental or not, this was information sorely needed by a sleepy town like a shot of heroin to a fiending addict, and nothing in the beings of the participants who made the trek various distances to view the body firsthand were likely to make any of them think or pretend this was any ordinary happening.

No, the people of the Tug Hills didn't get interesting news that often, and as hinted at previously, reveled in the macabre news story even more. This one, it would seem, was heaven sent – or sent from someplace just as supernatural.

"What a headline this will make!" Darien Woodsill bellowed forth from his massive gut, the benefit of many many chocolate covered donuts – with sprinkles – Woodsill was the editor of the only newspaper – or publication of any kind for that matter – anywhere in the province, stuffily titled *The Tug Hill Report* – provincial children had a good laugh about that title, to be sure; what exactly was there, in these boring, perfect for a witness relocation program recipient towns, *to* report? Indeed, the older generations quizzed each other as to the dubious innuendo hinted at in the title of Darien's pride and joy as well, albeit with much less outright disdain and apathy. Darien spoke the headline as it came to him, as he always did for effect, among the sweating throngs of a crowd – however pliant and still though it be – one of his few chances for attention and what a man of his nickel-and-dime background would, in honesty be heard to call a vice.

"Screaming Mad Widow Hit by Killer Doctor's Car!" he yelled, so thoroughly pleased with himself at how the words just rolled out of his mouth, he felt no editing as to length was necessary, the throngs – now really just a few stragglers and teenage hangers on with their bicycles and dirt bikes in tow – *enough to get a buzz going*, he thought – really didn't care for his morbidly campy ideas, or tabloidesque attention grabbing headlines, however enough people did buy the paper every Saturday – placed next to the more commercially viable national publications and magazines like *People* and *The Star* – to warrant changing the potentially damaging – and in plain old bad taste – format.

As can be expected, relating the previous happenings briefly thus far, our Good Doctor declined an on the spot interview with the not so scrupulous newspaper man. If such a doctored – excuse the term – tale *did* go out to the masses – *Hey Girty, look at this. A city doc bumped off old lady Shifton – the bag – geez, what a tongue lashing from God he's gonna get!* – then that was none of Doctor Haskel's concern at the moment. In sobering view of recent occurrences, it was of the utmost importance – to his own wellbeing as well as Sharon's sanity – to see Sharon and make sure she was alright. Anyhow, the sympathy of another familiar human being would do his nerves some good right now.

Make that your sanity as well, said the voice.

Unbeknownst to the grieving Doctor Haskel, however, Ms. Langhorn – his longest and admittedly best liked patient – was having enough problems of her own. But then, he was soon to find this out for himself, as well as the peculiar fact that problems – like a virus – have a way of *spreading*.

The little girl in the tattered old fashioned clothing – maybe turn of the century, maybe earlier, she could not be sure – eyed Sharon with a cool, even gaze, her large hazelish eyes taking on a watery quality that Sharon – who was being miraculously practical minded while in the presence of a ghost – supposed were tears – old tears, the kind someone might shed if they had not cried in years.

They just welled there in the corners of her eyes, as if they had forgotten to simply run down her cheeks and hit her mouth with a salty taste – as Sharon considered was the brain's usual command to the tear ducts.

No, this child – this sad looking, dirty, longing child – had held those tears, if not for years, then for *generations* in her pretty, expressive hazel eyes. It was a wonder that Sharon could calmly suffer the presence of such a tragic looking figure at all, being that she herself had been in such a deep, chilling depression since arriving at the mansion. If the truth be known, of course, she had been suffering emotionally for such a long time now, little things adding up to big ones... *little to big, and so on.*

Everything bothered her, as if the whole populace of the world were groping at her skin, trying to pull the still youthful supple flesh right off the bone – *rrrrrip!* – and the thieves, sated by their acquisitions, had taken her torn and bloodied, piece by piece, to some undisclosed private destination for safe keeping – Oh, the morbid tales one was prone to tell oneself when the bearer of dire loneliness, it was not to be believed! – her blood, the seething acidic life force to so many who were waiting for it – being stolen, quite daintily and with the utmost professional attention to not spilling or wasting a drop – that, if spilled, the vital liquid, being at once cleaned up and discarded into an available pocket for later proper disposal, it should be noted – by some ghoul, with ample obvious penchant – nay, experience and *relish*, for such macabre work as this, bending the dripping wounds to the floor to let gravity do its God intended job, to drip, and drip... *drip* until none was left, splattering into a large waiting goblet below, covered neatly and with prodigious care, as if its own repulsive life depended on it – oh, what a morose spectacle, to be sure! – for whatever reason, one would not want... Sharon shuddered, to think about it.

This girl in her tattered muddied rags – her budding teenage figure tightly outlined against her underclothes, which peeked through various holes in the patched over material of her house dress, was waving to her now, not a hello or goodbye gesture, but a circular motion of her right hand, asking – if not commanding, albeit gently so – to come with her somewhere. *Somewhere inside the house*, Sharon guessed, eyes on the vision/girl always. *In the house.* The words reverberated inside her head as if they were a ball in a ping pong match – back and forth, one to the other, to the other again... she felt herself rise slowly, the way she remembered she did for about a month after she strained a lower back muscle during a skiing trip with David – one of her few stabs at a getaway – twice more by herself – which had ended in disaster, physical and otherwise.

She put one foot in front of the other and shuffled along slowly like a sleepwalker. But was that not practically what she was, sleeping maybe for Sharon the eighty or so odd hours she had been here, a prisoner? A *stranger* to herself, left to ponder all the misgivings and mistakes she had made, all the parties she had never been invited to, but *knew* went on without her, the weddings office acquaintances had attended and talked about, which she had not been asked to. *It must have slipped their minds*, she had reasoned, checking her mail for an invitation even days after the event, hoping the mailman's *faux pas* would indicate the story she told herself. Many stories.

Right, left, back and forth, shuffle side to side. Terrible outrageous memories of a scared little girl who never really knew love, orphaned seemingly for some good reason, some benign righteous reason the thought of abortion maybe stirring some pathetic feeling of guilt toward the embryo that would be Sharon Langhorn, the surname not hers and the given name truly given by no one. Memories, dreams, traumas and nightmares better left unrevived and forgotten; yet there they were, in her head, since the moment of her arrival, the thought of it at the time too fantastic and unusual to swallow.

Who would have thought, a far off voice whispered intently through some empty doorway in her mind, a window opened suddenly, miraculously, in a house of boarded up shutters... crumbling with the ages, of memories suppressed or *transformed, changed* into a slightly abridged version of an original picture, like a doctored photograph – pimples and blotches airbrushed over, leaving the smooth perfect skin for the customer to gaze at and long for, eying his real life wife or girlfriend's imperfections against the vision in the adult magazine in disgust and contempt, taking the surgeried over the natural every time.

As long as the natural didn't have to be viewed first; that wouldn't be right then, would it? We're selling fantasies here, sir, not miserable bleak street reality, look at your whore wife, or your sagging bloated mother, and you will clearly need my version of reality, kind sir. My beautiful perfected version, free of blemish, stretch marks or scars of any kind. Life lessons, easily removed. Cleanly. With little or no effort involved. Very little effort.

The little girl stopped in her ghost tracks – sur tracks, maybe, would be a better description, Sharon decided – to turn around in Sharon's direction. It wasn't all that strange, of course, to spin about on one's heels as she had. Any new military recruit was taught this move as part of their training in every civilized warring country. No it wasn't that, Sharon pondered, nor the way her eyes – sur eyes, she reminded herself – glowed as though they were lit from behind, tiny flames almost flickering surely the way her own mind was seeing it most likely, being unimaginably in the presence of a living dead person like Jack O' Lanterns.

No, it was the cold trance like – even insect like way she turned, not stopping in her place, contemplating her next move, or just enjoying standing still for a moment before being called by her ... like we all did, didn't everything have to be done that way, one thing at a time, then again she had to remind herself – boy this was getting to be more than she thought she could deal with! – that this girl, vision, spirit or... well whatever – was not human. Not as she was.

Though if Doctor Haskel was around, she mused, I'd be able to dig up enough reasons to try and make him believe I've been turned into something less – or more – than human while being in this depressing shit hole.

That was it! She/it didn't pause before she turned around. Very creepy. Like in a horror movie. The Exorcist. Bratty Regan's head spinning in the film version, spinning a bit more, and in color. *Nasty business, following spooks all around a haunted mansion*, Sharon mused again, an invisible friend to her left preferably for some reason – madness, surely... such nasty, creepy crawly, shrieking business, this.

As she followed her benefactor down a sidelong corridor she didn't have the nerve to explore before by herself – By herself! The thought made her gag, short of breath. Was she alone here or wasn't she? Sharon couldn't help wondering what time it was, couldn't help wishing for the correct alignment of Little Hand and Big Hand, and wouldn't rest until she knew the damn time. Jesus Christ! What time was it indeed? How important this fact was, how little she had gotten her things in order – she cursed herself – how little. Her suitcase was not yet packed, her clothes not neatly folded and put away in the least. Leo, her savior; her Jewish Savior – the black humor of the joke made her feel like giggling again – would be here soon to whisk her away on his lawyer's chariot. Or why not his friend, what's his name? she couldn't remember his friend's name, the one who owned the used car dealership, who drove her the long way here – meeting her at her doorstep even – as a small favor to *his good friend Leo*.

Why did this sound to her like a scam? A ruse? A put on? Suddenly it all seemed – the easy paperwork, the widow's bucking at an easy – and admittedly shady payment plan put forth in all earnestness by her at the widow's home. Where she was *now*. At the widow's home. Could it be anyone else's? Surely not hers – Like pieces of a puzzle finally solved.

Easy. That was the word she needed to find – the part of the puzzle that had been missing for months, hobby temporarily discarded, put aside for another, readily assembled one before the missing piece with the word 'easy' is found by the family dog – *a cute medium sized one – as long as we're fantasizing Brain like – maybe a cocker spaniel or a Labrador – happy to be of service – but,* the head of the household says in Sharon's fantasy, in mock horror – *it's all chewed up! We'll never know what it said before, never know the answer to the myriad mysteries of the Shifton Estate, the widow's place on Tug Hill Road, where the murders took place! We'll never know!* Fantasy over.

Where did I get that from, Sharon wondered, still following the flame of the little stranger in front of her with dirty feet and no shoes, who she didn't know for sure was there or not, still talking to an invisible friend she knew wasn't there, short of their materializing, thereby he/she giving Sharon some well needed company in the edge of this mental storm.

Where did I hear that from? That there might have been killings here? Or, did I just make it up, running away with my imagination? "And puzzles," she said out loud – what's all this thought about puzzles? The teenager, maybe fifteen or sixteen, maybe less, turned her head around again, stopping in her tracks this time – possibly, if ghosts could think or surmise things about the living then she may have telegraphed the fact that Sharon felt uncomfortable by her bird like movements, and was trying hard to act more *mortal* – if that made any sense at all – casually, to give her charge a glance, an off handed one, a teenager's expression, as if to say *hey, it's cool that you want to follow me and all that, but you're gonna have to cool it if you want to hang with me.*

Just relax, the girl's eyes seemed to express, opening widely for a moment, for effect, and Sharon, for some reason almost outside herself, felt so, felt relaxed, even physically lowering her shoulders, which had been raised in a textbook perfect body language stance, which said, *wherever it is I'm going, I know I don't want to be there, even though I don't seem to have much say in the matter, that's for sure!*

134

Gee, Sharon giggled like a schoolgirl over this thought – one of many going through her mind recently – *the body sure can say a lot, can't it? I wish my shoulders could tell me what time it was,* she added. *I can't wait for my boy Leo to get here. Following ghosts on all these wild goose chases tuckers a body out,* she joked again, starting to feel her nerves rise up with her shoulders again.

The time, actually, was now 1:24 p.m. precisely, on this Monday morning, March 12th, 1996, if Sharon wasn't so taken by the young figure leading her down the basement steps now, no lights to lead their way – except of course the unholy glow that emanated from her guest. *As long as this place is temporarily mine, I guess – oh – I can have guests. Come on in, the water's fine,* the young girl said to her brothers and sisters watching at the edge of the pool, *it's fine! Nice and cool, you'll love it!*

With that she drowned, hitting the bottom of the pool like a sand bag. *Keep those thoughts up, Miss Langhorn,* Sharon scolded herself, while descending the weathered narrow basement steps – *and Doctor Haskel's likely to give your crazy little ass some kind of reward. Here's to the girl,* the toast will go, the Good Doctor's cup raised, feigning pleasure at the moribund festivities, *and to the honoree in question, who showed the greatest decrease in mental awareness, sanity and overall health, under my ... laxed and misdiagnosed care!* He addressed the nonexistent crowd, taking them all in with a grand sweep of his arms – outstretched in a generous expression of mirth and great joy – the deafening whoops and hollers of the nonexistent crowd going unsaid, and unheard.

This woman, he screamed, as if attempting to fend off an attacker, *is no friend of mine! No friends, she is sick, far sicker than anyone I have ever known, to masquerade as the merely mentally ill, or the crazy –* wetted his lips with his tongue, setting up for the crescendo. *She, my dear colleagues and esteemed acquaintants –* he paused, looking around the pretend room now – *don't be alarmed by the word, but –* and here was his Grand Ending – *this woman, this sick Sharon, Ms. Sharon Langhorn is, my friends, derrrranged! Oh! Oh!* The false audience – the one that wasn't there – gasped and squealed, unable to accept such an abominable word.

Suddenly, a fantasy Sharon appeared – in a jury box, no less – defiantly screaming *No! I'm not deranged!* – the cat calls and swoons rising once again – *Not in the least!*

That's what you think, heiress, the doctor countered. *You're now subject to punishment for the emotional, physical, mental and spiritual crimes committed at the Shifton Estate, and all accrued interest thereof.*

What interests are you talking about? Sharon spoke to him in an assertive manner, sure of her rights, though definitely unsure of the crimes – if any – she was being accused of.

The scene changed quite suddenly, as dreams are wont to do, from the 'dining scene,' to this court case set; a movie set, complete with overhead halogen bulbs hanging on high heavy boom stands, and two-by-four backing on the mock walls. *This, with all due respect, is a ridiculous charge, ridiculous, my good man!... Was that all I had to say on my behalf,* Sharon marveled. This had to be a dream! *Might as well cut my fool head off, then; where's Leo when I need the man to speak up for me?*

Karen turned to her once more, stopping at the foot of the next landing – *these stairs went on forever,* Sharon thought. *Forever?* As though hearing her new thoughts, making a face Sharon was having trouble trying to decipher – as if she could read Sharon's *small, mortal mind*, the fantasies there disturbed her, and she were agitated at the primitive fears and overactive imaginings. There was a mission here, a mission that Sharon and her guide, one Karen Nelson, had to succeed in accomplishing.

Whether Sharon knew this, could grasp it or do whatever she needed to *accept* it, was of little consequence to her living spirit, her dying memory. All Karen cared about, if a spirit *could* care, or show emotion at all, was that she be free of this house, and go on to her final true rest.

Sharon, meanwhile, was hoping this spirit that was leading her God knows where was the most benevolent happy-go-lucky spirit that ever existed – or didn't – *what was the right word?* – and, crossing her fingers, prayed the teenager on the landing before her wasn't leading Sharon to her – untimely – death.

The road to the widow's estate was bumpy, long, and pretty perilous too, as Doctor Haskel soon found out. The house he had *thought* Sharon was in, wasn't – having met another pair of aged spinsters – these, neither dead nor becoming so by some freakish accident on his part, unlike Libby and the widow, rest her soul – who pointed him in the right direction – however not without trying their damnedest to make him stay for a cup of tea, or two, or ten. Hell, they would still have been chewing his ear off, had he not pulled away from the Loneliness Vise Grip – an illegal hold in some states – one of them had on his forearm.

With brief goodbyes and even a couple of kisses blown from the doorway – which of course they lovingly blew back tenfold – for good luck – more his than theirs – he was out the door in a flash – smoke would have sparked off his heels were it possible. Hastily executed retreats *were* his stock in trade, however; as a therapist, he was always watching the clock. *The Almighty Clock, cousin to the Almighty Dollar, incestuous offspring born the Almighty Dollar Clock. Catchy, no?*

He had thought so, going so far as to share his self effacing creation with Trisha, who – to her credit – saw no humor in it whatsoever. Constantly checking his watch, again and again and again. Sometimes, he mused – to himself, between patients – how akin to an art form clock watching was to a man in his profession – *Mother had willed it, and so it shall be done*, especially struck his fancy. *Oh yes*, he was prone to say to anyone – excluding clients, who somehow looked as if they indirectly suffered or looked the fool by other people's summation when he mentioned this pastime – though Doctor Robert Haskel, not the most observant man in the world, failed to get the connection.

It's quite a skill, learning how to look at your watch without, of course, actually looking at it. A professor of mine at college confided this 'trick' to me, and it has fascinated me ever since!

Indeed, the listener would think, bored out of their minds, unless a more descriptive term popped into their heads.

The way it came to me was quite interesting actually... would look at the clock... too quick, too noticeable... a more sly look to the side would do it!... until I mastered it, the fine art of peek-at-the-watch-without-anybody-knowing-about-it!

Whoop dee doo and hallelujah, one and all! Did he really enjoy such droll, noticeably mundane 'hobbies'? One could only guess.

Doctor Haskel, it should come as no surprise – at least nothing major among his friends – was not known for having many friends. This fact or personality quirk if one ascribed to that train of thought; need not be the reason for his lack of companionship, nor the reason he came to work so early on the heels of Trisha Moore, the quintessential New York City Single White Female, why he was so prone to visiting his Mamma so often, even when she didn't need him, even when she would rather *not* see him! But...

The window at the rear of the house – third landing, he guessed – was open. There were many windows, and any of them could have led to who knows what room; having never stepped inside the estate before, he had no idea of the basic architectural outline of the rooms or the twists and turns of dinettes, servants' quarters and hidden alcoves, nor anything else one could think of that a mansion – he would never have thought one of his patients – people who, for 'one reason or another,' found it hard to cope with life's responsibilities and day to day drudges – would move into a bona fide mansion, which indeed, was what it was, not that he wasn't happy Sharon had made such a shrewd business deal on her average salary – might hold in store for an awestruck new guest.

He could see furnishings quite clearly through all the large, brightly reflected windows, past the glare of the hot afternoon sun, one could see much of the interior of the Widow's-soon-to-be-Sharon's house. Beautiful plush expensive carpeting on the floors; drapes of some rich, imported material no doubt, framing the windows still; acres of books along fine hand crafted quality bookcases, some undoubtedly nearly a century old; and then there were the furnishings. Oh, where to begin! Lavish dining room sets and boudoirs always held the doctor's interest, and he indulged himself for a moment to follow the shapes of the vision's strangely slanted, tilted – and even somehow reversed? – highly Victorian pieces, sparkling fittings and trims of chrome and gold plating – it would not have surprised many feeling as how the place was so well maintained and taken care of that some of the gold fittings were actually gold, not just plated, but through and through, before walking up the marble stairs to face the wide oak red stained door to ring the bell.

He pressed his finger firmly on the small white buzzer set into the heavy iron gate, and heard a pleasant *buh bong* coming through some recessed speaker he could not see – although he made little effort to look for the thing anyway. He waited. No answer. He rang again, longer this time. He waited again. Still no answer. An impatient man by nature, he didn't usually ring someone's doorbell more than twice – or spend more than six rings on the telephone waiting for them to answer – before giving up and saying loudly to himself; Hell. I. Tried. For a noted psychiatrist – he was twice asked onto *The Montel Williams Show* and even once on *Oprah* – he knew his willingness to sit still and whittle a stick while waiting for a tardy colleague or patient – he lacked many friends – wasn't exactly legendary, but now wasn't the time to draw a 'pros and cons' chart for himself, as he had done for many of his patients.

No, *his* chart – proven to work better than other mental/oral stimuli – would have to wait until he arrived home. *Home*, once he knew Sharon was safe, and not a danger to herself – alone, and judging by the tone of her voice over the phone, clearly *manic* – in that big house... somewhere.

He rang the bell again. No return buzz, no voice of acknowledgement, no sign of expectant or curious – she didn't know he'd be coming, only Leo, so he couldn't imagine her to be *expectant* – footsteps echoing thunderously down the staircase. *Nothing*.

If for no other reason, this shocking turn of events he had been – helplessly, without warning or provocation, so sickeningly thrust into these last two hours or so, he had to get into that house and tell Sharon about the widow, how she had run in front of his car

(?)

so fast for a woman her age, while he was trying to find her; the policeman he called to the scene, the widow's friend Libby understandably hysterical and shocked by the sudden death of her friend, the two old ladies who would rather mother him and chew his ears off talking than let him part – *for the sake of integrity*, the thought. He needed to speak with her now as her doctor, to break the traumatic news to her gently about the old woman's possible suicide –

(?)

judging by how her friend had described her state, a deep depression or type of *mania* seemed to have gripped her during the final moments before she ran into his car and...

(?)

Lest she get too shaken up about accepting the property as her own legally and outright. The paperwork, as Sharon had explained to him in one long nonstop blur on the phone – sounded to have been arranged to be exceptionally brief and to the point – being as how he actually saw now – from the outside at least – what his patient – and friend – stood to gain, especially against her paltry down payment.

The poor deranged sickly lonely old widow must have undoubtedly seen something in Sharon that she liked – maybe she had seen a version of her young self within Sharon – to have struck such an unholy bargain. Clearly, Sharon would be making out the better on the deal, and that in itself was worthy of some good natured questioning on the part of the good country doctor making his house call rounds – his first and most likely *last* – like a nice, Godless, science worshipping fellow that he was.

Leo the Great, her lawyer/savior, was to pick her up late afternoon today, sometime around four he thought she had said, this much he knew for sure. But as his personal fountain of anecdotes Trish Moore would say, *when you snooze, you lose!* Making an unpaid for house call out of the kindness of his cynical heart was one thing – killing widows with his homicidal dashboard was quite another. He was going to get to the root of this loophole ridden screenplay if he had to shout a soundman's ears deaf to do it!

Leonard Rothstein may have been arriving momentarily, but *he* wanted to be the one to know *first*. That way he could tell the hot shot Manhattan lawyer the story before he got his quick tempered paws on the doorknob.

Immature maybe, but in this case, warranted. He rang the doorbell again, his palms sweaty, his forehead and upper lip as well, and waited.

And waited.

And waited.

Leo found the address of the Tug Hill regional clerk, of all things, through an old friend on the divorce counselor corner of the office. The guy was a stickler for historical records on small nondescript towns in out of the way places, most of them not even on this map. The Tug Hills leg of the never ending Adirondack Mountains suited this quirky hobby perfectly, Leo reasoned.

His hunch paid off, as the attorney was more than happy to share unusual – and surely mostly forgotten, even to Tug Hill natives themselves – tidbits about this out of the way hick town.

'Hick' to Leo meant any people or place without a fax machine, but he also had the good sense and humility to know that he only said or thought something like that being around a computer heavy work environment such as he was at the firm. Had he worked at any other low main vocation – like most people who made a barely livable wage nowadays at some dead end job – he would be pointing his finger at *that schmuck* Leonard and his cell phone in all his downloading glory, along with the rest of them. Probably the first one, in fact.

Leo – despite his mother's constant scolding on the evils of this sort of behavior – *Good Jewish Boys don't make fun out of people. It is because of our great suffering that others look down upon us and laugh, so I will not hear of you, a Jew, my son, doing that to another* – always liked to get a charge out of people, and – *yes, Mom* – he didn't always do so with the other person's feelings in mind.

If memory served, he was more or less what he would call 'a good kid,' although he had barely escaped jail several times during his eye opening months just before starting Law School. If he prayed to *any* god, he joked in close company, then it must be narrowed down to the stuffed shirt balding man on the TV screen – Lieutenant Friday, Ironside, Perry Mason and others he could not now recall – who had indirectly spurred him on to using Mom and Dad's college fund to become another second generation snot nosed attitude L.A. Law watching hound – how funny how many Harry Hamlin, Susan Dey and Blair Underwood types – down to the facial features – there *were* at work, who had been there since he joined; part of the job – *the uniform*, so to speak.

He did not have the heart to tell them who he *truly* wanted to be were the Bad Dudes, the Villians. Oh, yeah, gotta love them villians! What was a cops and robbers show without the robbers? A *piss poor* boring show, that's what.

Soon enough, having been harassed by 'da pigs' for little more than being in the wrong place at the wrong time, he saw many cops *were* the bumbling fools, Keystone Kops come to two left footed life. Making a paranoiac big deal out of nothing most of the time. So, the Great American Hero Cop was out as a job for little Leo from the first.

Just as well, Leo thought, since he didn't like the idea of feeling the lifelong guilt of thinking – even for a second – that his Mom might have died a premature death of shot nerves and terminal worry, making dinner for her boy every night, waging mental bets in her head, wondering what the odds were that her boy would be coming home at all that night. No, police academy Jew boy was out. Lawyer Jew boy seemed so much more tried and true – God, what a lame expression – being that there were so many of them *already*, who would bitch about having to pay for one more?

So, Mom's happy to have a son who's a lawyer who – happy day – she, for some reason, could be proud of. Parents could be proud of the weirdest nonsensical things, and appear to be thinking their wishes betrayed by the most benign and loving ones. Yeah, Mom was proud of her Jew Child Leo, and Leo... he couldn't care less.

Sharon couldn't hear the incessant noisy doorbell ringing. Not where she was. Down in the catacombed remnants of what, years ago, was a fine wine cellar, but now was just a graveyard for dead insects – caught by a sea of spider webs, among a sea field of broken glass. The flood the house had suffered in the Spring of 1957 – quite a freak accident, actually – rendered everything that Old Man Shifton had ever accumulated forever and utterly lost.

A deep depression had come over him soon after those who knew the man – Old Man Shifton – ironically a nickname well before any grey hairs had appeared on his head – the nickname was probably based on his stoic demeanor and lack of *any* sense of humor – had noticed his change of temperament after the flood hit. Since his was the only house near the sloping hill – even Libby and her Frank weren't hit too hard by it – their home down the – flat – road from the Shiftons, while the storm took its effects, he was the only landowner to suffer any loss.

Mr. Shifton took this as a bad omen, being a man who put an unusual amount of stock in the winds of fate; to a man like Charlie James "Van" Shifton, such things as the Elements – Nature herself wasn't the creation of God, but *was* God, having spoken to him most frequently through the destruction of the only enjoyable pastime he had ever been given to indulging in his adult life. The gods, they say – or God – one deity, depending on the era one existed in and one's particular belief system – speak most times to those of a certain distinction, savoring their Lord's/Lords' words with an incomparable pleasure. *His* God, *Van's* God of Anger and Brutality, literally washed away an eighteen year dream of his, which had stemmed from his God given human brain – or so his Catholic faith led him to believe – speaking volumes to him as well.

Not being one of the Chosen, a pawned martyr at best, plucked from the dreaded existence that plagued most poverty stricken Holy Men; however, and having bought and paid for a quaintly designed estate – the remaining legacy of an eccentric who had fled the premises a scant three years after the property had been completed, leaving the ensuing bidding up to the State, and leaving no legal work to speak of per any relatives, either blood or marriage bound – complete with rather expressively commissioned custom furniture and trimmings, in his own mind, and undoubtedly removed his home, for whatever reason – only God knows – from the list of Holy Martyrdom. He still deserved a conference with the Creator, being a holy man trying to raise a holy family, when his wife Dorothy became expectant; this was not to be overlooked of course.

So the Lord, in His wisdom, showered volumes of truth down upon him and his wife's proverbial heads in the form of gallons of Holy Water. Gallons of water, pissed on him from the Lord's very own Mighty Bladder, showered his holy homestead utterly destroying the evil grapes of wrath – his wine collection. Some purchased, others more privately home fermented – *destroyed*, devastated, annihilated, null. The end.

Highly amusing, the biblical symbolism of it all – the cleanliness of Nature's purity – water – washing away the evils of Man's unholy Drink. Drink was the work of the Devil, after all. Maybe that was the reason why *nobody* helped him clean up the mess! And so, it was left there as a scathingly cruel testament to a middle aged man's unquestioned faith. Weren't the Saintly Disciples originally men who *didn't* believe in their Savior's abilities, but had been saved and rendered immortal for their troubles anyway? Very strange. Very beautifully bittersweet. And very very unfair.

All things come to those who wait. And wait. And wait. The ex wine C demeanor *did* indeed change, although not for the worst, as one might offhandedly guess with little respect paid to the background demeanor in the plot – often the more important – subtly so – than the *presumed* more visible front running cast members – of the story – but then, these were not the usual front row buying ticket holders, anyhow.

Chapter Eight

There – by way of brief example – are several screen versions Robert Lewis Stevenson's classic tale of dual personalities, The Strange Case of Doctor Jekyll and Mister Hyde. Some have been ambitious, some outstanding, some so-so, and a few just a waste of a producer's backing funds. The later versions of the tale – and even a couple of the early ones – both silent and sound – found it fashionable to portray the evil, amoral Mister Hyde, *not* as a throwback human; a primitive, a simian resembling brute, the guiltless, destructive, lascivious Missing Link... but as a Ladies' Man. No, handsome and debonair, the *well dressed*, externally *well mannered* Doctor Hyde of the soon to be computer generation, was a Man of the World, making women swoon with his gaze, his tender touch melting their flesh like a candle in the summer heat – not unlike the supernatural charisma of the legendary Count Dracula himself – irreproachable and full of kind polite phrases. A charlatan. A rogue. A fake; malicious in intent, anything but intimidating in appearance. While within this shell of maliciously planned lust and violence, an old, decrepit and/or agoraphobic Doctor Jekyll cowered, happy to be the life of the party – at least in part.

What happened here? What transformed Stevenson's ape like, drooling, hunched over Mad Dwarf into a Valentino? a Don Juan? Such is the fickle, unkind, uninterested-in-tradition Society of Man. One era's Ogre is another era's King. Robin Hood steals from the *rich* – who theoretically steal the life from the working class – ergo – it is not stealing, but a form of retribution...

Mr. Shifton, like our modernized Hyde, chose to turn the townsfolk on their ears, in a manner of speaking, by not doing the obvious – further souring his already sour puss – but going one better, to the amazement of his wife of then thirty four years – *smiling*, of all things on God's green earth. Smiling, and laughing, and acting more or less agreeable – traits Dorothy – the dutiful loving wife – his Angel he'd call her – while she loved him had not seen in him on their most emotional day together, their Wedding Day, October 14th – Dorothy's birthday – 1923.

Back then, a wife had to go with a husband's ills and sour disposition, wandering eyes, raised hands and more, without a word of criticism. *Criticism...* perish the thought! But a year after women got the Vote, things were looking up for the fairer sex – or so they thought themselves – so why rock the boat?

His new plan – thinking pragmatically, as he always did – was to have no further wasteful hobbies, draining in both time and money – he had endured the wrathful Holy Urine of God once – and only once! – before. That nightmare – counted and catalogued in a never forgetting Rolodex in his ever despairing mind – his new *anti* hobby would be a cliché within itself. *Kill 'em with kindness*, Charlie Shifton decided. That'll do it! And so, his plan was put into simple, and precise, effect. There would be no more children – they were both too old by now to breed and, even if they weren't, another miscarriage would devastate sensitive, guilt ridden Dorothy. Why women felt guilt over such things that were out of their control, such as sterility or a pregnancy that was not to be, was anyone's guess.

Charlie sat on the porch, day after day, looking up to the sky, much to the private consternation and worry of his dutiful, though now somewhat-more-equal wife Dorothy. Somewhere, he thought, up in the heavens, was a vengeful wrathful God who had taken away his Dream. A simple, uncomplicated dream about, well... about nothing that important really. He was just a man. Just a man, happy and content, looking forward to his early retirement from the police force with a mixture of sadness and relief, and... *something else*.

Was it grief, or the fear that something might be missing from his life? Was it fear of the unknown itself, of the mornings from now until it was 'his time,' when he could stay asleep or rise as he liked, with no morning clock to punch in or afternoon clock to punch out? No, that wasn't it. And then, that was it, and more.

He dismissed this when he looked out the window. *The window.* A marvelous invention, wasn't it! All good things – no, not good, but marvelous, great, stupendous! One of Man's finest hours. A painfully – to excuse the pun – simple – he mulled on this – invention. To see the Rest of the World. At least, the rest of the world as far as one's eye could manage to take it from that boxed viewpoint; that neatly measured and closed in glimpse of the world. Windows – made of glass of course, a material he'd humbly learned had little chance of its own inorganic survival when tested – were now a thing – or rather *things* of many shapes and intriguing designs – that fascinated him.

Fascinated him, his wife silently noted, while rubbing the points of her elbows nervously to the point of distraction. How the simple pastime of gazing out the window had uplifted him, or so she imagined to be the case – she imagined *many* things, many reasons which could account for his strange change of... was demeanor the word? or personality? or character? She was not a learned woman, in part due to the lack of opportunities – still – that presented themselves to women of her generation concerning learning a trade, or – male dominated – business skill, which, as far as she could manage to find out, had not required what she would have called 'skill' at all – and in part too, to an unwillingness, or lack of desire or *need* to be, without contempt, anything other than her loving husband had *wanted* her to be. So she told herself; so she believed.

The facts, to be painfully brief, were that, as a husband, and as far as husbands that she knew about, he was an exceptional one, regarding his treatment of her – and respect for her as a person – in relation to the tales of woe her women friends and acquaintances had volunteered – no doubt more as some kind of release, or even as a vindication, or even an excuse, than as idle conversation – to her in the past.

Whatever her lack of vocabulary, or her inability to grasp grandiose philosophical meanderings, she knew deep down in the place where she kept All Thoughts Kept Unsaid, that her husband Charlie – a recent retiree from almost forty years of police related activity; a decorated man, a *respected* man may, quite possibly, be losing his mind.

To Charlie Shifton, the glass he looked through during the early mornings when the sun was its freshest and brightest, and yet less harsh and more forgiving, more soothing, was a marvel. A testament to man's primitive ingenuity. At times – more *now* than when the flood had first come, a shock he had found a great burden to shoulder – he also reflected – as all 'good Catholics' must face the – sinful – duality of Man – that this thing, this transparent creation; baked bent and cooled, in a dizzying number of careful steps by skilled blowers – *artisans* really – was more the Devil's work; a cruel reminder of what Man had yet to accomplish *outside*, and what he had mastered to some degree, only to see the thing – whatever it was – slip through his fingers, all the while laughing at his uniquely human need to control *inside*.

What was there to be reminded of, he asked himself sourly, smiling like a fool at a carnival, *that We, in our human minds – our frail, cursed human minds – don't already repeat, over and over, like some damned machine? It's a curse, glass is,* he concluded, *just another thing to remind us – Man – of our inconsistencies and our petty moronic problems. Infantile problems, in comparison to the Grand Dealings of the Universe. Terrible things, windows. I hate them.*

He once raised his hand, holding onto the genial expression on his face – the smile – like a loose mask hastily fastened before the Ritual, in what looked to Dorothy like a gesture, simple enough, though to her frightening – of wanting to break the window. She hollered at him without hesitation to halt this action. Halt he did, but not without visibly slumping, as if a great weight had taken the action's place. He suddenly sobbed, as a baby would, without provocation.

At once, Dorothy dropped what she was doing and ran to him, pulling him to her breast, not sure of her feelings at that moment, aside from an agonizing confusion. She rocked him, wondering where the man she'd married had gone.

March 15, 1958 (?) – Many people keep many secrets, it might be said of a society, certainly a Western culture, where so much is condensed and made trivial – which was once Gospel – by so few. Dorothy began to wonder whether she really liked this place, this large house; so much larger and more spacious than was necessary for a husband and wife getting on in years. She thought about this as her Charlie napped in the next room, and managed a dry laugh at how pompous and spoiled of her that sounded. *Good heavens*, she pondered, *it was much too large and spacious for a wife, husband, ten children, plus servants besides!*

Why such a mansion, why such extravagance? Such thoughts often fall to the hard floor of the brain in times like these, when the health and wellbeing of a loved one are put in question. *Yes, we got an excellent price – a steal, to be honest – and a fine payment plan, extremely fair. But we didn't need such a place. Did not. Even if the babies were born, it just wasn't necessary, no matter the price.*

Charlie, meanwhile, was getting worse. He remembered the wine bottles, the broken wine bottles, along with the broken dreams. Dorothy would never know this; never, even until the day he died. A man superstitious about ghosts and fate, and – why not – Fate's ghost, following the hard luck cases of the world – for good measure, didn't cower easily in the face of hardship. Not Charlie Shifton, either. He had something to prove.

All religious men, raised in religious households, always came to a point in their lives when their content existence – especially for family men – comes to a sudden inexplicable halt or standstill. It is at this time that they can come to terms with what they were taught in Catholic schools, Parochial schools, the Church, Synagogue; whatever their faith, or whatever faith – through family tradition – they were forced to enter into – the faith invariably wavers.

It could be anything. A person finding out they have a fatal disease, or even one to invite social scorn and dishonorable rumors, if not deathly illness; a *loved one* can become ill, not oneself, and appropriate hard line measures must be decided upon; one can lose one's home, one's job, one's spouse, one's reason for living. Even, one's belief in God. *Any* god whichever name He or She goes by – if any – according to one's chosen… *beliefs.*

It is not hard to stop believing. In many instances, one needs but to notice one's surroundings as they are, and not as one's learned faith would have one wish they were; or maybe one would rather more pleasantly, philosophically ponder how one would be, as in another life, perhaps; or the use of some other crutch. Many crutches, to be sure. A cross, prayer, the lighting of candles – one or many – all crutches of some psychological form or another.

To Charles Shifton, this day came when God with his full bladder – no doubt having drunk a sea or two beforehand – unceremoniously pissed on Charlie's roof, flooding his wine cellar and bursting open his expensive, painstakingly cultivated – some one-of-a-kind – bottles of wine. A silly pastime to some – maybe the silliest insignificant hobby of all – but it was his hobby, dammit! *His!* Charlie Shifton's! Speaker of God's Law. A good Christian boy, later a properly married Christian man.

It came as no surprise when the ever smiling, obviously troubled husband of Dorothy Shifton wrapped a thickly linked chain around his neck, the other end around a water pipe – if one was to die by his own hand, he thought beaming; then irony is the way to go. Looking up at the ceiling, trying to envision looking up to a god he wasn't sure existed anymore, he stood upon Dorothy's upturned washbasin – which he had sneaked into the basement moments before – still looking up, tugged at the chain for tensile strength, and without fear, without anything but this dire moment; funny, he didn't think it would be that way – jumped off the flanged cylindrical metal – his helper into death – construct and floundered the eight or nine inches above the floor – kicking the proverbial bucket – to his early demise.

Was it 'fate' that did this to him – willed *him* to do it – or was he tempting It, tempting fate's hold on him, on all of us, just for a moment? A brief, glorious, freeing moment where, to purge oneself in self righteous honor – through a mortal sin and against his god – was the only way to free oneself from what Mother Nature, supposedly according to some eccentric convoluted plan of the Creator(s), even for that *briefest* of prided moments.

Pride in himself, in his human ability to think, to choose, to reason his surroundings, his health, his environment, quality of life, et cetera, and take proper action; the warrior choosing to take his own life rather than be dishonorably put to death in a public square in full view of his enemies and pallbearers. His enemies cheated of that sight of vengeance.

Who had Charlie sought vengeance upon; God or himself? Or was it both? In his heart of hearts, did he know the *truth*; that they *were* both the *same*, that no religious sect or literature – no matter how heralded, ancient or praised it may be – could now bind him? When Dorothy went into the basement to see what her husband was up to, she hadn't the hindsight or basic life experience – thanks, in part, to Charlie – to draw such wise conclusions about life, death, and allegiance to neither deity nor man, good nor evil – just to Be.

But one must *be* what one must. The tortuous visions of his prized broken bottles rising from their stained exposed graves on the floor of the cellar was too much for him. Every night, he had awoken to the pinching of the broken glass shards against his bare skin – just dreams, perhaps. Yes, dreams and nothing more, yet agonizing nonetheless. He saw these bits of glass through his window, the same window he had intended to smash – thwarted by a wife with a tenacious will to keep her husband safe and healthy, even though she knew – had she allowed herself to admit it – that it was probably too late for *that* too.

He would end his own life, the cop, the enforcer, the upholder of the Law, upholding his bony frame atop a simple washbasin turned upside down and used as a stepstool, a ladder ascended to meet the Reaper, face to skeletal face. *A pathetic end*, she thought, watching him swing there. *A pathetic end to a great man. Loving husband. Hard, conscientious, honest worker. Close friend to a few; the few who really knew him. Not as the Sourpuss of Tug Hill Road, but as a good fair man, made out of fine stock, the stock of his time. A great father he'd be – would have been –* this she felt strongly, and kept repeating this to herself like a Buddhist chant to deflect the shock of seeing such a horrible end come to someone so close, and at his own hand, at that.

Later, when time had come to bury him, many came out to pay respects to the deceased – mostly acquaintances from his job, some others she recognized as 'neighbors' who lived down the long steep path to the more populated area of Herkimer County proper. She didn't know most of them socially, except for girlfriends she met occasionally at the beauty parlor, or whom she had met through her long time best friend Libby. Libby held her hand – Libby's husband Frank in tow – a better friend of Charlie's, guessed the newly widowed wife of the man in the lacquered oak box – at the front of the church, below the altar – one was not likely to find.

As everyone said their goodbyes to the body, kissed the bereaved woman and cuddled her as they went, in an expression of loss and affection few among the throng actually felt – Libby opined to herself – she thought she saw a young girl, not more than fourteen or fifteen, make her way slowly down the middle aisle between the pews, a fistful of carnations in her hands – or tied to her wrist like a debutante – she was not close enough to be sure – in a straight line toward the half opened casket.

Dorothy's head bowed with grief, the visitors having no calming or soothing effect on her at all. Quite the opposite; their hand shaking, kisses, hugs and wishes of good fortune after this time would pass, simply reminded her that all this – the church, the altar, the long faces of priest and mourner alike, not to mention the man in the casket who, two days ago, was still her dear Charles – was real; horribly, chillingly, blood curdlingly real.

Charles had left a will with implicit instructions that Dorothy take the reins on what – in his opinion – she could, and included the phone numbers and addresses of reputable individuals to do the job on the business end that – in his opinion – she could not. There was not much to look after, nor many loose ends – *who didn't hate that expression, Charlie, who?* – to tie up, and so all those names, numbers and addresses went uncontacted – which was just as well, since none of them had the decency to get in touch with *her*.

Libby watched this girl as she dragged herself over to the crosshanded shell of Charles Shifton. *Dragged*, as if a weight pulled at her ankles, compromising her youthful posture. By the look of her tattered garments, she did not seem the charm school type – who *was* this person anyway, and *who* had she come with? – but that was no excuse for her *in*excusable attire, was it?

The girl looked in her direction after having peered into the casket at Charlie, and Libby felt a cold tingle rise through her back as she looked into the strange girl's clear hazel eyes. This person was not human, she thought, not human at all. Libby looked around, expecting the widow, or Libby's husband, or someone to take notice of this weird girl at the casket, but no one she noticed had seen her.

She looked up to get another view of this strange girl with the wry smile, the *cat who ate the canary* type of smile. But she was gone! She must have exited around the left aisle and hastily run up the side of the stained glass windowed wall, but another clear headed side of her, a side that did not care to be in this dreary church holding the widow's hand the way she was, her thick headed husband oblivious to all she saw – or *thought* she saw. She looked around to the large front doors of the Church, the only exit/entrance for parishioners.

Surely there were other entrances, other 'escape routes' throughout the cathedral. Must be. Bottom line was: whether this teenager *was* there, *wasn't* there, or was something she didn't care to even *think* about – in any case, it was forgotten.

Karen, on the other hand – a friend and surrogate daughter to the widow, who took care of the girl in her own bemused way – did not *want* to be forgotten.

Leo needed a map badly. The area he was perusing at a lazy seventy miles per hour – the limit there was fifteen – was, as far as the eye could see, all mountains, moss, rock formations... and nothing more that Nature herself had not made herself eons ago. He turned on the radio of the '88 Corvette – he had another one in storage – a cherry red 1969 model he had helped rebuild – to take his mind off the chilly monotony – that in his city bred mind, *was* upstate Ennui – of the road. AM Talk... FM Country... Maybe K.D. Lang or Bonnie Raitt. All those girl and guy singers sung the same, and the 'same' was precisely what he was trying to get his mind *off* of... Still FM. A song from the 70s he remembered from years back. A college roommate had this tape. Horns blazing, great riff. Weird stuttering drum beat. Cool.

...Feeling like I ought to sleep
Spinning room is sinking deep...

Oh yeah – 25 or 6 to 4. Chicago.

The air was heavy from the humidity. He popped open the glove compartment with his right hand and fished for his sunglasses, nervous about taking his eyes off the road for a couple of seconds to dig for his shades through a bunch of out of date papers, receipts from clothing and record stores, obsolete calendars, addresses, phone numbers, even *more* obsolete numbers of women he had met in bars and on lunch breaks – not that Leo was the bar type, but one got tired of Friday night overtime three weeks in a row – he had not gotten around to calling.

Social etiquette, at least as he understood it – said that it might be worse to call one of those available women *now*, than forget about them altogether – which was also pretty bad, too.

Damn. Why could he never get these things right? Eyes back on the road, sun glaring off the polished chrome. He spotted a sign. Thendera. Didn't sound familiar. If he was going to find his Little Miss Langhorn, he had better ask somebody where Tug Hill Road was. Soon. A small shack off the side of the road – in the middle of nowhere – advertised its dubious reason for existence – a small weathered sign in black, hand lettered script, which read – Leo wanted to laugh at this – Maps Maps and More Maps! Old Forge, Tug Hill, Big Moose, Little Moose, All Over the Adiro Mntns! *That's what it said – Adiro. Like abbreviating the name of an old friend. Like Leo from Leonard. And Mntns. Couldn't they have spelled out M-O-U-N-T-A-I-N-S?* Whomever had painted that sign, and sloppily at that, must have gotten tired near the end of writing it. *Gotten tired! Adiro! M-N-T-N-S!* Leo had been on the road too long.

Suddenly, a figure could be seen shifting around behind the tourist magnet's dirty window, as if this weren't actually a gag, but an honest-to-god place of business. A stick figure of a man bow legged his way out the rickety doorway – just like out of a classic desert movie set – the door had stuck a few times before opening, unbelievably like a bat out of Hell. Well at least a bat made out of four pipe cleaners and a few pieces of tissue paper covered in black shoe polish.

Leo's car had been parked outside of this beaten relic for about five minutes more than likely, and the middle aged skeleton bopping his way up to Leo's side of the Chevy had just noticed him now – probably just snapped out of a noon nap – one of many such entrepreneurs partook in during a workday, no doubt. Leo grinned at the old man – that cool, L.A. Lawyer grin that he knew so many people who saw him use it despised. He lifted his shades up onto his brow line to complete the Look. The look that said, *I'm glad I'm not stuck out here like you are, you moron.* The rube finally got up to the car and tapped the window.

"Hello there," the rube said, showing Leo he had many missing teeth. "Can I help you Mister?"

Leo lowered his glasses back where they belonged. This character did not need any hard times from him. "Yeah, as a matter of fact. I need a map, or directions if you have them."

"Directions to where, may I ask?" The man's voice was neutral, his clear blue yet bloodshot eyes finding Leo's past the tinted lenses.

Leo turned away, removing his sunglasses. "I need to know where Tug Hill Road is." He squinted at the rube, who grinned again toothlessly – this time, more sarcastically.

"Tug Hill Road?" The words came out of his chapped lips measured, almost reverently. "Why, Tug Hill Road is right 'cheer, mister, the rube asserted, pointing his free hand at the ground behind his booted feet, which were caked with who-knew-what beyond belief.

"Right here? What do you mean right here?"

The rube sighed, leaned on his cane, and studied Leo for a moment – which made him nervous. "What I mean," he began, condescendingly, "is that this here road *is* Tug Hill Road. Has been since you took that turnoff at Malone's Trading Post. Big sign. Can't miss it."

He spat.

It was true about the sign. He had seen it. The last person he had talked to had been at that trading post, bartending as only upstaters can; a sawed off shotgun for a rooster and two chickens – judging the condition of the weapon, he had gotten the better deal than the other guy. With that fellow's help, Leo had gotten up this far. Now came the harder part.

"Okay, I read you now," Leo said defensively. "Just didn't see any signs that pointed anywhere – either way – that's all." If there were signs that he had missed, well... he would hate to have a rube from an upstate ghost town take him for a city slicked fool.

The thin man thought no such thing. "That's alright! Happens to strangers around here all the time," he said, burrowing his cane into the dirt for no particular purpose. "You know, there ain't no signs around here for a reason." He scratched his head and spat again, the spittle landing near Leo's tire, and struck the tire with his cane – liking the firmness of it, probably.

"Could you please not do that, friend?" Leo asked cordially.

"Oh, sorry there, fella. Nice little machine ya gots here."

"Thanks."

Anyway like I was sayin, ya really wouldn't know that there ain't no signs around these parts... no, there's not," he reminded himself, then stared into space fixedly for a moment.

"Hello, I'm right here there, ru – oh, what's your name?" Leo asked, mainly for appearance's sake, still wary of being in this man's company. But if he was going to pick Sharon up in time, then...

The man gestured something that Leo could not comprehend, which resembled part of a mime act. More likely it was just local sign language, he figured. Strange guy, this rube. He straightened up, reminding Leo of Army roll call – at least what he had seen of it in the movies.

"Keller, sir," the rube stated in a deep voice he perhaps hoped sounded commanding, but did not. He saluted, and for good measure – choking back a laugh – Leo responded in kind. "Keller, that's the name. Daniel Boone Keller. But most people just call me Danny."

Yes I'm sure, Leo mused, cracking a smile. *The whole town calls him Danny*. All three of them, were he to include himself.

Daniel Boone Keller picked up in the grin, and tried to manage one himself. The outcome was not altogether successful. "Was there somethin ya found a bit comical maybe, mister?" Danny said, trying again to sound commanding, and again falling short.

Leo was taken aback at this. *Even rubes, it seems, have feelings.* He disregarded the question – back on planet Earth, he always considered a question like that not to be a question really, but a troublemaker's invitation.

"Is your name really," Leo again suppressed the urge to giggle, "Daniel *Boone* Keller?" He stressed the Boone – Boooonnne – not thinking the rube would notice the dig.

"Yes, sir," Danny proclaimed, indeed not noticing. "That is my real name. Heh; it's kind of a funny one to tell, I suppose – "

"Well, I really have to be someplace, maybe another –"

"My parents, *they* named me Daniel Boone," Danny said proudly, considering Leo's rudeness with one watery, wandering eye. "Yup, they were big fans of the T.V. show, you know? You know it – Daniel Boone?" he asked genuinely, as if the fictional character were only known within Tug Hill, Old Forge, and Thendera, and not an internationally published fable.

Leo went along. "No, I can't say that I've heard the name before... was he someone famous?"

The frontiersman's namesake took two muddy steps back, spiked his cane in the dirt, whistled – or tried to whistle – what came out was more like a dry bark, then set one motion after another, in deliberate and comical order. He smiled at the stranger who was – judging by his question – a newly discovered creature; a City Rube. "You mean to tell me mister –"

He paused, stifling an urge to playfully strike Leo's front tire with his cane one last time. *The City Rube doesn't like that.* "– that you never heard the legend of Daniel Boone?"

159

Leo shrugged, poker faced. *Was this character for real? Are the people really that stupid out here? He doesn't even know I'm kidding him.* "Can we talk about this another time Dan?" Leo said firmly, or with as much delicacy as his tight vocal cords could muster. *I've no intention of seeing this gentleman ever again, if I can help it.* "So you say that I'm on Tug Hill Road, so then how would I get to the Shifton Estate?"

At first Danny the Map Store Entrepreneur frowned at Mr. Rothstein, perturbed about not getting a chance to tell his famous *How I Was Named After the Legend of Daniel Boone* story, which all the other rubes in town – all two of them – had heard a thousand times. Nonetheless, he perked up when the subject changed to something else he knew about. "The Shifton Estate?" Danny thought this one over for a moment, scratching his head.

Leo sat silently.

"Oh you mean the widow's place, the *widow* Shifton," Danny stressed in local accent – *Wid*-der.

"Yes yes," Leo returned eagerly, "the widow's place... where can I find it, exactly? I had the house number, but I must have put the paper somewhere." Without thinking, Leo pressed his hands to the pockets of his sports jacket – the kind with the patches on the elbows – as if miming the words he was saying. He checked inside his shirt pockets as well, not so much because he thought he would find the address, but to pass off his nervous motion as something necessary. He knew from Danny's steady gaze though, that he shouldn't have bothered.

"What, are you nervous Mister?"

"No, not at all," replied Leo, placing his hands in his lap.

"Well, y'know, there's nothing *to* be nervous *about*," Danny said, stressing the words, sensing the man in the convertible's awkwardness in his presence. "You're almost there y'know. Right up the way here."

"Really?"

"One thing though," Danny sighed, and leaned to the left on his cane. "I don't know why you'd *need* the address, although –" he paused again to scratch his head.

Fleas, old man. You've got fleas? a deep voice with a British accent intoned in Leo's head.

"I do admit that I can't remember the numbers on the door meeself." He looked down at Leo like a grandfather imparting a wisdom to an uninterested grandson. "You don't need to though," he continued, taking Leo's silence as a cue to keep talking, "since the mansion's the only house at all on that land. About two miles' worth give or take, besides the other house; place. She's a *widder* too. Friends, they are. Good friends." He emphasized this by making the *O.K.* sign with his thumb and index finger, and then winking.

"Okay, I'm not sure Sharon mentioned her."

"Sharon?"

"Yep, the person I'm going to see. Well, not *see*, really – pick *up*."

"Is that *so*?" Danny queried, then said, "And how's that, if you don't think I'm bein too pryin or nothin, bein that ain't been nobody up there that *I'd* known about, cept the widder, for the longest!"

"No I don't mind," Leo said pleasantly, in that cordial tone of voice he had been trained to use at work. *This guy isn't a bad person,* he said to himself. *Not the brightest bulb in the drawer, but he's alright. Just extremely bored. I know that hell yes – I would be.* "She's staying there – Miss Langhorn, my client that is – up at the estate."

Danny didn't want to pry into Leo's business any more than he had, believing *a man is entitled to his own*, so he shifted his curiosity to the widow. "...And the old lady Shifton, she allowed it? Ain't like her to have visitors."

"I really have to be going Daniel, but thanks for your time and everything." Leo thought that sounded lame, being that Danny hadn't really done anything *for* him besides point him in the right direction. He paused, looking at the man in the muddied – he guessed it was mud – overalls and carpenter's cap. Danny looked sad, like a child who hadn't gotten the present he wanted for Christmas. *What the hell,* he figured, smiling.

The smile was infectious.

Let him in on some of the mess this deal is turning out to be. "Basically Danny, the widow let Sharon stay the weekend until now, sort of a good old fashioned spook out, if you get me. Silly, I thought, but they don't pay me to think, they pay me to do the paperwork and collect the late fees."

"And uh, why would your Miss *Lan* – what was it?"

"*Lang* Horn."

"...Langhorn be staying up there in that creepy place to begin with?"

"Well to be brief – I've really kept you long enough – *she*, I mean the widow – left Sharon there for a three day weekend – sort of a stipulation, you know, against the property. My *client* is buying it."

Danny straightened up, his exposed skin – his face, hands and forearms – turning pale, and whispered, "An old fashioned spook out, didja say?" repeating what Leo had said earlier.

Leo hadn't pegged him for a skeptic. "Now friend," Leo smiled, gesturing towards the shivering man before him, "no need to get all flustered like that, I mean... you're not inferring that the house is *haunted* now, are you?"

Whatever had set the map store owner off to turn so pale, had started him back up the sandy walk to his store in a hurry. The scared man turned to address the man in the Corvette one last time before retreating, permanently, within the confines of his desert sanctuary. "I'm not *in* furred *nuthin*! Whatever that is. All you's gots ta know is that place up there is *no good*, ya hear me. No good." He took three more steps before turning his head towards a confused and slightly annoyed Leonard Rothstein.

"Tell ya somethin else too," he offered, pointing a finger accusingly. "Might change yer mind about going up there."

Leo opened his mouth but had a funny feeling that if he spoke, he would regret it. He did so regardless. "And what might that be that's so important, Mister Keller?"

The rube spat again, and halfheartedly spiked his cane into the soft dirt sand for no visible reason. Then he spoke. Deliberately. Cryptically. "Word travels fast round here is all, and the latest is, that the widder... is *dead*."

Leo's eyes opened wide in surprise. The gusting winds – dry winds even, in the midst of this thick heat – may have stunted his hearing, he supposed... he guessed. *He couldn't have just said what I thought he said*. Leo placed his sunglasses back on to see the modern day Daniel Boone more clearly and free from the sunlight's glare. With any luck he could read Danny's lips. In moments, he realized there would be no need for that.

"Could you repeat that old man? I don't think I caught it the first time," Leo shouted, attempting to mask the sudden nauseous feeling in his stomach.

"Oh you heard me well enough stranger," Daniel smirked. "I know ya did. I see it on yer face, even in this sandy wind. Damn dry heat. I *hate* this shit!" He redirected his poker faced gaze at Leo. "What I said was – and I got it on good authority, so I know it to be the truth – I *said* the Widder Shifton's *dead*." He lifted his cane and pointed it at Leo. "And whoever's in that godforsaken *place* – that *evil* place..."

He continued, jabbing his cane to an indiscriminate point down the road ahead, and spat, "Whether it's yer friend Sharon – client or whatever – or anybody else – odds are they're dead too. History there, mister. *Bad* history."

He waved Leo on with a quick crossing guard motion. "You better get on now, ta check on yer friend – if you're still so inclined."

He went back up the walkway and shut his door behind him, checking the lock for strength as he did. "Not that awful place. Bad history there. Ain't no rest to be had there."

He raised a half empty flask of home brew rotgut, and toasted the dry air. "Here's hopin the widder Shifton's at her rest an' dat she's safe... her husband would've wanted it that way." Toast complete, clinking an imaginary glass – with an imaginary guest, and nothing else – and took a swig.

"Thanks for the floor show old man," Leo said out loud sarcastically, something he only did when he felt his time had been wasted, or something had been left unfinished – or in this case, both. Somewhere in his stomach – the nausea just barely receding now – bade him heed the rube's warning; not so much a *warning* as a belated newscast.

I should never have let her stay up there alone.

He started the car again, and coasted at a cautious ten miles per hour, not exactly eager to find out what further bad news awaited him at the Estate.

Okay, so the widow's gone. Dead. Wow. What to do, what to do. Let's just find Sharon. Leo tried to steady his breathing, keeping his eyes straight ahead.

He soon saw a parade, or what he *thought* was a parade. People gathered, hollering, arguing over *something*. He was unable to make it out. He had to stop the car. Too many people blocking the road. So crowded. So many people. The area had been deserted. Where did they come from?

If yer still so inclined. If yer still so inclined. Iffff yerrrr stillll soooo innnn cliiiined...

Chapter Nine

Doctor Haskel took a deep breath as he approached the gate of the widow's estate, and looked up, readying himself to scale it. *Pretty high. About fifteen feet at least, maybe twenty*, he thought. And panicked. And thought some more. *I don't usually do this type of thing, but...* He swallowed hard, quickly. *Fuck it.* He could not recall ever having been so worked up over something. She was only a client after all.

Only a client. Isn't that what Robert Haskel, Terminal Bachelor,

(?)

had always said? He remembered buying a compressed paperboard plaque saying that someplace off West 3rd Street. Near Bleecker Street, was it? *Terminal Bachelor*. He liked the irony, the scathing truth of those two words slammed together. Was it *truth?* Was it *his* truth?

(?)

He had many such trinkets and throwaway gifts in his office, and tucked away in any small space where he could stand them, hang them or nail them up. It made him feel that he was not so stuffy, that he was in touch with the common man – the ever present client – that he could have fun. Most importantly, he did. He *did* have fun. This journey was not exactly the type of 'fun' he had expected. He had run over that elderly woman

(?)

A disturbed woman. A mentally ill woman. Killed – although an accident –

(?)

by an awarded psychiatrist. Talk about karma. *Bit of a surprise, wasn't it old chap? Won't be able to talk yourself out of that come Monday morning. Nope. Can't do it. Want to climb this old wrought iron fence and rescue the fair maiden from the spooky who-knows-whats? No, can't do that either. Nope. Sorry. You're a doctor, not a gymnast.*

He looked around, craning his head to see through an open window. *No, they're not open. Just don't have the shades down. Can't see her. Can't see her at all.*

"Fuck it," he grumbled, trying to sound courageous – realizing he did not know *how*. "I'm going in. I've got to find out what's going on in there, for Sharon's sake. Was it for her sake? *Is it really? Or do you just want to play hooky from your high and mighty responsibilities and act the hero? Is that the real deal, Doctor Haskel... is it? You know you're afraid. You'll never make it. Nope. Never. You think cursing is going to give you instant courage. You curse like you rescue, my precious Doctor Has Kel. Not often, and not well. Poorly, in fact. You're a fool, doc! You'll never make it.*

He attempted to survey the design of the entranceway – gate, grounds, a couple of statues, small houses – sheds they were – weren't they? – sheds. Neatly trimmed and shaped hedges and trees... *never make it. It's too high, and you're too sedentary and out of shape. All your kind are. You sit on your ass all day, listening to people's problems – people who work for a living. Hard workers too; most for minimum wage, or slightly better. Maybe even below the poverty line, off the books. You know a lot of those don't you, my rosy cheeked I-have-everything-I-could-ever-want-and-there's-still-always-room-for-more Doctor Haskel, eh?*

167

Books. You've written a few of those, haven't you, my dear doctoré? Books so thick with nothing except notions of an average human mind, which are doomed to be ridiculed and used against you, defaming your character. Take you off the road tour book signing circuit. You like those don't you, Herr Doctor? Oh, to be read there, in this town and that, truly makes your weasly little heart jump, doesn't it? A million beats a minute it does. Gone! All gone!

You're so pathetic! There are things in that house you know nothing about, Robert. Nothing! Why take the chance? I don't understand you. I am you, and I don't understand you. Why do this? What do you stand to gain from it? Do you really think you can save her, this Sharon you pine for, from some unseen danger? All you'll likely succeed in doing is waking her from a peaceful needed nap. Or better yet: maybe you'll trip over a wire, cause an inferno and kill her. Kill her! Like you did the widow!

(?)

How do you expect the poor girl to pay the mortgage on this Rhett'n'Scarlett when the mortgage-ess is dead? Should I say it again in case you didn't hear? She's dead! You killed her!

(?)

Wait. Maybe you've forgotten. She's dead! You killed her!

(?)

So pathetic. Not a clue.

Doctor Haskel looked up to the grey sky, swallowed, took hold of the two lowest bars... and climbed.

Sharon looked around the forgotten recesses of the basement's secret niches, in awe of the design and construction of the beams and sharp corners of the alcoves – although she was not quite sure 'alcoves' was the right word, since that was a term for a design in a living room or den, was it not?

Sharon was not much for architecture, although she knew professional work when she saw it. And this – though obscured by decades of dust and grimy negligence – was the real thing. She decided to call the not-sure-they-were-alcoves alcoves 'indentations' for her own benefit, and perused these 'indentations' with an interest she had never expressed for such things before. Sure, she had been to the various de rigueur Manhattan museums – all those that were easy to get to by subway from her and Betty's apartment anyway – and had met her share of wannabe art dealer rejects and self important trivia nerds – *let's not forget the neurotic/compulsive liars* who tried to get her into an IMAX *private* screening at the Museum of Natural History.

This dusty stuff was okay to look at and all, but if she did not go back upstairs soon she might miss hearing Leo's car, or his rat-tat-tat knock on the door. *What am I doing here anyway*, she wondered. *Why am I down here? I... strange, I had no desire to come down here before, so why do so, so close to leaving?*

She felt a slight pain in her hand, and a squeezing at both temples. *Everything's fuzzy, I... someone was here. Someone was here and they led me down the stairs. Too dark to come alone.*

Sharon looked behind her, over her left shoulder. Her vision in the dark, even as a child, was usually good; even exceptional once she had a chance to become accustomed to the absence of light. But now, even as she searched for the cement and stone steps that had brought her here, she was unable to find them. She thought she saw their outline, but might have just imagined that she did, to make herself feel better.

Sharon took baby steps forward with her arms outstretched to feel for the staircase, its steps and sides gritty and lumpy with age. They had been crafted to resemble the stone walkways of European castles – as adapted for the sets of many Universal and Hammer films – which were mainly period pieces set in foreign countries – which suited its first owner exceptionally well.

He was a bachelor who lived alone except for a couple of servants – not much else was known of him, at least not in the modern town documents; much of the previous centuries' catalogue of minor paperwork not an interest to anyone – personal letters were said to have been burned by enemies of the owner. *Why* he'd had enemies, and what *they* stood to gain from suppressing any information from recorded documents, family information, notes, deeds et cetera was unclear.

A more 'reasonable' explanation might have been that after almost one hundred years, unguarded or improperly filed papers, shabbily set to a death sentence in the rusting metal drawer of a forgotten file cabinet by a temporary employee just trying to 'clean up the mess,' have a tendency to disappear. So no one really knew about the mysterious, reclusive man who commissioned this mansion – which, soon after completion, became his prison. Some locals always managed to keep some facts afloat however. Here are some:

The man, whose name was Abner Jameson – or Abner James as the nearby townsfolk re christened him – had been an early retiree, previously a tailor by trade. He had few guests, and ones he *did* have did not stay long – none in fact – coincidentally, Charlie Shifton would later repeat the same social tendencies, often against Dorothy's personal opinions on the matter, once they occupied the estate after him – stayed the night, nor were welcomed over the drawn out course of a weekend, even in the case of a holiday. Soon, Jameson became known as an opinionated man, and from the views he was prone to be vocal on, weren't to the agreement or beliefs of many servants, friends, nor family alike. Soon after, Abner became known as the grouchy sort, one not to be bothered with the unnecessary social graces of the day, more or less expected from a man of his accumulated wealth – and assumed intelligence as a shrewd, economically knowledgeable businessman who had built his own fortune seemingly singlehandedly.

His visitors – friends also formerly or still in the tailoring field or related endeavors and a select amount of family living, who mainly came calling unashamedly to ask for financial help – i.e.: a 'loan' not expected to be paid back – stopped making the day long carriage ride from the Old Forge train station – a highly imprecise and temperamental, often ill working *choo-choo* it was as well, it should be noted.

There were some children in the province, grandkids of the servants Abner had kept on the payroll – who subsequently found themselves without an employer or a job when the Grouch of Tug Hill unceremoniously fled his dream house one late afternoon without so much as a bindlestiff, never to be heard of again – who claim to have been told by their elder kin, the real reason for Jameson's retreat from the very house he had lived in – and had helped design. Many of the Tug Hill Acres farmhands and natives of the province especially believed at that time – superstitiously – that the estate had been built on 'cursed' soil.

The legendary death of Karen Nelson, indirectly caused by being neglected and later abandoned by her father, was widely known; its gory details recalled and repeated with interest and vigor, while the plight of the maligned memory of bachelor Abner Jameson went – almost ceremoniously – into the cobwebbed halls of obscurity. Although his famously hasty retreat was good tourist fodder for a time, years after Karen's gnawed, rotted, weather beaten body had been discovered in that terrible shed Daniel had kept her in as punishment – later callously nicknamed by the townschildren as Karen's Closet – Abner Jameson – the man – wasn't particularly interesting at all, and had not been remembered to have any particular vices, likes or dislikes.

A good legend, as everyone knows, is all about silver bells and tragedy, and not the antisocial crotchetiness of old men. Karen's remains were found when Jameson unearthed the courtyard that had previously been part of Daniel Nelson's – failed – farmland, the house Abner had envisioned being built was being constructed right over the spot where the house – the last relic of a former time, and only lasting testament to the missing Nelson's memory – had stood.

Daniel's house. His 'mansion,' he had always bragged would soon be built, went to the well and dissipated – as do all tall tales from drunken troublesome men – in these parts, during the last century.

But as one might have guessed, had one been following this narrative from the beginning, these things have a way of working themselves out. There was indeed a mansion built on Daniel's land – quite a beautiful one – both in its simplicity and function at that.

Karen had met her grisly, premature death on March 12th, 1896.

Tonight, Sharon looked around the grey unkempt walls of the reclusive Jameson Estate, which was later to fall into the loving hands of Dorothy and Charlie Shifton; the afternoon of March 12th, 1996. One hundred years had passed, since her unspeakable horrible death. Before the day was done, and the sun set in the distance for the evening, Sharon would unwittingly help a scared trapped little girl in a tattered housedress – a new friend of Dorothy's in a new world to the widow's, to do what her purged, desperate soul had often wished but was never granted until now; the one hundredth anniversary of her death. The teenage Karen Nelson, her father's Victim, would once more be coming home. Coming home one more time *for the last time*.

March 12th, 2:14 p.m.: In a grey shed, weather beaten and filthy from pig slop and dung, a teenage girl, barely fourteen years old, lay dead in the morass of rotted vegetables and excrement that would serve as her dismal tomb for twenty six years. Next to her corpse, which was ironically well preserved in the packed earth and fertilizer of the dirt floor shed – where the remains of many other skeletons – large animal shaped similarly preserved. When Abner Nelson stumbled upon this hideous graveyard of bones, dried up flesh and leathery animal skin, some still wrapped tightly around the bone – from malnutrition most likely – as age could not very much be blamed – being as how the manure and whatever else had once been thrown in there – a corral for the pigs when they were alive no doubt – had mummified them.

Pigs. Large, once healthy pigs, the kind a farmer kept to eventually sell to a slaughterhouse for the much prized pork. There are so many foods to be made out of pork and its related byproducts, that a man could earn a decent honest living just selling livestock – in this case overstuffed pigs – for that purpose; to be killed by a second party, and put to use in innumerable ways by a third party, fourth and fifth and so on – the farmer's conscience clear that he did not have to bear witness to or have anything physically to do with the actual slaughter of the animals he had raised.

Abner pondered this for a moment, scratching his head and holding up his lantern to get a better look. Didn't a farmer, obviously with an affinity for the land – and creatures besides himself that lived out their lives on it – and the ideal of a simple life – probably more than most – suffer an awful guilt knowing that a life reared on his land, that had eaten leftovers from his own hand, slept in quarters he had provided to protect them from the often harsh elements would sooner or later meet such a grisly fate; and that he had no small part in that outcome – have an awful guilt – a terrible wretched guilt – about holding so many lives in an unfair balance? Maybe it was true what they said; that one does what must be done, whether out of compassion, malice, greed or benevolence, deep love or blinding hatred. To these men, Abner thought, their cruelty was but a business, and surely one would not begrudge a man his living, as unsavory and unacceptable – to some – as it may be.

Does not a ditch digger make *his* living carving a path, through rigorous physical labor, for the recently departed, whose families at that moment are so relieved and unburdened such a profession existed, seeing how their relatives will benefit – even when, upon returning home, they most definitely would look at this same person with disdain and repugnance, when playing back that scene – the burial – in their collective minds? Who was to say then, what was the 'right' way to make a living, and what was the wrong?

These poor creatures – at least thirty that I can see, Abner reflected
*– have been left to a sad ungodly death here in this shack; a most
unsavory burial place.* But then there was the matter of these *other*
remains – clearly human – what could be the reason for that
discovery? Abner searched his jaded heart for the answer. Being a
formerly devout Christian, the only godly thing to do, he decided, was
to give the remains, at the very least – the human ones – an honest
burial. This, he resolved, should be acted upon right away, before
any further repairs or clearance could be planned. The entire
renovation may have to wait due to this 'discovery,' in fact; quite a
disturbing nasty business, this.

He choked back a surge of nausea which had risen in his stomach
when he considered, chillingly, that such a nonsensical hodgepodge
of dead carcasses – basically only two different creatures of God –
Sow and Human – may both have been due to some unfortunate act,
committed for the most unfortunate of reasons; this was a death
season he was witnessing. A death borne of madness. He opened his
encrusted eyes wider, and lowered his lantern, having never
expected anything like this. Nothing at all. These animals had – dear
God! – eaten this poor unfortunate alive. *Eaten alive!*

Abner turned away, making his way back up the staircase, which he
had forgotten in his frightened state, had boards laid upon some of
the steps – obviously left by some of the carpenters. He placed his
foot on one long piece of wood he had mistaken for a step, and which
had sat upon the concrete undisturbed. Until now.

Jameson fell backward through the air five steps down into the pile of
soggy mummified corpses – a few of which had not already teetered
entrenched in waste; which came loose and tumbled as he fell. He
landed with a wet thud on his back, the lantern gone – flung from his
right hand. Ribs – maybe sow, maybe human, dug painfully into the
middle of his back. He hastily lurched in an attempt to rise and find
his way back upstairs, or to call for help – he had no reason to
believe that none would come, but somehow he felt that no help
would.

Not for the stranger who dared live on the same land which that hated liar and gambler Daniel Nelson once called his own. And in many ways he would later reflect – when cooler heads had prevailed – it still was.

His left hand found a smooth rock, which was damp, mossy in texture – and cold. He grasped it tightly, meaning to lean on it and raise himself, when his fingers slid down the smooth surface and entered two wide orbital holes, side by side. Immediately reminded of the surrounding horror the lantern light had shown him, he knew he had found a human skull. Abner resisted the urge to shriek – he disliked the trait in women to shriek whenever a problem arose, and surely would not tolerate it in himself. He slid his fingers out of the eye sockets, and felt slightly below them for the skull's nasal cavity. He found it plugged up by the same dark filth that littered the floor, and which had most likely kept the carcasses *in situ* – including the inner skull.

A cold shiver raced down his left arm. Were these Karen's remains he had discovered? He was not entirely sure this was the only human skull interred here, and before he knew why, his body stiffened from head to toe. At first he reasoned this was shock from the fall – he surveyed the damage and wondered if his spine had been dislocated, and then doubted this, as up until now he was able to rotate from side to side – as when he had reached for the alleged rock. No, it was something less serious; although undoubtedly he had broken or misaligned *something*.

He felt the pain now. Oh yes; it was bad. A tingling sensation ran through his forearm. Even now, recovering from the initial pain of the fall, he knew – or surmised – that the sensation was not indeed internal – a byproduct of the trauma to his body – but enveloped it like a second skin, or a sleeve pulled over it gently by a mother dressing her child for the cold weather, after spring, summer and fall have taken their leave. The sensation progressed, more distinctly, like the kneading of fingers over his left forearm, massaging the cold skin.

He had not realized how cold his arm was, until he went to grasp it with his other hand – after having managed, quite slowly, to pull himself to a seated position. His legs were still pretty sore, and he felt he would rather not press his luck by moving too quickly – and he was struck how unnaturally cold it was. *Frozen.* Strangely, though, his arm sent no such message to his brain. In fact, his arm did not feel cold at all; only its surface when touched. In fact, although taking into consideration his shock from the fall – which he might have suffered without knowing it – his body temperature, all told, seemed perfectly normal. He had coincidentally been told by doctors and others that his touch was a bit cool, so he reasoned this as normal.

Within the darkness of the shadowy secret graveyard, the macabre scene was given voice, miraculously, one sound at a time.   Firstly, there was the sound of movement – the dull *rhumpf rhumph* of soldiers' footsteps through the faraway streets – or perhaps the teeming hooves of many animals collectively marching toward a new refuge for their clan. *Like horse steps – the clippety clop of hoofsteps.* Yes; that was what he thought he heard. Dull, distant hoofsteps. *Wild maybe… wild unshod horses roaming through a courtyard, or some empty patch of dry land.* Abner listened again. *Closer.* This time, instead of hoofsteps, they resembled another group of animals – but what kind? So many species ran in packs, it would be impossible for him to pinpoint. Wildlife in general had never really interested him all that much, though he was steadfast to come to the aid of any man or woman who decried the evils of hunting and slaughtering beyond the need of human consumption. This, he simply dismissed as some smug pecking order established by Man.

Abner Jameson was neither philosopher, poet, author nor playwright. So, intentions for the intended, he had said, and thought of other matters. For one; how to raise himself from this burial place beneath his new, beautiful home. And then, to remove these well preserved remains – they seemed so – some flesh still on the bones in places, muscle and cartilage entwined between yellowed bones. He again attempted rising to his feet, when a stabbing pain in his calves alerted him this may not be a good idea. The unusually cold sensation sheathing his jacketed arm as yet persisted.

Was this some form of stroke, he wondered, although general medical knowledge was not his forté, either. The sound also persisted, growing closer and clearer until he was absolutely certain what it was. *Absolutely certain*. It was then that the ghostly grip was released – the cold sure firm grip of death. An unrestful soul, reaching out to the living for something it cannot obtain on its own, but which it desperately requires in order to find peace in its own world; temporarily – for a purpose – among the living in our own.

Karen reached out to Jameson, however he refused the last Nelson her peace. The lantern tipped and touched fire to the mired carcasses, flames spreading and swiftly obliterating all he had found – all but one.

What had happened to Abner's mind after the incident in that secret basement space, friend, I invite you to speculate, for your guess is as good as any. With but the clothes on his back, and a mischievous grin on his lips...

When the servants rose from their quarters, saw the smoke and rushed to extinguish the fire, their employer was in a terrible state, shivering and rambling about a room full of pigs – *Pigs!* – and a beautiful sweet faced young girl who controlled those huge beasts within a secret cage – the invisible walls of her will. He repeatedly recounted his story long after the fire had been extinguished.

"This is getting ridiculous," Doctor Haskel said to himself under his breath, through gritted teeth. His attempts at scaling the tall iron fence had all failed, due in equal parts to his lack of confidence in the endeavor and a genetic disposition to profusely resisting any sort of limber physical exertion.

"Better I stopped in the middle and came back down now," he said, more as a comforting mechanism than a sign of tortured genius. Better than impaling himself on any of those 'Hello, my name is Eunuch' bar spears, which had been fashioned on Jameson's original design as a precarious 'salute' to the old moat castles in the day of King Richard and his prestigious Musketeers.

177

Charlie Shifton had taken lessons on and off in fencing, and though his aptitude for the sport could be considered fair at best, the obvious pun and scare factor to ward off criminals from his hard earned property was much too rich an idea to pass up. Over further years he had the outer casings recast in Fiberglas, molded over the original winding brass tips and iron bars, a shiny flat black epoxy. Dorothy enjoyed her husband's interest in the project – and his accompanying good mood up until its completion – so she decided not to meddle or give her opinion – however it was obvious to all she hated the wretched evil looking thing when it was done. She had thought the gate as it originally stood was *fine* and *beautiful* – shining and majestic bars dancing with rays of morning light – and simply abhorred it when it became *reborn*.

Charlie countered her sentiment – though he never knew of her true loathing toward his idea with an entirely opposite opinion. When *he* had seen the glowering round tipped spiraling bars of Abner's agate entranceway, he found it effeminate – old hat – pretentious – and most importantly not keeping with his simple unaffected tastes. After the renovated gateway had been completed, Charlie would stare at it from the outside with a servant standing nearby off to the side of his Creation, waiting for him to request reentry into the grounds.

The idea of 'restoring' perfectly good fixtures – which at one time had initially won the man over to buy the property to begin with – interested him more and more. The carpentry business was fine enough – although increased competition and the long drive from his freelance jobs in the state's more populated regions had bidden him slow down gradually, until it suited him well enough to live off his savings while awaiting his Maker. New York was huge, and the Tri State area during the early part of the 20th Century was becoming too densely populated – and downright scary with the rash of gangster related crimes becoming a perverse trend – definitely not a place for a family business. Too busy.

While he and Dorothy loved their first little-over-a-year together in his family home, the prospect of children sounded grand, something truly to look forward to – being a mother. Soon after a trip to the doctor during one of his days off, he received the news via telephone – good that he was home too, as he had not told Dorothy of the appointment and did not want her to worry there might be something wrong with his health – that his sperm count was too low to give Dorothy a baby.

Charlie kept this to himself until the day he died, and had always thought it peculiar that she never broached the subject of why they could not conceive, or expressed the natural womanly urge to see the doctor herself and undergo a fertility test – although at the time medical knowledge of this sort was still in its infancy by late century computer generation standards – and Charlie was unsure such tests for women even existed. Although the thought of denying her children through some defect in his person brought him great sadness, the thought that – possibly – neither of them were 'at fault' – what the doctor termed his 'genetic sterility' was God's will – and if he *was* sterile, that God had seen it to make things that way – had eased his mind considerably.

Charlie was a practical man with little time for indecision, and none for guilt. Whenever he considered the two of them there, in that immense house with no children taking up any of the seven spare bedrooms – live in servants excluded – he thought of the latter, suppressed the former, and felt better. It came as no surprise that his foreboding fifteen foot tall spike tipped personal welcome wagon – located a hundred feet from his massive front door – was to be the first 'renovation' brain storm as the flagship of this new hobby boring a creative hole in his brain… was to be the last. For the rest of their days together Dorothy and Charlie Shifton left their home just the way they had bought it; the way Abner Julius Jameson had wanted it – the way he had secured it.

Had Charlie known about the bones underneath the rubble, or of Abner's accidental fire? Of course he had. A carpenter's interest in scarce expensive woods being burnt to a crisp was to be expected, as well as in a roomful of blackened animal bones, with one *human* form among the departed. He had the balance buried by a servant and his son, both of whom had been sworn into secrecy. Lastly the human remains were collected and sealed into a tiny corner alcove in the basement proper, rather than the unusual open area where the bodies had been discovered, and the unknown corpse interred inside it. This area and the staircase were cemented over, no questions asked, no answers offered.

The charred remnants of what once were large specimens of slaughterhouse destined sow were now little more than fertilizer, what parts had not already returned to the earth. Karen's premature cadaver however – suddenly burned and entombed – did nothing for the soul of his find, even if no disrespect had been intended. In fact, Charlie had indeed thought sealing this Lost Soul into the very fibre of the home she hated and detested with all of her young being were the only Christian thing to do. It just might have been that, if not more. Sometimes though, dead is *not* better, as Sharon would soon find out – it simply prolongs the inevitable.

Chapter Ten

Leo stared at the large teeming crowd in disbelief. Why had there been such a large turnout in the middle of the road, and more intriguingly, where had they come from, in such a sparsely populated district, where houses were few and far between? The answer came to him rather quickly as he spotted the stretcher, borne by white uniformed emergency personnel, and the puzzle was completed by the bloodied elderly female body strapped into it.

(?)

Leo approached an apparent native – some inches shorter than he, though still around six feet tall – and tapped him on the shoulder.

The man's red and blue checked work shirt strained against overall suspenders adorned with two buttons, one on each strap – one 'What, Me Worry?' *Alfred E. Newman's* soundbite success, the other a smiling likeness of *Ren and Stimpy* against a plain white background. His face was rough and beet red, the result of exposure to constant sunlight – his pigment at odds with his outdoor activities. The heavy set man turned around and smiled toothily at Rothstein, admiring the fact that a city man would select him to ask any number of things – probably about the accident.

"Yessir, was dar a reason for a-tappin me on the back there?" Though he had said this without animosity, Leo, as a native New Yorker, found the choice of words confrontational.

"Yeah you can if you don't mind. What's the big pow wow about, and who's the woman in the ambulance?"

Yeah it's about the accident, the heavy man in the overalls sighed to himself. "Well dat dar's the Widow. The Widow Shifton," he said, pointing at the emergency vehicle as her dead body was loaded into it.

(?)

Leo was more than surprised – more than shocked – more than almost everything.

This was beginning to look like the afternoon of a very bad day.

The heavy set man noted Leo's confused expression with disinterest. He whipped out a small bag of Wise potato chips from what had appeared to be thin air – or perhaps Leo had not noticed the man holding it in one of his thick fingered hands.

"Knew her, didja?" the man asked, facing Leo fully now, his back to the throng that – only a few seconds ago – he had been a massive part of.

Leo put his hand up to shield his eyes from the sunlight. "Yes I knew her. A client." Leo justly figured polite conversation now might assist him in getting his head straight, and buy him some time to sort out this terrible news and its obvious residual effects.

"A client? What kind?" The man paused, squinting, and turned his head away from the sun's glare. "Like a defendant or sumthin? You a lawyer?"

Leo flashed a small smile and rocked on his leather loafers in a manner he hoped would seem non threatening – why did he waste so much time and thought energy on such inconsequential social matters?

"Yes and no," he replied demurely. "Lawyer yes; courtroom variety no. Talk to my Mom on that one, and that's... probably what she'd wished I went for. But I am instead the garden variety *real estate* lawyer. No fanfare please."

It was now the man's turn to look confused. He was not used to the oft heard mock putdowns of Manhattan's higher income working class, as they attempted to retain their dignity while separating themselves from their neighbors and colleagues, the Contented Vampire Drones. Leo didn't *like* suits and expensive shoes. It was just the uniform – or that is how he reasoned it to himself. No more; no less.

"Oh, I see," the man stated flatly, tamping down his excitement. "You have to fill out a report or sumthin about this, bein that you're involved with the –" He groped for the right word while fishing in his crumpled green bag for a few more chips. The bag – and his mouth when he chewed them – crackled loudly. The sunlight danced, pulsating rhythmically over the silver rim of the bag, mesmerizing Leo to distraction for a moment. The man pulled the word he needed from the air at last. "– plaintiff."

Leo knew this was not the appropriate term for what the widow had been to him, but seeing the rubbery skin around the man's mouth pull into a satisfied smile, Leo could not bring himself to tell him it wasn't. "If you wouldn't mind, my gentleman, I'll be getting along now. Enjoy your potato chips."

"Thanks mister!" the man yelled, as if Leo were already a block away. He then lowered his voice, and that peculiar impersonation of a smile spread across his face once more. "I hope you win the case." He placed a greasy chubby fingered hand on Leo's shoulder – the one he had been dipping into the bag. Leo gazed up the man's arm with only mild annoyance. The widow's death – and how she died, as its causes had obviously not been natural

(?)

was infinitely more to make a fuss about than a little patch of fried potato grease stain on his jacket. That – unlike the fatal condition of the widow's corpse – could be fixed.

Sharon thought she heard a rustling coming from upstairs someplace. It may have been outside as well – or even in her own mind for that matter – following a dead girl's spirit down a pitch black flight of stairs – that, without light to guide her, felt never ending – had wreaked havoc on a gal's cognitive skills. She joked to herself – was humor, as a last chance effort to retain a grip on sanity, to be considered 'joking?' Sharon did not think so, but she had always made light of life's peculiar twists and turns in what she had always thought was a straight no-harm-done road before this weekend – definitely the weirdest and most questionable weekend she could ever remember having – so why stop now. The on again off again artificial glow of flashlights seemed to appear and then disappear as if someone were making sure she had the barest knowledge of where she was, but then released her again to the darkness when she felt any familiarity or confidence in her footing.

For the last two or three hours – maybe more – a drowsy sensation, as if she had been injected with an antidepressant or experienced a forced light headed drunkenness from hard liquor – had attached itself to her person like a constant companion, aside from the feeling of 'company' while obviously under some sort of pull or mind control from the apparition speaking in her head – though she did not have the slightest idea how to describe such a thing if she had to. And she would, if it were the time she guessed it to be – around three thirty or four o'clock – then Leo would be due here any minute.

How would he know how to get to her, or even where she was? He would never have guessed she was here – far down the basement past a massive secret compartment well hidden from view in this maze of concrete blocks and Old World influenced beams. Even had he the good sense to *search* the basement, how would he get in? The front door was locked, and the alarms were all on – as far as she knew. The widow had explained the security system and how it could be shut off or implemented in case of a burglary attempt or other emergency if need be.

An alarm system – even if it were quite loud – with flags popping out of some recessed panel and waving about – James Earl Jones' booming recorded voice proclaiming over and over, "He's here! He's here! Get him! Intruder! Call the authorities! House in danger!" seemed a mite eccentric, or at the very least impractical for a building a quarter mile from the nearest neighbor, and a mile or more from anywhere else after that.

One question occupied her mind – as it would anyone else's had they been told of such folly: Who would hear it? Surely one took one's chances in these remote areas where – let's face it – privacy went hand in hand with foreboding helpless fear. Here a maniac would have full range to do as he pleased – carte blanche – while no one from the nearest community was the wiser. Indeed the low low price for such a luxury property was the main incentive which forced Sharon to get over that... real fear of hers – of being alone, helpless, and the target of some psycho – to be poked and prodded – a plaything, an amusement – before finally – quick! – he swooped down for the kill, his lips drawn back in a visage of triumph.

The apparition – the girl who had drawn her as in a deep sleep down this forgotten passageway – meanwhile – was crouched off to the side. Sharon sensed unhappiness. *How am I able to see her in this blackness*, Sharon wondered. *If I could just talk to her... comfort her somehow.* Sharon's thoughts trailed off as it came to her in another realization in a most remarkable day's worth of events – that a 'ghost' like this one – her companion could not feel any other presence but her/its own – then the sad crouched figure must not be aware of Sharon's existence here, right next to her/it – even if it were the one friend that made Sharon cognizant of this portion of the estate in the first place.

It was then that this phantom light ceased to illuminate that figure in the corner and moved away of its own mysterious volition – which Sharon thought she might have understood. Not all of it of course.

No one could, she reasoned without feeling – she had been without feeling for a long while – days or weeks – but in real time measurement, which outside those cumbersome concrete and stone walls and elegantly carved façade there was a definite date – and most importantly a definite time – 3:34 p.m. Monday. March 12th. 1996 – to be dealt with. Or had it been so already?

Through some mystical justice no living human being could grasp in its entirety, the spirit of Karen Nelson had been granted another chance by the Almighty to be at rest and at peace. Her bodily remains – thanks to the Christian-ish burial Jameson had bestowed upon her – were more or less – who is to say? – at peace. But it was not as most cultures – no matter how else they may differ in belief or practice will attest – the *body* that requires pardon from a higher power which wills all mortal beings to their ultimate ends – and new beginnings – but the spirit or soul, the lifeline of the animated, the living breaks from the departed when their time has come. The Soul.

It was Sharon's strong feeling that this person, spirit, soul or whatever was unaware of her presence – mortal or otherwise – in the least. No; she, Sharon, was being pulled and tugged to some ultimate End – an end, as many endings are – unopened and free to begin anew. Such was the case here – Sharon was sure of it. Watching this child cry in the creepy shadows that danced among this now-you-see-them-now-you-don't phantom light – it bade her relive her own troubled teenage years as a child abused by a jealous evil unforgiving poor excuse for a stepfather; and it hurt her brain to think about this all the more. Then came the strong, pungent scent of manure. A lot of it.

When Doctor Haskel had climbed all the way to the top of the gate on his fifth attempt, he was dizzy, out of breath and drenched in perspiration. He was so relieved to have made it to the top, he had not realized his button down dress shirt had untucked from his pants on his left side around the back, and gotten snagged on one of the pointed spear like tips. He had been careful not to touch these with his bare hands, but his shirt sleeve had become frayed – and it was then that he warily understood how dangerous this little climb was.

He cursed himself for being so impetuous and uncharacteristically intrusive upon anyone – especially a client – in their private life.

He began feeling woozy – almost faint. A glaze passed over his eyes, and he felt the salty sweat run down his cheeks – first one, then the other. He teetered upon the horizontal iron bar, balancing scant inches away from the sharp spikes before and behind him. He swung his feet as carefully as possible, as he attempted to gain a toehold. There was none of course afforded by this slim simple design – which had been designed expressly to dissuade breaching by any intruder. The wooziness persisted. He swung gently, holding the decorative iron bar – a foot below the sharpened spears – tightly with both hands. Doctor Haskel knew from the sizable rip on his dress shirt – sustained during one of his previous attempts at mounting the fence – that the tips were dangerously sharp.

Maintaining his balance was becoming increasingly difficult – tears stung his eyes, but he wasn't about to give up a hand in order to wipe them away. It had become progressively clear to him that he was indeed somewhat versed in the workings of the human mind – and medically versed enough to be aware of the brain's warning signals – that he was not going to make it down the other side in one piece. He began to laugh without provocation, thinking of nothing particularly *funny*, but out of mere panic. His voice rough and dry, he noted the humid false summer air thick in his throat – with no way to quench his thirst. Not now.

Haskel looked over the estate side of the gate, not interested in what might be going on where he was only moments ago – his car parked and waiting patiently for his return on the dirt road in the gleam of the hot sun. Had it been capable of thought, it would be thinking of returning with its driver back to the City – a bit of wisdom he now wished he too had thought twice about, instead of landing himself in this predicament – one leg out of trouble, and one leg planted deep *into* it.

His body was struck with fright and a strange sudden dizziness – *what was that coming down the walkway?* – alongside the cobblestone walk – now swarming over it. He thought he saw a crowd of – of all things – *pigs* traversing the grounds, spreading out as far as the eye could see. This was no doubt an hallucination, he tried to reassure himself, speaking as one would to another man waiting for the bus – pleasantly but cool. The scene was hazy at first, and he was relatively sure this strange mirage had been brought on by his sudden spasm of fear. *Vertigo – that's what they call it, right?* He shut his eyes for a few seconds, and tried to blink away the tears – succeeding only in bringing on a fresh bout of dizziness. Obstructing his judgment... not vertigo... that's the fear of... spiraling down. Down...

The pigs he saw on the grounds were grazing and nipping at one another, hooves stomping into the moist grass that grew profusely yet obsessively neatly – as the widow had preferred to see when gazing out her window – snuffing the soil in search of food, nudging one another playfully. It became increasingly clear to him – so clear in fact that he felt hard pressed to remember a time when his eyesight had been any better. One sow in front of the pack – the horde – looked up in his direction, and huffed. The doctor gripped the bar in panic. The stampede which would ensue once the hungry animals were alerted to his presence by the leader in front... the thought perturbed him. He would never survive the carnage. Never.

The creature in front shifted its forehooves through the thick grass like a horse in its stable, eager to be released from confinement. A few pigs behind and beside it looked to their leader, then raised their snouts in the air and pointed their large heads at Doctor Haskel. Petrified, slumped against the horizontal crossbar, fears both rational and irrational racing through his clouded mind, a two inch thick metal bar all he could hold onto – all he had between living – though crazed with fear and misunderstanding – and the All You Can Eat platter at *Piggly Wiggly's*, which he had a great chance of becoming in a precious few moments. A great chance – glowingly great – fabulous – Black Jack all the way – of being the Blue Plate family sized economy deal, in fact.

Still more pigs began to aggressively enact the behavior of the one Doctor Haskel had guessed was the leader – as well as the shrewdest, the smartest. The Pig that would get back at Man – the Enemy. *The Mass Murderers. Serial Killers.* As the pig stared directly at him, he looked right into its eyes – he could almost feel its brooding rage, as if it were transferred somehow to him. Definitely transferred – or *channeled*; the message, were one so inclined to call it a message – coming through loud and clear, to his fragile human psyche – his pathetic, overly complicated brain.

No more bacon for you, Buddy.

The thickness in the air appeared to lift; in fact, it felt as if there were no air anymore. *None.* Just a grey sky – a dull grey that would never elicit a second glance from a passerby, or much of a first glance, for that matter. He found, amazingly, that he could still breathe, despite the fact that the air around him had ceased to be. There at one point and gone the next. Did the rest of the world know about this? Surely the beasts below him had not noticed, for they were making more noise and creating a greater ruckus than ever before. At first, at a glance, they seemed merely idly curious. Now however they appeared positively hateful, huffing and snorting at the rank smell of Man with their wide flat noses, unable to get at him, but – no doubt; the doctor was sure of it – conferring among themselves in their own strange barrage of grunts, snorts and squeals – real *Pig Latin* to use against humans – about exactly how to do so – and fast.

They looked hungry – probably no one knew *less* about animal behavior and body language than did Robert Haskel – but even he could piece together that a lawn full of tubbies licking their chops with no prepared meal in sight spelled B-A-D-N-E-W-S. The pack was now steadily advancing on Doctor Haskel in near military formation – from his perch the movement was beautiful – graceful – as graceful as the shifting ungainly motions of such animals *could* be, he supposed. *Astonishing.* They all stopped, one after another, as soon as their leader had halted at the base of the gate. Cold and stiff like a machine – a mechanical pig maneuvered by a prop man off camera via remote control. Only this was no movie set – and he was no actor.

The leader pig raised its huge head, casting its cool hateful stare upon him. Its eyes were black with a core of – he could not believe he was able to see *this* from such a distance – intense *red* like a round flame undulating and rotating on its axis – or so he imagined – within each black orb. The eyes appeared crazed overall, and Haskel looked to meet the same death stares in the sockets of the leader's faithful followers.

Another typically banal expression popped into the doctor's head in keeping with his highly improbable and scared-as-all-hell unlikely change of scenery. *In a pig's eye.* He laughed as the saying crossed his mind, and the head pig huffed indignantly. *Should be; in a pig's eye there's one damned ugly eyeball... That's no good. Nobody would repeat something like that. There's no poetry in it. It just sounds flat. In a pig's eye... all good things can be... seen? Oh no. That's really awful.*

The pigs all voiced that much maligned tone often spelled 'Oink,' but pigs, as any farmer knows, in fact make no such noise – they grunt, noisily – they don't Oink. *In a pig's eye you can truly see that they don't Oink! No... In a pig's eye*, he thought, looking into the head pig's eyes. His dreams, his thoughts... his existence. *In a pig's eye, one can see* – try again – *In a pig's eye can be seen... the truth. That's it. That's the one. Too bad I'll be dead before I can tell anyone my great stupendous stupid assed saying. Jesus, I'm going to die up here.* He screamed to the sky – at no one in particular – just *up. I'm going to die in a den of pigs! Eaten! Sweet God!* He looked up again, straining in a desperate attempt to see some being – some higher power than his own – and get his/her/its attention. *Please help me!* No answer came – at least none of a divine nature.

Leo had finally made his way up to the front of the estate, and found a man perched atop the non entry gates, gripping the bars in what could only be a blinding fear of heights. He lowered his gaze to the ground, and then looked up again. The man screamed some gibberish while staring up into the sky, and then looked down again.
Leo thought he could make out a few words, and rolled his car window down – bleeding out the air conditioning as he did so – to get a better listen. Still sounded like gibberish.

The sandy wind whistled in his ears and stung his eyes – it had gotten worse since he had stopped in back of the large man to see the widow's body as it was removed from her friend's house down the road.

(?)

Bloody. So bloody.

(?)

making it hard to hear the raving man. *How did he get up there? Climbed. Had to. But why? Who was he?*

The lead pig had vanished suddenly, although the other pigs did not seem to notice – or they did not let on as such. They just kept staring up at him, waiting for him to come down.

Come down. Fall down.

He looked in the direction of the road, and though he strained to maintain his balance, his backside was hurting him considerably – having teetered so long on such a precarious roost it was a wonder he had not become sow food already. *Careful not to fall* – at this height he would surely die – *so out of shape, and getting on in years* – constantly reminding himself, as if foreseeing some bizarre death scene such as this, an act of perverse possible fate – Doctor Haskel reckoned quite level headedly – *That's if I fall down on that side.*

But – he hesitated – *if I fall on the other side* – he peered at the pigs, who seemed to be drooling heavily and livid with anger, hungering for the taste of his sweaty flesh – *they taste much better if they're scared... the blood flows and they have more of a taste that way... then I know it would be my ass! God I'm aching up here. I'm starting to lose my balance...*

Leo stepped out of the car and, with the window still open and bleeding air conditioning, slammed the door shut. *God, it's miserable out here*. He cupped his hands around his mouth and took a deep breath through his nose, shielding himself against the sandy gusts as best he could. He choked on the breeze – it was no use; it came from all directions. Leo ripped his shirt open, losing two buttons to the grass in the process.

"Hey you," he called to the man clutching for his life atop the gate. "Why don't you come down?" Leo enunciated the words slowly and without inflection so the man might hear him clearly, feeling the gritty air in his mouth, swallowing it, drawing it into his lungs. The stranger gave no indication that he had heard.

The leader pig had not disappeared after all. It was behind him on the other side! And it had grown to mammoth proportions. It was huge. On its hind legs, it might have been able to swallow him whole. *Did pigs rear up on their hind quarters, like bears?* Robert was unsure, but he would be damned if he wanted to find out right this minute. *I don't think pigs can rear up in that sit-up-and-beg position, but if this one has grown so large so fast, who's to say what it could or couldn't do?*

Had Leo known the doctor was far gone at that point – and that his attempts at getting through were only aggravating the problem and increasing the ferocity of Haskel's delusions – that there was no way to know who this man was and what if anything he had to do with Sharon – or the widow's death – even if he *wanted* to tell Leo who he was and what the hell he was doing hanging up there like a trapeze artist and screaming as if he were suffering a nervous breakdown – not now at least. Were he able, he would not have bothered. So he kept yelling into the wind, hoping for a response, or at least to let the man know he was there to help. It certainly did look like it would be needed.

What happened instead – in spite of his appearance – one Mister Leonard Rothstein, real estate lawyer, fun loving guy and Good Jewish Son to his Mamma, had turned, quite painlessly, into a large – make that *towering* – mean, hungry, hoof-beating-on-the-grass pig. Grand Daddy Pig. The greatest pig in the history of pigdom.

Better known in Doctor Haskel's Fantastic World of Man Eating Intelligent Beasts as *Leader*. Not that he had really changed at all. Oh, Doctor Robert Haskel, tightrope walker and dangerous stunts hobbyist, saw Leonard out there waving and yelling at him all right. Quite clearly actually. As clear as any pig he had ever seen in his entire life. The more Leo waved his arms to get Haskel's attention, the more – through Haskel's skewed vision of the world – the good doctor saw the incredibly tall wide hungry and *hateful* Leader Pig stomp its hooves and huff and snarl with Haskel's scent in its nostrils. *Doctor Haskel. Psychiatrist.*

Leo could make out this word and that, but not a full sentence – he had no idea what this man might be raving about – though the reason for the lack of fear on the man's face seemed pretty understandable. He was up there pretty high, and had probably gotten up there long before Leo had pulled up in his car.

The Leader Pig Leonard opened its tremendous mouth – the sight of its sabre like teeth froze Doctor Haskel's heart. The red cores within its black eyes burned brighter and brighter until the angry flames completely eclipsed them. Its nostrils flared wide in anticipation of his delicate flesh entering its mouth.

An electrifying bolt of pain rocketed through his body. He felt only fear before he died – but if Leo were able to see and feel what he saw and felt, he would have agreed that this was more than enough. *It happened again.*

Whoever he was did not matter. A robber perhaps. A rapist who somehow was able to discover that the house's most recent female occupant...

Leo considered his options and reflected on the events of the day. *It doesn't matter how. Not now. Something is going on here. Something doesn't make much sense. Not a routine way of closing a deal – yes I grant you that – and not the most tasteful or humane either.* Not that this was the most terrible house on the block or anything – it was the *only* goddamned house on the block. Geez, how Sharon must be going out of her mind in that house with nothing to do – no music or television to pass the time. That may be cruel, but – for only three days and a night – bearable.

Sharon's a City Girl through and through. What would possess her to grab one of these out of town properties is beyond my comprehension – that is if I read her right. Damned ass practical for sure – and a little frigid too looks like – but at this incredible price – just over fifty grand – I'm surprised more swindlers haven't pounded down the doors for a quick turnover to some private owner – or a smaller firm looking for a good Picture Postcard property to gain footing with. Nah – think that already happened most likely – and the deal's gone sour. Funny; we usually investigate a place like this much more accurately before shopping for a buyer. Shit – Old Man Shostrom would have come down here – chomping cigar and all – and handshook the whole deal closed himself. Lucky for Sharon – or for the late widow – that he had not seen this week's memos or review sheets, or the deal would not have gone down – if he had anything to say about it – for anything less than eight times the price. Really, he would not be so reasonable as to bang the table and demand it either.

Rothstein's Two Cent Appraisal in the harsh light – which made everything look better than it was – was that on the market it would gone for at least half a Mil. The eccentric add ons – and these Addams Family gates – you know all about those, my doomed friend, don't you? – would probably tweak the going rate some. *The celeb market could skyrocket it. Yep. The firm's losing a lot on this baby, but a Deal's a Deal... sigh... yeah.*

And the pigs, Doctor Haskel may have asked Leonard. What about the pigs?

The pigs were gone.

Karen was calling them home.

2:35 p.m.

Chapter Eleven

Sharon could see the figure in the corner clearly now. Quite an amazing spirit she was. *Nothing strange about her. Nothing at all.* Her tattered housedress looked as old as she must have been – however old she was. Sharon did not know, but it would be nice to try and find out when she got back into town – *if* Sharon got back into town.

What was that smell anyway? Sharon wrinkled her nose in protest of the foul mix of scents invading her senses – blending one at a time – until she felt dirty and nauseous. She knelt down to get a better look at her *companion*. She had been a lovely girl; that was clear enough. In a few years – had she matured – she would obviously be a knock out. The way you could tell by her role in *Pretty Baby* Brooke Shields would grow up to be a stunning woman.

"I suppose though that she's dead," Sharon said under her breath. And this is how she died – in that filthy dress, looking so unhappy. She let out a soft sigh, reinforcing this summation as a fact. *What a shame…* The words echoed in her throbbing head. The feeling of *otherness* persisted, as if she were outside herself, and the expected return of her usual pragmatic personality and bad jokes seemed far off in the distance. She was unsure how she was feeling right now – or at least since the little girl had led her down into the darkened basement – unusually cold for a warm spring's day. Though down there in the drab grey forgotten catacombs of the mansion's night creatures – that was, counting her brooding friend – she was a kitty in dire need of her comforting bowl of milk.

"I get out of this alive, and I'll never give David a hard time about militant women in the Independent Nineties ever again!" she whined aloud. She turned to face her teenage would be captor, who was clutching her raised knees in front of her bosom in a depressive troubled position. Sharon's night vision had improved steadily over the past hour, and she had a better mental picture of the young person in front of her, which pounded a destructive tune in her head from the inside out, through some unfathomable sort of telepathy – or, more accurately, *channeling*.

Sharon felt subsumed by a feeling of greater ease toward her surroundings as her fear of the slumped apparition across from her drained away – in fact, she felt more at ease in general. Given the extraordinary happenings of the last few hours – or days really – she hadn't felt this right since the widow had left and locked the door behind her on Friday night – into wide new consideration. And consider it she did – the move, the falling out with her new roommates, her failed romance with David and the poor excuse of a friend she was to him, this money she stood to owe – as reasonably cheap as the house might have been – and she *knew* it was a steal – over the next many years – with upkeep on a place like this she was well aware she would have little money left for installment payments, but they *had* to be sent, over and over.

The personage looked up – or mimicked a person looking up – then right, then left – side to side – then straight ahead. *It moved!* 'She' got up, appearing fully aware of Sharon's eyes upon her, padded on bare feet to the middle of the floor, and halted, facing Sharon, three or four yards from where she still crouched on the floor. The smell of manure, which had up until now been but a minor nuisance, was suddenly terribly thick in the air, wrapped around the duo like an old mildewed woolen blanket. The spectre spun on its heels and brought its right hand to bear in a gesture rendered obscure in the cloying darkness. *Could be a greeting*, Sharon thought for a moment, and then reconsidered. It, the Apparition, was waving something onward. *Another spirit?* Perhaps. *Or perhaps not.*

The spirit continued sweeping its hand counterclockwise through the air as the stench grew thicker and more nauseating to Sharon's mortal stomach. She heard a faint sound behind her, turned to face in that direction, then heard the same sound in front of her, and then all around her – the nasal grunts and dry snufflings of *pigs* had entered the basement. Doctor Haskel's maneaters. *Karen's pigs*.

Leonard stared transfixed at the dead body sprawled out in the moist grass on the other side of the gate. He could not believe he had just seen a man fall to his death – for no apparent reason. Leo hated it when he had no idea why something had happened – why a man did the things he did. Who this person had been remained a mystery, but the connection – if there was one – between his death and that of the widow – a suicide –

(?)

intrigued him. Why this man had plunged to his death he could not say, however it was an evident waste of time to help him, and time – 3:04 p.m. and counting – was at a serious premium. Something serious need be done if he were to make it in time to retrieve Sharon – and fast, too. *Not that this wasn't a great view of a dead man or anything.* The shade of blood from his head injury – *he must have struck a huge rock embedded under the soft grass – that must be it –* and the green foliage evoked a nice purple tableau in his mind's eye.

No it's not that I'm so damned worried about promptness – I couldn't care less – neither could Sharon probably, whether I got there in time or not – that I – I'm...

Leonard began feeling dizzy, and a throbbing pain like hammer strokes on either side assailed his temples. It caught him off guard, and he dropped to his knees. A cackling gnome with a long reddish beard – which cascaded over the chest of his faerie suit and obscured his pretty necklaces and frilly Christmas tree trimming and sequins around his glowing green lapel – was secreted in the grass manning a hidden strobe, which beamed a blinding white flash.

Within the flash he could see tiny faeries laboring inside a little faerie house. One faerie – let's call her Tina, shall we? – whispered into the ear of another – let's call him Thomas – something that must have been important, judging from the look of curious glibness – and then concern – on his pudgy hairy little face. They both ran away into the empty infinite light.

Leo's head was still pounding with an annoying stabbing pain – a *blunt* stabbing? – like an eraser tip stabbing into his right temple. He could almost see it through the blinding light, which was as intense as ever. Another tiny gnome appeared at his side, grasping the shaft of another pencil in its small grubby hands. And began stabbing into his left temple with the pencil's eraser. The light had reached searing brightness now – it burned like a bastard!

"Augh – my eyes!" Leonard shouted to no one in particular – or at least to the gnomes. The ones with the long red beards and the fluffy hats. *I have to get through that white light – Sharon's in there!*

A shriek of laughter shot through his skull – the gremlins had stuffed his ears with wads of cotton like those used to pack vitamin bottles. But you don't throw those away – oh no! – you're supposed to save them in a pretty new glass jar shiny with the prospect of snow white cotton dipped in a large thirty gallon vat of alcohol! Burning alcohol – the kind used to sterilize – oh it burns inside – burns a lot!

People in goofy makeup wearing playing cards on their chests. Playing cards? *That was strange wasn't it?* Jacks, Queens, Kings, Aces and the rest. *Little maids – pretty maids – all in a row.*

The Acid Queen wants her revenge.

The little people kept running. *Run little people, run! Run like your lives depended on it!*

Why run? Why run from the beasts behind you? The fat ugly beasts that kept chasing them, chasing and chasing until they were caught. The creatures – these creatures chasing them. *They're going to eat the little people! Nooooo!!*

Leo collapsed in pain on the ground – the inside of his head felt slimy like a slithering snake. He kept seeing things in his head. Silly nonsensical things. The men and women wearing cards on their chests winked at him through the bright light. Winked, ripped the cards gorily free and threw them away.

A horribly gory scene indeed. *Blood blood everywhere!*

Suddenly and with no apparent provocation, all the little people screamed – not the finger pointing screams of the past few minutes – how much time passes when one falls victim to such visions one cannot be sure – cackles of awe, if not outright high and mightiness over the Giant newcomer to their world – a tourist.

"Fair weather, that type," one male gnome said to another male gnome. "Never liked 'em. Always so damned curious with their beady little eyes always looking into your business."

"I for one would like it very much," the other little fellow shouted with a disapproving wink of his green eye – the skin color, not the eye color – that was black, "if they all just went back where they came from."

"Yeah," the first agreed. "Sounds good to me."

The second gnome snickered superfluously.

Leo overheard them quite weakly – the audio was not what it could have been due to the alcohol soaked cotton wads stuffed in his ears – it turned out these were the same two who had been tracing circles around his temples with rubber pencil erasers – one full pencil by one, and a pencil length eraser by the other, respectively.

Leonard quickly put a stop to that, once it became apparent who the culprits were. Yes indeed this was no laughing matter. Leo raised his hands up to the sides of his head and clapped them to his ears in an aggressive manner to prove to the little people that he meant business.

They ran around again – these green people within the white light always seemed to be running around for some silly stupid reason with hands flung over their heads – banging into one another with a sonic boom.

When Leonard again drew his hands back – flesh and bone came down hard on his eardrums – well worn now and in need of changing – bringing on another tidal wave of sound. All the little people tumbled off of Leo's head one by one, two by two and three by three, rolling, rolling back into the world of white light, and into nothingness. The singing, humming and sickening little cackles emanating from their fat ugly little mouths subsided to a whisper – and then nothing.

The pain in his head slowly dissipated as well as the seconds passed slowly by, until the glow was weak enough for him to see the quick growing grass once again. On closer inspection he realized that the grass wasn't wild at all, but had been rather neatly trimmed, as if it were a haircut just starting to grow out in uneven patches here and there.

None of this mattered at all to Leo, but he figured he had better focus on something – anything – other than what he had just experienced – the little people, the light, the throbbing pain in his temples, the mysterious galloping hoof steps – the suicide? Had he imagined that too?

No, that was real alright. The body was still right there, laid across the widow's lawn, right across from him on the other side of the fence. The ugly black dangerous wrought iron medieval looking fence.

Dangerous. Hmmm... Leo lit a cigarette and took a hard long drag, drawing the reassuring nicotine straight to his lungs, which wished a couple rounds of *Hey, how ya doin* to his heart along the way. He just stood there a moment enjoying his cigarette, gazing across at the grass, the house, the gate... the dead body. *Oh yeah. Couldn't forget that.*

He ground the cigarette into the sole of his shoe, then checked his right front pants pocket for his car keys. He had to get to the car and start it up. He had an idea. *If the Mountain won't come to Mohammed,* went the old adage, *Leonard Rothstein will break the fuck into that mutha.* Things were getting strange, and he was about to lose his lavish car over seeing something as usual as a dead body on the grounds of a dead woman's lawn – or little green men and women from the white light planet dancing the boogaloo and jabbing him in the head with stolen Number 2 Pencils – that was no big deal. Start that crazy peeper killin gate down, no welcome party necessary. *The jet's all I need.*

He walked to his convertible, opened the door, and settled into the driver's seat. *Comfortable?... Then let's rock.*

...First it's a Whisper...

...and then it's Nothing.

March 12th, 4:11 p.m.

Sharon looked across the darkened room at her companion, who again sat silent and cross legged on the floor. Gradually the room had become brighter – or, more accurately, Sharon's night vision had grown quite accustomed to the darkness – so much so that although there were no windows, she sensed what appeared to be the gleam early dawn – though she knew this could not be possible. The girl seemed to sense it too, from within whatever godawful limbo Sharon hoped she would never have to endure, be it life, death, or something in between – God willing, this person – this ghost sitting across from her – *God, it was a ghost, wasn't it? – dear God* – saw and felt everything Sharon did – and Sharon knew it. Somehow.

Sharon looked behind herself in a weak attempt to explain the false dawn – as if she could have explained anything that had happened that weekend. She looked for some hole in the wall, a crack through which some sliver of light might have crept in, from some intentional projection device – clearly installed without her knowledge, no doubt – *that's it!* As cliché as it may have seemed, and as tired weary and confused – and hungry – as she was, that was it. She knew it. It *had* to be so.

She attempted to deny it, but the most comforting reassuring thought was also the one that had to be true, and the *truth* was that this was all an elaborate scheme to spook her – an intelligent pokerfaced genius in the shadows orchestrating this nightmare – all cables, pulleys, wires and crank handles manned by some mad scientist adept at the Art of Illusion – Vincent Price in William Castle – *The House on Haunted Hill* – trying like Hell to break her spirit. *That's it! Someone working for that bitch the widow. The Widow Shifton*, she spat, and grimaced at the thought of the old woman's smiling face. The learned smile of pension, of affluence. The Grand Faker. The snake charmer. A bitch who had no more love in her heart for her or Leo than she could be expected to feel for anyone else, probably.

No wondering she had been willing to 'sell' this property so cheap. Fifty Grand... you've got to be kidding, woman! Do you think I'd fall for that?

Sharon spoke aloud, not noticing the Being in the room with her had heard every word. "That's why she quoted me so cheap, knowing I'd break my neck for the chance to call this place mine. Little Sharon Langhorn from Staten Island. Daughter of Dawn Connelly, Single Mom. No father, thank you very much. That old fossil had no intention to sell me the place, cuz she got some Bozo to rig the shutters and drop utensils and fling ashtrays across the damn room, trying to scare me half to death! but I'm onto you now you dried up old bitch! If you think I'm going to lay down and let you make a fool out of me, you're mista –"

"I don't think you understand what it's like to have a father," a voice from across the room interrupted Sharon's venting. A youthful hoarse hesitant voice. A teenager's voice. "Not likely you know at all." *Karen's voice.* "It's no picnic you know," the girl continued. "Not in the least."

Sharon's jaw hung open as she listened to what her ghost friend had to say.

"At least," she paused, searching Sharon for the right words, "I don't think we have a choice... in the matter... do we?"

One hundred years later, it was still March 12th, now 4:39 p.m.

"I'm sorry," the apparition in the tattered housedress said. Sharon could have sworn she saw her blush. *Blushing? A ghost? This was unbelievable.* "My manners... Miss Langhorn, my name is Karen."

Chapter Twelve

"How do you know my name?" Sharon asked, her mouth bone dry. "And, uh, that's Ms."

Karen's ghost regarded Sharon, grimaced, then shrugged.

"The *Miss*," Sharon explained, seizing her first opportunity to piss off a ghost. "Nowadays that's a no-no. That is, not among *my* friends. Not Miss. *Ms*."

"Beg pardon then, *Mrs*. Langhorn." Karen paused, looking at her wistfully.

"Married? No I'm not," Sharon huffed. *Man, these dead people are thick headed, aren't they? Funny how easy it is to talk to one after you spend a little time with 'em. Time for a bit of education.* "And it's Mizzzz, honey. It's pronounced *Mizzzzz*."

The strange word made Karen laugh. "Fraid I don't follow you Ma'am."

"Oh no. anything but that. I am *not* a *Ma'am*. My *name* is *Sharon*."

"Sharon..." Karen said perplexedly.

"Yes. Sharon."

Karen sighed, relieved. "Sounds like a fine name to me, Ma'am."

The two stared at each other for a moment, and then the ghost broke the uncomfortable silence, her gaze intent. "Why have you come to my home…. Sharon?"

"Well…" Sharon drew in a deep breath, and then let it out slowly. "At this point, Karen, I would have to say I… don't know. I guess it's… You haven't let me have much sleep here, you know." She attempted a sweet smile at the dead girl. "Not get much sleep at all, not with all that noise you've been making. I *presume* that was *you* then, making all the racket at night?"

Karen cocked her head to one side, then lifted her palms to her forehead above her eyes, as if in pain. Sharon was all too familiar with the gesture. *A migraine. A dead girl – talking to me as plain as day – is having a migraine.* Karen lowered her hands slowly, and again faced her human companion. "…*Racket?*"

"You know, crash boom bang. A mess. A *racket.*"

"Please, you misunderstand. I am not alone here," Karen said, looking around nervously.

Sharon could now see the face of this spirit plainly in the mysterious grey light. She was a beautiful young woman – fourteen, fifteen maybe – with quite a mature figure for her age – or so Sharon had gleaned judging by the loose dress she wore, which only exposed her smooth solid calves – and a bit of cleavage up top. If this were how she had looked before she died it had not been from any disease – or so it appeared.

"There are others. Don't be frightened. I know I might… scare you."

"Why would you say that? I find you pretty attractive for a girl your age. My roommate's nephew Phil would consider you a *fox.*"

"A *fox*? I have seen them sneaking around the neighbor's henhouse," Karen said woodenly. "I fail to see how I might remind this – *Phil* – of them." She spoke in a haunting lilting near monotone, at once beautiful and blood curdlingly waxen. Like a robotic simulacrum of a teenager. "*Fox*?"

Sharon smiled, beginning to find this exchange – although *chilling* – most fascinating. "Oh, it's nothing. Just another expression. Lots of words men use to describe a pretty girl they'd like to –" Sharon paused, not knowing if the young girl had yet to be told about the birds and the bees before her premature demise. "Most of the words they use aren't exactly complimentary – comparing a grown woman to a wild forest creature to describe her beauty – I find that a bit callous, if not outright insulting, if I might say. Now – tell me about these *others* – were they the ones *banging* all night?"

Sharon had many questions for this Being, but was afraid she may lose her train of thought, so she wanted to pose them as they came to her. "I could swear I've heard animals and, I don't know... *noises*. And *thumping*. Lots of thumping. For my *own* sake I'd decided that noise and all these weird happenings – sorry, that was *you* – were just some *moronic* play to *scare* my City ass offa this *property*. But *little* did they *know*... I'm *not biting*." Sharon stood squarely on her heels, satisfied with what she had said to this pretty yet nonexistent girl sitting across from her – *who did not exist*.

Karen, on the other hand, had no idea what this woman was so happy about. "This is strange, I must say... I've not spoken to someone in so long..."

Sharon could only stare in disbelief. In her heart she knew that Karen – or *some*thing – she had no idea what *kind* of something – and was nowhere near ready to deal with that yet – was right here – *existed* – speaking to her in an achingly lonely voice that so reminded her of the voice she had often heard in her own mind. The scared little girl looking for someone to talk to.

Anyone.

"Wow," Sharon gaped, half in shock at the possibilities that had transpired, the things that could actually be real. *Could they? Really? That must be...* There were no words for it. It must be so frightening. "What does it feel like, being... *here* again?"

Suddenly Sharon felt a surge of electricity, like a lightning bolt – or a creeping vine – creeping quickly underneath her skin, up in her heart, into her vital organs – seeping from some secret place – *Did Karen know about it? Was it her doing it?* Sharon panicked.

"Karen, what's happening? Something's... inside of me! *Help me!*" Sharon struggled to fight off the sensation, but was rooted to the spot. Her eyelids became heavy. The vines continued their ascent, encircling her ribcage – then around her liver... kidneys... something sat solidly in her heart. *Her heart.* A glow lingered there, assessing the reddish muscle, wrapping it in slender fingertips, and then enfolding the organ tenderly – curiously – studying its workings – its expansions and contractions.

The snake like fingers, exploring Sharon's inner cavities, made their way through her lungs until they found her larynx, and then wrapped themselves around her voice box. From there, it leapfrogged to her spinal cord, and made a beeline right into her brain – all its loops and whorls and breathable expansions nestled within, under and beside her grey matter – sending her into a state of temporary shock – *an induced stroke* – until they shot out of her eyes, ears, nose and throat – and disappeared into the darkness as mysteriously as they came.

With little emotion, Karen watched Sharon Langhorn 'die' – some sense from beyond told her the woman was not yet dead. However, had someone come in and seen the body sprawled on the floor, she would have appeared dead. *Clinically* perhaps, she was. No heartbeat, no vital signs, no brain activity – nothing.

Sharon looked across the room at the body she had occupied only moments ago – from the outside, she made a less than beautiful corpse – and Karen took her hand comfortingly. Sharon jerked her head back as she let out a hysterical laugh, feeling the familiar waves rise up in her stomach. It felt so good to laugh this way – a deep hearty laugh – as if all her stress and discontent had fallen away – all the nuisances of the mortal world.

"...into nothingness, and everything, all at once, is gone," said Karen, who rose, still holding Sharon's hand firmly, and stood next to her. Strangely, the overall feeling of relief and calm... felt different. Karen squeezed Sharon's hand to get her attention. "Come," she said. "We have to go somewhere... don't worry. You'll not be taken yet. They tell me."

"They?"

"Come. I have something to show you. You must see it. Now." Karen squeezed Sharon's hand again, and laughed – a dry silent cackle. Privately, Sharon thought, *an adventure – that's what it is – an adventure...* hysterical.

Leonard sat behind the wheel of his convertible and stared at the windshield, not yet turning the key in the ignition. He stared through the fence at the body around forty feet away. *Unbelievable*, he thought as he gripped the steering wheel, steeling his nerves. *Now, bright boy, knock those goddamned bars down like they were tissue paper. The woman you love is in that house, you poor soft bastard. How did you get this soft?* The voice in his head spoke sternly. *Don't ask me cause I don't know. It was just a job for you to come up here, wasn't it? I hope so, because it is to me. I take this job very seriously, Rothstein – I don't know about you.*

Leo began shaking mildly at first, his clammy palms grasping the steering wheel – and then felt the tremors become more pronounced, as if he were watching a stranger. *Oh that's fine Leonard – just fine. And you wonder why your mother still mothers you?*

You can't go anywhere without panicking can you Leonard Rothstein. Nice Jewish Boy from New York City. Slum Kid Who Made Good... Fuck it! Fuck it all! When it comes down to it you're not good for a fucking thing!

Leonard put his hand again to the ignition key – *Not a thing* – taking another breath, he turned it over – *not a fucking thing* – he revved the engine – *if you think this stupid plan of yours is gonna work then you're dumber than I thought! Let's see you break that gate down. Let's just see you do* – he stepped on the gas pedal. The car surged into life. He shifted it into gear – *how do you think this is going to end up, bright guy? And what about the girl? What about* –

The convertible slammed dead on into the black wrought iron gate. The lock busted on impact, the wheels burning through the manicured grass – *nothing you can do. It's too far gone to fix. You know what...* The car spun out of control and slammed into the house sideways just short of an exposed water pipe. *Too far gone. Too...* Leo crashed. The car skidded dully down the concrete walkway which surrounded the edge of the house. The car was not badly damaged. Leo however was another story altogether. *Poor bastard.*

Daniel, the Map Guy with whom Leo had exchanged some forced pleasantries a few hours ago, had been on the phone trying to get through to the Sheriff's office for the past twenty minutes or so – he could not be sure, as he had never been the kind for watches – especially the fancy kind – and even if he had the disposable income of a city boy his natural born sensibilities would consider brand name gadgets an unnecessary and selfish expense. Selfishness – and a few other evils brought on by Satan – or at least nurtured by him – were the Devil's work he would often say – and he suffered them very little before the onset of an argument even began – Daniel stating his misguided highly Presbyterian case to any onlookers who would stay put long enough to listen.

"No vices," he would begin in a preacher's fervor. "No vices do I have, ladies and gentlemen." He often added the pleasantry even if neither ladies nor gentlemen were present. "No vices a-tall. It is my lesson in life you shed foller – my single solitary lesson. And that lesson is... no vices – no shame!"

He was still on hold when he heard a car horn blaring incessantly. "Consarn it!" he cried out, and slammed a fist into his pockmarked dirt encrusted desk, which was littered and strewn with out of date papers – the only proper piece of furniture in the shack. Daniel took a deep breath and struggled to calm himself. Receiver still pressed to his ear, he walked over to the door and squinted through the window. Thick bass tenor notes filled the air outside, and Daniel saw the near musical tones had emanated from the horn of a Limousine. Daniel yanked on the stretched out phone cord, trying to pull the knots free and get a better look at this beautiful immaculate dream car while still stubbornly remaining on the line – as no one had picked up at the Sheriff's office as yet.

"Who is it Myrna?"

"Oh just that rattrap pest Daniel *Boone* is all. He's talkin some *mess* about a peculiar *stranger* come into town, and that the Sheriff should get on it pronto. How many times a day we get run down that road? This particular one got him so paranoid, I wonder."

"I wonder too Myrna. With all this uproar about the Widder Shifton *dyin* and all, mowed down in the street like a deer in the headlights by some uppity city *sicky*-a-trist person by so called *accident* –

(?)

and wanted for questioning – ain't nuthin I'd consider 'some mess' about it, girl."

The color drained out of Myrna's cheeks as she apologized for being unprofessional and passing judgment on a fellow member of the community.

"That's quite alright, girl. I understand how folks don't take that boy serious on account o'him living in that old desert show shack all by his lonesome, but at a time like this, woman, how can you *not* be tellin me everything with this *murder* an' all?"

"Oh I'm dreadful sorry, Sheriff, *dreadful* sorry. *Here*, lemme patch ya inta Daniel right *now*. I'm sure what he's got ta tell ya is *important*." The Sheriff sighed and nodded tiredly. "*Quite* important." He picked up the receiver and brought it to his ear. "Hello Daniel? Son... are ya there?"

Daniel admired the sleek shiny machine with its highly polished and buffed chrome hubcaps shining brightly, despite the gloomy overcast which had replaced this morning's harsh sunlight. *Another rainstorm like last night probably*, he thought. The phone cord made a 'thwack' sound as he continued peering out his dirty window. The receiver felt lighter in his hand, and it was then that he looked down at the cord tangling itself again, and realized he had pulled it so taut across the room that the entire phone and cord ensemble had yanked free from the wall. Unbeknownst to Daniel, the Sheriff had just that moment picked up the line.

"Cripes!" Daniel shouted. "Now I'll *never* get through again! *Dang* old *busted* rotary *dial* phone. And the jack's too close to the wall to plug'er back in. Oh hang me!"

"Where the hell could that damn boy have gone off to? Had'im on hold for fifteen minutes you say, Myrna?"

"Yessir – fifteen, twenty tops."

The Sheriff thought at first to maintain control over his temper and hand her back the receiver daintily – it was a dismally brief effort, and he bellowed, his face turning red, "Dammit woman, why didn't you call me sooner an' tell me the boy was on the boomer?" Apoplectic now, he drew the receiver up over his fresh crew cut like a knife. Myrna, petrified, shielded her head with crossed forearms, spun on her chair and crouched defensively against the drawers of her desk as far away from him as she could manage.

She was one hundred per cent certain he was about to bring it down, braining her in one swift and deadly arc. He caught himself, lingered for a moment, and realized he was about to bash in the skull of his desk officer for nine years. Seeing her cower like that made him uncomfortable – he disliked that scared look on his *wife's* face, and he sure as hell didn't care for it when it was is his *mother's* arms raised to fend off his father's fists.

He wasn't his old man.

The Sheriff slammed the receiver into the cradle, and Myrna cried out as if he had struck her. "Myrna, wass damatter wit ya woman? Didja think I was gonna slam you with the damn thing?"

Myrna, speechless and stunned, could only grin meekly and turn her flushed face from side to side.

"It's alright Myrna – no catastrophe. Just lemme know about all the other calls we gets in here today... will ya do that for me?"

Myrna nodded more perceptively and, eyes on the Sheriff, got back in her chair.

"After all – this may not be the LAPD, but a murder's a murder, y'ear?"

"Yessir," Myrna, still shaken, replied.

Daniel opened his door slowly and strained to get a closer look at the driver behind the Limousine's tinted windows. No such luck – from this distance they looked as black as night – a deeper creepier black night than he had ever seen before. City Night. Oh he had seen big cars like this pass him by, but none had ever stopped long enough for him to get a good look. He approached the car slowly and carefully – as if it were an alien spacecraft, instead of a standard issue Limousine. UFO or not, the machine mesmerized him.

Whomever had been sitting inside took notice of Daniel, and lowered his power windows with a familiar *whirr*. The driver – no interstellar alien – was a large framed man in his thirties with a wide yet severe face, eyes obscured by dark glasses as dark as the tinted windows had been. He wore a black chauffeur's hat and uniform topped off with a black overcoat. The man pursed his lips sourly and flexed his knuckles.

Leather racing gloves too, Daniel noticed. *Status statements leather was to his kind, and an expensive kill-an-animal-just-to-look-good statement at that*. Daniel disapproved of wearing a dead animal for warmth when cotton was just fine. *Didn't crease either*. Now that he had thought of it; it seemed that aside from his face – which was pale for this time of year – everything about this man and his automobile was solid black. Gruesomely black gleaming with a hedonistic shine and smelling of new leather. It then struck Daniel as less of a Limousine and more of a *hearse* – a *Death Car*. He shivered at the thought despite the warm afternoon.

The driver curled a finger, beckoning Daniel closer. "Say pop," he began in a deep voice which matched his stern expression, "have you seen my boss Mrs. Shifton? You must see a lot of stuff being out here all by yourself." He smiled a dark and unnatural smile which split his chiseled features stiffly.

"Alone yes – but not lonesome," Daniel countered as curtly as he could manage while standing in a muddy shit patch – or that's what the driver had guessed by looking down at Daniel's feet, and by the condition of his place of business – which probably doubled as his home. This yokel didn't look the type afraid to get his hands dirty. *Must fucking love it as a matter of fact*. He grimaced as the smell of manure confirmed his suspicions.

Daniel correctly construed the man's sour expression as a personal attack, and burrowed his hands into his stained overalls. "You mean the *widder* Shifton?"

"Yes, uh," the driver said, pausing to adjust his sunglasses, which had slid down his nose from perspiration. "The widow Shifton. Have you *seen* her?"

Daniel grinned like the cat who had eaten the canary – his eccentric sense of humor was tickled most at times like these. Whomever this man was, he would be in for a surprise. "Oh the *widder*, she..." he spat, and rocked on his heels for a few seconds.

The driver did not appreciate this at all – he was already late in picking his employer up at her friend Libby's house where she had stayed the weekend, and he was wasting even more time talking to this retard – it was not making his predicament any better. Most likely he was at least a half an hour late, and this *hick* wasn't going to make it a full *hour*.

"Now take it easy my friend. Don't get upset."

The driver fumed. "I'm not *upset!*" he yelled, and Daniel put up his hands signaling 'no contest.' Neither man wanted any trouble, each for differing reasons. "Where *is* she? Have you *seen* her?!"

Daniel continued rocking his heels in the watery fertilizer. The driver removed his sunglasses, revealing cold grey eyes that completed his face's stony appearance. *Probably a body guard too*, Daniel mused, absentmindedly mouthing the words.

The driver realized raising his voice would get him nowhere with this type of man – the type of man who stands around in puddles of shit for fun was not going to be intimidated by a little yelling. His face, though, gave Daniel the willies.

"Oh I *heard* of the *widder* alright," Daniel began. "Whether I *seen* her or not is a whole 'nother baller *wax* now, *in*nit?"

Clearly, the driver thought, this 'conversation' was going nowhere. He might have to hurt this man if he kept this act up. He hated glibness, especially in lowlife upstate backwater rednecks. He looked straight into Daniel's blue eyes and, stepping out of the car and towering over the smaller man – Daniel guessed six foot six – warned in a cold flat voice, "Look. I'm trying to compose myself in front of your sorry ass as you can plainly see." He swept his hands out, affecting the movements of a male model on the runway.

Daniel merely spat and frowned at having been called a *sorry ass*. "I under*stand*," he answered slowly. His father had told him always counter a bully with kindness – throws their game right off. If this city boy wanted his shit thrown off, then Daniel was only too happy to oblige. His walking stick was propped up behind an empty trough, and his shotgun was a short run away back at the shack.

"Good," the bully said coolly, believing the runt to be sufficiently scared by now. "I'm glad you understand my situation." He pressed a leather gloved right fist into his left palm.

"*No* actually," Daniel answered, scratching his head. "Come to think of it, I *don't* understand your situation. Not tryin to be difficult, but I don't even know who *y'are*. I'm *guessin* some sort of show *furrrr*," he drawled.

The frustrated man shifted his weight from one foot to the other. How long was this going to take?

"But *whose* and what *fer*, that sir, I jess *don't* know."

The driver sighed and attempted to collect himself. *No biggie – don't blow a fuse over some loser goober. Not worth it.* "That's fair. I see where you're coming from. I'm Mrs. Shifton's private chauffeur and bodyguard."

I knew it! Daniel thought.

"...And I'm late to pick her up and take her back to her estate. Saw some people milling around figured something was up – thought you might have some insight. If I'm wrong I'll be on my way." The driver reached into his car for his sunglasses, and slid them back on. "I've wasted enough time here as it is."

"The *widow*, sorry to say, is... *dead*," Daniel said, and winced involuntarily, expecting to be hit. *Dang, I wisht my shotgun was out here.*

"What?! *Dead?*"

"Tha's right. Dead as a doornail. Bout an hour ago, maybe more."

"An *hour!*" The driver yanked his car door open so roughly Daniel thought he might rip it off. He swung his bulk into the driver's seat, slammed the door shut and banged repeatedly on the steering wheel with his fists. "It's all my *fault!* I shouldn't have let her spend the night at Libby's – not with that *woman* in the house." A terrible thought crossed his mind. Maybe *she* did it. "Shit!"

"I know it must be an unbelievable shock to you, but –"

"Is the lady – Sharon – still up there at the estate?" he asked, his shaking hands gripping the steering wheel for dear life.

"Sha – Sharon? Sorry no, that name don't ring a bell," he muttered to the driver, as if to say *I might be of some help here.* "I seed this *city* boy come up in a con *vert*ible."

The driver looked out his window into the distance, and then at the dirty faced messenger who had delivered him such dire news. *So early in the day for death to strike*, he inwardly snickered, focusing his eyes on nothing in particular. "Was this fellow's name *Leonard* by any chance?"

Daniel slapped his knee and smiled broadly in recognition of the young Jewish lawyer. This here woman Sharon's lawyer – yeah!

217

"*That's* it! Leonard Rof – uh – *Roth* steen! *That's* the man! Know him?"

"I know *about* him, thanks. You've been a great help –"

"Daniel!"

"Okay Daniel – the widow at the hospital?"

"Yep. Old Forge General. Up past these trees quite a ways away though. Aimin ta head up there?"

"Yeah but," the driver paused to take a breath. "If what you say is true then somebody's got to go up there and get Sharon – if no one has yet that is." Under his breath he added, "I gotta find out what she knows about all this."

"Oh," Daniel said theatrically, "it's *true* alright."

"Shit!" the driver yelled as he drove away. "*Shit!*"

Randall Alcott – the widow's chauffeur – arrived at the estate and gaped at the dead body lying on the grass, as well as the convertible which had crashed and skidded along the side of the house. He stood there staring in disbelief – not shock exactly, as Randall was not like most people. A kickboxing enthusiast and NFL hopeful, Randall – for various reasons, mostly involving women – had more bar fights to his credit than he would care to admit, and kept his sensitive cerebral side more or less in check, choosing to rely on his intimidating size – genetic, he would tell his friends, not steroids – *Au Naturále, my man* – and quick temper.

What he saw made his blood boil as his temples throbbed ala *the Funky Chicken*. He had not a clue who these people were or why they were lying around dead on his elderly boss's property – who incidentally – if that dirty grinning fool could be believed – was *also* supposed to be dead. Randall checked his watch before reaching into his pocket for the key to shut off the hidden alarm system. *Why hadn't it sounded?*

It was 5:25 p.m., much too late for the widow not to be out on the doorstep by now, arms folded and lips pursed, ready to reprimand him for his tardiness.

If these two had been able to get in without sounding the alarm, he thought, who's to say someone else was not this moment ransacking the place for valuables or... Randall returned to the Limo, reached his large arm into the window and across the dashboard, opened the glove compartment – and fished out his gun. Randall, born and raised in a lower middle class section of the Bronx, had – like most of his friends – grown up a television junkie, and shared a common thread of escapist fantasies of known – but disproven – master criminals and various other deviates, all taken in and processed as the Partridge Family, Get Smart, and the Mod Squad played on – to name a few. He palmed his Colt .45 revolver and eyed it for a moment – admiring its gleam; even in the afternoon's overcast gloom it shone like new. He placed it in his sidearm holster for safekeeping, incase his paranoia were justified. *It's good to be paranoid*, he would tell people matter of factly when the subject was brought up. *You live longer – so if I'm paranoid, so be it!*

He approached the bloodied body, which lay on its back. *Head's a mess – probably a concussion. Not much to see here. Fancy duds though. Must have had a few bucks in the bank. Cartier watch too.* Randall felt like *Kojak* or *Columbo*, as he stepped over one of the corpse's sprawled out legs, and then the other, and approached the banged up Corvette. She was a beauty – gorgeous candy apple red with tailfins – if not the real '65 McCoy, then a startlingly good reproduction nonetheless. He noticed no modifications when he peered into the interior, then returned to the body and nudged it with the shaft of his pistol to more closely assess the damage done.

He cased the vehicle for weapons and contraband – seat cushions, back seat and glove compartment came up clean. Unless something had been stashed in the trunk. Could an assassin be secreted there, ready to shoot? If so – despite being armed himself – there was little chance for escape. He walked steadily along the side door, past the accordion of the retracted black cloth roof, knowing he would be unable to enter the house before checking everything outside first.

And so – the trunk. Randall held his pistol at the ready, took a deep breath of warm thick air and tried the trunk, finding it locked. False alarm. He replaced the gun in its holster, then reconsidered and redrew it.

He walked back towards the front of the classic automobile and admired – despite the damage – how well cared for the car appeared to be – showroom condition even. *Just needs a once over with a cotton cloth – that is, after six months in a repair shop and a small fortune to get this baby up and flying again. I wonder what those Dukes of Hazzard boys would do...* Randall allowed his fantasy to play out, envisioning that *Daisy Duke's* shapely figure. *Man, that show was the best...* The fantasy veered dangerously close to X Rated territory. *I'm Bo Duke. Take off that t shirt Daisy, and let me toss your melons around for a spell.*

Randall heard a groan, and at first attributed it to the imaginary *Daisy. My they sure are a gorgeous pair Daisy girl...* He realized though, that the sound had come from somewhere more down to earth. Leonard stirred slowly in the driver's seat, raised his head gingerly off the steering wheel and attempted to focus his eyes. He saw Randall approaching him, and groaned again.

"Hey guy, are you *awake?* Can ya *hear* me, fella?" Randall inquired. Leo, not yet fully conscious, rolled his eyes in Randall's general direction. Leo could only think of sleep – the sweet stress free sleep of surfing the incredibly radical waves between life and death. Randall patted him on the shoulder, and addressed him more forcefully.

"Hey *buddy*," Randall said as he poked Leo in the shoulder with the index finger of his free hand. It struck him that this man may well be badly injured and in dire need of medical attention, and that his little game of *Secret Agent* may have put his life in further jeopardy. The fellow on the ground looked even worse, the man's likely broken neck reminding Randall of Bela Lugosi's *Ygor* character from *Son of Frankenstein*, when displaying where the hangman's noose had caught him – but not killed him.

After the townsfolk had watched Ygor 'die,' he had painfully removed the noose from around his neck – which had deformed him and severed some key nerves, resulting in his famous hunched posture. This man's complexion resembled Jack Pierce's makeup work on the film, but this was no movie, and this guy was surely *dead*. Randall, for good reason or bad, knew dead – occupational hazard. And this time there was no mistaking it – Dead was *Dead*.

But the other one…

Karen paced the floor with a desperate urgency, mulling over the death of Sharon Langhorn. Had this been an act of God, or had it been her own doing? "Oh *please*," she spoke upward to a Lord – a Heaven – she had never seen in a hundred years. "I did not mean for this *creature* – your *creation* – to lose her life." Karen held her hands to the fallen Sharon's face, grief stricken. *Curse this woman for bringing me back… like this.* She looked at her human hands – a body which could be hers – saw them in the flesh, could almost feel the blood flowing in her veins, her heart beating, the ache in her mind as she brooded over the suffering silent purgatory she had spent in this House.

"Miss?" Sharon's spirit called to her – a faint and otherworldly voice – she could not tell from where. She examined Sharon's body – a broken and battered form, overrun by eldritch vines which had appeared from nowhere as if sent by some vengeful demon – her *father?* Karen's mind flooded with the awful unspeakable details of her death, the painful memories that bade her reenact the scene day after day, moment by moment. *It is as it was supposed to be* – here she was back at the threshold of the mortal realm, with all its own brand of suffering. *Damn her! Damn this place! Damn this woman Sharon Langhorn! damn her for bringing me back this way!*

"Karen?" Sharon called – the voice of a woman caught between two different worlds. "Karen, are you there?" Sharon – the spirit – reached out like a scared child separated from her mother in a crowd, and was worried that she did not receive an answer. "Karen!" she yelled, and it was then that the brooding ghost answered her.

221

"I am here, Sharon," the spirit spoke bitterly, pronouncing the name with distaste.

"Wh – what's happening?"

"You are as I am now." Karen's cold sharp brusque tone emphasized the shock and anger she exuded.

"You mean... *dead?*"

"*Are* you?"

"What's the matter? You sound... *different*. Has something... happened?"

"*Happened?* Has something *happened?!*" Karen barked indignantly, livid with anger.

"Karen, please don't be mad at me..."

Karen looked at her, and murmured something unintelligible. Sharon – her body anyway – clutched her knees to her chest and began crying softly. Karen glanced over to where the shell sat huddled on the floor – at the spirit Sharon, whose face was also streaked with tears – and cocked her head, quizzically.

"I'm... crying, I guess." Sharon wiped her eyes with the balls of her palms, just realizing that the was – in this form – crying.

"Why?" Karen asked softly. And why indeed? It was she who had wept incessantly for all these lonely miserable years – for a lifetime and more – alone. It was her fate and punishment for having perished without a proper burial – in the eyes of God – her punishment and her right. Angered again, she looked at Sharon head on. "Why have you come here and *done* – this – to me?"

Sharon struggled to hold back another wave of tears. "What *I've* done?" She folded and unfolded her hands nervously, and then pointed across the room. "Look at *me* over *there!*" The tentacles were back now, writhing and enveloping the hollow form – seeming almost imperceptibly to wither it away. *I'm – my body – is becoming something's dinner.* "You have your nerve you know – *real* fucking nerve. I'm dead over there bitch – *dead!* Maybe that doesn't mean a hill of *beans* to you cause you're fuckin dead *already*, so you've gotten *used* to it, but not *me!*" Sharon's voice trembled with the knowledge of what she had just said. She – Sharon the *Second*. Like it or not, the ghost named Karen was all Sharon had in this – *whatever* it was – and it would do no good to alienate her, if she could be of any help. "Oh sweet *Jesus*."

"You cuss like a common harlot. Jesus, our Savior, the Deliverer, will not hear a word from your foul mouth. It is a sin, how you speak."

"*Listen* sister," Sharon retorted, her repressed anger rising. "God, Jesus – if they listen at *all*, they listen no matter who you *are*, what you *do*, or how you fuckin *speak*, okay? If God and his Chosen Son are so damned *righteous* as to dismiss some poor soul from the Pearly Gates based solely on their *grammar* – when besides that they tried their hardest – like I try my *damnedest* – to be a good person through so much twentieth-goin-on-twenty first-century adversity and *bullshit* – trying to believe in a paradise, a *Heaven*, a place to go where I'll be safe and *cared* for when I die – then finding out there's a *catch* to all the shit they force down your throat in school – like, 'Oh you can't curse, that's part of the rules,' *sorry* then – fuck it all to hell – I don't *wanna* go. You *hear* me God?" she yelled, looking up into the featureless void. "I don't wanna *go!*"

"Look at me," Sharon whispered, feeling suddenly drained and defeated, and slid down the wall, splaying her legs out in front of her like a young girl, looking at and through her translucent hands with transfixed horror. "I'm not anything anymore. I can think, I can feel... inside... and yet I don't... exist."

Karen eyed her as if suddenly discovering Satan himself in her presence. "Blasphemy," she decreed, in a ghostly – of course – whisper.

Sharon was struck with the realization that she must follow these unimaginable happenings until their very end, and if it indeed meant her death, then so be it. She knew the outcome of this grand scheme at once, like a lightning strike – and knew she must play it coolly – for everything had happened for a reason.

"Blasphemy? Even you don't know what truly happens after death, if you've been stuck here all this time. I don't see," Sharon continued, getting back to her feet, "how you can't see my point, Karen. You look like you're... were... a fine, smart young lady." Sharon stretched out her arms with fingers spread, skin taking on a faint greenish hue. "You know ah'm raht girl, jest as sure as ya know mah name." Sharon's eyes sparkled with a maliciously luminous bluish glow to contrast her waxen skin – glaring burningly, directly at Karen – into her soul. Karen could sense something was terribly wrong.

"You... you're not Sharon Langhorn." Karen spoke haltingly, as if losing herself. Although long dead, she felt within herself a distinctly human fear. Sharon had come to her. Alone. A savior at last. But the tide had perceptively changed. This Sharon was... *possessed*. "You're not her at *all*. Who *are* –"

And then Sharon's eyes – her greenish countenance – was familiar. *Too* familiar. Karen looked over at Sharon's corporeal form, still riddled with those unholy slithering things, which she knew were feeding on her. And she knew she again was facing her abusive father Daniel. He flashed that same half smile he always had before he would inflict his worst on her – the face was Sharon's, but the expression was unmistakable. He had tricked Karen into believing Sharon was dead, and that Sharon's spirit had come to her aid. Oh he had been cruel – but now she saw there was no *end* to his torture.

She had died as a hideous byproduct of his neglect – didn't he *know* what would have happened? That without any money coming in, the pigs would have nothing left to *eat?* Her reticence to plead her case to the storekeeper – surely he would understand her predicament and come to her aid. The storekeeper however knew of no such need, as she had not approached him and told him of her father's abandonment – as she should have. And so he remained as shocked as the others upon hearing of the horrible truth – how the pigs had not been fed. Had that somehow been her father's doing – had he willed her to stay put and not seek out help – to become a meal for these hulking beasts? "Eaten alive, father – alive!"

The masquerading form stood over her, grinning, and draped its fingers around her tense shivering neck. Karen screamed.

Chapter Thirteen

"*Hey* buddy," Randall said loudly, poking Leo further with his outstretched index finger, "you *alive? Huh? Answer* me!" He grasped Leo's shoulders in his large firm hands and began to shake. Leo opened his eyes and then closed them, repeating the sequence several times over, until they remained closed. He wasn't dead, that much was certain, as the driver of the convertible made a weak attempt to shrug him off. Randall moved to shake him again and reconsidered, as moving an accident victim may do more harm than good. Randall cursed himself for having been so impatient – for all he knew this man had done nothing wrong, and had nothing to do with the widow's disappearance.

He at least had to allow this man – who was badly in need of a doctor – the benefit of the doubt. The man's head, which had rested on the car's plush covered steering wheel, was bleeding more than before – a red trail running from a long gash on the man's forehead down the length of his white shirt. Randall searched his own pockets for his keys – in particular, for the one to the front door. *Garage key – glove compartment – gym locker – my house keys – got it.*

Randall paused for a moment. If this was the right thing to do, he hoped he would not get into trouble for it, or get *dead*. The police should be notified about these people on the lawn, and about the crashed car. If not they might think he had not called for a *reason* – and that would mean trouble for *him* – and a lot of 'where were you' numbnuts questions later.

Yeah, come to think of it, it looks pretty bad doesn't it? He looked around at nothing in particular, and then at the bodies. He looked hard at the bodies, putting two and two together. "Shit," he said aloud. "They might think *I* did this. Damn – what da *fuck!" Like I knew this was gonna happen, right? Shit!*

He fumbled putting his key into the lock, his hands shaking just enough not to line it up with the keyhole. He had left his prescription glasses in the Limousine. He found the opening on the seventh try, and then took a deep breath to collect himself. *Okay – you're going to go in – calmly – pick up that phone and dial 9-1-1. When they pick up, you're going to tell them about the widow missing somewhere,* and *those two dicks out there really fucked themselves up.*

What was that one thinking, playing cat burglar? Whatever – just check yourself – get it together. The desk officer took all the basic information down in a simple even tone of voice that put him more at ease.

"Do you think they'll blame this on me? Will I be considered a suspect?" Randall blurted in an uncharacteristically high desperate voice. Myrna responded in the only way she knew how, briefing him on what would be expected, while pulling her desk drawer open and drawing out a tabletop cassette recorder with a suction cup microphone attachment which she had christened Ol' Crime Buster. As she'd often said, *When in doubt, record it.*

"Okay, Mister –"

"Randy – *Randy'll* do for now. I work for the widow Shifton, as I said and I need backu – I need *help* here. There's two dead bodies here

(?)

one on the lawn with his neck broken," he said, agitation building. "That must have been a nasty one. The other in a car with a long gash on his head."

The tape recorder was running by now, but despite the man's distress he sounded more like a guilty party than someone who had just *happened* to find two dead bodies.

(?)

But there's no way to be sure until someone goes out there and gets all the facts.

"Hello *ma'am?* Are you *there?*"

"Yes sir. I'm reaching out to the Sheriff on his beeper, but he's out right now on another *call.*"

Randall sighed on the other line, not knowing what to say next.

Mister... Randy," Myrna began in an attempt to swerve the conversation – *tape is still running.* "Are you aware what happened to Mrs. Shifton? The accident I mean."

(?)

A chill ran up Randall's back. Something *had* happened to her. *Dammit!* "Wh – *what* accident, Ma'am? I was just supposed to pick her up at her friend's house."

"Would that be Libby?"

"Yes! Libby. Mrs. Shifton stayed the weekend, then today I was supposed to meet her at three, three thirty – but I was running a bit late – which is not a habit of mine, believe me. I was a bit pissed at myself for that..." Randall paused, and realized he could no longer postpone the inevitable. "I'd better get back outside. That man in the car could be *dying.*" Randy put a hand to his sweaty forehead – another sinus headache was coming on. Then Myrna asked the question he had tried to avoid.

"*Excuse* me, but... are you *aware*, the *status* of your employer? Sir, do you *know* the outcome of the *accident*?"

(?)

"With *all* due respect *Miss* –"

"Sir –"

"*How* could I know the freakin *outcome* if I didn't know there was an *accident? Please* make sense."

"I apologize sir," Myrna said, as she switched off the cassette recorder.

"Me too." Randall forced himself to take steadier breaths in an attempt to ward off the headache.

The presence in Sharon's body pressed its hands against Karen's throat as if this act alone would elicit a scream, but all that came out was a terrible dry wail – more like the howl of a faraway coyote, heard over sagebrush from a distant hilltop. The eyes of this false Sharon were alive with suppressed emotion as they came to life once again. Not the kind of life we mortals know, but some shadowy manifestation of the being Sharon had unwittingly called back from whatever abyss it had languished in. "No," Karen pleaded of her aggressor as the grip tightened around her throat. To an outsider, the forms were as a double negative photographic plate, both there and gone at the same time – solid, yet transparent.

The *real* Sharon shifted under the weight of the heavy vines, as she struggled to remove them in fits and clumps – there were so many of them, and they writhed like snakes. What were these things, and where had they come from? *Perhaps from whom was the better question* she thought, her mind somehow still loosely tethered to her body. That sad screaming moan was maddening, and as much as Sharon wanted to free herself, she realized there was little she could do to help. After all these things were not human, she thought, remembering the strange noises and nightly visitations of the previous three days, including in the room as she slept.

What excuse do you have for that one Sharon? How do you explain poltergeist activity, short of coming out and sayin it's plain fucking poltergeist activity? Oh but we couldn't do that, no. Just couldn't buckle under the pressure and admit a couple of dead people – one of whom could be your clone – are wrestling right across the room from you. And you – squirming underneath a pile of smelly mutated reptilian vines you're not fucking sure even exist outside your stupid freakin mind. This whole Bat Mitzvah might all be in your damn mind – did you ever ponder that one, Brainy? Huh? Huh?!... I thought not.

Karen slammed her palms flat into the fake Sharon's face, scrambled to her feet just as the other did the same. *Pretty fast – and bigger than me too.* Karen trembled at the thought of it again touching her – of it *hurting* her. Karen knew for a fact the identity of this antagonist spirit, as well as she knew her own death.

"Karen," the doppelganger said. "Don't leave me please." The voice – strangely – was not entirely female, yet strived to express... regret? "Karen, you know me," it said drily.

"Yes," Karen said. "I *do* know who you are."

The real Sharon by now had managed to remove a good deal of the slithery creatures from her body, and sat unsteadily upright. *God,* she thought. *I have no idea how these things didn't crush me to death, they're so heavy. Somebody must be looking out for me.*

Karen looked over, seeing Sharon had almost freed herself, and shouted, "It's my *father!* He's *here!*"

"*What?*"

"It's *him! Please* look! He wants to take me *with* him!"

"Your father..." The last ten minutes under those suffocating vines had felt like a lifetime – had she died then and come *back?* – and she pried and kicked her legs free enough so she could rise tentatively to her feet. She attempted to focus on the two combating forms, but some entity definitely did not want her to get involved.

"Forgive me... Karen, don't run from me. There's so little time... That woman," it said, indicating Sharon – who heard none of this ghostly exchange, "has given me a chance." Its voice, hoarse and out of breath, was definitely male now. "The chance... to beg your... forgive –" It was clearly her father Daniel Nelson's Voice. "*Forgive...*" it said again, and then slumped to the floor, trembling weakly, as if terrified that it would have to go *back* without getting what it needed from Karen.

"So... weak," Karen said, both perplexed and fearful, and looked to Sharon quizzically.

"Forgive me for not being up on the latest Tarot card nonsense, but after seeing my ghost *twin* try to *kill* another *ghost*," Sharon scathingly responded – surprised at how *alive* she felt, "but I always thought for ghostdom you already hadda be *dead!* But like I said, I'm not an *expert* on the subject." Karen eyed the spirit disdainfully.

"Sharon Langhorn, have you no *respect* for the d –" Karen spat out, her eyes blazing with a bone chilling hateful glow, yet still unwilling to address her own death. "I've been *here* – like *this...*" she ran her fingers through the air, "for so long..." She repeated distastefully, "So *long*. Trapped in the nightmare of that day, the day I was *taken...*" Her voice trailed off. "...before you came *here*, to my *home*." Karen, now commanding Sharon's full attention, approached the other – corporeal – woman, temporarily dismissing her father's masquerading form, cowering on the floor. "I didn't remember any of it. Not the pigs, not... *any* of it."

"I'm sorry... *pigs?*"

"Yes," Karen answered simply.

"I think I get the idea. You've been stuck in this house all these years in some form of limbo, trapped here because you were murdered or something, and now your soul cannot rest."

"I..." Karen muttered, startled. "You *could* call it murder." She pointed at the pathetic husk on the floor. "Murdered – by *him!*"

231

"Your father? Your own father murdered you? I find that hard to believe."

"What you believe doesn't matter. No one has to be somewhere to murder someone. People die... *many* ways." Karen lowered her voice, remembering, almost against her will. "They die neglected... *unloved...*"

Sharon nodded.

Karen's eyes again blazed – an unholy shade of magenta that frightened Sharon into backing away into the nearest wall. *If only I could step through that wall and out of this place.* But of course she could not. "How is that, if I may ask?"

"No, you may not." Karen closed her glowing eyes and rotated her head in what looked to Sharon like some sort of Yoga warmup exercise. When she stopped her eyes remained closed.

Within the mysterious light which illuminated the basement room, Sharon looked over at the ghostly twin of hers whom Karen had inexplicably referred to as her father. If this creature was to die, she considered with growing unease, what would happen to her?

"Are you... *alright?*" Sharon asked, immediately realizing how stupid she must have sounded asking that question of a dead girl. Karen reopened her eyes and cocked her head, regarding Sharon stiffly – mechanically. *Like a puppet.*

"I am... fine," Karen replied. "There is nothing wrong with me." Karen uncocked her head and again looked dead straight.

"You've... changed. Are you al... are you still... you?"

"Yes I am," Karen replied politely – coolly. A gentle smile played on her full young lips, lending an unsettling chill to her beauty. "I am quite alright, after all." Karen's smile deepened and grew wider, and she let out a giggle so wholly out of context it made Sharon shiver.

"Though it has been quite a bore doing the same thing over and over again for an eternity." She lifted her hands, miming the sewing of a dress, ignoring Sharon completely. Sharon tucked her head down in her arms, closed her eyes and wished she were anywhere else, in bed, asleep.

Randall searched the house carefully but was unable to find any sign that either of the men outside had been *inside*, or had attempted to rob the place. He remembered being told to expect a lawyer of sorts – come to pick up a young woman – Sharon – in the early afternoon. *Strange. This all seems like trouble, but I can't prove a damned thing. If that guy in the car is the lawyer, then I'm in hot water boy, unless I can prove those two had a fight – which was probably the case.*

He stood in the walkway connecting the living room and the master dining room to see whether he could hear anything, but the house was completely silent – even the floorboards. This in itself disturbed him. The woman dying in an accident

(?)

was *one* thing – he could in no way be blamed for *that* – but *those* two... and the *car*... it didn't add up. He called the Sheriff's office again, afraid that if he didn't, it would be his ass. *Busy...*

Karen walked over to the lookalike Sharon – the masquerading Daniel Nelson – which was completely motionless now. It neither raised a finger nor batted an eyelash. The man who had subjected her to so much pain over such a long period of time – such harrowing, dehumanizing abuse... was gone. "He's not here anymore," she said more to herself than anyone else.

Sharon raised her head drowsily and looked about, having lost her night vision. "Karen? Did you say something?"

"My father – *look!*" Karen pointed at the spectral double, which was now surrounded – and then engulfed – by a glow like an orgy of bright lights – lights so bright that *things* could be seen in them. The form writhed and convulsed – or so it appeared. She realized it was some sort of supernatural illusion meant as an assault on her senses – it was only the light playing its tricks like a nightclub strobe.

And then it was no longer an illusion. The Other Sharon's features began to shift around like a pile of loose puzzle pieces being scrambled together by a small child, or a deck of cards manipulated by a skilled magician's sleight of hand – the jumbling up into unusable configurations of real muscle, skin and human flesh. Not *real* real, but real enough – as real as a swarm of slimy constricting vines. This ghost woman – a carbon copy of herself – was slowly and painfully shapeshifting into... a man. A man, battered and worn, maybe in his late 40s – it was hard to tell in the overpowering glare. He was naked – that much she could make out – but his form passed so quickly that his features had no chance to register. The entire unbelievable scene had become too much to bear, and Sharon turned away just as the body disintegrated into a blinding glow of light and became... dust.

Gone. As though it had never been there at all.

Karen watched her living companion turn away in combined horror and confusion with a calm intuitive understanding. After all, the things Sharon had seen were completely alien to her. The apparition felt sorry for the living human being – and at the same time angry at the woman for bringing her back to the horror Karen equated with that life – terrible suffering and loneliness – angrier than she had been with any other creature in her life that God had created in his wisdom. As much as she held this female in contempt – as if her very presence were spoiling death as she had come to understand it over the past century – which admittedly was not very much at all. Had she been called back to pay for her father's indiscretions, or as some other hellish breed of punishment? It was not her place to see these things. Karen screamed within herself a terrible silent scream, her eyes blazing in her rage.

Sharon swallowed nervously and managed to croak, "So... that's... that was your *father*, eh?" She forced herself to look at the spot where the creature had lain. To her surprise, not a trace remained. "Karen... where did he... where did your father... *go?*"

"Away. I would suggest, for your own sake, that you did the same."

"Before I go, I have to tell you I did not come here to stir up any cosmic unrest, but I'd have to admit that this all scares the living *shit* out of me and... I've never felt this way before – I can't explain it – what I'm *feeling*... Jesus *God!*" Sharon screamed. "I had these fucking... *vines* all over me – like *snakes!*" She ran her fingers roughly through her hair and stomped her feet. "And I fucking *hate* snakes alright! Dammit! *GAH!*" She glared at Karen. "I can't *handle* this shit! What the hell is going *on* in this fucking house? What?!"

"More than you know," Karen answered matter of factly.

Randall heard a scraping outside the door, as if someone were scraping his shoes on the welcome mat before coming in. He figured, though he had not spoken to him directly, that desk woman Myra or whatever must have tipped off the Sheriff. *Crap,* he thought. *If she blabbed everything I told her, he won't wanna hear shit about what I think happened... not fucking sure about what happened, but I better come up with something quick or I'll be one stupid mumbling motherfucker on my sorry assed way to jail.*

Four sharp knocks on the door confirmed his suspicions. The knocks – a neat *thwack thwack* he admired despite his fears of being blamed for a double or even triple murder – such things never went by him unnoticed – reverberated nicely through the heavy oaken door. He remained seated in the tall, finely carved wooden chair at the far end of the living room, the main entranceway visible to his left. He turned to watch it with nervous interest – the whole scene dryly fit the mindset of this small town, its sparse population spread out and isolated from each other with a huge expanse of acreage dividing them.

Such ostentatiousness was a pet peeve of Randall's and, having worked these years for one of them, he saw firsthand just how wasteful *their kind* could be. Spoiled or not, it was his own *ass* that he had to worry about. He kept his eyes on the locked front door.

Four more loud crisp knocks broke the silence. *Thwack. Thwack. Thwack. Thwack.* More rustling at the doorstep like he had heard earlier. He gripped the oversized rounded edges of the chair's armrests and waited for a *voice.*

"Hello. Mr. Alcott? This is Sheriff Malcolm of the Old Forge Police precinct of New York State... We're aware of the situation out here with the two bodies..."

We? Randall thought. *There's more than one of them out there?*

"...and we'd like you to please open the door so you can answer some questions. Please," the voice on the other side of the door continued firmly – although it could have emanated from the other side of the world. "Don't let's make this harder on you than it already is."

"Shit!" Randall exclaimed without thinking.

Sharon sensed Karen's presence approaching her, even though she had lowered her head again, and hovered in and out of sleep. "Yes Karen? What is it honey?" she asked, feeling a surge of affection for this young girl – the words 'spirit,' 'ghost,' or 'apparition' no longer sat right on her tongue – and even a sense of kinship – why; she did not know. They looked into each other's eyes.

"I'm... *sorry*," Karen said.

Sharon smiled. "Sorry for *what* dear?"

Karen began pacing about, looking at the floor. "My manners before... I'm not usually like this... But that night... the night I..."

"Yes?"

"I'd... rather not *talk* about that now."

Sharon nodded and wiped her eyes, wishing she had her contacts in so she could take all this in more clearly and commit it to memory. *Just two days ago I never would have thought this possible.* How many times had she berated David and Beatrice so smugly and self righteously regarding their passing interests in the occult and mysterious 'other' religions of the world?

"I don't yet feel quite right here... the *assimilation...*"

Sharon croaked, her throat dry. "Assimilation?"

"Your *world* – your manners – so *strange* to me..."

"I understand but – how would you *assimilate* as you are now?"

The girl fluttered her tattered housedress in a pretend wind, looking more like a playful girl her age than a long dead – *God, could it be true?* – ghost. Karen sighed. "I am part of you now – am I not?"

Sharon looked at the spirit quizzically. Karen continued, answering herself.

"Yes I am." Karen smiled, pleased with the sensation the words left on her cold dead lips.

"I don't follow you..."

"*Like* you. *Part* of you. One *person*. In time, one *mind*. It's becoming *clear* now. I can *feel* it..."

"I still don't get it. I'm new to this, being..." Sharon swallowed, her throat parched.

"I was like you... *alive*... there are so many levels to this existence..."

"Is that the word for it – *levels?*" Sharon laughed nervously, her voice hoarse. "Then again, you would know better than me." She swallowed again drily and leaned against the concrete wall, trying to relax. She had never felt so drained before. "But…"

Grinning, Karen repied, "Yes, please go on."

"Have you seen… God?" Sharon looked directly into Karen's clear hazel eyes in anticipation of her answer. Karen pirouetted, her fluttering dress stirring up a welcome breeze in the stale basement air. That can't be, Sharon thought, alarmed at what this implied. *How can I feel that if she doesn't really exist, and I'm not… dead?* Karen, smiling, continued spinning, and said nothing, until her beautiful youthful face became a blur of motion in the darkness. Sharon drew into herself and fell to her knees, hands to her tightening temples.

Sharon pondered her question, thinking how foolish an educated woman like her could be some times. So foolish, so numb to subtle nuance and shading. Life was like a painter's palette, so many colors and hues therein – from primary colors to tertiary and still more yet to be mixed by the artist at work. Thousands of colors yet to be blended, named, blended again, and forgotten. *You couldn't be blinder, Sharon Langhorn*; she scolded herself, *even if it were daylight down here. Stupid – stupid – stupid! Sharon* had received her answer – loud and clear. And yet the girl danced, and said nothing.

"Hello Mr. *Alcott!*" the thickly voiced man – probably a chain smoker – yelled impatiently.

"I have some men at the back of the house, so odds are – short of a miracle – you'll *not* be going anywhere without us knowing about it, so I ask you *again* to *please* open the door before this gets any *worse* for you son. I will *not* ask you nicely a *third* time."

The Sheriff looked around at the skeleton crew of half a dozen would be bounty hunters he had assembled in hopes of flushing out the 'bad guy' holed up in the widow's house – correction – her *ex* house. Right now the place belonged to no one he was aware of – he knew nothing of any next of kin the widow may have had.

The Sheriff, who was not even in uniform – Myrna had raised him at home – removed his cowboy hat and fanned himself, then looked down at his khaki pants, thick grey cotton shirt – which had brought on the sweats in the first place - white V necked undershirt, black nylon socks, and dark brown Hush Puppies, which completed the ensemble. His dedicated yet undernourished deputy bore a striking resemblance to that map feller, Daniel Boone – who had also been called into action as an *emergency* deputy shortly after the situation was brought to his attention. Also present was Jack, a local star from the High School football team, and Jimmy, a friend of Bobby's at Al's Bicycle Shop.

Jimmy scratched his head with a free finger of the hand holding onto his omnipresent baseball cap, still trying to piece together

1) A stranger – near death – in a busted up convertible
2) A man apparently fallen to his death, and
3) Another man, barricaded in a dead woman's house for no reason he could fathom.

Bizarre. Just fucking bizarre. Did I mention we're standing around here scratching our asses like a buncha idiots?

The Sheriff walked back and reached into the open driver's side window of his private car – Old Forge was not the most generous of municipalities. *God knows the townsfolk wouldn't shell out for an actual Sheriff's car. Would a few bucks each kill 'em?* He looked around at his makeshift posse. *And how about an actual police force?*

He pulled out a rather worse for wear bullhorn and, after speaking a few vowels to test out its speaker, said, "Alcott? If you knew me son, you'd know I'm a *patient* man. But once you've made me get this old *thing* out, then you'd know my saintly patience is wearin a *little* thin. So Alcott – *Randall* is it? – *please* just open the door and let's talk about these two *men* we've got out here. One's near *dead* son – the other done went off to meet his Maker a long time ago. Doctor's on his way – should be here shortly."

He put five sausage thick fingers over the bullhorn's mouthpiece – though he could have simply released the button – and called over his shoulder, "Did we get in touch with Doc Allen yet over at the Yarbroughs' place?"

"Still at the house," the deputy replied. "Delivering twins, ya know!"

"*Shit!*" the Sheriff replied, finger still on the megaphone's button, and spiked his hat football style off the ground in a manner which would have done Jack proud. He stopped short of stomping on it, and turned to address the deputy. "Just get that man on his beeper again, *will* ya – twins or *no* twins. To *hell* with 'em!"

"Yessir," the deputy said, and ran to put in a call to Myrna on his car's two way radio.

Leonard, meanwhile, teetered on the edge of consciousness, and wondered why the elephant in a cowboy hat kept on playing a hotwired clarinet in a distorted Jimi Hendrix style solo through an arena sized array of classic tube driven Marshall cabinets driven by a series of daisy chained power amplifier heads. *Wow*, Leo thought, *I didn't know elephant clarinet could rock so hard! Party on – party to the max! Uhhh...*

Randall, meanwhile, knew the private party he had thrown for himself would be over real fast. *They'll break the door down if they have to,* he thought, resigning himself to the unsavory image of being forcibly yanked out of his chair by who knows what band of inbreds Malcolm had scraped up. Suddenly he had the impression he was not alone in the room – he saw no one, but felt someone right next to him.

He followed the presence with his eyes as it moved toward and hovered over the doorway, where it flowed down the door and sank into the carpet. He tried to ignore it and concentrate on the matter at hand. *The matter at hand – what a stupid expression. God I'm in deep shit here.*

Chapter Fourteen

"There's someone upstairs," Karen said, "Large – tall – a tall man." Karen looked at Sharon and again cocked her head. "Do you know him?"

"Well, I'd need a better description – that's pretty vague... Wait a minute!" Sharon bolted upright, rising quickly to her feet. "It must be Leonard! He must have gotten into the house somehow! Karen, he doesn't know I'm down here! I've gotta try and contact him and tell him about you too! Won't you help me find the staircase so I can get out of here? It's getting dark in here."

"Not really – your eyes are betraying you. I can't let you leave until I've shown you something you need to see."

Sharon felt shaken and disappointed by the ghost girl's response. "Now listen *here* Karen," she asserted. "It's just great how we've *bonded* here – human to *dead* person and all that – you really gave me some *pointers* on that *afterlife* stuff. *Really*. But my ride's here – and I'll have to be *going* now."

"You don't seem to *understand*, Miss *Langhorn*, you –"

"That's Ms. Langhorn. *Miiizzzzz!*" Sharon interrupted, and broke down in a fit of nervous laughter.

"I still don't understand."

"*Miss* Ms. *Messurs* Misses *Miiizzzzz!!* What a *crock* of shit! Fairer *sex* my liberated *ass*."

Karen cocked her head again. Sharon continued.

"Words are the foundation of a civilized society, don't you think? Sort of a hobby of mine. I wouldn't say you were the delicate type. I'd say you're strong and you don't even know it."

"*Me*, miss? I don't think you're talking to the right girl. *Strong?* I'm not so sure. The things I've had to... *live...* through... *Sassy* is what *he* would say." Karen motioned to indicate the spot on the floor her father's spirit had occupied moments ago. "But *strong?* I believe you're mistaken. I've tried to be *civil*, though, even to *him*. It's how God has intended. That's what we learned at school, and at church. Sometimes I'm not sure about the teachers, but no one would dare question the Holy Word."

"Times have changed... Never mind. I gave you a compliment and I'm sticking to it."

"Extraordinary..." Karen spoke the word in a breathy reverberating tone which reminded Sharon the girl was no longer human.

"Who, *me?*" Sharon responded. She found this young spirit fascinating, and felt a reassurance from somewhere deep inside – inexplicably – that this being from the past would *not* harm her.

"It is *you* who are strong. I find it... refreshing. For so long I've been in this place... not *this* place," Karen spread her hands wide and moaned, "but a terrifying empty place of white light."

"Did you say *light?*"

Karen, unmoving, locked eyes with Sharon.

"You don't have to answer if you don't want to... I... think I'll *rest* awhile." Sharon again lowered her head, and closed her eyes.

Karen lowered her head as well, her body seeming to shimmer and undulate like a kite in a strong breeze – trapped in a kaleidoscope of subdued light. Sharon opened her eyes and stared. *This is what she must look like when she's... sleeping? Do ghosts sleep? Why did I bring her back?*

The best way to play this, Randall thought, *is just to open the door nice and easy and ask them what the fuss is all about. Tell them you were downstairs – upstairs – whatever – just tell them you were doing something for the widow and you couldn't hear them.*

"Randall I won't ask again. You open this door now – hear?"

No, that won't work. What work could you say you were doing for her? She's dead.

"Boy you in there? The longer we all hafta wait..."

Just stay calm. Don't shake. Just open the door nice and easy-like.

"...the worse off for you it's gonna be."

Just open the door, stupid. He did, and met the Sheriff's surprised expression – a perfect match for his own. The Sheriff's fist was pulled back and poised, apparently frozen in mid knock. An uncomfortable silence passed between the two men for a long moment. Then the chubby man in the cowboy hat and makeshift uniform spoke.

"Are you uh, *Randall*, the widder's *chauffeur*?"

"Yes Sheriff. Yes I am."

"*Well* then – we been *out* there for the better part of an *hour* – ah ain't got muh *watch* on – *Jimmy!*" He looked over to the young de facto deputy standing on the front lawn beside Haskel's dead body. "Is that *right* son? About an *hour*?"

Jimmy checked his watch, nodded and shouted, "Yep. *Bout* right."

"Fine – *see*," the Sheriff said, looking back at his potential suspect. "I'm not the typa man who talks all this My Time Is Money malarkey, but the thing is a man can get mighty *antsy* standin around out here lookin at his *toes* while there's not so much as a *peep* comin from behind thet *door*."

Randall paused for a few seconds before answering. He knew it wasn't necessary to answer the man, seeing as he had not – in so many words – been asked a question. However he felt under the circumstances that he should say something. "I know how you must feel Sheriff, but I was down in the basement, and it's really hard to hear anything down th–"

"Sheriff!" Daniel, the other emergency deputy shouted, waving his arms to rally the small group around the Sheriff's car.

The Sheriff considered the wisdom of turning his back on the man in the doorway, then shrugged and took the chance. "What *is* it Daniel?"

"Sheriff," Daniel shouted again, and pointed off towards the convertible. "One o'them *bodies!* It's *movin!*"

Back at the office Leonard's co workers were gossiping over why he had yet to return from or call them back about the Shifton Langhorn property transaction. Leonard Rothstein was known by his colleagues as a highly conscientious and considerate man – if not a little hot headed and impatient at times – a true rarity among 'his breed,' the big business corporate set. Old Man Shostrom, the most visible and involved member of the firm's founding power trio, often called Leo into the main office for a fatherly pat on the back and a steady stream of 'how you doin son,' along with a wide smile stretched across the thin lips of that wrinkled – extremely rich – face.

Shostrom's middle son had died in combat during the Korean war, and of the two sons he had left, none of them warmed his heart as much as this idealistic fiery driven Jewish boy fresh out of college, who – against all odds and at the risk of being thrown head first out the door by security – marched into Shostrom's own private sanctum – occupying the final 'gauntlet' level at the rear of the firm's lush – some would say excessive – five thousand square foot main office, and demanded – in the nicest way possible – he be made 'part of the team.' Leonard had always been Shostrom's favorite employee for years since. The Old Man would often buzz each cubicle to inquire, "Where's Rothstein?" making Leo something of a legend among the newer recruits – which only made him want to work harder. And harder.

Now – with Leonard gone less than one whole working day – his absence was deeply felt among the cubicle jockeys. No doubt panic and hysteria would break out had anyone found out about his accident. The fur would really fly in the kennel then.

"I wonder if Rothstein sealed the deal yet," said James T. to Cloe, the twenty something A student and hacker *wünderkind*.

"Dunno. I guess the *Genius* has something really *hot* going, or else he would've *called* us, no?"

James T., the Junior Advertising Executive's apprentice, was not satisfied. "Sure, but I don't *buy* it. No, I think something's *wrong* in Wonderland. The Son is never far from the Manger. I don't like it."

"Settle down little man," kidded Cloe. "It's probably not as bad as all that. I'd advise you to enjoy your late lunch, sip your coffee, grab your coat with a clear conscience and *go home*. So Cloe *says*, and Cloe is *never* wrong."

"*Oh* is that *so*?"

"That's *right*."

"Okay Sybil, whatever you say."

"Dare you doubt my *power?*"

"I'm not. It's just that it doesn't feel *kosher.* But you're right. No use wasting a good workaholic's lunch hour thinking about the *Messiah.*"

"There you go – the Genius is a big boy. If there were any trouble – God *forbid* – then I'm positive he'd blow the whistle pronto. Okay *Pancho?*"

"Fuck you *Cisco.*"

"That's my *man* talkin. Now be a good little girl and finish your sandwich."

"Riddle."

"Shoot."

"Whadda ya call two office workers who do two times the overtime and wanna grab lunch before burnout?"

"I uh call it Cloe and Jimmy – the Twinkie Twins, the only two jerks lame enough to take a lunch break at four thirty in the afternoon."

"Four thirty *two.*"

"I stand corrected, James T. *Kirk.*"

"Hey don't call me that."

"Man you couldn't help it if your parents were both diehard Trekkies, now could you?"

"*Ha* ha."

"*Now* you're talkin. I see the ham and cheese is finally kickin in."

"Hey I don't play around. I pay big bucks for this, bitch."

Cloe leaned in close. "I love it when you talk dirty."

Jimmy reeled in mock horror. "Aaaah, *Cooties!*"

"*Excuuuse* me!"

"You're excused. Another thing," Jimmy said, taking a big bite of his sandwich. "It's James and *Cloe*, not Cloe and *James*."

"Sir yes *sir* mister fancy pants apprentice to the junior advertising executive *sir*, says the lowly miss key puncher."

"A key puncher who's saved my *ass* more than a few times."

"Don't you forget it."

"*Yes* sir – *no* sir."

Randall had been attempting to plead his case – with little success – to the Sheriff, who was now too busy with the man in the convertible. The deputies had abandoned pinning him down at the door with guns drawn. Randall himself was curious – not in the least because the man's survival drew heat off himself, but also out of simple concern. *Who was he, anyway? And why was he here in the first place?*

He highly suspected that this was the lawyer Rothstein whom the widow had been expecting on Monday. Here it was almost Monday evening, and odds were good this well dressed individual was he. Randall thought about tapping the Sheriff on the shoulder and telling him this, but then decided against it. It had been the Sheriff's contention that the widow's chauffeur had guiltily holed up behind the woman's locked door. Attempting to set things right at this point might make matters worse. And lately, 'making matters worse' seemed a new addition to his job description. He wisely decided to put it off until the Sheriff asked for his opinion. Which he did not.

"So," Myrna's voice called over the police radio – an early model which should have been retired years ago, but instead stood proudly as the only link between the Sheriff's office and the outside world. "What's going on out there fellas? Come in – anybody out there?" All she could hear was static – loud brassy static that Myrna recognized as an incomplete connection – one of many conversations unconsummated.

Myrna clicked off the radio with her thumb, feeling she had given ample time to have garnered a response, and resigned herself to waiting until someone thought it important enough to call back.

"Sharon."

Sharon slowly came around, remembering where she was, and whom – or what – she was with. "Yes?" What could this spirit want? Sharon, who had no idea, was not about to ask directly, but kept her strong suspicions to herself.

"Sharon, *please* wake up."

"Leave me *alone* – I need to *rest*..."

"*No* Sharon," Karen commanded in an authoritative adult tone. "There's no *time*."

"Time... for *what?*"

"I brought you here for a *reason*. It is not mine to forge my destiny alone, nor can I without your attendance." The spirit seemed bathed in a fog of conflicting emotion. "Awaken so I can take you to where... *it*... happened."

"Attendance? What do you mean? What do you need me for?"

"Aren't you listening? You are a stubborn one." Karen intoned, hands on her hips like a mother in disapproval of a willful petulant child.

249

"David would always call me that," Sharon replied, thinking *I miss him*.

"Get up! I have no time to waste on any more of this foolishness!" Karen made as if to pounce on Sharon, who danced back out of her grasp.

"Wh – where do you want me to go?"

"Not far... you're almost there," Karen said, beckoning the living woman around a corner and into another alcove. "I *must* have you accompany me."

Sharon looked about her. "What's so *special* about this place anyway? Isn't it bad enough you won't let me *leave*? I'm supposed to be *out* of here. I've already had to pee in the corner – and I can still *smell* it! What about Number *Two?*"

"You must *understand* – the sooner you *help* me, the sooner you can go back to your *life*... out *there*." Karen pointed upward, but Sharon knew she spoke in far broader terms than the house itself, or even the surrounding town, but instead referred to the cold impersonal confusing world of the living.

"Who are you," the large man in the cowboy hat asked Leonard. "We been waiting for you ta snap *out* of it for some time now. Speak *up* son." The Sheriff removed his hat and turned it over in his hands. "*I'm* the *Sheriff*. Sheriff *Malcolm's* the name."

"You the *wha* –?" Leonard blinked his eyes hard and then rubbed them with both hands. "Sh-*Sheriff?*"

"Yep. I'm the *Law* around here – me and my *deputies* that is." He looked Leo over and did not like what he saw. "*Listen* fella – that's a pretty nasty *gash* you've got on your *head* there."

"...Gash?" Leo hesitantly put his hand up to his left temple. All he felt was dried sweat.

"*No* son – the *other* side."

"Oh." Leonard touched his left hand to his right temple, which was moist and sticky with what felt to him like warm maple syrup. He knew without looking at his hand that this had to be blood, but he looked at his palm anyway. *Uh huh. You got it. Blood.*

"You *alright* fella?" the Sheriff asked. "You've been out for a while. There anything we can get you? *Jimmy!*" he yelled to the deputy. "We get through to the Doc yet?"

Jimmy lowered his head. "No sir."

"Damn. Well mister, we'll just have to make do with a little Old Forge hospitality until the cleanup wagon arrives." *If it arrives*, he echoed silently.

"Great." Leonard glared at the grey haired man balefully, and winced as a sharp pain stabbed through his temple. He instinctively clapped his right hand to the wound – an obvious mistake – the pain in his arm was far worse. *Probably broken.* He was not prepared to deal with it. Leonard was a fairly accomplished amateur athlete – he played more for the exercise and the opportunity to small talk clients in a non work environment – people had a tendency to be more open about their wants and needs when he and the client could both break a sweat together. Breaking any bones in his body was a tragedy he had hoped to avoid in this lifetime.

"My arm," he said, eyes squeezed shut so he could not see the man rotating his hat in his stubby fingered hands like a wheel. "It's *broken*, I think." He took a deep breath, which hurt – *everything* hurt – and he strained to keep his voice level and calm. Not like those gasping idiots who managed a few nonsensical last syllables before biting it. If he could *sound* okay then maybe he would *be* okay – he had nothing to lose in trying. He lowered his voice, but still gasped, "My arm. Broke. Broken."

"I – we – kinda figured that." The portly man momentarily stopped rotating his hat in order to scratch his head. "Can't get ahold of the doctor – not just yet anyway."

"Great," Leo said again. "I can't wait. I'm certain the local medical staff in this one horse town is top notch, Sheriff Clint."

The Sheriff stopped scratching his head. "This is *no* time to start acting *smart* now mister. I'm just tryin to piece together the *story* here real *neat* like – if you were not aware – and there are a *lot* of missing pieces."

"Few things in life are ever that easy."

"Ain't *that* the truth."

"And as for *me*, I don't think – *ouch!* – all the King's men are about to wipe up this mess just yet. I guess... you'll be wanting my *name*, Sheriff."

"It'll help."

"Rothstein. *Leonard* Rothstein."

"Glad ta *meetcha*. I'd shake your *hand* but you've broken enough bones already."

"*God* is it that *bad?*"

"I'm no doctor, but I'd lay pretty good odds it's bad enough – as bad as you'd want it to be anyway."

"That's the problem," Leo said wryly. "I don't *want* it to. I'm a *lawyer* by the way."

"Lawyer?"

"Yeah. I'm supposed to pick up a Sharon – Ms. Sharon *Langhorn* – my firm's client – at around four o'clock. By the look of the big hand I'd say it was *way* past then." He heard a noise behind him and turned his head, but the pain in his neck was so sharp it stopped him – there was no one back there anyway. "Listen, why don't you forget about me for a few minutes – I don't even know what I'm saying."

"Well I can't do that but I'll give ya a little breathing room until you're able to answer a few questions."

"Ow!"

"What is it – something *hurt?*"

"*Everything* hurts – but that's *beside* the point – I understand your predicament. The '*Ow!*' was for a cop asking a 'few *questions*.' No offense."

"None taken. And that's a good word for it – *predicament*. I'd say a feller in a crashed *car* – a *City* type *lawyer* for Christ's sake – and a *dead* man on the *lawn* in a sleepy old town like Old Forge – I'd say that's pretty much a *predicament*, I will tell you *that*. An even *bigger* predicament," he continued, putting his hat back on his thick silver head of hair, "is that *no one* here is telling me what's going *on*."

"Well, having never defended Jesus *Christ*, I'm *flattered* at the *prospect* – but since I've been *out* for I don't know *how* long, I *couldn't* have answered you *anyway*."

"Are you *always* such a *smart* aleck?"

"Hey, it's what they *pay* me for. Being *smart*."

"Now just wait *here* – "

"I don't *think* I'm going *anywhere*."

"Uh, yeah. I'm gonna get that fella *Randall*. I don't like his face. Drove us *crazy* with his bullshit – not answering the door when I knocked."

"Who's he?"

"The widder's show *furr* – that's what he *says* anyway. Don't remember seein *him* before, but I don't know *everyone* round these parts either. The widder – God rest her soul."

"Yeah I just *heard* about that. Right after the *doctor* crashed *into* her.

(?)

I don't suppose that's him over there."

"Is that right?"

Leo, suddenly agitated, said truthfully, "I don't *know*. I have no *idea*... I'm not really in the *mood*, okay? I could be fucking *bleeding* to death *internally* here."

"I *know* you're injured – *Rothstein*, is it?"

Leo nodded.

"But it's my *job* to find out the truth, *especially* if it's about *murder*."

"I don't know about any murder. All I know is when he –"

"Yes? *Go* on."

"*Wait* a minute. You don't think I *did* that to him, *do* you?" Leo said, as he pointed to the stiffening corpse on the grass.

"I don't *know*. Just like I don't know *why* a man *crashed* a perfectly good *expensive* car into the *side* of a *house* – or why *another* man is *dead* and stiff as a *board* with a face like somethin scared the *bejeezus* out of him. In *that* case, I don't *know* much of *anything*."

"No you don't," Leo said, offended at the insinuation of him having to do with some wild man's suicide.

"Sir... oh hell," the Sheriff muttered between clenched teeth, and took off his hat again, intending to spike it – yet stopping in mid pitch in a comical display of vain restraint – he simply did not want to get his hat dirty. "I'm not that *good* at bein *coy*, Mr. Rothstein. I ain't no high falutin' Manhattan *lawyer* like you."

Leo could almost taste the hatred this man must be harboring. "I can't complain."

"*Okay*, Laughing Boy. I'll talk to *you* after you get the rest of that *sass* out yer system." Malcolm turned and faced the first deputy he saw – a man sporting a hang dog expression.

"Oh *God*," Leonard moaned – depressed and helpless with the pain. "I'm really up shit's creek now, and without a fuckin paddle."

"Whattsa *matter* deputy? You look like your *dog* just died."

"Sir?"

"Yes man – what *is* it?"

"The *suspect*, sir."

"*Randall?* What *about* 'im?"

"He..." The deputy swallowed hard and braced himself, expecting really soon to be yelled at by a man in a cowboy hat. "He... got *away*, sir."

The blood ran entirely out of the Sheriff's face. "Why don't you just say that *again* – *clearly*-like," he hissed from between vise grip teeth. "Cause I *didn't* quite *hear* ya right the *first* time."

255

"Well…" The first deputy scratched his head, hoping to stall for time for lack of a better plan, until he came up with a better explanation – with the way the Sheriff looked, he was more worried about getting *shot* than *fired* – but was unable to come up with one. He simply looked at the Sheriff, shrugged meekly, and closed his eyes tightly, waiting for the sound of a gun's hammer being cocked. The portly man shook dramatically in an Actors' Studio portrayal of restrained anger worthy of *Boss Hog* from *The Dukes of Hazzard*.

"That's all you've got to say? *Weeeeaaaaalll?!* You *dumbass!*" the Sheriff screamed as he spiked his hat against the ground. "Now I don't know *Shit* from *Sherlock* about this case. Goddammit Christ Almighty *Jesus* and the *fucking* Holy *Trinity!* Am I the only poor *bastard* who cares about this *job* – who thinks it's *important* – am I the only *one?*" Jimmy stood silent for a bit as he thought it over. The rest of the posse froze in place and tried to turn invisible. Both men looked everywhere but in each other's eyes – and at the two bodies – one living, one dead – which had brought them here.

Bobby swallowed. "Well uh… I wouldn't go as far as callin you a bastard…"

"I don't wanna hear *one* word outta *you* boy – not *one* word. You tryin to make *excuses?* Shut *up*, ya *hear* me?!"

"Bu-*buhhh…*" Bobby stammered as the other deputies stifled their urge to giggle – and thanked God they weren't being raked over the coals instead. The Sheriff struggled to calm himself down.

"Go home, deputy. Just… go *home*."

"Shuh *Sheriff*, he said he was going for *help* – said we had the wrong *idea…*"

"Well I had the wrong idea about *sumthin* – about *you!* Go for help my *ass* – he *killed* that feller! Do you *understand?*" the Sheriff asked, not expecting to receive an answer.

"I… guess so?" the deputy responded, and immediately regretted answering.

"You *guess* so? I'd say more like you *know* so, *if'n* you're mah *deputy*." The Sheriff paused, picking up his hat and dusting it off with his left hand before placing it back on his head with his right. "So why dontcha jest take yerself on home and think about it for a spell. I can handle these two for now." He turned around dismissively and regarded the remaining deputies.

"Yes *sir*," the deputy responded, as he did an about face and headed to his mother's house without a further word in his defense. *He'll cool off. Maybe.*

Too bad about that Randall character, the Sheriff thought. *I'm not sure he did anything, but that Bobby… I'd better round up the boys and get a handle on the situation.* He walked over to Jimmy and Daniel Boone. Daniel jerked back nervously at the fatherly hand the Sheriff placed on his shoulder. "Daniel, would you please fetch that boy there Jack and ask him to come on over?" Daniel nodded, and sprinted towards the rear of the house.

Just as quickly, Jack emerged, eager to be filled in on what had happened while he was chain smoking at the rear of the estate over the past half hour. The Sheriff gestured to include them as a group. "Not much else to see here boys. Who wants to stay back and see if this feller comes to and gives us an official type statement? After all this is a man in *pain* with some serious injuries – where in *hell* is that damn *doctor*?"

To the credit of the deputies appointed, they all expressed an interest in and willingness to stay by the injured man in hopes he could tell them something they didn't know – as they really only knew very little. The Sheriff smiled at their dedication, but noted that now the escaped suspect was top priority. The Sheriff selected Jimmy, whom he had guessed to be the sharpest of the three, to stay – and said a silent prayer that the other two would not be that great a distraction.

"Son?" he asked Jack.

"Yes Sheriff?"

"Don't be *lightin* up in muh *car*, y'*hear?*"

"Yessir."

Jesus Christ, the Sheriff thought, *I picked the wrong man to send home. Myrna's right though. I can be a bit hot headed.*

Karen stood in the alcove for what seemed like an eternity over a drowsy gritty Sharon Langhorn – whose entire body was caked in dried sweat and reeling from waves of heat and cold. In her semi dream state, she was overcome by a creeping sense of foreboding, and it was then that she sensed the spirit standing nearby, her dress still fluttering in that otherworldly breeze. Where is it coming from? Sharon thought. There aren't any windows – hardly any air to breathe.

The breeze stopped as the spirit offered Sharon a soft cool hand. "I feel dirty," Sharon moaned. "Can't you just leave me *alone?* If it will put you to rest, or end this *nightmare,*" Sharon weakly begged, "then please tell me what it *is* and I'll *do* it. If this is your *home* I don't *want* it – I don't even *like* this house – I've been here too long *already!*" Sharon's voice rose along with her ire. "I don't wanna *be* here anymore!"

"Come," Karen beckoned warmly, hand outstretched invitingly. "Soon this will pass and you may do as you please, but first you must help me, Sharon."

"I... I need a shower," Sharon stated, her voice an apathetic monotone. *"Me?* Help *you?* You don't even *exist!"*

Karen ignored the insult. "You *can* help me – you're like a *mother* to me."

"Oh *God*."

"*Please*. You're all I *have*." Karen replied – an innocent girl with a sweet smile playing across full sensuous lips.

If she'd only made it to adulthood, she'd have been quite a beauty. She's already stunning, despite the filth. For the first time it dawned on Sharon this was not dirt, but blood. God! Dried blood!

"Take me back," Karen said, "to the place where it... *happened*." The spirit seemed to sigh, as if mourning its own passing. Sharon sighed as well, considering her own fate.

"I... don't know if I *can*," Sharon said, still shocked that this dead girl had called her, 'Mother.' *Why do I feel so much pressure to help this thing?*

"Because you *have* to," Karen said, completing Sharon's thought. "It is meant to be. Your past and mine are intertwined – our fates will prove the same. Help me find *my* way, and you will find *yours*, Sharon Langhorn."

"I don't believe it."

"Have you no idea what's *happening* up there?"

Sharon felt curious yet offended. "Of *course* not – I've been stuck down *here* all this –" She stopped herself short. Of course this creature knew what was happening in this house. She *died* here. "What makes you think there's something going on? There's nobody upstairs – you're just trying to confuse me – and I'm scared *already*."

"What about the *dreams* you had – the *murders* – the large man *chasing* you – and the pigs – the *pigs!*" Karen shivered, and Sharon felt herself do the same.

"I *do* remember... was that *real?* Was that *you? God* how you *suffered* so."

"End my suffering then. I cannot go there alone." Karen pointed off into the darkness – so close – however to her impossibly far. "End his deception, which sought to entrap you."

Sharon shuddered. "Oh jeez. You mean those worms or vines or whatever? I thought I'd suffocated – dead – *Deado!* I still have no idea how it happened. I don't even think..." Her voice dropped to a whisper. "...it *did* happen."

"An illusion," Karen said. "As much as I am."

Sharon shorted. "I should have *known*."

"Always so smug. Do not *test* me, woman." Karen raised her arm palm out to Sharon, and a warm glow emanated from Karen's hand, seeming to bloom in Sharon's belly. Sharon's head felt heavy, and Karen's intent expression blurred and swam in her view, engulfed by a red warm mist that permeated the air around them. Sharon blinked rapidly, fighting to stay awake, however her effort was proven fruitless. She collapsed gently to the floor as she lapsed into a deep comatose sleep – helpless and oblivious.

Karen crouched over Sharon and placed both palms in the living woman's lap. The spirit stared unflinchingly at her unwitting savior, pondering the now dull recollection of her former life – other than the circumstances of its end – and probing Sharon's own living mind to confirm she had chosen correctly, before she did what she knew must be done.

The act itself was immensely easier – and less painful – than she could have imagined. In less than a minute, it was complete.

Randall ran through stalks and wild fields of corn, barley, peas and whatever Daniel Nelson had left to run its course. No one in the universe cared less than he for the fineries of agriculture, having grown up spoiled by the convenience of middle class city life. As he had gotten older and made his own way in the world – rife with mistakes and touched by his family's complacency – his father would often point out the difference between working 'hard' and 'smart.'

Well daddy would be a bit peeved about now, Randall thought as he pushed a clump of barley stalks away from his face, *cause I've been working hard all my life ever since I left home. Why did this have to happen to me? I'm not even supposed to be a fuckin driver! I didn't know the widow was in danger. Where the fuck am I?* Randall surveyed the endless expense of green – what *were* those things? – with deep regret. He saw neither road nor sign, and the anonymity of his surroundings was strangely comforting – at least it would be difficult for that Sheriff and his bullshit deputies to catch up with him and keep asking all those *stupid* questions.

They'll never find me here. Never did nothin, and they'll never find me... where the fuck am I anyway? Any direction he looked revealed nothing but more crops, and yielded more frustration for Randall Alcott, chauffeur to the now departed widow Shifton. *I might die out here in this heat*, he thought.

And he did.

Leonard, meanwhile, was found to have fractured both his legs, and was carted off to the hospital. And Sharon?

Chapter Fifteen

The body of Doctor Robert Haskel was driven back to his Manhattan apartment after a hysterical Tricia faxed the address to Jameson's Funeral Home in Tug Hill. Tricia went on – after a lengthy depression riddled two months of unemployment checks complete with a new addiction to sleeping pills – to work for another psychiatrist who originally had someone else in mind, but who ultimately took Tricia on after hearing of her circumstances after the tragic loss of a familiar colleague. His death had left her temporarily jobless, however for his wife –

(?)

the widow Haskel –

(?)

the trial had much deeper residual effects – not the least of all being the loss of a beloved mate. The children

(?)

were well taken care of through trust funds, half of which Katherine had funded – much to the private chagrin of Robert Haskel's hyper evolved ego. After all his thriving practice did provide him with an exceptional income – which would have rendered him a candidate for the Millionaire's club – had he not furnished his house – and his family – with the best there was, including several trips around the world for his daughter and son

(?)

'Several' had indeed been trimmed down to one, with both siblings taking in and immensely enjoying the sights together – despite the fact that the two blood Haskels had taken the sojourn to forget. After a time the Haskel children moved into their own apartments a brisk walk from one another in the multimedia Tribeca district, where artistic types hobnobbed with the homeless and S & M elite – as well as the homeless artists who occasionally dabbled in S & M in order to offer a cash only thrill to wide eyed tourists and bloated voyeuristic natives.

After a time, the two were able to put their father's death behind them, and sought the solace of companionship from the opposite sex – usually by frequenting local weekend club nights – only the respectable ones of course – unless they mock innocently allowed themselves to Le Bar Bat, the Space or Downtime. Both of Doctor Haskel's children managed after a bout of commitment free dating to fall into semi serious relationships – very *New Yawk* – which they had both, in their own way, found fulfilling. The daughter Minya

(?)

dubbed 'Meanie' by her brother

(?)

soon moved in with the man she was dating – subletting her choice apartment – incase things did not work out – to a girlfriend in the meantime. Branford, the son

(?)

dubbed 'Bran Flakes' by his sister however disliked the idea – at least at this particular time in his life – of 'moving in together' with someone. The thought of marriage – to anyone – was a far off bad dream in the back of his mind. Minya

(?)

too felt a bristling distaste for the Altar, and her brother knew – as some friends had surmised – that her 'commitment' to her boyfriend was not exactly cast in stone either. Their mother understandably bore the greatest burden regarding her husband's death – second only to Haskel's mother – who through rigorous crying jags, which *her* husband compliantly and sympathetically shared with her – if not in tears, then in the bitterly shared feeling of loss – was beside herself with grief – falling – literally – into a deep, brandy induced depression. The irony of resembling the out of favor washed up actress cliché was not lost on her; she and the Good Doctor had frequently launched into politically incorrect sendups of figures each had observed at work, the doctor having had a much deeper well of offbeat characters to choose from than Katherine – a political analyst – by sheer choice of profession – though some might argue this belief.

"I, the *great* Katherine B. Haskel," she would begin in her most convincing bombed actress/tramp voice, "am no longer needed by my endearing public. So it is through *no* small feat or teary eyed regret that I posthumously remove myself from the life of the Jet Set, and become a recluse – the Great Katherine *B.* Recluse – I *remarried* you know – and find myself no longer able to fulfill the duties of being your Silver Screen Queen – a title which I have held with both honor and vigor. Don't get me *wrong*; I loved being your queen – but I am also indebted to another – a man by the name of Robert. *Boy* he's a *swell* guy, isn't he? All of you – my loving subjects – have probably seen me in the trades – at this Gala event and that... he's one in a million – not the greatest in the *sack* maybe – but some of you male admirers of mine who have written in for my signed glossies – I hope you got 'em all and enjoyed them Honey – *swig* – have expressed an interest in wanting to... let's see, how do I put this *delicately* – *swig* – since there are so many rolling cameras watching

– *sip* – it behooves me to remain ladylike – so allow me to just say it as I know how. Many of you men out there," she continued as she pointed to an imaginary crowd, "have expressed an interest in me – and I'm flattered – to give me a good roll in the sack – you know, gulp down the old Gator Ade, spit in both hands, rub 'em together – *sip* – and go for it, giving this *body* a good old fashioned *workout* like the old man never did. Just push me down, rip off the jewelry and the silk blouse," she tugged at her own blouse for effect, "the bra – if I'm wearing one that day – I'm still pretty *firm* for my age – and just *plug* me *up!* Just – *haha* – put something in *every* hole I *got*. Just *fuck* me *bow* legged! Stick it in my *mouth* and everything! Now I don't want to appear *ungrateful* – read: how *dare* you *propose* such a thing? – did you really *think* I would *go* for it?! – but I think in a case like this, cooler heads have prevailed – do ya *get* me? – all I'm sayin is *thanks* for the memories kids, especially all of you who have been with me from the start – tracing my career from the screen tests, the magazines – *swig* – from the first movie to the last – gee that was a bomb wasn't it? – and everything in between. Again thank you," she bowed, "and from the bottom of my heart," here she placed her hand on her bosom, "I love you *all!*"

"Mother."

It was common for Minya

(?)

or Branford to find the place a mess after she binge drank – oh Meanie! Bran Flakes! You missed the premier! – which sadly was most days. The remaining monies from her personal savings – and the Haskel joint account – would keep her afloat in Brandys ... and the politician she worked for had let her go over two weeks ago, having cited 'controversial behavior in a political setting', and 'inappropriate unprofessional behavior in an employee' as grounds for dismissal.

Word spread fast in the cutthroat government game, and a highly visible 'aggravated discharge' could now almost *guarantee* unemployment later. Maybe for *years*. The kids dropped by on a regular basis to clean out the house

(?)

they grew up in – now the house she *threw* up in – and put their alcoholic mother to bed. They lacked the heart to grill her about seeking help, or mandate she enter some type of program. They were unable to figure out why – they *did* talk about it – however it never *seemed* like a good idea at the time, and she never seemed sober enough for anything they could offer in her best interest to penetrate. So they did the same thing, every time – small talk.

"You're looking *better*, Mama..."

Then clean her up, put her to bed, clean house, get out of there. It *seemed* like the right thing to do – although things were a mess – to keep it that way, at least for a while. Their father, rest him, was missed.

When his legs had healed, it was business as usual for Leonard. After a few friendly dates with Sharon, he wished her well and hoped she had a good life – and if she ever needed legal advice or counsel, to please – for the love of God! – go elsewhere – he had enough problems at work already.

Due to the unusual residual effects of the Shostrom Langhorn property transaction to the firm – those would be two broken legs and a dead body – it was best for morale – and Rothstein's nerves – to transfer responsibility for any remaining legal paperwork to another department.

Shostrom himself personally sent the files to the grand ballroom office of one of his elder statesman colleagues and – after explaining – rather laboriously and long winded for a reserved man of such few words – how he felt for the young future company Vice President – *hell, maybe even president after I retire* – and what a tragedy this one time standard loan had brought to the people involved... best if the matter was handled by another party – was – and in a *reputational* sense in the very least – the Shostrom offices had to hear the names Langhorn, Shifton and Haskel no more.

Leonard had found out through the grape vine that Sharon was still going to therapy – religiously and more regularly than ever before since the incidents at the estate had become but a sore memory better forgotten by all directly – or indirectly – involved – and that she could no longer hold her job as an executive secretary, and had to go on Disability – a 'choice' forced upon her – although nothing to be ashamed of, the medications she took for depression and sleeplessness were counterproductive to maintaining a busy weekly schedule – and she had gotten used to staying up until early mornings and sleeping until late afternoons anyway – for her trauma, Leo – perhaps a bit smugly – though he felt entitled to be so – personally felt slighted by this, if not thoroughly jealous or vengeful - neither of which proved to be the case.

From his perspective – not so different from that of the common man, however modified for those of Jewish faith – Sharon got the easiest free ride – the best priced first class plane ticket – out of all of them. She managed to rescind her contract with the widow – which he had hastened to own up to and blame himself for – a seemingly by-the-book buyover that had exploded in everyone's faces in one way or another – and now she sat at home on her ass and received government checks. *I'm so happy for you Sharon*, he seethed. *Have a couple broken legs with your Scotch and Soda on me, why don'tcha. What a crock. I get to go back to work with a buncho' sick days against me – real nice – while Sister goes and whoops it up with Oprah! There's no fuckin justice in the world! What I went through...*

Leonard's mother noticed – with some alarm – the attitude change in her son; however she dismissed it as a byproduct of the accident, and hoped the Sheriff and his trusted deputy 'Bobby-O' went on – business as usual – as did the by now long *un*deputized nomads Jimmy and Jack – as well as the famous Tug Hill Map Store Guy Daniel Boone – complete with coonskin cap – whose business was finally thriving – *Exploded in one way or another...*

Daniel soon took a wife, was happy his recovery was a swift one – and would stay married as long as she would have him. He still had the peculiar habit of standing contentedly in mud and manure while overlooking traffic on the new throughway being constructed down the road through the old Shifton place – which gave him a weird disjointed sense of pride. *Somehow, in some way, I'm responsible for this town comin into the 20th Century.* It was something Danny – the goofy lanky product of an incestuous brother/sister common law marriage – had sorely needed. Admittedly, he could never eke out more than a pauper level living from his map store dream – after all, townsfolk would scoff, men passing by his pitiful dirt road shack and realizing there were only so many places to go in Tug Hill and Old Forge, and most of them were farms, for God's sake! *Who needs maps to find private land? If you're standing on a dirt road*, went another peculiar saying brought into vogue in town after the suicides, *chances are you're already where you want to be!* That one was sure to garner guffaws from at least two onlookers no matter how often the saying was repeated. This was after all a small town. Daniel's wife Bess did not mind any of this. She had a husband, so let them all be damned.

The Sheriff kept one small memento from the incident at the Shifton Estate – The Big Murder Case, as he referred to it – no doubt demoting it to Second Biggest Murder Case if the town were to suffer another such incident with a body count of three or more instead of two – if it could even be called a memento, since no properties were taken from the scene some five plus months ago other than freezer bagged residuals from the crime scene – mostly pieces of bodies found here and there – which later were cremated.

(?)

Instead he kept the miniature pocket sized calendar on the side of his desk. The town was in the middle of the usual late August heat wave, and still the Sheriff had his calendar turned to March. Thusly he and Bobby sometimes mistook March for the current month. March 12th 1996 to be precise. The day Old Forge was put on the map.

Dave brought Sharon a drink and excused himself so he could go to the bathroom. The floorboards squeaked when he walked on them. The wood had warped, and he had conceded several times they could be fixed, yet this had never happened. It would mean taking a day off from work to watch workmen pull all of the old boards up – he would advise only the 'bad ones' be replaced – since he did not trust union carpenters as far as he could throw them – and that would be too far. *The boards can stay as is, I suppose*. He switched on the bathroom light, unzipped his fly, went about his business, put his head back and sighed in relief.

I can't believe Sharon's come back to me after all this time. He flushed, zipped up and fished in the medicine cabinet for an aspirin, as Sharon had said she was suffering from a splitting headache – and Dave felt no subtle hint that she may have been lying. She had not been sleeping well lately – some nights she slept not at all – and she would have cancelled the dinner date without thinking twice if it had not meant a lot to her to try and patch things up between them.

Friends is fine, he supposed, but having her to myself is better. I hope this evening isn't going to go bust. He found the bottle and checked the date stamped on the back – *still good*. He ran his hands over the hot and cold knobs of the sink, slid both palms underneath the faucet and splashed his face with a few handfuls of warm water. Exiting the bathroom, he found Sharon waiting outside the door, just standing there with a half smile playing on her face.

"Hey – you gonna be there all *day?"* Sharon kidded, poking him in the abdomen with her index finger.

"Careful – *hey!* Don't *do* that! My *stomach!"*

"Oh I'm *sowwy*. The *baby's* got a boo boo." She paused, fixing her hazel eyes directly on his brown. He gazed back curiously.

"What's *with* you, Sha?"

"Whadda you mean?"

"You never used to be *like* this before." He backed against the door without realizing he had done so. For a split second Sharon thought he might be trying to get away from her. She wrapped her arms around his waist and smiled. "I mean, it's not that I don't *like* you this way – a little *goofy* – but –"

"But but but," Sharon interrupted coyly. "But me no *buts*, mister. And *speaking* of *butts*..." She grabbed his backside and squeezed softly, feeling him through the roughened cotton.

"Hey! *See* what I mean? I'm not *used* to this from you. I mean, it's not that I don't *like* it though..."

"You're *repeating* yourself, dear boy," she returned, cutting him off again. "*Stop* it – *okay*?"

Dave warmed, gently taking hold of Sharon's wrists and removing her hands from his buttocks.

"Whatsamatter?" Sharon asked. "Can't I play *around* with you anymore?"

"Sure – if it was something you always *do* – but we *both* know it's not like you."

"Oh, and I *suppose* you know what's like me all the *time*, don'tchoo?" Sharon, offended, was the one to step back this time, arms folded over her chest.

"Now don't be like that," Dave said, as he walked down the short hallway towards his dresser. He opened the top drawer, picked out a bright orange *Florida, the Sunshine State* t shirt and pulled it on over his damp hair. "It's just –"

"It's just *what?*"

"It's *just* that you've been... *different* lately... *that's* all."

Sharon lowered her head, hurt that her rare show of affection had been met with so much cynicism. "Well I *am* different, *Mister* David, or hadn't you noticed? I'm going through some hard times here, you know? All I want from you is a little love and *attention*, so I can help myself *forget*. It's already one *half* of the year *gone*, and I've got nothing to *show* for it so far."

"You're way too hard on yourself with this I've-got-to-get-things-done business. You've gotta calm down."

As Sharon continued quietly brooding across from him with arms folded, Dave picked up on something she had said. "...forget *what?*"

Sharon's shimmering hazel eyes dimmed in the unlit hallway – which was only partially illuminated by sunlight filtering in through the large paned bedroom window, as if some terrible secret had just been revealed. She stiffened, then slumped, wringing her sweaty hands, trying to keep her distance. She responded flatly, "I... don't want to talk about it."

"What don't you want to talk about? See, this is what I mean – these mood swings are getting to be too much. I have to finish getting dressed. I have to meet a client for some afternoon cardio. Before that, I have lunch with my old boss Elaine. She might have some work for me to do."

"Good looking *woman* for her age? I *bet* she has something she could *use* you for. You've planned yourself a busy *day*, I see."

Dave froze, facing her. "You *know*, Sharon – if you have anything to *say* about me trying to earn a living – *anything* – I'd appreciate you speaking to me like an *adult*, instead of your usual pot shots." He paused, then continued, smirking slightly. "What do you have against Elaine?"

"Nothing. I have nothing against *Elaine*. Doesn't she have a last *name?*"

"Yes."

"What *is* it?"

Dave felt an uncomfortable stirring in his stomach, and he placed a hand over it instinctively. This time he took *two* deep breaths, while Sharon waited for an answer. "What is this *about*, Sharon?" he asked, deflecting her intrusive question. "*Surely* this cannot be about *you*, since this is *my* life we're talking about here – not *yours*." He paused for a moment, considering what he had just said. Still Sharon said nothing. "And yet, maybe it *is* about you – about *us*. Having mixed feelings about this, are you?" Dave dropped to the floor and put on his socks and shoes, while attempting to ignore the hurt in Sharon's face. He considered his last words to her harsh, and he would have liked to take them back, but there was one thing he knew about having heated conversations with women, and that was to stand his ground – no matter what.

"Maybe after *lunch*," Sharon said coldly, "*she'd* like you to hold something against *her instead*. I've heard older gals are horny. Go for it and maybe *you'll* get lucky *too*."

"*That's* it. Make yourself breakfast if you want – or lunch – you *sleep* so damned much I'm not sure you know which is *which* anymore." He took his windbreaker off the door hook and stood facing her dramatically, jacket in perspired hand. "I don't know what you're trying to *be*," he spoke matter of factly, "or who you're *becoming*, if that's the case – I don't know…"

Karen, sheepishly, interrupted, "I don't know either."

"Well then. That's the problem then, isn't it? That's the whole damn *problem* alright."

"Dave, I'm sorry. I went too far..."

"Too *far?!* You think I give a *damn* about you going too *far?* What am I, some little *shit* who gets offended over every little thing you say or do? I'm *worried* about you, that's all. *Nothing* else. I don't see you getting better Sharon. You mope around here, thinking I don't know *what*, then when I ask you how you're *feeling* you give me, I don't wanna *talk* about it."

"I *am* getting better, honey. It just... takes *time*."

"How much time is *enough?* I took you in when that stuff happened at the big house and Beatrice didn't want you *there* anymore, and I'm *glad* to have you with me – that goes without saying. But you've gotta try and *motivate* yourself at least a little more than you *have* been – cause I can't stay home and *babysit* you, Sha. I've gotta get some work *goin* for myself. And with you *like* this – up and down, so moody, not letting me help you, not even letting me see if I *can* – then I can't keep my mind on what *I* have to do, *worrying* about you like this."

"I'm sorry about that, Dave. I've just never felt so... down before – so desperate for something to *happen* – to *make* it happen. I just can't do it right now." Sharon hung her head in defeat, hiding the fact that she was on the verge of tears.

Dave took his keys off the dresser and managed a half hearted 'see you later' wave – his footsteps receded downstairs – and then, with the clicking of a lock, he was gone.

Sharon moped her way down into the kitchen/dining room, dragging her feet on the carpeted stairs, half hoping she would trip on her fuzzy slippers, fall the rest of the way and break her neck. These last few days had been miserable for her. David was right. *So right, and so patient.*

What was *wrong* with her? What did Dave see so clearly that she had missed? She didn't feel the same as she had before, this was true. But what to *do* about it? Seeing Leonard like that – *Oh God, he looked awful.* What a terrible weekend. So many terrible things had happened. *The doctor. My Doctor Haskel. Poor man. His wife*

(?)

must be a mess. Still! And the widow. She might have been a little strange, but for the woman to be in the street alone in a trance,

(?)

and for Robert to hit her...

(?)

dead... what a freak *accident!* What are the odds that he would *hit* her?

(?)

Hit and run.

(?)

The whole situation was freaky. *Hellish.* Cursed. A mistake. *Leonard... I haven't heard from him in weeks. I don't blame him. He probably thinks I'm a jinx! After all this... maybe I am. Those tentacles... eels... whatever they were, all over me...* She shivered with the memory of lying there smothering while Karen had watched – the work of Karen's dead – *also* dead – father. *I was alive.* She shivered with the thought. *Alive and in the presence of dead people. I can hardly believe it. I wouldn't – shouldn't believe it – except I know it's true, that... it had to have happened.*

274

Sharon ran her clammy hands over her forearms, scratching an imaginary rash – one of a few nervous habits she had picked up. *The Old Maid who sees Dead People – who Talks to Little Dead Girls – Ghost Girls. Okay, pull yourself together. Let's not get into this again. Just breathe deep and make yourself some coffee.*

And so she did – black – no sugar. But she couldn't stop shaking.

Is this a nervous breakdown? How can I be sure? She let out a dry, nervous tic of a laugh. Irony. *Sharon, you can't even fall apart properly, can you? I feel like I never left that dark stuffy basement room.* She cupped the mug – one of Dave's – and sipped the tasteless hot beverage. It was tempting – repeatedly – to spill its contents. *Anything for attention. I'm tired. Don't feel like greeting the day just yet.* "I'm going back to bed," she deadpanned out loud.

Sharon trudged up the stairs again, spilling her cooling coffee on selected steps as she went. *Shit, that'll stain*, she reprimanded herself, slapping her robed thigh with her free hand. "Oh *fuck* it. Let him *see* the stain I made. Ooh, Sharon made another mess. I'm so *sorry!" Who gives a shit? Really! His fault for having so much carpeting – who needs it! I always hated – despised – carpets! They just get dirty – bugs grow in there – fuck that shit! Carpets.*

She made her way into Dave's guest bedroom – her room – which wasn't so much a second bedroom, but an unused den with a futon in it – set down her coffee on the night table – or was it a footstool? – and flopped into an instant and deep sleep. Dust particles danced in the sunbeams playing among her streaked light brown tresses. Sharon had dyed and trimmed her hair perhaps a bit severely, believing her trip to the stylist to be therapeutic – or so ran the rumor. When she arrived at Dave's apartment

(?)

hat in hand, the 'renewed woman' quickly left, never to return. *Maybe marked woman would be more appropriate.* As she slept, the same faces and scenes occupied her mind: the widow's sly secretive smile, Leo's ride with her to the estate, the Confident Driver, picking at the dinners she had cooked herself while she was alone over that terrible extended weekend – Four days! What was I thinking? – allowing herself only the smallest amount – just enough to stay alive, walking through blinding sunlight from that crippling darkness to see a body covered with a white sheet, blood seeping through the spot where the head must have been. *I remember everything. And I wish I didn't.*

How they suffered, she thought, as she awoke from her nap. A few moments later, she nodded off again, and she was back in the basement with the spirit of Karen Nelson. She envisioned the two of them frozen still like display window mannequins waiting to be posed by some horny male teenager on summer vacation. The ghost, suddenly animated and glowing – an eerie otherworldly illumination in the darkness. The specter reached out to her in the twilight, its cold hand warming in hers as Sharon held on for balance, feeling her footing somehow unsure, even though she knew she was really only sitting on cold concrete in the black, deserted hidden room.

"Come," the apparition commanded. "You must help me find my resting place. My father called where he would leave me my 'closet.' It wasn't a nice place, Sharon. The pigs would crowd me at night, and it wasn't easy for them to sleep with me there. They knew I shouldn't have been there, where they slept. They knew…"

"Yes… I understand."

Karen held Sharon's hand tighter, her phantom grip an excruciating spectral vise – and yet Sharon felt no pain.

The closet. Karen's Closet. And so many pigs…

"*See* it, Sharon," Karen's voice resonated from within her mind. "See it *all*, as it happened – or I will not rest."

There, in the basement, Sharon fell into a comatose state. And she saw. And she felt. And she heard.

The damp grimy pen smelled rank with moist soil, and a large group of animals were milling about her. And there in the corner of this drab unimaginative simply built structure was the girl – crying. In the darkness she lost her train of thought. All she could hear were the shuffling hoof steps of these incredibly large... pigs – remarkably quiet for their size. *Surprisingly quiet*. Whoever gave sows a second thought, except when they were on a plate as part of someone's breakfast?

Sharon didn't. She felt the self gratifying socially righteous need to lament her twice a week – often more – plate of bacon and eggs – crispy and sunny side up – respectively – to expound an existential ... or would be animal savior... the doomed fate of the lowly piglet so poetically and admirably drew a crowd fresh out of a Save the Earth/Whales/Ecological System rally – and within minutes became their newsworthy spokeswoman. Yes, before her first heaping forkful of pork, Sharon Langhorn was as sorry as a woman could be about having to eat this fried dead animal flesh.

Amazing wasn't it – how quiet they were. It was so dark – no windows or lighting whatsoever – that all Sharon could count on to stop her from falling were the bristly meaty bodies constantly passing her, brushing her roughly from all sides. Their densely packed forms made her quite warm – almost feverish, if this illusion were to be believed. Her mortal self, of course – left behind on the bed – the physical shell of her – she knew did not suffer any illness – if her manic depression and suspended sense of self and overall lack of feeling *there* – in the moment – could not be counted as illness. Within this cramped world of beasts, Karen was all but obscured in the complete darkness. Panic set in, slowly and undeniably.

This is what it's like to be blind – totally and unendurably blind. The blindest one can be, I suppose. Oh, for your eyes to be wide open and yet seeing nothing – it's maddening! I wish these creatures could step back, just a little.

Ow! One of the pigs stepped roughly on Sharon's left foot, and in response to her involuntary cry the noise level escalated quickly to a fever pitch – the shrill guttural sounds became deafening. How this could have happened in reality, even the most ardent fastidious farmhand could have never explained in his lifetime.

Somehow – even though she had no way to know – she had been transported to another version of the same room. In this strange all encompassing moment of clarity she knew that none of this could be the miracle it seemed. After all, she did not believe in God. And only God could furnish a bona fide miracle – wasn't that the way it went? Miracle or not, Sharon felt unintimidated.

Doctor Haskel's Widow Elizabeth

(?)

stirred in their Queen sized bed – which she swam in now that her Robert was gone – shaken awake by a strangely reminiscent dream. She opened her eyes widely, and then closed them again after lazily rubbing them free of crust with the back of her forearm, then flopped her head back down onto the warm pillow as she struggled to recall the dream which had awoken her. *Robert.* She had been dreaming about Robert. No – not *about*, directly – but something else. The story of another – yes – a woman – trapped inside some horrible place. Sharon. This woman, running through a great white pathway – no – not white – greyish maybe – she could only see it foggily. A tunnel of some sort – an entranceway – and it was moving. Not so quickly as to knock this woman over, but by God, it was definitely... *moving.* Shifting slowly. *Undulating* like soft waves embracing a calm beach during low tide. Slowly – ever slowly, the waves broke again. This time she could make out different shapes – separate, yet somehow linked to the greater whole.

Then she saw what it – they – were, and her dream self panicked, raising the back of a hand to her mouth in perplexed horror. It was not so much that the animated scene with this lone woman – the catalyst? – was particularly grisly – thank *God* that wasn't the case – though a streak of foreboding which made her hair bristle warned her that – quite soon – it *could* be. All she knew was the poorly lit entryway had filled inexplicably and completely with animals – *creatures* – by the dozen – crowding the woman, lifting her off her feet and shifting her about at the whim of their massive combined weight – or so it had appeared.

Immediately it came to her what type of animals these were, however even that failed to explain their gargantuan size. *Pigs*. Large noisy filthy *pigs* – many if not all bearing the mark of encrusted excrement and fresh soil – or moist manure – on their hooves, upper legs and flanks. The woman grimaced automatically, closed her eyes, and raised her hands up to her temples in response to the deafening mass call of the creatures. Elizabeth

(?)

caught her stumbling – nothing could pull her dream gaze away from this scene now – not now that sufficient light had seeped in from – where did that light *come* from? – allowing her to see – plainly enough – the perplexing movements of woman and beasts – almost united as one as a single entity. The woman reached up overhead, seeming to grab for something to assist her in pulling away from fear of being crushed – even if that had not been their intention. As she groped in the darkness – her own *private* darkness, which Elizabeth

(?)

as the dreamer, was not subject to...

Elizabeth

(?)

was right of course – Sharon was unable to see anything. She was wrong however on another account. The beastly bodies did move, yet they merely shuffled about without really going anywhere. The entire group remained stationary, milling around in a paranoid dance of survival. This woman, the dreamer feared, would surely be crushed. Before her, the dance became a steadily accelerating spiral of porcine flesh... and then the woman was gone. The animals dispersed one by one, as if by magic, until all were gone. The dreamer counted down, half expecting to see the woman lying down crushed on the floor beneath them.

Seven. No sign of a body yet. *Six.* Only the panicked bodies of the pigs – as dirty as they were large – could be seen. *Five.* The body of this woman seemed to have all but disappeared, although there was still hope... *Four.* The next pig exited, and things were looking grim for this stranger, as the dreamer wiped away a tear that had not yet fallen. *Three.* Grimmer still. *Two.* It was impossible that there was no trace of her. *One.* No hope remained. *And Then there were None.*

Elizabeth

(?)

felt a hand on her shoulder, shaking her awake. She bolted upright in bed, exhausted yet completely alert. No one stood by her side – neither of the children

(?)

who had often awoken her from a nap – wanting something. Not Ann.

(?)

Not Peter.

(?)

Just her own conscience taking hold and jolting her out of a strange and curious dream. When she went back to sleep, her slumber was welcomingly deep and dreamless, before the children, Ann and Peter

(?)

nudged her awake so she could prepare dinner. Just a strange dream.

That woman, she later recalled. *She just... disappeared. How could such a thing be possible? Strange... I don't usually have weird dreams like that. Or maybe... Robert is trying to contact me. Didn't they say something about animal prints being found in the basement of that house? Oh God...*

She forced herself not to think about it.

Chapter Sixteen

Leonard's mother had prepared one of his favorite meals for him – corned beef hash – non Kosher for a change – and eggs with *ham*. *This* was a surprise. She didn't usually allow pork in the house, for religious reasons. Leo was not fastidiously Jewish when it came to learning the doctrines of Popular Orthodoxy, however he knew enough to know Kosher food – most of the time – gave him indigestion – although his mother would probably take this secret to her grave with private guilt if he ever told her.

The fact was – without a doubt – he was the most McDonald's patronizing *Jew* he *knew*. He caught himself laughing at the wry rhyme, but not before his mother gave him the Eye.

"Leonard," she called – in that clipped, two syllable fashion which he despised – Len *Nerd*.

"What is it mom?"

"What reason do you have for giggling at the table like an *idiot?* There's no one else *here*, son."

Leonard answered her in less than cordial tones. "Can't a man have a laugh in his own *home* without someone telling him he looks *stupid?*"

"I'm not just '*someone*,' Leo – I'm your *mother*. And this is *my* home more than it is yours. But I didn't *mean* to use the word 'idiot.' That was a little bit *strong* maybe."

"Never mind. That's not what I meant. I know you're not just anybody, but I wasn't speaking to you – Huh!" Leo raised his hand resolutely – a trait among Italian and Jewish people alike – fingers joined together, creating a fan like shape, as if to say, 'I give up.' His mother folded her arms over her considerable bosom – which he thought tipped the scales at almost his total weight.

"And who would you be talking to, my son, but me? I'm the only other person standing here, besides you sitting there, unless you're seeing something I can't see. Are you?"

"No of *course* not – don't be *silly* – it's *just* that…" Leonard struggled to express the recent discontent he felt regarding his station in life without sending his stability loving mother into a panic.

"*Yes*, Leonard?"

No going back now. "Oh," Leonard began, eying the dream breakfast before him balefully, kicking himself for having no appetite for a meal he had wanted so much, and by the last four words had lowered his voice to a whisper. "It's *just* that… I'm *not*… I'm not *happy* at the firm like I was before… if I ever was."

"I didn't catch the last part. Speak *up* my boy," his mother replied brusquely, a frown forming at the corners of her mouth and extending beneath her first chin. It was a look Leonard avoided provoking in her as much as possible. Everything was different now, he realized. As different as the All American Breakfast – with Pork – looking back at him from his plate – uneaten and cooling fast.

"I *said*," he repeated, stressing each word clearly, "*If. I. Ever. Was.*"

"What are you *getting* at Leo?" she said softly, hoping it wasn't what she thought it might be. She sat beside him with her arms folded on the table. Leonard was not the type to ruin a woman's reputation by getting her pregnant, so there was no way it was that, and he would never leave the firm without anything as a backup.

Leonard took a deep breath before he spoke. "I *think...*" he began, and instead stabbed his fork into an unholy amount of ham and scrambled eggs, and proceeded to stuff his face with it, without remorse.

His mother gasped, yet said nothing. *My Leo is having a problem – this much I'm sure of.*

He attempted unsuccessfully to speak through that formidable mouthful. "I'zzz *dinker* abber *lead* duh *orfice* soom, Mudder." He realized he just sounded ridiculous, and once more lamented the beautiful meal that he was not even tasting.

Leonard's mother went into one of her mild panics. "*What*? Son, swallow that *awful* pile of pig. Whatever possessed me to *cook* that for you, I have no idea. I think I'm doing the right *thing*, and now my son is going *insane* from Pork *Fever!*"

"I'be *nod* gobbin *inzun* wid purk *febber!*" Leonard mushmouthed, and then swallowed as much of the mostly unchewed food as he could – attempting to pass the large slices of ham down his throat – hoping he would not choke – wishing he had not tried something so stupid. He would end up having gas pains for sure after a stunt like this. "I *said*, uh..." he said breathlessly – *that felt bad going down*, "that I'm..." he swallowed the rest, and tensed himself in anticipation, "*thinking* about *leaving* the office soon, Mother."

"Oh is *that* what you were trying to say?" Leo's mother said steadily, looked at him sidelong, and willed herself not to become angry. "I find it *important* to know exactly what it is you are talking about so that I am quite capable of responding in a proper manner. So *here's* my response." She paused. Leo fidgeted.

"Yes?"

Leonard's mother glared at him, then blurted out, "Are you *crazy?* Leave the *firm* and jeopardize your *pension*, not to *mention* any promotions? You're *not* getting any *younger...*"

Here we go again, Leo sighed.

"Where is this all *coming* from all of a sudden?"

"All of a *sudden?* Ma, I've been feeling like this for *months* now. I've been going over this in my *head* and –"

"*Hold* it!" his mother yelled. "Maybe *you've* been thinking about this for who knows how long, but *I'm* your *mother*, and it's *news* to *me*. I *hate* seeing you like this, son. All *nervous* and pacing the *floor* like an *inpatient* like."

"They're called the mentally *challenged*, mother."

"*Please* Leonard, we're having a serious *conversation* – this is *no* time for jokes."

"*Jokes? You* called me an *inpatient*."

"Quit changing the *subject*, for *Christ's* sake." For a devout Jewish woman, Mrs. Rothstein bandied about the name of that son on a stick quite often.

"They're mentally challenged *people*, Ma."

"And who's talking about *retards?*"

"Now I'm having a nervous *breakdown*."

"For the *life* of me, I can't understand *why* you have to be the patron saint of *vegetables*."

"Vege – *Ma!* You *know* how I feel about that word! They are not *vegetables!*"

"I'm sure *some* of them aren't. But there's no *way* you're gonna catch *me* mopping up after any of *them* – not a one. It just goes to show that their *God* makes *mistakes*."

Leo waved his hands, miming desperately for closure. "I am *not* going to get into an *argument* about *reta* – *now* you've got *me* saying it!"

"You might as well. That's what they are. And worse."

"I'm not going in to work today, mother. I'm not feeling too well."

"The way you *inhaled* that *mountain* of *cholesterol* like *some* sort of *heathen*, it's no *wonder*. You didn't even *chew*."

Leo's steely resolution came to the fore as a moment of clarity overtook him. "I'm going to *sit* right here and finish my cold breakfast – cholesterol be damned – and then I'm going to *walk* myself back upstairs and lie down."

"But you're already *dressed* son," his mother soothed, resting her hand on his. "We can talk this over more civilly once you come home tonight. Have a chance to think about it on the train I say, that might be better."

"Alright," Leo guiltily acquiesced. "I'll go in today, but no promises."

"*That's* my boy. Now give your momma a kiss."

Leo did so, and flashed a detached smile. "G'bye ma." He left the house, took the train as usual, made small talk with his coworkers as usual, and then walked directly into Old Man Shostrom's office and gave his immediate notice of resignation, as highly unusual. Leonard wasn't the 'flat leaver' kind – he was the type everyone depended on. People like him didn't do things like that – didn't act irresponsibly.

But that had all changed now, ever since March – hadn't it? What had being the on-time-all-the-time saint done for his sleeping habits? Not much, in fact. He pressed himself to think of the last time he had been able to sleep the night through – without any nightmares. Acting responsibly had won him two broken legs and a busted arm – nice for someone who had never gotten even a parking ticket.

'Driving Under the Influence.' Wasn't that what that pathetic county Sheriff had charged him with? Ah, the feeling of being whisked into an ambulance, thrown into a strange hospital bed, waking up with cast after cast of hardened plaster over broken bones and lacerated skin.

That's what I get for being Saint Leo. Well this Jewish momma's boy can't play the saint anymore. It's too damned hazardous to my health! Why me? That's what I still can't figure out... why in fuck did it have to be me?

Leonard walked away from the cubicles which had been his weekday home, in addition to his home on many late nights and overtime Saturdays – walked away, cane in hand, from the fatherly bear hugs and pep talks of his aged boss, *THE* Mister Shostrom, Esquire. One of the old Bloodhounds – still standing, still sniffing out the next deal, the next takeover, the next great win in a court of law.

The New York Game. Well, sorry to disappoint you, sports fans, but Old Number Thirty Three – Rothstein – can't play anymore. It's not that his momma don't want her boy to get hurt – or that she minds a few mud scuffs on the linoleum – that's not it at all. In fact; the mother – I have it on good authority – was dead set on opposing his retirement from the active roster. No, sports fans, the Stein Machein is hanging up his cleats in crippled defeat. He can't play this fucking game anymore. So, adios, mon amore. He's off to see the Wizard, in hopes of getting a new brain. And a couple of brand new legs...

I'm gonna need 'em.

And so Leo left the office – past a gauntlet of shocked faces and a pall of impending Martyr gossip – never to return.

A copy boy later asked one of Leonard's old cubicle jockey friends whether the tales of the famed Crippled Man's walkout were true.

"You'd better believe it kid," was the answer, the co worker's eyes lighting up at the memory of that famous – at least among immediate Shostrom staff – day when Leo click clacked his way – albeit with dignity – out of that office, that job, and ultimately out of the post Baby Boom lifestyle.

"That *Rothstein*," the man said, raising his hands from his computer's keyboard and leaning back with fingers laced behind his head, sitting back in his wheel away hydraulic lift chair. "He had some pair of *balls*. A tough *motherfucker*, boy..." He paused to absorb the look of shock on the copy boy's face in response to the easy profanity. He shrugged this off with a laugh. "He *will* be missed. *That's* for shit-sure. We *all* learned from Leonard – from the *Master*."

Leo's mother both hated and resented his decision to leave his lucrative in house lawyer's position at the firm for a less than a life's alternative of backpack hitchhiking and eating out of cold Chef Boyardee cans – was that stuff Kosher? – she didn't think so – but it was either make peace with his choices or lose her son to the wind. *The wind should be so lucky.*

She came around eventually, when he came back to New York periodically – he always returned with a smile, a hug, a small gift, and a new story to tell...

He was right – that skinny map store fella, Leo recalled, as he drove home after his dramatic career ending departure. *I was a weasely little stuck up Yuppie shit. Thank Yehuda for these precious few moments of clarity we all get, Amen.*

Leonard's mother accepted that he had found happiness – that deep kind of happiness that she had felt walking down the aisle in her mother's gown, to marry his father. She had loved him so much she alienated her own family by getting married in a Catholic church – to start a new family with this man, her husband.

They eventually came around, knowing that he was a good man, who had raised a good son. His illness and subsequent death, to his credit, was mourned by both clans and, in an unprecedented move at that time for American marriages, offered his bride – aborting Catholic hegemony – to keep her maiden name, and to pass it on to the baby boy as well. Shocked, she accepted, as did both families, to their mutual shock.

Brian Alfonso, an Italian kid from Bensonhurst, Brooklyn, had little use for tradition – which, during the late 1940s, had alienated both friends and enemies alike. Although he did not go along with the staunch machismo and stubborn old hat beliefs of his generation – and among his ethnic group especially – people soon found his intentions to be true for the most part, and accepted him as an honorable man among the community. Traditions – brought from the Old World to America – still ran deep then, and Alia to this day was barely able to fathom how an Italian-Jewish couple, raising a son Jewish – with a Jewish last name – had not been disowned by his family, *stoned* by the neighborhood, and run out of town, in short order.

Had Brian not been the man she had known and loved, things would have been different. All she wanted was for Leonard to know the peace of mind that love brought, as she had. Yes – wasn't that the most important thing? He had proven to her – and himself – beyond a doubt that he was able to accomplish something that she had held as important, and to thrive at it, the way he had thrived at the firm, as an understanding lawyer and real estate agent to the needy – a man with compassion, in a humanitarian position – which ironically was quite rare. He had performed his former duties with professional precision, acute understanding, patience and aplomb. If he really needed to shuck all that now, to truly be happy, *then so be it*.

Sharon, fully clothed, stirred in her bed, tossing the neatly tucked outer covers about in unconscious restlessness. The dream – a slightly abridged version of her now suppressed actual memories – ran by at breakneck speed, images flitting by in eerie Day-Glo pastels, as if a tumult of strobe lights had invaded the scene, assaulting her acutely raised senses.

"What is this place?" Sharon yelled in the general direction of where she had seen a little girl crouching only seconds before. She very well could not have been there, for all Sharon knew – the room where she teetered, upswept by a vast display of myriad beasts, was an endless tomb of darkness.

"You know very *well* what it is," a voice called to her through the blackness. "It is my *Hell*, miss, and you are a *guest* here."

"But *why?*" Sharon replied sleepily, suddenly lulled by the strange dance of the pigs milling and passively bickering about her. "All I *remember* is... a *staircase...* and then..."

"You were *lost!*" interrupted the strange, barely female voice – the hateful disdain was plain, although Sharon could not comprehend its motivation.

"Where *are* you? Are you *hurt?*"

"I am where he *left* me," the raspy cryptic voice responded. "And hurt? I'm... *dead.*"

"I don't *understand* – let me *help* you – *Uhh!*" Sharon struggled against the ever churning warm sea of bodies around her, which only drove them into further unrest, and succeeded in jostling her about more roughly, knocking her backwards so her back was arched like that of a child dangling off the edge of a large bed, blood rushing to her head, making her dizzy and nauseous. Her fall of course had been broken by more creatures behind her, and so she was not afraid. Frozen and helpless with shock and confusion, yes, but not afraid.

"Do not disturb them," the spirit warned wearily. The far off voice continued. "*Listen* to me. I *know* this place. It is where I *died*. These beasts are too *strong* and too *many* – they will smell your panic. You must be *still* – or they will *crush* you. *Mind* me, woman!"

Sharon lowered her head. The echoing shuffling hooves and grunts that reverberated throughout the seemingly endless chamber were deafening.

"This is no *game* – you should not have come here, to my *home*. No good can come of it!"

A sudden tremor – like a lightning strike through torrential rain – blinded Sharon in a shock of light. Sharon, who had unwittingly opened her eyes wide in the pitch darkness, forced herself to train her sight on some shape, anything that might clue her in to the nature of her surroundings. She saw nothing, and the pain of this unholy brightness felt as if it were piercing the backs of her eyes as her overwhelmed lenses signaled her brain to heal themselves – as retinal fibers felt their way through to the wide pupils, her hazel eyes now almost uniformly black from the shock of accepting so much white light – a painful rebuttal from the nervous system. She shut her eyes in remission, and for fear of losing her vision – *God forbid!* – for good.

"Open your eyes," the voice commanded. "You are safe here."

"No," Sharon cried, "I don't believe you."

"Open your *eyes*, and see what you were blind to before."

The voice had changed – the cavernous reverberation, which reminded her of the church she had frequented as a child... *wait! I never went to Catholic school. I –*

"For the last *time*, woman, open your *eyes!*" The voice – now clearly that of an adult – was also clearly, if not pleasantly, female. Was this a new voice of yet another strange being among these unruly beasts, or were her ringing battered ears deceiving her?

The voice continued, as if answering her thoughts. "It is I. *Karen.* Now open your eyes. The light here cannot harm you."

Amazing. The question had been plucked directly from her mind as it had come to her. Against her cynical better judgment, Sharon decided she had better listen to this being, be it demon, ghost or spirit – or else perish in resisting her. And so she did.

Hesitantly, slowly, Sharon opened her eyes.

The invasive, blinding white light which had maliciously and indifferently sought to blind her – be it God or not – was gone. What luminescence remained resembled summertime sunlight filtering in through a morning window. Sharon *screamed* when she saw how many pigs had surrounded her, and how *large* they were – nudging her off her feet and lifting her in fleshy waves; she knew nothing *but* to scream in total confusion at this nightmare. The voice – this *Karen* – living, dead, or *un*dead – strove to calm her. This thing meant for her to live – she could feel that now; although an overwhelming part of her brain teetered with uncertainty within milliseconds. *Don't trust this! Don't trust what you see! Don't trust what you feel – it's a trick!*

"Your mind betrays you. Do not scream. Even I did not scream so when their teeth ripped my flesh. Enough!"

The air was thick in Sharon's lungs as the air about her grew thin – as if the pigs had consumed all available oxygen. As they huffed and puffed around her, she could almost see white streams of vapor shooting from their nostrils. Sharon began to wheeze heavily.

"Sharon!" Karen screamed from somewhere out in the distance. "Do not leave – I need you *with* me now – I need your *strength!*" The voice faded away and was silent for what seemed like minutes before it continued, raspy and breathless. "We *both* need your strength now." None of the voice's apparent former malice remained – instead it seemed weary, as if the ghost – *but it's just an illusion!* – also felt the lack of air. Something about it had changed.

Sharon struggled to draw in what breath she could before responding. "Wh-what do you mean we? I'm the one who's su-suf-focating."

"Without you I will be unable to attain my resting place. We *must* not fail."

"Wh-who *are* you?"

"I am Karen's cursed passenger. I am *bound* to her in this place." Yes. The voice was different now.

Sharon looked to her right, and discerned a ghostly form she took to be Karen, illuminated by a flash of light. Sharon was conscious of having sweated profusely, pressed among a huge clot of agitated pigs – *of course – they can smell me – but how do they even know I'm here?* Again she screamed, though no sound escaped her dry lips. *Cursed passenger... all an illusion...* Not attempting to make any sense of it was a small relief. She called out to Karen – the Karen she knew. After a few seconds a voice responded.

"Yes – I am here – I am always here. It is our lot to be here... all of us."

A humid breeze touched Sharon's cheek. She answered slowly, dreamily. "Do you mean... the pigs too?"

"Yes."

"Wh-what do they have to do with –"

The second voice interrupted. "*You*, Sharon Langhorn, were chosen to bring this child's body and soul to her final rest. Is this so *difficult* for you to understand? We two are the *same*."

"Whadda ya mean *we?*"

"Do you not listen?"

There was that warm breeze again. It beckoned her attention. It coaxed her gaze in Karen's direction.

"Your souls are twin spirits – both of you lost a mother, and were left with a monster. Both of these monsters... *took* you. *Violated* you. By your suffering, you are *one*."

Sharon shook her head in vigorous indignation. She had spent decades struggling to shed that part of herself, like an empty husk – to cast it off forever. Like a bad dream better off forgotten. Like someone else's story. She responded, choking back tears. "And what does that have to do with Karen?"

"Look!" the voice commanded. "Look at what we have become!"

"No!"

The warm breeze caressed her face, and drew her gaze to face the morose, malnourished countenance of the teenage Karen – which was no more. Only the mummified remains of a blackened skeleton propped up against the wall where the young girl had huddled.

"Karen... is that... you?"

"It is as we are now, in the flesh. In spirit, we are another matter. Help us to leave this place, Sharon Silverina Langhorn. We grow weary of this hell."

Sharon pushed herself mightily yet sluggishly forward, wading against the sea of squealing bodies, straining against head and belly, flank and rump. At long last she reached the far wall, and braced her sweaty palms while bending at the elbows against the lumpy unfinished concrete wall – had this been part of the basement's original design? Sharon felt compelled to curve her fingers into claws... and dig, straining against outcroppings of sand and mortar.

"Damn this place! Damn this wall!" Sharon felt her mind slipping, drawn in by the undertow of formerly suppressed memory. She remembered something her mother had said to her long ago, after her frightened daughter had, through many hesitant fits and starts – and for fear of reprisal or worse – admitted that her stepfather had molested her.

The memories came flooding back all too clearly – the undressing – the fondling – the assessing hands – *watching you turn into a woman*, he had said – brushing her budding pubic hair with his calloused workman's hands – probing her – first with his fingertips – then inserting one finger – then two – bleeding her – making her touch him. Later – guiding her lips to his penis when they were alone – swallowing his seed – the same seed that had borne him a daughter.

"Take it all Sharon," he would say after climaxing in her mouth. "It's good for you."

"It tastes awful Daddy... what is it?"

"Don't worry sweetheart," he would say, pulling her close to him. "Whatever we do is right. I'm teaching you the right way. I'm your father. Now swallow it all."

Near the end – when she told – he took her from behind – mildly for him, but excruciating for her. That huge thick *thing* halfway up into her... *invading* her... back and forth... until he finished. The image slammed into focus – the look on his face – losing himself in the moment before release – in that selfish instant of ecstasy. Taking his own virgin daughter. Knowing he made her squirm. Knowing he could never have his wife in quite this way.

He pinned her down by the wrists – not that she struggled – that would have done her no good – most of all, it would arouse his rage. And besides, he was teaching her about life, which most fathers did not do. In his words, he bore her no malice – he held her tightly as would any man, sharing this moment with his partner. Sharon locked onto the recollection, holding it firmly at the front of her brain. And she saw – and remembered – everything.

"Yes," Sharon addressed her own dark vision – the buried horror of her youth – forgetting for a moment her current supernatural surroundings. "Yes he *did* that to me, the son of a *bitch!* Fuckin *bastard!*"

So that was the point. This young girl – Karen – must have endured the same torture as she had – only worse. *Oh Jesus yes... much worse.*

"Sharon. No man must do that to you – ever – again. This disease must not win. Your world is different now. What he did to you was a heinous horrific crime – and he *will* be punished. I will see to it. I love you, Sharon."

In her mind, Sharon took the voice to be that of her mother, and she allowed herself a faint smile. "Me too, Mommy. Always."

This had to have happened to Karen too, she reflected, dragged back into awareness of her surroundings, straining to retain her balance as another pig jostled her with its large belly. She forced her bloody palms to grip the sharp edges of weathered stone, bracing herself against stinging laceration. *One wrong slip and I'll go under, pummeled under dozens of pairs of sharp fat filthy hooves – crushed beyond recogni – wait! That's it!* Sharon smiled triumphantly in spite of the gnawing pains that racked her overwrought body. *That's how Karen must have died! They can't see me though, so I'm not in danger...* "Oh God."

She yelled as the form of the large grunting animal – clearly disturbed at being prodded and shoved by something it could smell, yet which remained unseen – poked its snout in her direction. Sharon easily maneuvered out of its way. The room was again jet black, and she could only feel her way. After hours in that sauna bath of wild bodies – with no way to escape – and where she had resolved herself to her imminent death – her ingenuity – and stamina – lasted barely twenty minutes.

"Funny," Sharon whispered, when her pulped hands, now slightly more than butcher's goods, finally touched something other than solid rock. "How I mustered the strength to fight against all those bodies crushing against me." She looked down at her soiled jeans. "*Shit!* I even *pissed* myself! I've gotta get *out* of this nightmare."

"Sharon, please *help* us – *please!*"

"Jesus, I can't *breathe*... just sit still... relax..."

"Sharon, you are *free* – now free us. Free *me*."

"Wait a minute. Did I *hear* something? Something... *here!*" Miraculously, Sharon's eyesight had become accustomed to the darkness – everything cast in greyscale. She examined her upheld bloody hands, and looked down to her feet. She regarded the cavity she had ripped into the surface of the wall – the culmination of all her recent nightmares – all this suffering – this horrible hellish three day weekend of spectral visions and mental anguish... gone.

Karen's remains lay sprawled before her, her housedress still visibly clinging to blackened sooty bones, the fabric now tattered, bleached and frayed with age. Sharon stood there stiffly, stunned at her discovery, and yet far too tired and spent from her recent trials to go into total shock.

Shock is for people who have never experienced life, Beatrice had once said. *How very true.*

Chapter Seventeen

When the men had come to exhume the body – halfway encrusted in leftover slop and manure – which had created an amazing chrysalis – the remains of Karen's Pig Army were also found. *They ate her*, Sharon mulled. *And here she died. How horrible.* She shivered.

Sharon would tell no one how they had all come to share this strange common burial – the teenage mistress, alone, probably abandoned, and her starving charges... her ultimate executioners. The visions of her ghastly end remained with Sharon in a nightmare of cartwheeling gorefests, the grisly truth playing itself out in her fertile raw mind. Horrible yes, without question. But she would tell no one.

As the grimacing men hauled the rotted remains from inside the secret hideaway tomb around the bend from the main chamber – more a storage area than a room – Sharon felt a pang of closure. Many emotions coursed through her, however surprisingly few stemmed from the immediate real world she was forced to address once the town had learned of the find. This made for big news in Old Forge and Tug Hill; however Ms. Langhorn did not much feel like being interviewed.

Not many emotions at all. But so much hurt – so much indecision. *Gone* – like old friends – healthy, then suddenly dying. *Right away. One after the other.* Robert – *dead*. Leonard – *seriously injured, but he'd live*. David – *oh my poor David! What a fool I've been!*

When he had feverishly rushed to her side, to take her to his home, forcing his way through the neighborhood throngs – all of Tug Hill must have congested onto the widow's lawn on the morning of March 13th, 1996 – to sweep her into his arms, hold her tightly, and proclaim his love to her. This was the widow's home, not hers. She could have it, now that she too was gone.

Ironic end for you – eh, Doctor Haskel? The Widow Shifton. Dead.

None of it fazed her now. Not *anymore*.

"Take me *home* Davey," she murmured into his chest as she clung to him hard, her voice brimming with tears. "I want to *leave* this place." And they both did, as the bemused crowd watched his car drive off into the distance – regarding first the empty house, then the empty road, then the empty house again, in unison.

I hope you've found your peace, Karen. And God willing, I'll find mine. Someday.

David, alarmed by the wide eyed animal occupying the body of his normally reserved calm girlfriend, sensed an urgency in her. "Are you alright Sharon? I mean besides your –"

"*No*," Sharon uttered coldly. "I'm not. Let's go *home*." *God, Leo must hate me now.* She looked at David, who turned his head and smiled at her. *If he does, then so be it. Everything's different now. everything…. He'll be alright. And Robert's wife!*

(?)

How she must be over this, I can't… I have to start worrying about myself now. Sharon felt like crying, but instead fell fast asleep.

Back at David's place, Sharon unpacked a few things she had not gotten to before, and folded the few blouses and pieces of underwear she had brought for her three day stay.

The weekend.

David gave her a couple of drawers for her to use for her own stuff.

Did it really happen?

Beatrice's friend Mike said that he could drive her over some more of her clothes later that night.

That was nice of him, she thought. *Very nice.*

He was going to take Sharon's place as Bea's roommate, which was just as well. Sharon had felt uncomfortable there before as it was – and now that she had been veging out over the Widow Incident – as she began calling it, she didn't know why – she'd be a nervous hand wringing wreck there altogether. *It was for the best.* Beatrice expressed her genuine concern for Sharon's horrible mysterious experiences at the estate – at least Sharon hoped her concern was genuine – you never really know – and the two women straightened out the few – according to Beatrice – generational issues she had considered the reason the two had initially parted – as best they could, which meant they were still estranged – and Bea was left with more verbal ammunition to wield at Sharon if need be – *more issues* – or if she were simply bored and the party needed more gossip. So be it. *It's all different now. I'd have been in Mike's pants by now if she hadn't gotten him already. I hope she's happy.*

Sharon tried reaching Leo at home, with less than positive results – his mother answered the phone.

"Hello?"

"Is this Alia, Leonard's *mom?*"

"That's the name. Who is *this?*"

"This is his *friend* Sharon Langh –"

"*You!*" she yelled vehemently. "You *crippled* my *Leo*. You are *evil*, Mizz *Lang* Horn!"

"But I *didn't* –"

"*Horns!* The long horns of the *Devil* is what your name means!"

Sharon minded not the senseless attack – she was more concerned for Leo's health. "How... *is* he?"

Alia Rothstein laughed heartily. Sharon's mind was completely muddled. She couldn't figure any of this out.

Is this a put on? I just want to know how her son is doing.

"*So,*" Alia responded with an audible smirk. "The Devil *herself* asks me how *my* Leo is doing, eh? He is *crippled*, Devil, by your evil *deeds!* Your witch's hold on him – *bah!* – it is no *more!* He is *away*, my Leo. And you have *driven* him away. Witch. No more will you speak with my Leo. No *more!* Long Horned Devil, *begone!*" The elder Rothstein slammed the receiver down as hard as she could, the jarring report making Sharon wince on her end of the line.

That went well. Sharon shrugged, and then began packing away her clothes. *Why – why is this so hard?* "I won't be needing you now," she said, addressing her light cotton blouses. Fall was coming on – *fall already?* – so pack 'em all away. She deposited them in her dresser, closed the drawer and crossed over to the wall mirror to take a critical look at herself. "Boy you really messed that up with David back there, jerk. Look at you. That hair's attro – who's there?"

Something was there, she could have sworn, behind the half opened closet door. No. *Someone. A girl. Long brown hair. Ill fitting tattered dress.*

"Who's *there?* I *saw* you! Come out *now!*" Sharon ran across the room, threw open the closet door and rifled through David's coats. *No one.*

A memory. That little girl – a teenage waif – dressed in rags – huddled in a corner – smelling of urine and feces. *The pigs... that girl... Karen. A ghost? Just my imagination.* She looked... like *Karen*. Sharon again remembered her mother's call, and her own response.

"Me too, Mommy. Always."